Cat Telling Tales

ALSO BY SHIRLEY ROUSSEAU MURPHY

Cat Coming Home

Cat Striking Back

Cat Playing Cupid

Cat Deck the Halls

Cat Pay the Devil

Cat Breaking Free

Cat Cross Their Graves

Cat Fear No Evil

Cat Seeing Double

Cat Laughing Last

Cat Spitting Mad

Cat to the Dogs

Cat in the Dark

Cat Raise the Dead

Cat Under Fire

Cat on the Edge

The Catsworld Portal

Cat Telling Tales

A Joe Grey Mystery

Shirley Rousseau Murphy

An Imprint of HarperCollinsPublishers

This book is a work of fiction. The characters, incidents, and dialogue are drawn from the author's imagination and are not to be construed as real. Any resemblance to actual events or persons, living or dead, is entirely coincidental.

HarperCollins books may be purchased for educational, business, or sales promotional use. For information please write: Special Markets Department, HarperCollins Publishers, 10 East 53rd Street, New York, NY 10022.

FIRST HARPERLUXE EDITION

HarperLuxe™ is a trademark of HarperCollins Publishers

Library of Congress Cataloging-in-Publication Data is available upon request.

ISBN: 978-0-06-208869-7

11 12 13 14 ID/OPM 10 9 8 7 6 5 4 3 2 1

*For all those who help lost and abandoned pets,
who feed, shelter, and care for them, giving of
their time and love.*

Some abandoned cats adapt quickly to feral life, but others have great difficulty learning to survive outdoors. Often the newly strayed cat will look dirty and disheveled, fitting right in with the common image of the feral cat, while the feral cat will look clean and sleek because it's not spending all its time trying to learn how to survive. . . . Building a cat-owning consciousness that precludes abandonment is . . . within reach and being worked on throughout the humane movement.

—ELLEN PERRY BERKELEY, *TNR: Past Present and Future: A History of the Trap-Neuter-Return Movement*

Cat Telling Tales

1

The tomcat didn't believe in prophetic dreams, he didn't believe in insightful visions of future events or past events or whatever the hell that was that woke him yowling and clawing at the cushions with sweaty paws. It was the middle of the night, the sky outside the windows was clearer than the glass itself, the stars hung high and bright in their universe; the cool night was tucked around him as if to say that all was good, all was right with the world.

But he'd awakened frantic, still caught in the violent storm of his dreams; black wind driving rain at him so real that, rising up, he licked his paw expecting it to be sopping wet, expecting to have to lick himself dry all over.

That was a dream? What the hell was that?

He didn't mind lifelike dreams of, say, a rollicking hunt with his tabby lady, feasting on rats and gophers, happy dream-memories that did nothing more than enrich his restful sleep. What he didn't need was this kind of storm-filled nightmare so real he could still hear the wind howling. Didn't need this chilling experience of humans he didn't know, caught up in some violent personal battle, the dream's aura dark and so damnably loud that his poor cat head pounded and his ears still hurt: rain pelting down hammering a thin roof, two women shouting and screaming at each other with a terrible rage as rain beat against the thin walls of their little wooden shack, both women's anger elemental, irreconcilable.

Even in the stormy dark, he'd somehow known the shack stood beside a low hill that was flattened off at the top, a fence running along up there. That a small grove of trees stood below, some distance from the shack, sturdy saplings bent nearly double by the driving wind. He had a sense of several cats crouched at the base of the trees, terrified and shivering. Rain drove like hammers against the cottage, its drumming mixed with the women's shouts, and then he was inside the shack itself, the air cold and stinking of onions fried in rancid fat. A thin greasy light from a bare, overhead lightbulb, only a hint of warmth seeping from a square metal heater, the smell of butane fumes. An old woman, kinky gray hair, her wrinkled face screwed up with rage. The young woman slender, maybe in her twenties, her oval face flushed with anger, dark hair, long and wet and tangled, her brown eyes huge with vengeance. He could see a cot in the far corner, a child curled up beneath thin blankets into a miserable ball like a little animal, hugging himself against the women's rage.

"I didn't do any worse than they did," the girl shouted. "You think just because I was—"

"You were stupid and foolish and now you're paying for it, now look what you've got. If you try to pressure someone like him . . . You don't know half what he's capable of. And your own sister—"

"I was doing just fine until you poked your nose in. If you'd left it alone—"

"*I* poked *my* nose in? I've kept a home for you when your own sisters won't have anything more to do with you, and who can blame them, after how you've behaved?"

"Why are you so mean! You don't care about me and the boy, all you care about is how things look, what people think. Where do *you* get all puffed up, living in this shack! An old drunk living in worse than a slum. You think *I* like living here?" She whirled around, crashed out through the warped door into the driving storm, the wind wrenching the door from her hand, blowing it in with a crash. Out in the turbulent dark another figure moved, easing deeper into the windy blackness as she passed, a tall figure, flapping dark coat torn by sheets of rain. The watcher lifted a hand but she didn't see him, she disappeared running hard into the storm, the rain almost horizontal, as powerful as water sluicing from a fire hose. Over the storm's pounding the tomcat heard a car start, its headlights blazed on, cutting through the downpour, in the dash lights he saw the woman's pale face, saw her jerk the wheel as the car took off skidding a geyser of mud up against the house. Behind her, a second set of headlights flashed on, a second car loomed out of the blackness skidding against the hill and then straightening, following her fast, its red taillights quickly lost in the driving rain.

The tomcat had awakened so suddenly, shivering from the storm, amazed to find himself dry and warm within his own cushions, looking out at the calm, still night from within his own cat tower. Safe in his own digs, blessedly alone in his personal tower atop the second-floor roof, its tall windows dry and free of any rain, its timbers strong around him, his pounding heart the only residue of those violent moments. He sat looking out at the calm night, thinking about the violence of the dream, the women's mutual hatred so real it had sucked him deep down into it, seemed to have left part of him still there with them, shivering with perplexed fear. What the hell was that, where the hell had that come from? It was more like a vision than a dream, an ugly message maybe portending a view of the future— or was it a look at the past, a glimpse of painful conflict that had already happened, and that he might soon have need to know and understand?

Except, he didn't believe in that stuff.

So-called visions had nothing to do with real life, what folks called psychic portents were nothing but make-believe, temporary derangement. Life was right here and right now. Life was fact, what you could see and smell, what you could touch with your whiskers or an outstretched paw. Life was what you *saw happening* or could figure out for yourself without any kind of cockamamie ethereal message. No one, cat or human, could call forth a future that hadn't yet happened. No one could see into a past he'd never witnessed. *That* was sure as hell nonsense.

Rising, he pushed out through an open window to the roof, onto the dry, rough shingles that no storm had touched this night. He sniffed the cool, fresh breeze, the homey scent of pine and oak trees, the iodine smell of the sea from ten blocks away, and the sweet stink of a skunk hunting for grubs in one of the neighbors' yards. He thought about the two women in the nightmare, tried to think if he'd ever seen either of them around the village.

The old one looked familiar, as if he might have glimpsed her now and then among the shops; Molena Point was small, it was hard not to know the locals. But the young, dark-haired woman was a stranger to him. Oval face, ivory complexion, cleft chin as if a dimple lodged there. A pouty mouth, a sullen, selfish look about her that, whatever the argument had been about, made Joe want to side with the older woman. When he thought too hard about the dream, his paws began to feel cold and wet again, his fear gauge to shoot right through the roof. But at last he tucked the nightmare away, shoved it to the far dark at the back of his feline thoughts along with other matters he didn't much care to dwell on, with incidents he'd bring forth into the light only if they were required.

But he slept no more, this night.

Leaving his tower, he prowled across the rooftops of the village cottages and shops, brushing among overhanging branches of the oak and cypress trees, peering into cozy second-floor bedrooms still dark and peaceful and into the occasional rooftop penthouse. Galloping up and down the steep roofs, he wondered if his footfalls woke anyone in the rooms below where even the patter of a squirrel might be heard by a light sleeper. And the dream ran with him, shattering his sense of what was real, almost made him question his own convictions. Prowling among the shadows of roof vents and warm chimneys, he watched the sky pale from deepest gray to its first predawn silver streaked with wisps of blood-tinted clouds and still he couldn't put the dream away, couldn't know if it was a prediction or some mysterious voice from the past—or simply damn foolishness? Badgered by futile questions, he snapped back to the present only when he caught the first smell of coffee from the cottages below and the aroma of frying bacon. As hunger jolted him back to reality, he spun around and raced for home, his soft paws pounding across the rooftops, thinking of breakfast. To hell with stormy mind games, with nighttime portents and with visions he didn't want, and didn't believe in.

2

The rising sun fingered in through the glass walls of Ryan Flannery's upstairs studio, and a fire burned on the hearth against the dawn chill. The brightening room smelled of fresh coffee from the pot on the big worktable where Ryan and Clyde sat surrounded by stacks of real estate ads and flyers. The lingering scent of frying bacon and waffles had drifted upstairs, too, mixed with a whiff of Joe Grey's breakfast kippers. He lay purring, stretched out across the mess of real estate come-ons, his hind feet anchoring a pile of foreclosure notices, his front paws idling with a stack of price lists and specs the couple had been collecting for weeks. Licking a bit of maple syrup from his whiskers, he marveled at the propensity of his two favorite humans to complicate their lives—they needed another falling-down cottage to renovate like he needed a bed full of hungry fleas.

Ryan had pulled a sweatshirt on over her jeans, its white fleece setting off her dark, tousled hair, her sea-green eyes and high coloring. Her Latino and Scots-Irish heritage had blessed her with the delicate beauty of both races—as well as the volatile temper of both, which, most of the time, she kept pretty well reined in. Across the table, Clyde looked a bit shabby this early morning in ancient, faded jeans and a colorless, threadbare T-shirt that, in the gray tomcat's opinion, had long ago been ripe for the ragbag. Beneath the soft lamplight, both were examining eagerly the color ads for the small, neglected houses spread across the table, as if each cried out to them with the insistent voice of temptation: Buy me, remodel me, make me beautiful again.

Clyde and Ryan had been married just a year next week, but nearly from the moment Clyde slid the ring on her finger and engulfed her in a bear-hug kiss, they'd celebrated their marital bliss by throwing themselves into buying run-down houses, taking advantage of the falling market to launch into the small but challenging remodel projects that were a sideline for Ryan, turning each dilapidated shack into a bright little home so appealing that, despite the economic downturn, it sold often within days of being listed. This, on top of her full schedule of new-house construction, indicated a form of insanity that could beset only the human mind.

Though maybe, Joe thought, Ryan's creative inner fire was, after all, somehow akin to the same burning drive that made a cat stalk, capture, and kill; maybe, indeed, the same single-minded kind of obsession and commitment. Looking around him at the studio Ryan had designed and built atop their home, he did have to admire his housemate's talents: The heavy wood beams of the studio and its three tall glass walls had turned what could have been a dull second-floor addition into a treetop aerie, the space skillfully tied into Clyde's adjoining study and the master bedroom beyond. Those two rooms, she had built some months before they were married, expanding what had been a poky one-story cottage into a spacious and imaginative environment.

As the sun lifted, the glass walls of the studio seemed to melt away, the surrounding tree branches to become even more a part of the airy room, mingling their shadows with the oak worktable, the computer desk and old drafting table, the long, antique storage cabinet with its wide, thin drawers that held Ryan's drawings and blueprints. In the far corner, two campaign chairs, fitted with deep blue canvas, faced the blue daybed where Ryan's big silver Weimaraner lay on his back, his four gray legs in the air, snoring, his upside-down rumbles soft and rhythmic. The little white cat slept curled against his shoulder, safe and trusting. Rock was Snowball's guardian, she felt deliciously secure under the big dog's stewardship.

Ryan, having given up her small apartment when she moved in with Clyde on their wedding day, had started constructing the studio the minute they arrived home from their honeymoon. Frantic for a place to work, she'd been just a bit cranky as she tried to complete the designs for two new houses and four remodels, place orders for materials, do her invoices and bookkeeping, all in the downstairs guest room where she'd crammed in her office furniture, while at the same time starting construction on the studio, and supervising three building crews. Those first months of marriage she had, in short, not been your typical lighthearted bride. Thank God Clyde could cook. Or life might have degenerated into an endless round of frozen dinners for the humans and, too disgusting to contemplate, canned cat food for Joe himself.

Now, since she'd moved into her comfortable new studio, you'd think she'd take a break, but no way. She and Clyde had bought and completed two remodel prospects and were burning to buy more. Joe tried to keep his opinion, and more scathing remarks, to a minimum; he made no comment now as they passed real estate ads back and forth, discussing the possibilities of each little house, its charms versus its drawbacks and weaknesses. Rolling over, he edged into a patch of sunlight that shone down through the clerestory windows; the bright shaft streaming past him picked out, as well, the carved antique mantel with its hand-painted tile insets, each bearing the image of a cat—cats whose history often perplexed Joe, their uncertain origin an aspect of life that sharply unnerved the tomcat, that told him more about his own ancestry than he cared to dwell on.

Ryan and Clyde had found the mantel while on their honeymoon up in the wine country northeast of San Francisco, in a musty antique shop, and of course they had to bring it home. They'd left for their wedding trip driving a borrowed Cadillac Escalade. Two weeks later they arrived home with Ryan hauling a trailer behind the SUV, and Clyde following in a large, rented U-Haul truck, every available inch of all three vehicles loaded with dusty relics unearthed from junk shops all along their way: six antique mantels, twelve stained-glass windows, old hand-hewn lumber, detritus from people's basements and attics and torn-down houses that fit right in with Ryan's remodel designs. Amazingly, Clyde had been just as hyped as Ryan over their cache, the onset of feverish love apparently affecting his mental health, generating this new obsession that replaced his erstwhile preoccupation with antique cars. Oh well, such was love, and the tomcat had settled in, to adjust to household changes that, while frenetically busy, were far cozier and more charming than the careless environ of their austere bachelor pad.

Now as the sun rose higher, its warming rays touched not only the cat tiles of the mantel, but the letter that stood on top, a small pink envelope propped against a stack of architecture books. A letter that seemed to Joe as insistent as a blinking neon sign, awaiting Ryan's attention, a missive he found both repugnant, and worrisome.

When the letter first arrived, in the regular afternoon delivery, he'd had no idea of the dilemma it would cause. The small, note-sized envelope, addressed in a clumsy and unskilled hand, seemed unimportant, hardly worth noticing as Joe pawed idly through the mail Clyde had left on the coffee table. The writing seemed to be a woman's, someone who had plodded through grammar school at a time when the teaching of cursive was out of fashion, a woman who had apparently spent her entire adult life still laboriously printing her awkward little messages.

There was no return address, and the postmark was too blurred to make out the point of origin. The envelope was directed to Ryan in her maiden name, Flannery, which she still used professionally, and not to Mrs. Clyde Damen, but it did not appear to be of professional content; it didn't have the polish of a business letter concerned perhaps with the design and construction of a new house or with the proposed requirements for some costly and extensive remodel. When Ryan had come in from work in her jeans and boots, and opened it, when she scanned the letter, her green eyes narrowed to a frown. She'd stood a moment rereading it, as if to make sure she'd gotten the message straight, her dark, short hair windblown and sprinkled with sawdust like the sparkles from some children's party. At last, making no comment to Joe or to Clyde regarding the contents, she'd turned away, carried the letter upstairs and left it on her studio mantel where it now resided, the open note folded atop the envelope, the corner of a photograph visible underneath. As if the message wasn't exactly private, but she didn't care to discuss it. Of course the tomcat had followed her and, when she went on about her business, had leaped up and read it for himself.

The message carried an aura of disaster, of bad karma, if you will, that made his fur twitch and his paws tingle with sharp misgiving. The fact that Ryan didn't want to talk about it was sign enough that the request was going to screw up their lives. What was really worrisome was that, though she'd set the letter aside, she hadn't ignored it to the point of laying it facedown and slapping a book over it, or dropping it in the round file. This unsolicited bid for bed and board would, sooner or later, require her dutiful response. Joe knew what answer *he'd* give, but he guessed Ryan wouldn't follow his advice. Social courtesy is a human trait that most cats don't consider of much value. Except, of course, when that courtesy is toward the cat himself.

Now he watched Ryan select a dozen real estate ads, and lay them out beside him. He flattened his ears when she propped three ads rudely against his gray flank as if he was some kind of cute copyholder. She gave him an innocent green-eyed look and scratched under his chin until his ears came up again, of their own accord, and he felt a purr rumbling. That was the trouble with Ryan, her charm got him every damn time.

Some of the little houses were so cheap the brokers hadn't bothered with flyers or color pictures at all, had simply placed small black-and-white newspaper ads. Some were tiny old guesthouses, behind larger dwellings, which had apparently been sectioned off into their own lots. Two of the cottages were foreclosures, three were bank sales, all had suffered dizzying drops in price, as the economy fell. But in Molena Point, even the bottom of the barrel was still of value, every bit of land on the central coast was at a premium, and ocean-front lots were as dear as gold, even the smallest parcel worth as much as some Midwest mansions.

But that didn't mean Ryan and Clyde had to snap them up like a cat snatches mice from the cupboard. Rising impatiently, Joe sent the ads sliding off his side and across the table. Ryan gave him a look, and picked them up. "You needn't be so grumpy."

"You're collecting economic disasters," he said coolly, "gambling on a collapsing market, just begging to lose your shirts with these expensive toys."

"Market'll pick up," Ryan said gently. "You're just not big on patience."

"I'm patient on a mouse hole."

"You are patient tracking a felon," she said, reaching again, to scratch his ears. She always knew how to get to him. "I'd like to know who's bought up so many of these old places, though, grabbed them before the list-ings even hit the street." While expensive homes and estates had taken a tumble, it was the small vacation cottages and the homes of those who worked at the ser-vice trades that had been hardest hit.

But then suddenly many of these had been pur-chased overnight, including three of the cottages that Ryan and Clyde had badly wanted, that would have lent themselves to just the kind of renovations they enjoyed working on. And then after the houses went off the market so quickly, they had stood empty for months. No resale signs, no renters, no work crews making repairs to put them back on the market at a quick profit. They simply sat. Empty and uncared for, the weeds growing tall, the lawns turning yellow even with the early spring rains, the old paint peeling like the skin of an onion. This was not like Molena Point, where most of the cottages were carefully maintained, their paint fresh, their front gardens lush with bright blooms and flowering trees and bushes.

In two cases, in the very neighborhood where Ryan and Clyde had made their last purchase, the neighbors had begun to see hushed activity late at night around the neglected houses, soft lights behind drawn shades, strange cars pulling quietly into the drive and soon slipping away again.

And now here they were this morning, still looking at that blighted neighborhood despite the neighbors' unease and the whole country's worry over the real estate market—as if nothing here, in this village, could stay down for long.

But as the two diligently sorted through the ads, forever optimistic, Joe was more interested in the problem of the moment. In the letter on the mantel that needed decisive action before their happy home was invaded by some strange young woman in the throes of a divorce, with two cranky-looking kids in tow, a woman severely driven by a sudden lack of a home and income. If this Debbie Kraft gained a foothold, if she moved in with them as she was pushing to do, she might linger for months, as persistent as a bad case of mange.

Leaping from the table to the mantel, he read it again, looking pointedly at Ryan. This, not pie-in-the-sky real estate investments, was the dilemma facing them right now. He looked at the photograph of Debbie herself and the two little girls that she had enclosed hoping, perhaps, to charm an invitation from the Damens. There wasn't much charm apparent. She was a scrawny young woman with an angry scowl on her face, long, dull hair hanging loose down her back, her ankle-length denim skirt sagging at the hem, both children clinging to it like baby possums grasping their mother. The kids were maybe four years old, and twelve, both as ragged as their mother. The older child's expression was as sour as her mother's, too. The younger girl didn't look at the camera but stared at the ground, huddled into herself, perhaps in a fit of shyness, or perhaps fear. The best-looking one of the group was the cat, and even he didn't look too happy.

The older child held the big red tabby awkwardly in her arms, squeezing him so tight the cat's ears were flat to his broad, tomcat head. The camera had caught his ringed tail blurred, swinging in an angry lash, the cat obviously practicing great restraint in not slashing his juvenile captor. Debbie's letter didn't mention the cat, until the very end.

Dear Ryan,

It's been such a long time since our art school days in San Francisco. I tried to write to you at your old address. When the letter came back, I called your husband's office. What a shock that you'd divorced, and then he died. Well, I managed to wiggle your address out of them, anyway.

My situation has changed, too. I have two little girls, and now Erik has left me, so I guess men are all the same. He took all our savings. I have no money, even to pay a lawyer to try to get the child support he isn't paying. He stopped paying rent, so of course we were evicted, he did that to his own children. I have to be out by next week and I have nowhere to go. I have nothing, and no one who cares, but you. I have no job, and don't know what I'll do until I can get some money out of Erik.

He'd never dream I'd come to Molena Point, he knows I don't have anything to do with my mother, and that I don't see my sister. Of course he and Perry Fowler still own Kraft Realty and he's right there in the Molena Point office, that's all the more reason he won't expect to see me, he'll think I'd go far away from him. But I don't know where else to go, except there to you, there's no one else to help me, only you and Hanni, you and your sister are the only real friends I have. I'm glad Erik doesn't know about you, at least I kept some things to myself. I'm leaving Eugene the end of the week, but the drive down from Oregon will take longer with the kids, they always have to eat and go potty. Here's our picture that my neighbor took last year, the girls were cute then but they've gotten so gangly now. In the picture, Tessa is four, Vinnie is eleven. We don't have the cat anymore, Erik used to throw things at it, so I guess it ran away. A neighbor said it hung around the nursing home up the street, that they took it in, but then that burned down. The kids won't stop whining after it, so stupid. I'll see you soon, I do hope you have room for us, otherwise I don't know where we'd go.

Your friend and eager houseguest, Debbie Kraft

This was just great, just what they all needed, a whining houseguest with two kids, one that looked like a royal pain—and practically on Clyde and Ryan's anniversary, which they'd planned to spend having a quiet dinner with close friends. Joe looked again at the picture, focusing on the red tomcat, a handsome young fellow with wide, curving stripes. There was a certain look about him, a sharp awareness in his wide amber eyes that made Joe wonder, that made him pause with a keen curiosity. Debbie didn't seem to care that he might have died in the nursing home fire, in a shocking and painful death. Had she even bothered to look for him? Or was a child's lost cat like a lost hair ribbon, of only passing note and no value?

But the strangest part was, they had lived in Eugene. There was the home of Misto, the old yellow tomcat who had left Oregon before Christmas, hitting the highway to begin his journey south to Molena Point, searching for his kittenhood home. Both cats were from Eugene, both had the look that Joe knew well, that was not the look of any ordinary feline.

Misto had left three grown-up offspring somewhere in Eugene, he had lost track of all three as they ventured out on their own into the world.

Could this cat be Misto's son? The picture was taken a year ago. Now, was he even still alive? There was no one to ask, no one to know his fate or to care. When Joe looked down from the mantel, Ryan was watching him. "Stop frowning, Joe. She's not staying here."

Joe wasn't so sure. Ryan might be a no-nonsense businesswoman, but she had a soft spot for the less fortunate that, Joe feared, would make her cave right in, would let that woman move on in and take over their happy home.

Clyde said, "Why can't she go to her mother? What's that about? She's broke. No job. Two kids to feed. Let her go to her mother or her sister. The Fowlers are loaded, why can't she stay with them?"

"How can she?" Ryan said. "Perry Fowler's not only her brother-in-law, he owns half of Kraft Realty, he and Erik are co-owners. He'd be sure to tell Erik she's here." She shook her head, perplexed. "I don't know what the estrangement's all about, Debbie was always secretive, often for no reason at all. She told me once, years ago, she and her sisters would sneak around, sneak out at night. That she married Erik to get away from the village and from her mother, but she didn't tell me why. They ran off before she finished Molena Point High. Later, when she moved up to San Francisco, she was in some of my classes in art school, and in some of my sister's. Hanni couldn't bear her, no one could. She'd hang around on the edges of a group, pushing in, interrupting whatever you were talking about, always with a problem of her own that was far more important, always a dilemma she wanted someone else to solve for her. She'd borrow tubes of paint, lengths of expensive canvas, never return anything. She'd say she forgot, then say she didn't have the money. She cheated on tests, begged for rides even when it was miles out of everyone's way. Tag along if we went out for lunch, and then never have the money to pay for hers. She was just there one summer semester, she never graduated, and she never did much with what she did learn. Hanni was one of the gifted ones, and Debbie tagged after her. As if, if she stayed close, Hanni's talent—or her grades—would rub off on her."

After listening to Ryan's description, Joe considered packing his figurative suitcase and moving out for the duration—he knew Ryan wouldn't refuse this woman. He could move in with his tabby lady, take refuge with Dulcie and her housemate. Wilma Getz spoiled Dulcie worse than Ryan spoiled him, she'd serve up fillet, salmon, anything he asked for. The imminent descent of Debbie Kraft, with one kid who looked mean as snakes and another who was as yet an unknown quantity, made his head hurt and his skin twitch. If Ryan and Clyde wanted kids, they'd have some of their own. Looking again at the photo, he could find sympathy only for the cat.

"I always wondered," Ryan said, "what could possibly be so bad between mother and daughter, that Debbie never even phoned her, never wrote to her? Well, I guess any number of things could, but I can't get my head around it." Ryan's own mother had died of cancer when Ryan was small. They had been a close, happy family. The idea of hating your mother was foreign to her, and repugnant.

"Letter's dated eight days ago," Clyde said. "It's only a two-day drive down from Eugene. She says she has nowhere else to go, so where is she?" He glanced away in the direction of the street as if she might materialize, standing out there looking up at him. "Even the cheapest motel," he said, "the cheapest restaurant, is expensive if you're flat broke and have two kids to feed."

Joe said, "We could pull the shades. You could pull the cars on through the carport into the garage, pretend we're out of town."

"Quit worrying," Ryan repeated. "They're not staying here."

"Where, then?" Joe and Clyde said, together.

"Maybe the Salvation Army has room," she said, referring to the army's charity shelter.

"Did she write to Hanni, too?" Joe asked hopefully.

"She did. You know Hanni has no room, with their two boys." Ryan smiled. "Hanni said she wasn't inviting Debbie Kraft there to lift the good silverware and trash the house." Ryan's sister Hanni was among the best-known interior designers in the village, a glamorous woman with striking prematurely white hair, a penchant for bizarre and beautiful costumes, fabulous jewelry, and sleek convertibles—but with an even deeper attachment to old jeans, a fine hunting dog, and a good shotgun, an indulgence that, these days, she got to enjoy only rarely.

Ryan said, "Don't even suggest Charlie and Max. Though," she added with a wicked smile, "it would do Debbie good to live in a cop's house for a few days." The Harpers lived up among the green hills, happily alone except for their dogs and horses. Joe could just imagine the havoc two unruly kids could create among the defenseless animals, not to mention the danger, leaving gates open, letting the horses or dogs out onto the highway. And of course getting themselves stepped on by a hard hoof or snapped at by a usually patient mutt, and then blaming the Harpers. Charlie Harper worked at home, she didn't need the frustration of nosy houseguests underfoot. A published writer and a successful artist, she had commission deadlines, publishing deadlines, and had neither the time nor the patience for such an intrusion. Restlessly Joe dropped off the mantel. "Going for a little hunt," he said impatiently.

"You two can work out the logistics—just send her somewhere else."

Trotting from the studio into Clyde's office, he leaped to the desk and up onto the nearest rafter. Padding along beneath the ceiling, he pushed out through his rooftop cat door into his tower, into his hexagonal glass retreat that rose atop the roof of the master bedroom. This was his private place, daytime suntrap, nighttime lookout beneath the scattered stars—and now suddenly a trap for inexplicable nightmares that, he sincerely hoped, would not return.

Pausing among his sun-faded cushions, he nibbled at an itchy paw then pushed out a window onto the roof of the master bedroom. With the rising sun warming his sleek gray coat, he leaped away across the shingles into a tangle of oak branches and across these onto the neighbor's roof, then the next roof and the next, heading for Dulcie's house. He needed Dulcie to talk to; needed a good run with his lady by his side, needed to stalk and kill a few rats and work off the unease. The woman hadn't yet arrived, and already he was clawing for fresh air.

3

"You could be wrong," Dulcie said, licking blood from her paw, the sun gleaming off her brown tabby fur. When she looked up at Joe, her green eyes were questioning. "Debbie could be a perfectly nice person, just broke and alone. And scared, with two little kids to care for." They had been hunting all morning, had caught and devoured four fat wood rats between them. The hills rose emerald green around them, patterned with an occasional twisted oak, the land fresh with the scent of new growth and with the salty tang of the sea; the sea itself, down beyond the village, gleamed deep indigo beneath the wide, clear sky.

"She didn't ask if she could move in," Joe said, "she *announced* that she was, she did her best to make

Ryan feel sorry for her—played on her sympathy like a panhandler."

Dulcie flicked her tail. "You can move in with Wilma and me. Except," she said, cutting him a look, "you'd miss all the excitement and high drama." Having washed her whiskers, she nibbled delicately at the new winter grass, then looked down toward the village rooftops. "Kit's off with Misto again," she said with interest, thinking of Misto's ancient tales.

Joe laid back his ears. "She'll forget how to hunt. Misto's a fine old fellow, but . . . Does he have to fill her head with so many stories, with all that foolishness?"

"Not foolishness! He's taking her back through past ages, through our own history. Even the old myths grow from real history, Joe."

Joe sneezed. He didn't like tales of ages past, he didn't like all those yarns of peasants and nobles and magic that so pleased Dulcie and made Kit purr as if she'd rolled in the catnip; the tortoiseshell was enough of a dreamer without Misto's help. Pretty soon she'd hardly care what was happening here and now, and where could that kind of foolishness lead her?

Dulcie said, "Let her be, Joe. Misto's the closest thing she'll ever know to a father. She hardly even knew her mother, the only way she could hear the old tales was to crouch in the shadows at the edge of the wild clowder, just a tiny, scared kitten, listening. Not one of those cats wanted her there, no one wanted to love her and care for her. And as to the tales," she said softly, "if we don't understand our past, Joe, if we don't know where it all began, how can we understand what's happening now, all around us?"

Joe gave her an impatient look, and turned away. He didn't need to know what happened ten centuries gone, to make sense of life around him. He didn't need stories to tell him right from wrong, tell him the difference between good and evil. Both cats came alert as a band of coyotes began to yip, back among the hills. The beasts were very bold, for the middle of the day. With an alarmed look at each other they raced for the nearest oak tree, scrambling up its gnarled branches to safety, above the reach of prowling beasts. There, curled up together in a fork of the heavy branches, they slept. The sea wind whispered around them, the sun warmed them, and the coyotes remained busy looking for other prey. Dulcie dreamed of medieval villages, but Joe dreamed of Debbie Kraft, her invasion bolder than any hungry coyote, and then his dreams turned darker still, caught again in storm, and human rage, and a strange prophetic fear. When he woke, the bright day was gone.

The clouds were nearly as dark as his nightmare, heavy clouds hanging low above them, hurrying night along. They yawned and stretched, and smelled rain on the wind, and the wind itself had grown colder. Weather in Molena Point, which was notional any time of year, could never be trusted this early in the year. One moment the sidewalks and rooftops were burning hot, an hour later the streets and roofs were soaked with rain. Ever since Christmas the weather had swung from heavy storm, to idyllic spring, to days as humid as summer; only a cat could tell ahead of time what the day would bring, and this time of year even a cat might be inclined to wonder. The coyotes were silent now; the cats listened, and sniffed the breeze. When they detected no scent of the beasts nearby they backed down the rough oak trunk and headed home, thinking eagerly of supper.

Below them in the village, high on the rooftops, tortoiseshell Kit and Misto barely noticed the weather or cared that rain was imminent, they were deep into another time, another place, as the old yellow tom shared his ancient tales. The tide was out, the iodine smell of the sea mixed with the scent of the pine and cypress trees that sheltered the crowded little shops. As Misto ended a tale of knights and fiery dragons, as if in concert with his words the last rays of the setting sun blazed red beneath the darkening clouds. And when they looked down from the roof of Mandarin's Bakery where they sat, a thin stray cat, a white female, was slipping along the sidewalk and into the alley— toward a baited trap redolent with the smell of canned turkey. Maybe tonight she'd spring the trap and end her wandering.

Neither Kit nor Misto moved to stop her, to scramble down and haze her away from the waiting trigger that would snap the mesh door closed and shut her inside. This stray was starving on the streets and too fearful to approach strange houses for food, she was a dumped cat, an abandoned household pet with no real notion how to hunt for her living. Her instincts to chase and catch were still kittenish, without focus, without the skills wrought by training. She was a charming little cat but, in their opinion, helpless as a newborn.

It hurt Kit that so many unwanted pets roamed the village, animals often sick, thrown away by their human families. Coddled from kittenhood in warm houses, then suddenly evicted, they had little chance to survive on their own, no notion how to snatch gophers from the village gardens or snag unwary birds on the wing. Many still lingered hopefully near the very homes from where they'd been abandoned, houses standing empty now. Families without jobs, moved away suddenly, leaving the village to search for cheaper rent, cheaper food, for the possibility of work somewhere else. Families who dragged away their grieving children and left behind the little family cat, to make it on her own.

Only the boldest cats would yowl stridently at a strange cottage door demanding to share someone's supper, only the most appealing cats were taken in and given homes, while the shy and frightened and ugly were chased away again into the cold night.

Some of the strays didn't even belong to this village, they had been dropped from dusty cars stopping along the highway, the drivers tossing them out like trash and then speeding away among the heavy traffic, leaving a little cat crouched and shivering on the windy roadside. All across the state, more animals were abandoned as more houses were repossessed, or leases broken. With taxes rising, fewer customers and fewer jobs, many stores had closed in the village, their windows revealing echoing interiors furnished only with a few empty boxes left in a dusty corner. Ever since Christmas Kit and Misto, and Joe and Dulcie, had watched their human friends trap the strays and settle them in volunteer shelters. Sometimes one of the four would entice a stray into a trap, a strange occupation, helping to capture others of their kind—or, almost of their kind. There were no other cats in the village like these four.

No other cat who carried on conversations with a few favored humans, who read the local *Gazette* but shunned the big-city papers, who hung around Molena Point PD with an interest as keen as any cop—an interest no cop would ever believe. Misto was the newcomer among them, the old cat had shown up in the village just before Christmas, a vagabond who had once been a strapping brawler but was now shrunken with age, his yellow fur slack over heavy bones, his big paws worn and cracked, his yellow tail patchy and thin. But he was a wise old cat, and kind. Now, as they watched the white cat below, Kit gave Misto a shy look. "Tell about the cats from nowhere. Could some of these strays in the village, the ones we've never seen before, who seem to come from nowhere, could they be the same as in that tale?"

The old tom laughed. "These are only strays, Kit. Pitiful, lonely, scared, but not magic. Magic is for stories, just for make-believe."

Kit nipped his shoulder. "We're as different as the cats in the stories! And we're not make-believe. Do my teeth feel like make-believe?"

Misto swatted at her good-naturedly, and licked at his shoulder. "We're not magical, we're just different.

If those poor strays had any magic, do you think they'd be wandering hungry and lost? They'd have made something better happen for themselves."

"I guess." Kit cut her eyes at him. "Tell it again anyway," she wheedled. Above them the heavy clouds had dropped lower still, and a mist of rain had begun to dampen the shingles and to glisten on their fur. The story Misto told came from France; he had heard it among the docks on the Oregon coast, listening to the yarns of fishermen and sailing men while pretending to nap among the coiled lines and stacks of crab traps.

"Five centuries ago," Misto began, "in a small French town, dozens of cats appeared overnight suddenly prowling the streets, attacking the village cats, slashing the dogs, chasing the goats and even the horses, and snarling at the shopkeepers. With flaming torches the villagers drove them out, but secretly a few folk protected them. Next day, the cats returned, prowling and defiant, and they remained, tormenting the villagers, until on a night of the full moon they all disappeared at once. The moon rose to empty streets, every cat was gone.

"The villagers came out to celebrate, they danced until dawn, swilling wine, laughing at their release from the plague of cats.

"But when the sun rose, the villagers themselves had vanished. In their place were dozens of strangers, cat-like men and women who took over the shops, moved into the deserted cottages, settled onto the farms. It was their town, now. Not a native villager remained, except those few who had sheltered their feline visitors. Only they were left, to live out their lives among the cat folk, equitably and, I'll admit, with just a touch of magic," Misto said with a sly twitch of his whiskers.

Kit smiled, and licked her paw. Ever since she was a kitten, such tales had set aflame her imagination, had brought other worlds alive for her. Around them, gusts of wind scoured the rooftops and tattered the clouds ragged, and soon the rain ceased again, blown away. The sun appeared, swimming atop the sea in a blush of sunset, and below them on the nearly deserted street, an ancient green Chevy passed, heading for the sandy shore. Kit rose, the white cat forgotten, and the two cats followed, galloping over the wet rooftops until, at the last cottage before the shore, they came down to the narrow, sandy street where the old green car had pulled to the curb. The driver remained within, watching the shore.

Only three cars were parked near her, all familiar, all belonging to the nearby cottages; and there was not a pedestrian in sight. At last the driver's door swung open and an old woman stepped out, tall and bone thin, her narrow face and skinny arms tanned and wrinkled from the sun, her T-shirt and cotton pants faded colorless from age and many washings. Her walking shoes were old but sturdy, and as deeply creased as her face. She carried a brown duffel bag that Kit knew held soap, a towel, a toothbrush, clean clothes as thin and worn as those she wore. Heading for the little redwood building at the edge of the sand that held two restrooms, MEN and WOMEN, she disappeared inside.

Three days ago Kit had followed her, in the early morning, followed her into the dim, chill restroom, not liking the cold concrete beneath her paws, which was icky with wet sand. Wrinkling her nose at the smell of unscrubbed toilets, Kit had watched from behind the trash bin as the woman stripped down to the skin, shivering, and gave herself a sponge bath. How bony she was, and the gooseflesh came up all over her. She had to be homeless, living in her car, she was always alone, keeping away from crowds, careful to move away if a police car came cruising. Kit had watched her dress again in the fresh clothes she took from the duffel, watched her fill the sink with water, squeeze a handful of soap out of the metal dispenser that was screwed to the wall, watched her launder her soiled clothes and wring them out. Back in the car, she had spread her laundry out along the back, beneath the rear window. If the next day turned hot, they should dry quickly. If the morning brought fog or rain, the clothes would lie there wet and unpleasant and start to smell of mildew. Did she have only the one change of clothes? Had she always been homeless? She was nearly as pitiful as the stray cats of the village. Except, she had more resources than they did. She could speak to others, she could find some kind of job, she had a car and she must have enough money to put gas in the tank.

On several mornings, Kit and Misto had watched her carry a plastic bucket down to the shore, scoop it full of sand, and return to the car, leaving it inside. "Is she building a concrete wall?" Misto joked. "She's filling a child's sandbox," Kit imagined. "She's making a cactus garden," Misto replied. "She has a cat," Kit said, "she's filling a cat box."

But this evening the woman didn't bother with the sand. Reappearing from WOMEN, she spread her clothes out in the car, then, carrying a battered thermos and a brown paper bag, she walked down the sloping white shore halfway to the surf. She took a wrinkled newspaper from the bag, unfolded and spread it out on the sand, sat down on it as gracefully as a queen on a velvet settee. She unscrewed the thermos, poured half a cup of coffee into the lid, and unwrapped a thin, dry-looking sandwich that she might have picked up at the nearest quick stop—or fished out of the nearest trash. Eating her supper, she sat looking longingly out to the sea, as if dreaming some grand dream; and Kit and Misto looked at each other, speculating. Was her poverty of sudden onset, had she lost her job and her home? Had her husband died, or maybe booted her out for a younger woman? Or was she an itinerant tramp? Maybe a con artist, come to the village looking for a new mark?

But now as dusk fell, Misto rose, gave Kit a flick of his thin yellow tail, and headed away to his evening ritual. Kit watched him trot away along the edge of the sea cliff that climbed high above the sand. When she could no longer see him, when his yellow coat was lost among the tall, yellow grass, she spun around and raced for home, a dark little shadow leaping across the roof-tops and branches from one cottage to the next. Her two elderly housemates would have a nice hot supper waiting, and Pedric might have his own tales to tell, as the thin old man often did. But even as she fled for home thinking of a cozy evening with the two humans she loved best in all the world, the image of the bony old woman disturbed her, the sense of a life gone amiss, of pain and worry wrapping close the lonely woman who had no home and, Kit guessed, no friends.

4

A quarter mile to the south where the cliff rose high above the sand, a little fishing dock crossed the shore below, a simple wooden structure. A tall flight of wooden steps led up the cliff, to a path that met the narrow road above. The sun was gone now, and above a low scarf of dark clouds the evening sky shone silver. On the pale sand, long shadows stretched beneath the little dock; winding among them, a band of stray cats waited, circling the dark pilings shy and hungry, rubbing against the tarred posts, waiting for their supper, listening for the sound of an approaching vehicle. There was little traffic on the road above, though earlier in the day tourists' cars had eased past bumper to bumper, the occupants ogling the handsome oceanfront homes on the far side of the road, homes innovative in their architecture and surrounded by impressive gardens. That was a world apart from what the stray cats had ever known; they didn't go up there among humans to hunt, they kept to the wild and empty cliff and its little sheltering caves strung above the shore. Now, when they heard the van coming, still three blocks away, heard its familiar purr and the sound of its tires crunching loose gravel, they crouched listening, ears up or flattened, tails waving or tucked under, depending on how each one viewed the approaching human.

The van stopped on the cliff above, they heard the door open, listened to John Firetti's familiar step approaching the cliffside stairs, the soft scuff of his shoes as he descended the wooden steps.

He was a slim man, well built, his high forehead sunburned where his pale brown hair was receding. Mild brown eyes behind rimless glasses, a twinkle of compassion and amusement—and perhaps, too, a barely concealed expression of amazement. Even as he approached the cats, Misto came racing along the cliff to meet him, lashing his thin tail with humor, beating Firetti to the bottom, looking back up at him with a silent laugh. The veterinarian carried a big, crinkling bag of kitty kibble and meat, a paper sack of scraps that smelled of roast beef, and two fat jugs of water.

Descending to the sand, man and cat moved together beside the dock, from one feeding station to the
next, setting down bowls of kibble, rinsing and filling
water bowls. The bolder cats rubbed against John's
ankles, and none of them shied from Misto. Only two
cats kept away from the crowd, peering down from the
cliff above, half hidden in the tall grass. The two young
ones had arrived together, most likely dumped there,
and were shy and new to the group. Dr. Firetti and
Misto pretended not to notice them.

John Firetti had grown up in the village and had
never wanted to live anywhere else. Vet school at U.C.
Davis, and then his years at Cornell, that was a time
in his life when he studied hard, got his degrees, then
hurried home again to practice in his own small village,
near the open hills and the sea. Returning from college
he joined his father's practice, and joined, as well, the
older doctor's care of the seashore ferals, feeding them,
trapping and neutering any newcomers, giving them
their shots then turning them loose again. The two
veterinarians were among the first practitioners of the
Trap-Neuter-Release programs that were now at work
all over the country, helping sick and hungry stray cats,
and preventing the unwanted tide of homeless kittens.
Father and son had worked together in this venture,
just as in the practice, until John's father died of a

sudden massive stroke. They had, tending to the needs of the homeless band, harbored a dream that only a few people would understand or believe. John Firetti was nearly fifty when that dream came true—though the cat he had waited for was not from the feral band as he and his father had imagined. He was not one of the new generation of feral kittens that they had hoped would be born with special talents. Often such a skill skipped generations. In fact, after waiting and watching for so many years, John didn't discover the cat of his dreams at all.

The cat found him.

The good vet was only sorry his father wasn't there to share the wonder of their visitor. That meeting was the best Christmas present John, or Misto himself, could have imagined. John and his wife, Mary, were still amazed to be sharing their home with the talkative old tomcat, they never tired of hearing Misto's adventures. As for Misto, what could be more comforting than sharing his true nature, and his stories, with a pair of humans he knew he could trust? Having found his way back to the village after a lifetime of wandering, he'd received, from Joe Grey, a history of the Firettis more complete than any cop's background report; moving in with the Firettis, he felt as if they had always been family. Evenings before the fire, the three of them trading stories, was a dream answered for all three of them.

This evening Misto watched the wild little cats eating nervously and glancing around to make sure no dog or human came up the beach; but when John went back up the stairs to approach two humane traps that he had hidden in the forest of grass, Misto followed him.

The doors of both traps were bound open with bungee cords; Misto sniffed at them, then looked up at John. "They've been inside," he said, his whiskers twitching at the scent of the two half-grown kittens. "Been in again, licked the plates dry again."

John pulled out the empty dishes. "I think it's time." He put in new dishes that smelled of freshly opened tuna. He removed the bungee cords from the doors, so they would slam shut the instant a cat moved deep inside and stepped on the flat metal trigger that looked like part of the cage floor. The slamming door would scare the captive but in no way would harm him; he'd be deep inside, two feet away, when it sprang closed.

"They're only kittens," Misto said. "Maybe you'll find homes for them, maybe the people who dumped them will find a place to live and come back for them."

John turned to look at him. "Would you give them back?"

Misto lowered his ears. "I guess not, I guess they wouldn't take any better care of them the second time around." Man and cat shared a comfortable look, and headed away together where they could watch the traps unnoticed. They were halfway to the van when Joe Grey came trotting over the roof of a sprawling clifftop home, and paused to watch.

Having left Dulcie among the roofs of the village shops, he'd watched her head for the library where, during the busy evening hours, she would preen among her admirers, always dutiful as the official library cat. He had to smile at the number of pets and hugs she'd receive from patrons all unaware that, moments earlier, the tabby's sweet face and dainty paws had been grisly with the blood and gore of freshly slaughtered rats.

Too full of rat himself to go home for supper, he'd headed for the shore, for the little ceremony of the evening feeding. Moving over the rooftops, he had appeared as only a gray shadow within the shadows of the sheltering oaks, his white markings dancing along like pale moths, white stripe of nose, white paws and apron as disembodied as the Cheshire cat's fading smile.

Dropping down onto the low roof of a jutting bay window, he watched John Firetti step into the van. The vehicle was unmarked by the veterinarian's name or the name of the clinic, just a plain white Dodge van that was almost a hospital in itself, equipped inside with cupboards, drawers of medicines and bandages, animal stretchers and cages enough to handle most emergencies, to care for sick and hurt animals while transporting them to the clinic. Joe watched Misto leap to the abbreviated hood of the van and stretch out against the windshield. He watched John, in the driver's seat, unscrew the cap on his thermos, and he smelled the aroma of rich coffee. Joe remained still and apart for some time before he scrambled down a jasmine vine, trotted across the little road and leaped up onto the hood beside Misto.

Together they watched the traps that were just visible among the tall, yellowed grass, just as John was watching. Joe had thought, coming across the roofs, that someone had been watching *him*, but it was only a feeling. He saw no one, and now that sense of another presence was gone.

They watched the grass twitch and shiver as the two young cats peered out. In the cab, John Firetti was very still, not a movement, no smallest sound, only the smell of coffee, no different than if it had come from the nearby cottages. The trapping took as much patience as watching a mouse hole, patience not only to trap the cat but to care for him, doctor him, prepare him for a new home or, if he was feral, to notch his ear and release him again into his own wild world. The only changes in the cat's life were that he would be healthier, and that he'd miss all the fun of making kittens.

Now, the two young cats slipped out from the grass, nervous and wary but yearning toward the smell of tuna. The pale silver tabby was maybe a year old, the scruffy black kitten half that age. They crept belly down toward the reek of tuna, easing toward the cages, sniffing eagerly through the mesh walls. Once they dodged away, then crept close again. Impetuously, the black kitten skittered into the nearer cage; she paused just inside, shivering. When nothing bad happened she crept toward the back where the tuna waited. The silver tabby started to follow her but tonight something alarmed him, made him draw back.

For a week, the two had been taking their supper in the traps, the tabby always wary, slower to enter the bungeed trap but at last following the black. They would clean up one bowl together, then move to the other cage and do the same. They had no notion that at every meal they walked over an inactivated trigger—cats know nothing of triggers. The kitten had no clue that tonight, before she reached the tuna, the door would spring closed behind her and . . .

Snap. It slammed down as loud as a gunshot. The kitten bolted into the wire mesh, stepped in the cat food, bolted away into the closed door and then into the side again, throwing herself at the wire, clawing frantically at it as Firetti swung out of the van and ran to drop a big, dark towel over the cage.

At once the kitten quieted. The terrible thudding stopped, all was still within. A trapped creature, a feral cat or raccoon, a bobcat or cougar kitten, will fight an uncovered cage until they are so badly cut and wounded they will die or must be killed. Even domestic cats will do the same, terrified, wanting out. They can see outside, and they fight to get out there. Only the dark cover, blocking their view, will calm them.

The pale tabby had disappeared back among the grass and poison oak, where he would be peering out. John was sorry not to have caught him—now he'd be twice as hard to capture. Carrying the covered trap, and opening the side door of the van, Firetti didn't see, behind him, the silver tabby come out to follow him. Only Joe and Misto saw.

The young cat approached nervously, bravely following his friend. Above him, Misto looked through the windshield, back into the van, and caught John's eye. He twitched an ear toward the tabby. John looked, and froze.

For a while, he stood immobile. Then silently he lifted the cage up onto the floor of the van and backed away.

It took a long while for the silver tabby to approach. He looked up at Misto and Joe, but seemed unafraid of them. Misto, taking a chance, dropped down from the hood, padded casually to the open door, and leaped into the van. He lay down a few feet from the cage and stretched out, purring.

The tabby, watching him, crept closer; but every muscle was tensed to run. He looked in at Misto, then at the cage. Looked up through the windshield at Joe. Looked back at John, who stood far away.

At last he hopped up into the van. Misto remained stretched out, limp, as the silver tabby nosed under the towel, where he could see the kitten. When he had made sure she was all right, he settled down halfway beneath the towel, his rear end sticking out, his striped silver face pressed against the wire, close to his young friend. This was not a feral cat, the beautiful tabby had been someone's pet. Slowly Misto strolled out of the van, dropped to the ground, and John eased the sliding door closed.

It was now, behind them, that a shadow moved across the street among the tall bushes, a thin figure, watching them.

"Someone's there," Joe said softly. As John turned, the figure stepped out of the shadows. A woman, bone thin and tall, deeply tanned, dressed in ancient jeans and colorless T-shirt. The cats could see, down the street, the bumper of her battered green Chevy where it was angled into someone's drive, half hidden by a wooden fence.

She approached the van, studying John's face. She was just about his height, her brown hair slicked back in an untidy bun, her sun-browned face wrinkled and leathery. She peered past John, trying to see in through the van's tinted window. "Where are you taking them? What did you mean to do with them? Those are my kittens, I'll take them now."

"Why would I give them to you, after you've abandoned them?"

"I couldn't help it. I thought they'd be safe here with the other cats, I know you feed those cats. I live in my car, you can't leave cats in a car, the heat would kill them. What did you mean to do with them? Who are you? Open the door, they're mine."

"I mean to feed them and care for them," John said. "You haven't done that, you abandoned them. The little one needs defleaing, and they need their shots. Kittens—"

"They've had their shots."

"Which shots? Which vet? There are only two clinics."

"Dr. . . . I don't remember his name. The one on Ocean, behind the Mercedes agency."

"Firetti's Clinic?"

"Yes, that's it. Ask them, they'll tell you."

"Which doctor?"

"I don't remember. Dr. Firetti, I guess."

"That clinic has only one doctor. I'm John Firetti."

She looked at John a long time, her face crumpling, a dampness welling in her brown eyes. "You were going to take them somewhere that would put them down."

"I wouldn't take them to a shelter that kills unwanted cats. But these kittens aren't ferals, they shouldn't be abandoned and on their own."

"You'd take care of them?" she said, not believing him.

"Of course I would."

"You'd keep them safe, and I can come for them when I find another place? I lost my job, I couldn't pay my rent, I have no place to keep them."

How many abandoned strays, Joe wondered, was John Firetti already sheltering at the clinic? Actually, the woman looked worse off than the kittens, half starved, badly used by the world.

"What's your name?" John said. "How do you manage, living in your car?"

"I'm Emmylou Warren. I was renting a shack on the Zandler property, there along the river, one of the old workers' cabins. I lost my job bagging groceries. Well," she said crossly, "my neighbor *could* have let me stay with her until I found a place, even if she *does* have only the one room." Her anger made Joe uneasy, or maybe it was her mention of workers' cabins along the river, though he couldn't think why. Dropping to the ground, he caught Misto's eye, then glanced away toward her car; both cats were of one mind as they slipped away through the shadows of the darkening street to where the nose of the Chevy stuck out among the bushes.

The windows were open. The interior of the battered Chevy smelled of banana skins, crackers, damp clothes, and still smelled of the two young cats. When Joe leaped in through the back window, he sank alarmingly among a mass of bulging plastic bags and folded blankets. Misto followed, scrambling over the sill, descending carefully down among the clutter.

Beneath the bags and blankets were cardboard boxes of canned goods, paperback books, and pots and pans. Stretching up to peer out the back window, making sure Emmylou wasn't headed their way, Joe dropped down again among the detritus, sniffing at the tied plastic bags, pawing into the boxes. He didn't know what he was looking for. He wanted to know more about the woman, to know why she made him uneasy. "She's living in her car, all right. Her blankets could stand a good washing." Pawing into a box among paper plates and kitchen utensils, he unearthed a padded brown envelope, the kind lined with bubble wrap. There was something hard inside, making it bulge. No address on the envelope, no writing at all. It wasn't sealed. He peered in, reached in with an inquisitive paw. At the same moment Misto hissed like a den of snakes and Emmylou's thin shadow came soundlessly along the side of the car, approaching the driver's door. The cats exploded through the opposite window, hit the sidewalk in a gray and yellow tangle, scorched into the bushes as Emmylou opened her door.

They listened to her start the engine, watched her pull away. She had no clue they'd been in the car—but what would she care, they were only cats. Behind her, another pair of headlights blazed on and the white van came down the street, moving slowly as John Firetti looked for them. When his lights flashed in their eyes he pulled to the curb, reached over and opened the passenger door.

"What was that about?" he said softly, having apparently watched them toss the car. The cats padded out of the bushes grinning with embarrassment, and Misto hopped up into the van. They both looked down at Joe.

"Headed home," Joe said, not wanting to explain his nosiness. *Just curious,* he thought. *Just . . . something about Emmylou Warren,* he thought, puzzled. He watched them pull away down the street, the pale van melting into the darkening evening, its red taillights growing smaller as they ferried their two little captives home to a good meal, a flea bath, a session with the hair dryer, and a nice warm bed.

Then, scrambling up a pine and up the shingles of a steep roof, Joe galloped away across the rise and fall of the crowded peaks, across heavy old oak branches that embraced the village houses, racing for home himself, wondering if the soft staccato of his thudding paws startled the occupants below, made them think they had rats in the attic.

5

It was two days later, just at dawn, that Joe woke in his rooftop tower to a bright red sunrise flickering up against the clouds above. *Flickering?* He leaped up from his cushions, saw flames licking and dancing among the eastern hills. Fire, running wild just where the Harper land lay along the crest. He reared up, staring, praying it was down the hill below their pastures, not their barn or house afire. He bolted in through his cat door onto the rafter, dropped to the desk below shouting, "Fire! Fire!" then realized no one was there. Remembered hearing both the car and truck drive away before ever it was light. Clyde had headed up the coast to look at a client's 1920 Rolls-Royce that had inexplicably quit running, and Ryan left even earlier to trap one of the feral cats; the night before he had watched her tuck her cages and cat food into the pickup among her ladders and wheelbarrow.

Spinning around, he hit the phone's speaker and pawed in 911, his heart pounding.

Were the Harpers' horses trapped in their stalls, helpless? Had Max already left for work? Had Charlie seen the blaze or had she, too, left early, out with Ryan and Hanni, trapping strays? The day before, half a dozen more homeless cats had been called in, and already the three temporary shelters were full. He was still shouting at the night dispatcher when he heard a siren whoop. Quickly he broke the connection, raced into Ryan's studio, leaped on the daybed where he could see out the east windows, reared up slamming his sweating paws against the glass.

The sky was barely light, streaks of gray and silver, the hills still dark except for the lick of orange flames rising up mixed with smoke darker than the heavy dawn clouds. If the flames reached the Harper land, reached the Harper barn with the horses still inside . . . Even if they had already been turned out they'd be at danger, terrified by the fire, running blindly into the fences. A panicked horse could injure himself so badly that, sometimes, he had to be destroyed. Leaping for the phone on Ryan's desk, he punched in the Harpers' number, shivering with nerves.

When Charlie didn't answer he tried her cell phone. "Come on! Come on!" He was trying to calculate just how far the blaze might be from the Harpers' pasture fence when he heard the shriek of a police car following the fire trucks. He prayed it was the siren on the police chief's pickup, prayed Max was on the way.

Charlie had left the ranch long before daylight, she was up above the village, kneeling in the side yard of a small clapboard cottage among a mass of scratchy holly bushes, setting a trap for an old black cat who had been hanging around the vacant house. She was about to put the bait in when a work crew pulled up in front, a truck laden with ladders, lawn mower, gardening equipment. Pretty early for a gardening crew to be coming to work.

The driver was a handsome Latino boy she didn't know, and there was no logo on the truck indicating any of the usual village gardening services. A car full of Mexican workers pulled up behind, parking at the curb. She watched the driver crimp the wheels in the wrong direction, assuring that if the brakes failed, the vehicle would careen backward down the hill clear to the bottom or until it crashed into a house or car. Five Hispanic men got out. They were dressed in jeans and sweatshirts, but something about them was off, they didn't look like garden workers, they were too focused on the house, too quick yet wary in their movements. Quietly she picked up the cat food, closed the cage door, and headed away. This stray wouldn't come around now anyway, until these men had left. It was only a few days since the department had raided a meth house just two blocks over, and maybe she was extra wary. Or not, she thought. The meth raid had been a nasty shock to every one of the few families still living in the small neighborhood. She was wondering if she should set the trap up the street, wondering how far this cat roamed, when her phone vibrated. Picking up, she spoke quietly.

Joe's voice came loud and clear, shouting with a mewling panic, "Fire! Fire below the ranch, below the north pasture. Fire trucks on the way."

She grabbed the empty trap and rose, had hardly hung up when the phone vibrated again. "Fire below the ranch," Max said. "Where are you? Can you help get the horses out?"

She ran, swung the cage into her SUV, and headed for home, punching in the single digit for Ryan's cell phone as she barreled down the hill. Ryan was out trapping, too; Charlie had talked with her once and she already had one young stray safe in her truck. Ryan answered in a whisper, "The cat's approaching, I'm in my truck. Can I call you back?"

"There's a fire below the ranch, I'm going to get the horses out. Come when you can."

For an instant, Ryan hesitated. The cat was so close. A black-and-white shorthair, a tuxedo, very thin, his fur all awry. If she scared him off, it might take weeks to lure him back again. But the horses . . . She held her breath as the cat stuck his head in the trap, but then he paused. She'd give him a minute longer. He must be starving. He hesitated, sniffing the smell of freshly opened tuna, then something spooked him, he spun around and took off.

Half defeated, half relieved, she threw the cage in the backseat of her king cab and took off fast for home, pausing for tourists and for stop signs so the few blocks seemed to take forever. Skidding into the drive, she ran in hauling the one covered cage, and shut it in the guest room. The cat would be all right for an hour or two. Racing back out, she could hear Rock pawing indignantly at the back door. She left him in the yard, she didn't need an excited Weimaraner racing among the frightened horses. Maybe it was those old shacks below the pastures that were burning, those ancient workers' cottages from years ago when the river delta was farmed for artichokes. She thought they were rented now, though how much rent could you charge for an old wooden cabin that let the wind whistle through? The three places were tinder, that was sure, dry as a bone. She could see thick gray smoke ahead, rising over the lower hills, hiding the Harpers' pasture.

Turning up the hill beyond the village, speeding up the narrow two-lane, she watched the fire licking up below the north pasture. She had to slow to pass a dozen cars that were pulled over to the side, their drivers rubbernecking. Why did people do that, why did they feel compelled to get in the way, slow down the firefighters and police? She was nearly to the Harpers' turnoff when she heard Joe scramble up from the backseat, felt his paw on her shoulder. "Can't you drive faster? Those poor horses."

"I can drive faster and get us both creamed," she said, glaring at him. At home, when she'd settled the cat cage in the guest room, she'd called out for Joe but there was no answer, and that had been worrisome. Racing out to the truck, she'd prayed he hadn't gone galloping up into the hills alone headed for the fiery canyon, had told herself Joe had better sense, that he wouldn't do that. She turned, scowling at him. "Now that you've made your presence known, would it do any good to ask you to stay out of trouble?"

"Does anyone live down there?"

"An old woman, I think. I've heard she's a pretty heavy drinker, maybe she accidentally started the fire. And her grandson—Billy's a nice kid, he works for Max and Charlie sometimes, feeding, cleaning stalls. I guess Hesmerra's the only family he has." She sped up when she'd passed the gawkers, turned left onto the Harpers' gravel road. No point scolding Joe for slipping into the truck, no point telling him he'd be in danger around the fire, it would only make him bolder. She parked on the shoulder where the lane was blocked, where Charlie had shut the gate to the yard. She got out and slipped through the gate, Joe Grey trotting beside her. Ahead, Charlie was leading her sorrel mare and a boarder across the yard at a trot, toward the south pasture. Already Ryan's eyes stung from the smoke as she went to halter two more horses.

Charlie couldn't see the fire below the hill, could see only dark smoke rising up, as she moved the first two nervous horses through the north gate into the stable yard, her mare snorting and pulling back. She could see in her mind the three weathered field hands' shacks that stood below the hill huddled at the edge of the floodplain beside the river. Surely the old woman and Billy had gotten out, those places were so small, only a few steps to the door or a window. Hesmerra

Young. Everyone called her Gran. Charlie thought of her and Billy waking to flames, the blaze licking at the walls and ceiling, and she felt her stomach lurch. But surely they were safe, the fire trucks were there now, and she tried to ease her worry. Billy Young was only twelve, a silent, shy boy, with gentle hands for a horse or dog; he worked for the Harpers at odd times when they needed extra help. Maybe, when the fire broke out, he was already gone, off on his bike to work at one of the other ranches. Often, as Max headed to work before daylight, he'd see Billy somewhere on the road on his bike, and give him a lift, throw the bike in the back of the pickup. The boy did odd jobs for many of the local horse people, cleaned stalls, fed, cleaned tack, lunged and exercised the horses. She guessed he went to school when he chose, maybe in the afternoon. She didn't know how he managed that, maybe he had a work permit like their young friend Lori Reed, who was learning carpentry as Ryan's part-time apprentice. Charlie liked that a kid wanted to learn a hands-on skill, in addition to getting a formal education. If Billy was gone when the fire started, if his gran was alone there sleeping off a hangover, had she gotten out, had she even smelled smoke? Redwing reared again, fighting the rope, but the boarder, a bay gelding, was calm and sensible. By leading them together, she got them across the yard and into the south pasture, as far from the flames as their land went. As she eased the mare through, her phone vibrated. Latching the gate, she picked up. "I'm moving the horses," she told Max. She looked up as Ryan's truck pulled in.

"Shall I come up?" Max said.

"No, Ryan's here, we're fine. I'll call if we need help. Shall we hook up the trailers?"

"No, they have it under control, not a breath of wind down here," he said curtly.

He sounded strange. She said, "Is everyone all right?"

"Everything under control," he said shortly. "I have to go." He hung up, startling her.

Something was wrong, he hadn't wanted to talk. She told herself they were busy, the place must be chaos, the men cleaning up, to keep the last of the blaze contained, not let it creep along and start in the surrounding fields. The bottomland along the river lay fallow now, gone to coarse grass and weeds, the owner waiting for an upturn in the market, for some developer to give him an inflated profit. She didn't like the thought of condos or tract houses down here, destroying the open land where she liked a nice gallop along the trail that ran beside the river. Max said no one would build houses on the flood bed, they'd have to be certifiably crazy. But all over California, people had done just that, built on cheap lowland, and then were surprised when, during heavy weather, their living rooms filled up with river mud.

She could hear the firefighters' shouts, could still hear the hiss of water hitting the buildings, the dull chunk, chunk of shovels as if the men were cutting back dry weeds or pitching rubble and loose boards away from the hot spots. Ryan joined her at the north gate. They haltered the other four horses and led them across the yard, Max's buckskin gelding snorting, strung with nerves. Probably the fire wouldn't climb the hill, with no wind, but the horses sure could smell it, and that was all they needed. At least the new green grass was rich with moisture, not tinder dry. But still, a sudden wind whipping up the cliffs from the sea, and who knew what the blaze would do? Well, the trailers stood ready if they were needed, the tires inflated, and all their horses would load easily. It was that, or tie the bunch of them head-to-tail and lead them all at once to safety, to one of the neighbors' pastures.

Slapping Bucky on the rump she sent him trotting away, the other three following him closely, as if Bucky might protect them. Ryan's short dark hair was atangle, the collar of her jacket turned under as if she'd pulled it on fast, leaving the house in a hurry.

With the horses moved, Charlie let the two big mutts out of the barn and put them in the south pasture with the horses. They took both vehicles, heading for the blaze, Charlie following Ryan's truck. She could see Joe Grey sitting tall on the back of the seat. A right turn, and right again a quarter mile down the hill, and they bumped along the narrow dirt track that skirted the bottomland, heading into the smoke and the tangle of men and vehicles, the confusion of fire hoses spewing water, undulating like muscular pythons. They parked short of the burn, against the hill, and got out. Charlie smiled as Ryan threatened Joe Grey.

"You stay in the truck, Joe. I mean it."

Joe sighed, put his head on his paws, his ears down, as if browbeaten. He couldn't say a word in front of the firefighters. How was that fair?

"Don't scold him," Charlie said softly. "It was Joe who called in the report." She reached in to stroke his head, and gave him a wink. "Ryan worries about you," she said. He gave her a smile and a cranky sort of purr.

As the two women headed into the burn, a little smoky breeze whipped ashes in their faces. Most of the flames had been smothered, but where the blackened walls had fallen in, their remains burned cherry red. The smell of wet, burned wood was mixed with the odors of melted plastic, melted electrical wires, burned food, a stink that made them gag. Four men were raking refuse farther away from the smoldering boards, piling it against the hill beyond a tangle of old timbers, wooden barrels, and an old door with peeling veneer. Past the black, sodden remains of the shack, the white EMT van stood parked near the two fire trucks. The firemen and two medics stood there in a circle with Max. His thin face was streaked with soot, black smears stained his western shirt and jeans. He had turned away from Charlie and Ryan. That, and the look on the medics' faces, made Charlie go cold; turning, she took Ryan's hand.

Not twenty feet from the burn, the other two cabins stood untouched, their rough wood siding soaked from the beating water, the roofs dripping. As Charlie and Ryan moved toward the group of men, a sick smell reached them, the stink of meat singed too fast on a hot barbecue. The circle of men nearly hid the portable gurney beside the EMT van. They could see it held a stretcher, strewn with a heap of blackened rags.

But not only rags. Charlie made out a frail body tangled among burned blankets.

Max turned to look at her, his mouth and jaw drawn tight. "She never left her bed, Charlie. She was there under the blankets, dressed in her flannel nightgown." Charlie pressed her fist to her mouth. Max said, "There was glass in her bed, shards of glass under the blanket, as if a bottle had exploded in the flames."

Behind them, up the dirt road, the coroner's white van pulled in off the two-lane, and behind it came a kid on a bike, leaning over the handlebars pumping hard, kicking up dust as he skidded off the highway onto the dirt lane, following the van. Skidding to a stop beside it, dragging his foot in the dirt, Billy Young sat looking at his burned house and the group of silent men.

6

Joe crouched on the dash of Ryan's truck looking out through the windshield, watching Billy. The boy sat on his bike looking at the black and smoking remains of his home: the heap of fallen timbers, steam rising up from the alligatored wood. His fists were clenched hard on the handlebars, his face gone white. He was so thin his protruding wrists looked like the bones someone would throw to a hungry dog. His face was long, his cheeks sculpted in close, his brown eyes huge with shock, a look that made Joe's belly twist, that made embarrassing cat tears start—this was as sad as watching an orphaned kitten whose mother had been hit by a car.

He was dressed in frayed jeans limply shaped to his legs, run-over boots, a ragged khaki jacket that might have come from a local charity. Brown hair clipped short and uneven as if Gran took a pair of dull shears to it once in a while. Joe had seen him out in the fields when he and Dulcie and Kit were hunting, they'd see him scrounging the mom-and-pop vegetable farms, picking up culls, dropping them in a black plastic bag: cabbages that had been accidentally cut and were left to rot, ears of corn that might have been wormy, tomatoes that had been missed or that the birds had pecked open.

Max stepped over, blocking Billy's view of the gurney, and put his arm around the boy, but Billy had already seen what was there. The firemen and medics had turned away, with their backs to him, so as not to stare at his grief. Joe watched Billy try to get his mind around what had happened, try to come to terms with the body on the stretcher.

Did the boy have anyone else, besides his gran? *What happens to an orphaned boy?* Joe wondered. *Will some county authority take him away, tell him where to live, put him in a foster home or institution? Tell him he can't work anymore, that he's too young to work? Confine him in a straitjacket of legal hierarchy? Is Billy Young nothing more than county property now?*

Max walked the boy away from the stretcher, talking softly; they talked for some time, Billy hesitantly asking questions, Max's answers direct and brief. When Billy turned again toward the medics' van, Max shook his head, discouraging him from approaching the burned body, and guided him instead toward Ryan's truck. Watching them, Joe dropped to the seat and curled up, his chin on his paws, his eyes slitted closed.

"No one else has been around here?" the chief was saying. "Anyone who might have accidentally started the fire?"

"No one ever comes here," Billy said. "Except Mr. Zandler, to get the rent." He didn't bother to wipe the wetness from his cheeks. Joe knew Zandler, he was the kind of scruffy and rude old man that a cat made a wide path around. A lanky and stooped man, shaggy black hair and bristly beard, old black three-piece suit, grubby white shirt, a necktie loose and crooked and dark enough to hide some of the grease stains. Billy said, "Sometimes my uncle comes, my aunt's husband. He likes Gran. But Aunt Esther never comes, neither of my aunts do. Gran's own daughters."

"That would be Erik Kraft," Max said.

Billy nodded. "I need to tell him. So he won't come, find the house burned." Joe thought if he were to reach out a paw and touch Billy, he'd feel him shivering, the kind of tremor you didn't really see, that came from deep down inside.

"Did your uncle come often?" Max asked.

Billy shook his head. "Maybe three or four times a year. He'd give her spending money, fill up her whiskey stash. He said if her daughters wouldn't give her money, he would. Said it was no one's business what she did with it. He said her daughters didn't realize how hard it was on her, raising me alone. But I always worked," Billy said, "ever since Mama died I worked to help out."

"I know you have," Max said. "The other two cabins, they're empty? Isn't there another tenant?"

"A woman lived in one, Emmylou Warren. After Christmas she lost her job and couldn't pay, and Mr. Zandler made her leave. Gran . . . Gran wouldn't let her stay with us, she said we didn't have room. Well, there is . . . was only the one room. Emmylou's my friend, but I don't know where she went."

"And the other cabin?"

"It's empty, half the roof's fallen in, the floor rotted. The back room, where it doesn't leak, I have some cat beds there, for my strays. I need to find them, they'll be so scared."

Max nodded. "Go on, then," as if he was relieved to see Billy distracted for a moment, or going off in private to get himself together. As Billy turned away, Max said, "If you can corral them, we can take them up to the ranch. You don't want to leave them here alone, the coyotes will take over now."

Billy turned to look at him. "I'll still be here. I can sleep just fine in the room with the cats. Until Zandler kicks me out," he added uncertainly.

"You can't stay here alone."

"Why not?" Billy said defiantly. "You going to turn me in, Captain Harper? Send me to some home? What about my cats? No one can keep me in a home, I won't stay."

"You can't stay here," Max repeated. "The minute someone at Child Welfare hears about your grandmother's death, they'll come nosing around. Go find your cats, Billy. There's room for you at the ranch. You and Charlie can move the cats up the hill, shut them in a stall until they settle in."

Billy looked at Max for a long time. He turned away at last, moving off toward the little stand of willow trees farther along the hill, wiping his sleeve across his face. The little wood was a natural shelter where the frightened cats would have fled from the fire and noise, from the trucks roaring in, from strange men shouting, from the flames and smoke and from the violent jets of water. Walking away, Billy avoided the burn. Circling away from the fire truck and the medics' and coroner's vans, his shoulders were slumped, grief clinging around him as he went to gather up his wild little cats. Maybe they were the only real family he had left, Joe thought. The only creatures in the world who cared about him were there, crouching hidden among the willow grove. But then, looking toward the grove, Joe suddenly felt the skin along his back twitch violently, and he was thinking no longer of the frightened cats, he was seeing his stormy nightmare, seeing the same grove, the same stand of willows; but in his dream they had been blowing wildly, whipped by the driving rain. The same cliff rising up behind, rising up to the Harpers' pasture; and the two shacks that the fire had left standing were surely a match for the rain-drenched hovel of his dream. He felt sick, he was shivering. What was this, what was he seeing? Or, what *had* he seen, in that midnight violence?

That dream had been Kit's kind of wild fancy, or could even be a product of Dulcie's imaginative vision. Such dreams were not a part of his own nature.

And yet this was not fancy, he *had* dreamed of this place, this cluster of derelict pickers' shacks that he must have seen dozens of times while hunting the field along the river but which, until that night, until now, had no special meaning for him.

Billy returned sooner than Joe would have thought, with a dark tabby tomcat wriggling in his arms. He shut him into the fallen-down shack and had turned back to find the others when Charlie and Ryan caught up with him. They talked with him a few minutes, then

Charlie swung into her SUV and pulled away, turning up toward the ranch. Ryan headed for her truck and, opening the door, seemed relieved to see Joe safe inside. "Billy'll be all right for a little while," she said, "rounding up his cats. We'll just run down to Firetti's, borrow some cat carriers. It'll take the most frightened ones a while to come to him."

"Is he all alone?" Joe said. "Except for his aunts? What's that about, that they never see him? Where's his mother? His father?"

"His mother's dead. His father . . . no one knows," Ryan said. Turning right onto the two-lane, she glanced over at him. "Why would his aunts leave a child to grow up in that falling-down shack with that drunken old woman? Everything I've heard, she started sucking up whiskey first thing in the morning, the minute she rolled out of bed. She did work, though. Worked nights, cleaning offices. I guess she drank and slept during the day, apparently held her liquor well enough to function on the job. Some drunks are like that. That was her old Volvo parked off against the hill."

"When the fire started," Joe said, "could she have been so drunk she didn't even know, never tried to get out? Those shacks aren't as big as a one-car garage; she could have rolled out of bed right into the yard. Was she so passed out drunk, she never knew?

"Or," he said, "was she already dead when the fire started?"

Ryan gave him a sharp look. "You didn't hear the coroner? He said maybe she was dead. Said it was hard to tell, she was so burned. We'll know more once he gets her back to the lab and has a look." She turned onto Ocean, heading for Clyde's shops, and reached for her cell phone; she hit the single digit not for Clyde's automotive shop itself, but for Clyde's cell. "You back from up the coast?"

"Just pulled in," Clyde said.

"Can you have lunch?"

"Sure, what's up?"

"We're just pulling up outside. It's about Billy Young, about his grandmother."

Joe thought maybe it was Hesmerra who had once worked with the night crew that cleaned Clyde's shops and the Beckwhite dealership that occupied the other half of the sprawling, Spanish-style building. Some old woman Clyde had complained about, had said she'd better not be drinking when she cleaned his shop. But in a strange way, Joe thought Clyde must have been fond of the old woman. He said once, she held her liquor well—no brawling street fights, Joe guessed. No vicious cussing matches.

Ryan ended the call, made a left across traffic, and pulled onto the red tile paving of Clyde's wide, commercial driveway. The automotive shop occupied the north half of the Beckwhite building. The white, one-story structure, with its red tile roofs, was brightened by climbing red bougainvillea and stone pines alternating against its pale stucco walls. Clyde came out through his garage-sized entrance, removing the white lab coat that he wore around the shop, revealing a red polo shirt and jeans, and brown leather Rockports. The satisfied look on his face told Joe he'd probably repaired the Rolls-Royce just fine and wouldn't have to haul it down the coast to work on it. "What about Hesmerra?" he asked, getting in, giving Joe a nudge to the shoulder by way of greeting.

Ryan filled him in. "Why was Billy living with that old woman? I know his mother's dead, but what about his father? Doesn't anyone know where he is?" Ryan had been in the village only a few years, so she was not the rich source of gossip that Clyde was, having lived in Molena Point off and on for most of his life

Clyde said, "I don't think anyone knows *who* Billy's father is. Maybe even his mother didn't know. One of the boys at the high school, most likely. Greta had something of a reputation. She was still in school when Billy was born—she was the youngest of the three sisters. She and the baby lived with Hesmerra. Billy was eight when Greta was killed in that car accident. Both

Debbie and Esther were married and settled by then, but neither aunt wanted Billy. I guess, from the time he was born, neither would have anything more to do with Gran."

"What was that about?"

"Maybe because she let Greta run around and get pregnant," Clyde said. "Like it was Hesmerra's fault. What made those two so righteous? I'm not sure they were any better, in high school. Max was chief when Greta was killed, he'll know more."

"Don't you think it strange," Ryan said, "that Erik Kraft was such a close friend to the old woman? Big-time Realtor, new Jaguar every year, but he goes regularly to visit that drunken old woman?" She turned to look at him. "And isn't it strange that just now, right after the fire that killed Hesmerra, Erik Kraft's wife is back in the village and moving herself into our house? Or, she thinks she is. What is this? What's going on?"

Clyde just looked at her.

"What?" Ryan said, making a right off Ocean, pulling to the curb in front of Jolly's Deli. "What?" she said again.

"Debbie Kraft is Billy's aunt," Clyde said. "Hesmerra's middle daughter. Somehow, I thought you knew Debbie's mother was that old recluse. Debbie said in her letter she didn't want to have contact with her mother, that they didn't speak."

Ryan looked at him, frowning. "She only told me she grew up in the village. I never cared enough to ask anything more." She sat a moment, taking that in. Ryan had lived in the village only three years; she'd done a lot in that time, shaken off the baggage of a painful separation and then widowhood, established and run a profitable construction business, fallen in love with Clyde and begun a new life with him. But there were still a lot of things about the community she didn't know, connections Clyde often expected her to understand because they were part of the fabric of his own life. Getting out of the truck, she gave him a shrug and a grin, and headed for the deli, the bell jingling as she slipped inside.

Drinking in the heady smells from the deli, Joe felt a sharp urge to nip around to the alley, see what leftovers George Jolly had offered today outside the back door. But, considering the purchases Ryan was making, he stayed put, watching through the big window as she picked out a selection of cheeses and meats, coleslaw, and three kinds of potato salad. "She'd better get crab salad," he said, peering up over the dash.

"You can make life so difficult."

"What's difficult about crab salad? You're so cheap. A couple of bucks for a little carton of something special, to cheer up your poor beleaguered cat."

Ryan returned, sliding a white deli bag into the backseat of the king cab. Joe could smell the crab salad mixed with the aroma of ham and other delicacies. Winking at him, she headed for the veterinary clinic. "What I don't understand," she said, making a left onto Ocean, "is why Billy was living with Hesmerra, when she drank so heavily, why Children's Services hadn't stepped in, if his own aunts refused to take him. Was she his legal guardian?"

"I think everyone who knew him, their one neighbor and the ranchers he worked for, kept the situation under wraps. The boy is stubbornly independent, he wouldn't have tolerated a foster home. I'm guessing everyone pretended things were just fine. Hesmerra *was* his grandmother, she was family. She was working steady, too. She seemed to be one of those drunks who hides it pretty well. Apparently she gave no one, including the school authorities, any real reason to interfere."

Clyde shrugged. "You might say a lot against Hesmerra, but I think she would have fought as hard as Billy himself to prevent him being taken into custody. Who knows, maybe Kraft intervened, too. He'd have pull enough."

An interesting tangle, Joe thought. *Billy's one willing guardian turns up dead, his one defender is out of town for an undetermined length of time, and what's going to happen to Billy now? How much can even the chief do?* He imagined Max butting heads with a cadre of county do-gooders, and that made him smile. *If I were a gambling cat, my money would be on Max Harper.*

Ryan turned off Ocean to the next block and parked before the clinic against a tall border of Mexican marigolds that made the air smell like cat pee. Both Ryan and Clyde went inside to haul out the carriers.

The two cottages that formed the clinic had been joined together by a tall solarium, its glass walls rising above their dark roofs. The complex housed boarding and hospital rooms, large kennels, examining rooms, offices, and surgery. On the roof of the front cottage, beneath the shadows of a cypress tree, Kit and Misto sat looking down at Joe. Dulcie wasn't with them. This was story morning at the library, she'd be curled up with the children on the big window seat, their little hands stroking her as the librarian read to them. Tourists were enchanted when they found the pretty tabby hanging out at the library and learned she was the official library cat. Many made a special effort to visit her, as, of course, did all the cat-loving locals. As Joe sat thinking of Dulcie, and looking up at Kit and Misto, a leap of recognition hit him, a moment as startling as a lightbulb blazing on.

Rearing up to get a better look, he studied Misto's shoulder, the pattern of swirling stripes. The configuration of pale cream and dark yellow was a dead ringer for the circular pattern on Debbie Kraft's lost, red tomcat. Even their long faces showed a likeness, and the way both cats' ears were set at the same jaunty angle.

Joe never did believe in coincidence. So what the hell was this? *Eugene,* he thought. Misto had left his grown kits in Eugene, where they had all lived. A tom and two girl cats, all three as red, Misto told him, as fresh rust on a paintless fender. He looked up as Ryan and Clyde came out hauling five cat carriers and loaded them in the back of the truck. "What about Rock?" he said. "You leaving him home alone?"

"I called my dad," Ryan said. "He's taken him to run the beach. I didn't want him to scare Billy's cats." Rock didn't do well by himself in the Damens' small yard; the big Weimaraner, high-strung and full of energy, didn't like being left alone, and was inclined to tear up Ryan's garden. He wanted to be out and busy, wanted to be tracking felons as Joe himself had taught him, or out running with the horses.

It was after one o'clock by the time they met Charlie back at the burned house. Billy had managed to corral all seven cats and shut them in the back room of the half-fallen shanty. Slipping in with the carriers, he came out a few minutes later hauling three carriers heavy with cat, then went back for the other two, the plastic cages emitting a chorus of yowls and snarling through the mesh sides. As they loaded them into Charlie's SUV, Ryan said, "Dr. Firetti wants you to bring them down for shots, and to make sure they're healthy before we take them up to the ranch."

"They're healthy," Billy said, bristling. "I don't want to take them to a vet, they're already scared half to death." His thin face was still white with the shock of the morning, with the death of his gran and, now, with an imagined threat to the only other creatures in the world who meant anything to him.

"My cat goes up to the ranch," Ryan told him. "So do the cats of our friends. We don't want them to catch something that your cats might be carrying."

"Sometimes," Charlie said, "cats can carry a disease that they don't have themselves, and they can pass it on to others." Billy looked unconvinced. "Firetti's a kind man," Charlie said, "the cats will be fine. I don't think we'll need to leave them, just get their shots and bring them home again. Maybe take a little blood for testing, and he can call us later with the results."

Billy looked at her for a long time. He'd worked for Max since he was nine, and he trusted both Max and Charlie. At last he nodded, and climbed in the back of the Blazer, crowding in among the cages. Ryan looked in at him through the window. "We'll clean up a stall, so the cats can settle in. If we turn them loose too soon they'll hightail it right back down the hill—to the delight of the local coyotes."

Joe thought, when Billy and his gran were in residence, the predators might have kept their distance. He imagined Billy and Gran out in the front yard at dusk, maybe throwing rocks at the coyotes' slinking shadows. He wondered how the old woman's aim was, with a skin full of whiskey. He watched the SUV head away for Dr. Firetti's, Billy wedged in among the carriers to keep his little charges calm. The seven cats were a mixed crew, all sizes, all colors, from kitten to codger. Joe knew they'd be fine at the ranch. He hoped Billy would be, too. Though a number of questions gnawed at him as he rode between Ryan and Clyde, in the deliscented pickup, up the hill to the Harpers'.

7

The Harpers' pastures spread away above the cliff untouched by the fire, the grass green and lush and tall from the winter rains, weaving up into the wire mesh between the white fence rails. The north and south pastures were separated by a narrow gravel drive leading in from the highway to the pale frame house and stable. A big hay barn rose at the rear, stark against the dark pine woods. The old house had started out small and plain but now a tall new great room, all glass and timbers, looked down across the pastures to the falling cliffs and the sea below. Max and Charlie, with happy disregard for convention, had turned the old living room into a new master suite, had converted their old bedroom to Max's study, and joined the two smaller guest rooms together to give Charlie a spacious new studio.

Now, the stable's big sliding doors stood open, allowing the roofed alleyway between the two rows of stalls
to catch the ocean breeze. Joe watched Clyde fetch the
wheelbarrow from behind the stable, watched him and
Ryan wheel the heavy bags of feed from the back stall out
to the hay barn, emptying the stall for Billy's seven cats.
He watched Ryan sweep the stall's hard dirt floor clean
of straw and attack the cobwebs along the ceiling, then
carry in the five old Styrofoam coolers that Billy used for
cat beds. Turned on their sides, with the lids taped on
and new doors cut near one corner, they made cozy little
houses, shutting out the chill. Clyde lined them up along
one wall, while Ryan washed Billy's chipped crockery
and filled a bowl with fresh water. It was nearly two hours
before Billy and Charlie returned with their little patients,
and Charlie backed the Blazer down to the stable door.

Getting out, Billy stood looking into the stall, then
looked shyly at the three adults, his cheeks coloring
with pleasure. Then he went to fetch his cats. Setting
the carriers in the stall, he left them closed while he
headed out to the hay barn.

"What?" Charlie said.

Billy turned back. "Getting straw for my own bed.
If—"

"You'll be sleeping upstairs," Charlie said, "over
the stable. There are two bedrooms, you don't need to
sleep in a stall."

Billy looked at her quietly. "I'd rather, if it's all right. The cats'll be easier if I'm with them. And . . ." He grinned at her. "More like home, maybe. And I like the smell of the horses, I'll like hearing them around me at night."

"You're sure?"

He nodded. "I can park my bike in here, too, out of the way of the horses, to keep it dry."

"All right, then," Charlie said. But as Billy turned to head for the hay barn, Clyde stopped him.

"We have a folding cot down at the house, and some camping blankets. Leave the straw until you try that." There was even a half bath up by the tack room, a convenience that saved Charlie and Max and their boarders from tracking mud and hay into the house. The tomcat could just imagine what kind of bathroom had been in the burned shack; even a litter box would be more luxurious.

Sure as hell, he thought, that old shack had been ripe for the smallest spark to break into flames. But why not the other two? Why hadn't they burned? And why *hadn't* the old woman gotten out of there? *Or,* the tomcat thought again, *was she dead before the blaze started?*

Padding out the big door into the stable yard, he watched Ryan, Charlie, and Billy start off across the south pasture to bring the horses back. Clyde headed for the pickup to go fetch the cot, then turned to look at Joe. "You coming?"

"Think I'll hang out here for a while," he said innocently, as Max's truck turned in from the highway.

On the narrow lane the two trucks paused, driver to driver. Clyde said, "Billy's moved in. The kid . . . What's wrong? What have you got?"

"Coroner's preliminary," Max said. Joe eased closer, along the pasture fence, as Max glanced toward the stable. "Where's Billy?"

Clyde nodded toward the south pasture. "Bringing the horses in."

Max nodded. "Looks like Hesmerra was poisoned."

"What, spoiled food? Billy wasn't sick."

Max was silent.

"You mean deliberately poisoned? With what? Why the hell would anyone poison that old woman?"

"Coroner hasn't done the autopsy yet, but he's thinking wood alcohol. There's isopropanol in the blood. He'll work on her tonight. Alcohol could have been easily added to her booze. Heavy drinker like that, she probably never noticed the difference."

Easing deeper into the bushes, Joe wondered if the old woman might have been so hard up for booze, she'd purposely drink rubbing alcohol? But that didn't make sense, she had all the whiskey she wanted, Erik Kraft bought it for her.

Would Erik give that old woman poison? But why? Who else was there? She lived practically as a hermit, only her grandson around most of the time, and Billy sure hadn't poisoned his gran. He wondered about the neighbor who had moved out, Emmylou Warren, the woman who had come to the fishing wharf looking for her two cats. Could she have poisoned Hesmerra's whiskey before she moved out? But why? A lot of questions to be answered, Joe thought, laying back his ears.

Max glanced away to the south pasture where Ryan and Charlie and Billy were coming back with the horses, Charlie carrying a grain bucket that would now be empty, a little enticement to catch the nervous mounts. "I need to talk with Billy," he said, and drove on into the yard. Joe watched the sorrel mare buck and snort as Charlie and Ryan turned the horses back into the north pasture. But it was half an hour later, after they'd all eaten a bite of deli lunch around the big kitchen table, that Max took Billy aside. As they walked outdoors, Joe followed, slipping into the bushes as the two hoisted themselves up on the pasture fence. They sat in companionable silence, their boot heels snug on the lower rail, their backsides nudged occasionally by the small bay mustang who, always curious, had come up to be friendly. The chief looked down at Billy. "Did Gran keep wood alcohol around the place?"

"Wood alcohol? Rubbing alcohol?"

Max nodded. "Maybe for aches and pains, sore muscles?"

"Not that I know of, I never saw any. If she had a sore muscle she used Vicks rub."

"Do you remember rubbing alcohol around your neighbor's?"

"Emmylou?" Billy shook his head, frowning.

"Did Gran ever try to drink wood alcohol?"

The boy's brown eyes widened. "She wouldn't do that, that's poison. Gran might be a lush, but she had better sense than that. She could hold her liquor all right, too. She drove to work every day, five days a week, and only ever got one ticket. Why would she do something dumb like drink poison?"

Max said, "Are those your trash cans, out by the highway?"

Billy nodded. "I took them out this morning before I went to work. Mr. Zandler's real strict about that, said he didn't want rats around the place." Billy smiled. "My cats took care of any rats that showed up. Well, Zandler paid for the garbage pickup."

"Where did she keep her stash of whiskey, Billy? She must have had more than one bottle."

"She usually had a case. There's a cave under the hill, behind that stack of boards and doors, maybe an old vegetable cellar. She'd bring home a couple of bottles at a time, stash them in the cardboard box. And Mr. Kraft, when he came, he'd bring four or five." Billy looked at Max a long time, his brown eyes searching the captain's face. "You're saying she drank wood alcohol? If she did, someone gave it to her. Put it in her whiskey?" He swallowed. "You're saying she was poisoned."

"The coroner thinks she was. He should have a definite cause of death by tomorrow. He says she didn't die from the fire, she was already dead when the fire started. She didn't feel the flames, Billy."

Billy's tears welled. "Thank you. But how could she be poisoned, no one would do that. I'll show you where she kept her whiskey. Could one of those bottles have been that way when she bought it?"

"They were bottles with labels, and sealed? Not someone's home brew?"

"From the market, yes. She didn't suffer, then? Except . . . she must have been sick from the poison. But she was dead when the fire began?" Billy couldn't seem to get beyond that. He wiped his sleeve across his face, and Max put his arm around him.

"Did your neighbor know where she kept her whiskey?"

"Emmylou? Probably. Gran always had a bottle. If Emmylou watched Gran much, she might have seen her go in the cave. You don't think Emmylou hurt her? She wouldn't. If she saw anyone else go in the cave, she'd have said, she'd have told Gran."

"Did they get along all right?"

"Yes, they'd go back and forth for coffee, breakfast sometimes. Emmylou doesn't drink, but they got along fine. Emmylou tried to see that Gran ate, she'd fix something for the two of them, and for me if I was home. They were fine—until Emmylou couldn't pay her rent." Billy shifted on the fence rail. "Gran wouldn't let her live with us. Emmylou asked if she could, just for a little while, until she found a place to rent, but Gran said our house was too small. Well, there was just one room, our two cots, the stove and table. That's the only argument they ever had. Emmylou had nowhere to go and I guess not much money. She has another friend in the village, but she's gone off somewhere. Gran wouldn't let her stay, but they didn't fight, exactly."

"Do you know where she went?"

Billy shook his head. "I guess she'd have to live in her car, an old green Chevy, a four-door."

"Did Gran keep money in the house?"

He looked down at his worn boots. "Under her bed, under the floor. At least some of it was there. She thought I didn't know. She'd cash her paycheck, give me some for food, keep the rest for whiskey. Mr. Kraft always gave her money, a wad of money. Maybe she kept that somewhere else."

"She didn't put it in the bank?"

"No. In a little tin box under the floor. She thought the box was fireproof. That's all I know of. Maybe it all burned up."

"You think Emmylou knew where the money was hidden?"

"I don't know. I knew, so I guess she could have."

They were quiet, Billy scraping his boots on the fence rail to dislodge the dried mud from his heels. When Max asked who he should notify about Gran's death, besides Erik Kraft and Billy's two aunts, Billy said, "There's no one else. And my aunts . . . Gran hasn't seen Debbie in years, she lives up in Oregon. Aunt Esther lives in the village, but she hardly ever came to see Gran. Except at Christmas. She'd bring a basket of food like we were some kind of charity case. She hated that we lived there, she was always so snooty. She hated that Gran drank, she always acted mad at Gran. She didn't like me much, either. I don't know why she came."

"Did your gran ever get any letters, did your aunt Debbie write to her?"

"I never saw any letters. Usually Emmylou brought the mail in from the highway before I got home. I guess

Debbie could have written, but Gran never said. Why wouldn't Gran say, why would she keep that secret? I saw Debbie's phone number in Gran's little address book, but Gran never said she talked to her. I guess the book got burned, too." The boy's voice was flat, shut down. These two aunts had never been his family, had never tried to be. The two people he cared about had both been taken from him, his mother when he was eight, and now his gran. Now he had no one. A lone child, trying hard to become a man.

Max said, "You don't know who your father is."

Billy shook his head. "Before Mama died, she said it didn't matter, that I only needed her. But then she died."

Max shifted his position on the fence.

Billy said, "Gran would never talk about it, she said Greta wouldn't tell her which boy she'd been with, she said the high school was way too lenient, letting the kids do anything. Then she'd start drinking more, and didn't want to talk to me about it—like it was my fault I had no father. I didn't understand all of it, then. I was only eight.

"Well," Billy said, "no one came looking for me. No one ever came there saying he was my father." He turned to scratch the ears of the bay pony, hiding his face from Max. "After the accident, after Mama's car went off the bridge, Gran said it was her fault, it was her fault Mama died."

"Why would it be her fault?"

"Because they fought, because Mama got so mad she ran out in the storm, took off in the car, got in a wreck and died."

The boy's words startled Joe. Brought his nightmare reeling back again: the stormy night, the two women yelling at each other, the child huddled on the cot. Shivering, he pushed the memory aside. He didn't want to think about it, the unbidden nightmare sickened and scared him.

Billy said, "Gran would never tell me what they fought about that night. If I bugged her, she'd just drink more. Before Mama died, she didn't drink so often. That night, the night Mama died, they were yelling and screaming, and when I tried to make them stop, they yelled at me, told me to go to bed and shut up. It was raining hard. Mama screamed at Gran that she didn't understand anything and started to cry and slammed out, I heard her take off fast up the road, for the highway."

Ducking his head, he straightened the pony's mane. "That was the last I ever saw her. Except for her funeral. That night after the cops came to tell us Mama was dead, Gran said she should have stopped her, should have grabbed her keys, made her stay in the house. But she couldn't have," he said angrily. "You couldn't stop Mama, she'd never listen. You couldn't make her listen."

Joe sat shivering, stricken, seeing the scene Billy had painted, reliving his nightmare, every word and every move, the feel of the rain, of his soaking fur. Savagely he licked at a front paw, wished he could lick away the dream as easily as dislodging a blade of grass—wished he could lick away the cruelty of the world, all the ugliness of humankind.

"After Mama died, there was always a bottle. By the stove, by Gran's bed, under the covers. She stank of whiskey, and it made her mean. I hate the smell. She didn't want to eat, she'd come home from work with no groceries, nothing in the cupboard, maybe crackers. That's when I started working at the Peterson ranch, cleaning stalls. They didn't turn me away because I was so young, I'm good with animals, I did good work for them. I earned enough to buy beans and bread on the way home."

Joe looked up the lane as Clyde pulled in off the highway, the red king cab kicking up gravel and dust against the taller grass at the edge of the long dirt drive. He parked near the stable, got out and slid his old, folded camping cot out of the bed of the truck, along with some folded blankets and a striped mattress just about thick enough to make a small cat comfortable. Billy dropped down off the fence, took the load from him. Max said, "Get your cot set up, then I want to walk down the hill, have a look at Gran's cave."

Billy nodded and disappeared into the stable, as Max fetched a heavy flashlight from the cab of his truck. Joe waited until the chief and Billy headed down across the north pasture, then he slipped into the rank grass outside the fence and followed, slinking along unseen, the tall blades tickling his ears.

8

Where the pasture fell away to the delta below, Joe crouched under the fence among the tall weeds, looking down on the burned shack. Detective Garza was moving slowly through, sorting among the debris, his jeans and blue sweatshirt smeared with ashes, the pockets of his dark windbreaker bulging with what were surely small items of possible evidence, each secured in a paper or plastic bag. Garza's tan Blazer stood parked near Hesmerra's rusty old Volvo with its thick coat of smoky ash. Directly below, Max and Billy were clearing the cave entrance, moving the rotting doors and cobwebby boards away from the opening.

As Max ducked down into the cave, shining the electric torch across dry earth, Joe slipped down the cliff between the two cars and under them, where he could see into the cave. Inside, the light of Max's torch swung slowly back and forth across the earthen ceiling and walls, across the heavy posts, the rough crossbeams and hard dirt floor. On an earthen shelf stood a cardboard carton with five screw-top whiskey bottles sticking up. Max pulled on a pair of cotton gloves and examined the circular strips of black plastic that sealed the lids, then picked up the carton and backed out. "Erik Kraft brought her whiskey, but he didn't know about the cave?"

"Not that I know of," Billy said. "She'd put them in here after he left. I don't know why all the secrecy, but Gran was like that." Billy peered at the bottles. "Are you thinking *he* poisoned them? Why would he do that? He liked Gran, he was kind to her, he gave her money, brought pizza, things to eat. He bought medicine once, when she had the flu." But then the boy went quiet, very still, as if perhaps letting his thoughts touch something new and unwelcome.

Max studied his face then moved away, carrying the carton. As he set it down on the open tailgate of Dallas Garza's Blazer, beyond him Emmylou Warren appeared, coming down the lane from the highway. Joe could see a glimpse of her car, of its back bumper and a patch of green sticking out past the bushes that grew along the edge of the two-lane. Max and Billy saw her at the same moment.

Billy moved as if to go to her, but then seemed to change his mind, to think better of it, and turned his attention back to the whiskey, studying the seals more closely. "If none of those was poisoned, poison could still have been in the open one."

Max nodded, his attention on Emmylou. She had stopped beyond the cars, stood watching Dallas sifting through the rubble. When Dallas saw her he came to join them, looking back at Emmylou. "I sent her away once. When I got here she was parked right down at the yellow tape, sitting in her car, crying." He looked down at Billy. "She was worried about you. I told her you're all right."

"Go on," Max said to Billy, "go talk to her."

Billy ran. When Emmylou saw him she let out a whoop and ran, too, flinging her arms around him and nearly toppling them both. Joe was crouched beneath Hesmerra's car, not six feet from them. Emmylou's sun-browned face was as wrinkled as crushed leather, her jeans worn and soft, her colorless T-shirt thin, with two holes in one sleeve. "You're all right!" She held Billy away, looking deeply at him. "I was in the market when I heard about the fire, about your gran. No one knew where you were, what happened to you. Where are your cats, are they all right? Where will you go, do you have—"

Billy nodded up toward the Harpers' place. "They're in Captain Harper's barn. I'll be staying there, too, for now. Did you find a place to live?"

Emmylou gestured toward her car. "That's *my* home, for now," she said, grinning. Behind them, Max watched Emmylou, his expression thoughtful. Was he, like Joe himself, curious about why she'd come up there? Wondering if she'd only been worried about Billy, or if she'd had some other reason?

As broke as she was, would she come nosing around looking for Hesmerra's hidden money, however little it might be? Had she meant to make off with it before the fire inspectors and detectives appeared on the scene? She *had* arrived before Garza. Had she already rooted through the burn and, knowing where Hesmerra hid the tin box, already stolen the money that was rightfully Billy's?

Max stepped over to join them. "We'll want you to come down to the station, Emmylou. For routine fingerprinting."

Emmylou just looked at him, the expression in her faded brown eyes wary.

"A matter of elimination," Max said. "If you were in the house, your prints could come up on broken dishes, glasses. With a set on file, we can eliminate you as someone who shouldn't have been there. I'd like you to come in today, if you could," he said gently, "so we can move on with the investigation. Any of the officers can take your prints."

Emmylou frowned. "You're saying someone *started* the fire? On purpose?"

"It's possible," Max said. "Both the fire and Hesmerra's death are under investigation."

She was quiet, studying his closed face. "I'll come," she said, subdued. As she put her arm around Billy, Max turned away, stepping over to the burn to talk with Dallas. Billy said, "You can't live in your car for long, the street patrol will arrest you, or the sheriff will."

"Remember my friend, Sammie Miller? She worked with Hesmerra for a while, cleaning? She came here a couple of times?"

Billy nodded. "You feed her cats when she's gone. Can't you stay with her?"

"She's away now, but this time she didn't leave her key. When she gets back, maybe I can stay there." She smiled down at Billy. "I'll be fine, I'll come to see you. Maybe pick you up at school, give you a ride home. We can tie your bike on the back." Before she turned away, to head for her old Chevy, Joe shot through the grass along the top of the cliff and dropped down to the car, where the driver's window was open; he shot through and into the backseat before she was halfway up the lane.

Pawing through the rubble, he scented among the clothes and blankets for the faintest smell of ashes, looking for Hesmerra's lost money, burrowing among cartons of canned goods and paperback books. How did she sleep in here? Actually, though, the plan was pretty neat: everything tucked on the floor up to the level of the backseat. A thin foam pad was folded up against the door; he imagined her laying it across the seat and her stacked belongings, to make a wide bed. She'd have to pull her knees up, though, as tall as she was. He was peering between the pad and the door when he heard her outside brushing off her jeans. As he turned, his hind paw slipped, sliding against cold metal—and he smelled burned wood and wet ashes.

Digging aside the blankets and some newspapers, he uncovered a tin box, tall and narrow, made to hold office files. His exploring paw came away liberally dusted with dirt and ashes. He froze when she passed the window. But she went on to the back of the car, and he heard the trunk pop open.

The latch of the box was of a kind hard for a cat to snap open, one of those affairs where a lever is pulled down, securing a metal bar into a hook. He fought it, shifting position until he had his claws under it, took a deep breath, pulled with all his might, praying he wouldn't tear his claws right out of their sockets.

Snap, the latch popped open with a scrape so loud she heard it, the trunk slammed and there she was at the side window. Quickly flipping the box open, he got one glimpse of the contents: not money, but letters and business papers. He clawed through sheets of figures. The name on the letterheads was Kraft Realty.

Behind him, the door jerked open. He spun around staring up at Emmylou with all the forlorn fear he could muster; choking out a shaky "Meow," he backed away.

She laughed and reached to pet him. "You poor thing. What are you doing in here? You're not one of Billy's cats. Where did you come from?"

Joe looked at her helplessly. He was crouched to bolt past her when Max Harper appeared behind her, looking in.

"What the hell? Get out of there, Joe. What are you doing in there?" With no ceremony he reached in, lifted Joe gently by the back of his neck and one hand under his belly, and deposited him outside on the ground. "Why the hell are you so nosy?" he said with a dry little grin. "Get your tail up to the ranch, Clyde will be looking for you!"

Joe vanished. Scorched up the cliff into the tall grass, pretending to race away. Max Harper seldom touched him, and never unkindly, only sometimes to scratch his ears if Joe was lounging on his desk. Below him, Max and Emmylou stood talking, Harper making clear to her again that she was expected to come in and be fingerprinted, Emmylou still looking reluctant. As her car headed away up the narrow, rutted road, and Harper and Billy started back to the cave, Joe hightailed it for the ranch, his thoughts on the metal box and the documents it contained. Some were emblazoned with the letterhead of Kraft Realty, but there were half a dozen other real estate firms, as well, names that meant nothing to Joe. All the letters and documents he could see, in that quick glimpse, presented neatly typed accountings of funds ranging up into the high seven digits— ten million, twelve million. A financial smorgasbord that Joe found singularly interesting, considering that, from the burned smell, and the ashes and dirt coating the container, the collection had come from the burned house, had perhaps been buried in the earth, beneath the floor. Many of the dates were recent. Where had Hesmerra gotten these and why? Why would Erik Kraft give his business papers to Hesmerra Young?

Could she somehow have stolen them? But why? What good would his legal papers do her? If Kraft was her friend, why would she steal from him at all? Even if he was only a convenient source of whiskey and cash, why would she jeopardize that? Or had the old woman, when she died, been quietly pursuing some other agenda involving Erik Kraft, driven by some motive of her own?

9

Debbie Kraft arrived two days after the fire; she showed up just after midnight at the Damens' front door repeatedly ringing the bell, dragging Ryan and Clyde from sleep, sending the big Weimaraner into a fit of barking, ripping Joe Grey straight out of deep and pleasant dreams. Grumbling, he slipped out from his cushions, left his tower, and padded across the roof to the edge to look over.

They were crowded on the little porch around the front door, a young woman, two kids, three threadbare suitcases, a pile of ragtag carryalls and cloth bags with the contents oozing over the tops. The skinny woman, clutching her arms around herself against the night's chill, was dressed in black tights, a puffy black jacket, high-heeled black boots. The two little girls clung to her, the little one silent and still, the older kid whining and pulling on her. Above them at Ryan's studio window, Ryan appeared like a ghost in her white gauzy robe, looking down just as Joe was looking at the little group, at the dusty brown station wagon parked in the drive behind the king cab, the back so full of jumbled belongings the windows might as well have been boarded over.

The porch light went on. The front door opened. Clyde stood there bare-chested, in his sweatpants. Debbie's voice was shrill and animated, a gushing greeting from a woman Clyde had never met and, from the look on his face, didn't want to meet. There was a short exchange, then Debbie and the two girls swarmed in around him, dragging what baggage they could carry. Clyde, turning away resigned, left the door open so Debbie could haul in the rest.

Joe watched for only a minute, torn between the fear he'd miss something, and his sure knowledge that the rest of the night would be chaos, the woman's high, emotion-driven voice reaching up even into his tower. He wouldn't get a wink of sleep. If he had any sense he'd get the hell out of there. Whatever drama the night might hold, as the Damens got Debbie settled, he'd hear about in the morning.

He went. Heading across the rooftops toward the center of the village, beneath the bright full moon, he leaped over rivers of moonlight and over shadows as black as hell itself. If Dulcie was prowling the library, exploring among the books, maybe *she'd* give him a little sympathy for this midnight eviction that was, after all, the next thing to a full-blown home invasion.

From the roof of a shop behind the handsome Spanish-style library building, with its tan stucco and heavy timbers, he peered down at its back door that opened on the narrow alley. Yes, the faintest light shone out through Wilma's little office window, the ambient green glow of the computer. He caught Dulcie's fresh scent, too, on the tile roof and among the leaves of the bougainvillea vine as he descended. Nosing up the flap of Dulcie's cat door, he pushed on inside.

Wilma Getz's office was small, crowded, and cozy, her desk placed between two tall file cabinets stacked to the ceiling with books. Dulcie's housemate worked only part-time now in her position as a reference librarian, but she'd managed to keep her tiny office. Much of her work was done in there, on peripheral projects, including the library's old-fashioned vertical file. The library saved clips from the local paper and local magazines, historical information about Molena Point. And—because of Dulcie herself—they maintained an extensive collection about cats who lived in libraries across the country. Having a special interest in working cats, they saved, as well, clips about any number of cats in shops and business offices, a tribute to the talents and skills of even your ordinary, everyday feline.

Dulcie sat on the desk, her back to him, silhouetted by the glow of the computer, her peach-tinted ears nearly transparent in the light, her nimble paws playing across the keyboard, so engrossed she didn't hear him push the door in. Only when the plastic flapped back into place did she spin around, startled.

She stared down at him, her green eyes wide, guilt writ large on her sweet, striped face. What was this? What was she up to? What was so secret that she didn't want him to see? Leaping up beside her, he nestled close to her warm shoulder. When she lifted a paw to darken the screen, he swiped it away. She hissed, and cut him an irritated look, her striped tail lashing.

The short lines of type on the screen, even to the antiliterate tomcat, were obviously poetry. Was she reading dirty verses, something ugly that humans had put on the Web? He'd never known his lady to go for smut. But then, scanning the lines, his eyes widened.

There was no title, no author's name, nothing but the nine lines of poetry, and he could feel her shy embarrassment as he read.

What a lovely cat she is
Posed behind the curtain's gauze
Like a princess robed in gold.

Coy her gaze through laces gleaming,
What dainty vision does she embrace
Behind that dear, exquisite face?

I step to the veil, draw back its folds,
And there it lies, at my feet,
The bloody rat she's brought to eat.

"You wrote this," he said, grinning. Her tail went very still, he could feel the uncertain tremor of her heartbeat through the warmth of her tabby fur. He read the lines again, and at the last line, he couldn't help it, he let out a loud guffaw that echoed through the office and into the empty library. "How long have you been doing this? Is there more? You're writing from the human viewpoint."

If a cat could blush, her little striped face would be pink as cotton candy. "It made you laugh," she said, pleased.

"Does Wilma know?"

"How could she not? It's her computer. I guess I could have set up an access code, but . . . She thinks . . . She's pleased," Dulcie said modestly.

Joe nuzzled her cheek. "I like it. It makes pictures, it does make me laugh. How do you do that? How do you even begin, where does it come from?"

Dulcie's tail swung more easily. "I don't know, it's just . . . there. In my head. I write it down before it gets away."

"Can I see more?"

"Not tonight, you didn't come to read poetry," she said, looking deep into his eyes. "What's happened?" she said. "What's the matter?"

"Debbie Kraft. Arrived at midnight. Enough luggage to stay a year."

She gave him a sympathetic nudge. "Ryan and Clyde don't need this. You think they'll let her stay? But she must be devastated, grieving for her mother. No matter what Billy says about Debbie never seeing her."

"She didn't sound devastated. She sounded rude and pushy."

Dulcie was quiet a moment, then, "I was thinking about the fire, about Emmylou prowling in the rubble. About the tin box she apparently took from Hesmerra's, the Kraft Realty papers. Wilma was talking with Chichi Barbi, and *she* said Hesmerra applied with her for a job." Chichi Barbi had, late last year, bought Charlie Harper's cleaning service, Charlie's Fix It, Clean It. "Chichi said when she hired Hesmerra, the old woman dickered and argued about locations and hours. Said she was dead set to get on the crew that cleans the house of one of the Kraft Realtors. And then later, the minute the Realtor moved away, Hesmerra quit her job."

Dulcie gave him a sly smile. "Next thing you know, Hesmerra's working nights for the firm that cleans the Kraft offices. And now, Kraft papers turn up in her burned house? How does that add up?"

"How indeed," Joe said. "Particularly when her two daughters are married to the two owners of Kraft Realty?"

"When Wilma suggested Hesmerra used her pull with one of her daughters to get the Kraft job, Chichi said she doubted it. Said those girls aren't friendly with their mother. And, she said, Kraft has a strict policy about hiring family. She thought the cleaning company didn't know who Hesmerra was."

Joe said, "Maybe Erik Kraft put in a word, bent the rules to help her out? Or, again, maybe he didn't have a clue. And, if she did lift those papers, what did she mean to do with them?" He licked his whiskers, thinking. "First she cleans for one of the Kraft Realtors, then turns up cleaning the Kraft offices. Then she turns up dead. Which Realtor's house?"

"That Alain Bent woman, the tall elegant one. That painted white brick up on the hill above where Ryan and Clyde bought their last cottage, where so many houses went vacant, that's her house." Dulcie rose from the computer. "Alain Bent and Erik Kraft worked together, they were sales partners, like a team, until she left the village. She kept the house, maybe until prices go up. Come on, I'll show you, their picture's spread all over." Leaping down, she pushed open the inner door to the big, echoing reading room.

The high-raftered room seemed vast when it was empty of patrons and lit by only the soft glow of the moon shining in through the tall windows; moonlight threw twisted tree shadows across the reading tables, and across the leather couches that stood empty before the tall stone fireplace.

On the table nearest to the magazine racks, Dulcie had laid out half a dozen brightly colored Molena Point magazines. They were older copies, as if the newest volumes were still on some librarian's desk. Each was open to a two-page real estate ad, the corners of the pages dimpled by the marks of little cat teeth. The full-color ads, arranged with four elegant residences to a page, included all the best real estate offices in the village, and each ad included a picture of the listing salesperson. In nine Kraft Realty spreads, partners Alain Bent and Erik Kraft were featured together, in their handsome two-agent sales pitch. Both were tall and slim, Alain's dark hair sleeked back in a chignon at the nape of her neck, her black business suit trim and well tailored. Erik's black hair was short, neatly trimmed, his sport coat casual and expensive, his open collar showing a deep tan. In one shot he was wearing white shorts and a white polo shirt, his legs and arms tanned and well muscled.

"Nice-looking couple," Joe said suspiciously. "Debbie's ex-husband, and his beautiful sales partner."

Dulcie's tail twitched, and she smiled a wicked little cat smile. "You're thinking he could have left Debbie for Alain?"

Joe shrugged. Who knew, with humans?

"So," she said. "What does this add up to? Erik Kraft and Alain Bent work their listings together. Hesmerra stole papers from the Kraft offices, and was snooping in Alain Bent's house, then turns up murdered. Emmylou Warren steals the papers. Hesmerra's two sons-in-law own Kraft Realty. And, to add to the mix, Debbie Kraft arrives in the village just two days after her mother is poisoned."

Joe rose and began to pace, padding across the magazine pages looking down at them as if the puzzle might be all laid out before him, but not yet making sense. Dulcie had started to speak when she spun around. Together they stared across the room at the tall windows as a scratching sound was repeated, soft but insistent.

A branch swung against the glass where no other branches moved, there was no wind to stir its wild sweeping back and forth; then they saw the dark shape swinging on it, riding the pine limb. The branch went flying as Kit dropped to the windowsill.

She pressed her face to the glass, looking in. When she saw Joe and Dulcie her tail lashed with impatience, and she disappeared again, dropping to the ground. In a moment they heard the cat door swinging, and Kit came bolting through into the reading room. She leaped to the table, sliding on the slick magazines and nearly careening over the side.

"What's all this? What are you doing? When I couldn't find you I went to Joe's house and in on the rafter but you have company, a woman talking and talking real shrill and a whining kid, and when I went in Ryan's studio Rock and Snowball were huddled up on the daybed so miserable they scared me, and then I saw the picture on the mantel standing up beside a letter and I jumped up and—"

"Slow down!" Dulcie and Joe yowled together.

"Who was that woman?" Kit said, her yellow eyes wide. "I read the letter, what nerve. But—"

Joe said, "You saw the red tomcat, the picture of him."

"He looks like Misto, only younger," Kit said. "Red stripes instead of yellow and Misto said his son was that color and his name was Pan and I raced out to find you and they lived in Eugene where that letter came from, too. He *looks* like Misto and did you see he has exactly the same mark on his shoulder and the letter said he just got lost and they didn't even look for him, they didn't try to find him, they didn't care where he went, they didn't care if he's hurt or dead and—"

"Slow down, Kit!" Dulcie hissed, her ears flat.

Kit tried, but she couldn't contain her excitement. "If he lived in that nursing home we can find him on the computer, there are all kinds of things about cats and dogs in nursing homes and hospitals and—"

"Stop!" Dulcie cried, losing patience; of course Kit was right, she'd seen hundreds of entries about animals in hospitals, cats in a children's hospital, therapy animals—if she could just find this cat, this particular nursing home. Leaping down, she raced for Wilma's office, Joe and Kit right on her tail, and the three crowded onto the desk around the computer.

It took her a while, her paws pinched tight as she carefully pressed the keys, pulling up a number of subjects until she'd found the Eugene nursing home and then a clip about their amazing therapy cat. Kit was so fascinated she pawed eagerly at the screen, her eyes widening at the young red tom, who was held in the arms of a white-coated doctor—a strapping red tabby with a thoughtful expression, his knowing look far wiser than that of any ordinary cat. And the pattern on his shoulder was just the same as Misto's, a clear medallion of concentric swirls narrowing in toward the center. Kit was so excited she was shivering. "We have to tell Misto, we have to go right now and wake him up and show him the picture and—"

"Wait," Dulcie said. "Maybe we don't want to tell him." She scrolled down through a number of articles about the red tomcat, pausing at a headline that silenced Kit.

Did Nursing Home Cat Die in Fire?

The remarkable red tabby cat who began, on his own, to visit infirm patients at Green Meadows Nursing Home nearly a year ago has not been seen since a midnight fire burned the complex to the ground . . . "We haven't seen him since three hours before the fire broke out. . . . He came to us as a stray . . . ."

They read it together, crouched on the edge of the desk. At the last words, Kit sat silent, her ears down, her tail hanging over, limp. "What if he is Misto's son? What if he's dead? Oh, we can't tell Misto . . . But he so misses his son. If he is dead . . . Oh, fire is a terrible thing. I don't understand. All at once, that woman dead in a fire, and now this fire . . ."

Dulcie said, "No speaking cat would get caught in a fire, he'd have gotten out, he'd be too clever to get trapped." She looked to Joe, begging him to help ease the tortoiseshell's distress.

"That tom would have saved himself," Joe said. "If he is Misto's son or maybe grandson, you can bet he's smart enough to get out of there, one way or another." He pressed a paw on Kit's paw. "He's somewhere in Oregon, Kit, right now. And you can bet he's safe."

"But what if he was hurt in the fire, what if . . . ?" Her yellow eyes blazed at them. "We have to find him, we have to go and find him."

"Then we have to plan," Joe said patiently. "Do you know how many miles it is to Eugene? Do you remember how long it took Misto to get here, months, hitching with truckers and tourists? And then, when we get to Eugene, what? How do we find one lone cat in all that city? He could be anywhere."

"Maybe," Kit said, "maybe Misto would know where he might have gone. Misto knows Eugene and he—"

Dulcie said, "What if that is Misto's son? What if he did die in the fire? You want to tell Misto that?"

"We can tell him we think we've found his son but not tell him about the fire."

They both looked at her.

Dulcie sighed. "He'll want to see the pictures. If we pull up those articles, he'll read about the nursing home and about the fire. Maybe he'll try to call them. If the nursing home burned down, does it even have a phone?" Dulcie dropped her ears, giving Kit a stern look. "We can't tell him, not yet, we need to find out more."

But, watching Kit, she knew Kit would tell Misto, that they couldn't stop her. Or, if she didn't tell him, and as flighty and irresponsible as the tortoiseshell could be, would she take off alone for Oregon in a fit of goodwill and passion and not much common sense?

Or would she and Misto go off together, an old cat too frail to survive a second journey halfway up the California coast and up into Oregon, and the flighty young tortoiseshell? Again, Dulcie looked at Joe for help. They'd backed themselves into a corner. Now, either they distressed Misto by telling him before they knew enough, or they abandoned Kit to her wild and headstrong passions.

"We'll tell Misto," Joe said softly. "We'll show him the pictures. Tell him the whole story. We can't tell him only half." Maybe, Joe thought, Misto would show better sense than Kit and wouldn't go racing off with no plan, no notion where the red tomcat might be.

"There are all kinds of animal rescue groups," Dulcie said, "Humane Society, SPCA, Animal Friends. Maybe they can find him. Or maybe he's already chosen a home, maybe he's already settled in with someone, is rolling in luxury lapping up cream and he has no need of our help."

"But he'd want to find Misto," Kit said indignantly, "he'd want to find his father, he doesn't know where Misto's gone, he might be worried about his dad, wandering all over Eugene looking for him."

Joe just looked at her. Kit could get pretty worked up.

"First thing in the morning," Dulcie said, "I'll call Eugene. Maybe I can find out if anyone at all saw him after the fire, or saw him escape the fire. Maybe by this time, someone has come forward, called to say he's all right. If I can't locate anyone from the nursing home, Wilma can, that's what she does. She spent her whole career running investigations. Missing humans, missing cats, what's the difference? Wilma can find out what happened to the red tomcat."

10

It was after three in the morning when Joe left Dulcie and Kit, and headed home. As he trotted along above the village streets, the night sky arced clear and vast around him; below him, the streets themselves were deserted, even the late-night party crowd seemed to have packed it in. He sniffed the wind and knew, though the stars shone diamond bright, that weather was on its way, he could smell a storm gathering, could smell cold weather coming down from the north. The shingles, damp from the ocean air, were only slick now, but soon rain would sluice down the steep peaks, rushing into the gutters. Racing onto his own roof, Joe caught the scents from within, the smell of a strange woman's perfume, the unfamiliar smells of people he didn't know and didn't want to know.

But at least he could hear no voices. Maybe, with luck, they were all asleep, Debbie Kraft and her kids bedded down in the Damens' guest room, stuffed like sardines among their ragtag belongings. Stepping to the edge of the roof, he looked down at the old battered Suzuki wagon with its thick patina of road dust, its windows smeared with little handprints, and blocked by the jumble of blankets and cardboard cartons that Debbie hadn't dragged into the house. A skateboard pressed against the glass, and a ragged teddy bear. He could just imagine the smell in the closed car: hamburger wrappers, broken crayons, half-eaten candy bars, the smell of little children shut into a small space for many hours. He imagined the same smells in the rooms below.

Maybe, with great good luck, they'd remain asleep until late morning and he'd be gone again. Or, if the gods really smiled, they'd get up early, collect their possessions, shove everything back in the car, and head on down the coast for some other unfortunate "long-lost" friend.

Or, he thought, Debbie would make up with her sister, after all these silent years, and move on up there to the wooded hills high above the village, where half-hidden and expensive homes stood in self-satisfied privacy. Turning away from the roof's edge, he pushed into his tower and on through into the house to have a look around, to see how the land lay.

Crouched on the rafter, he peered down into the dark study, and into the master bedroom where Clyde and Ryan sprawled, fast asleep, Rock and little Snowball curled safely across their feet. Both animals flinched when Joe dropped down onto Clyde's desk. They looked up at him frazzled, their ears at half mast, their coats bristling from the stress of dealing with a small, rude child, their eyes reflecting a frantic unease that left no doubt Vinnie, the older girl, had been at them.

Joe looked at them with pity but turned resolutely away. There was nothing he could do, just now, to ease their misery. Dropping to the floor, he padded down the stairs, his nose twitching with annoyance at the smell of strangers that rose up the steps. Below, he descended into a chaos of abandoned sweaters, grubby dolls, children's dirty tennis shoes dropped at random down the hall. In the kitchen, a blue plastic cooler stood on the floor dripping water across the tile. The table was strewn with food-crusted paper plates, a package of cupcakes with one bite out of each. Two thermos bottles stood open, smelling of souring milk. He had to guess that Ryan and Clyde, losing patience, had left it all for Debbie to clean up—if she was so inclined.

The guest room door stood open. Despite the fusty smell of sleep, he slipped inside, skirting the two duffel bags, the clothes draped over the rattan and cane chairs and the desk, and the rattan game table. On the handmade Konya rug, an open suitcase lay, revealing a tangle of sweatshirts, big and little, a woman's lace panties, a makeup case, a grubby white brassiere. The room smelled of the same perfume, of unwashed hair and dirty socks. In the queen-sized bed, Debbie and the two children slept tangled together, the girls snuggled up to their mother, their long pale hair strewn into her dark hair, their arms around her as if, at least in sleep, the little family found solace in one another. Looking at the sheer volume of their belongings, he imagined them camping in his home until Christmas, and he backed out again feeling depressed. The only upside to this woman's arrival would be whatever he could learn about her dead mother, about Debbie's relationship with her, and maybe about Hesmerra's interest in the affairs of Kraft Realty. Hurrying back up to his tower in the black predawn, he burrowed deep beneath the cushions, shut his eyes, and listened to the rising wind, its wail as miserable as he felt.

Joe woke at first light; as he rose up out of the pillows, the sharp sea wind harried and chilled him, blowing in through his open windows. The temperature had dropped. The treetops loomed in dark islands, and in the east above the black hills one finger of light streaked across below the clouds, blushing pink from the hidden sun. He could smell coffee, pancakes, bacon, but this happy greeting was broken harshly by Vinnie's shout, "I won't, I won't! You can't make me!" He heard no word from Tessa. Didn't the smaller child ever talk?

Slipping inside, onto his high rafter, he looked down at the empty king-sized bed, the covers tossed back in a tangle. On the leather love seat in the study, Snowball slept curled against Rock, the two animals staying sensibly clear of their houseguests. He froze as childish footsteps pounded up the stairs.

Twelve-year-old Vinnie raced to the top, her curly blond hair rumpled from sleep, her eyes as dark as Hershey bars. Dog and cat watched her warily. Ignoring them, Vinnie looked around the study with a keen and destructive eye.

Stepping to the desk, she picked up a ruler and, turning to the love seat, she began to poke at Rock. The big silver dog looked at her, shocked, and hunched away. When she poked harder, he stood up on the couch facing her, glancing around for a way of escape but unwilling to abandon Snowball. But when Vinnie turned her attention to the little white cat, Rock snarled at her and in the same instant Joe dropped from the rafter to the desk and made a flying leap to the kid's head, his claws out. Snowball exploded over the back of the love seat and beneath it, and Rock gave Joe a grateful look and raced away down the stairs. Joe was still clinging. Vinnie snatched at him and then hit him. He scratched her hand and leaped clear, and she ran screaming down the steps behind the escaping dog, hit the kitchen bellowing that the cat had attacked her. No wonder that red tom had fled the Kraft household. He heard the dog door flap as Rock bolted for the backyard. Smiling, he sauntered down the steps and into the kitchen. When Vinnie saw him she screamed and tried to twist out of her mother's hands. "It jumped right on me! Get it away, it tried to kill me!"

Debbie was busy dabbing at Vinnie's head with a wet paper towel. Turning, she fixed her gaze on Joe, her dark brown eyes blazing, her brown hair tangled across the shoulders of her skintight black T-shirt. Vinnie, cradling her bleeding hand, backed away from Joe. At the table, Ryan and Clyde watched the scene tense and ready to move—Joe had no doubt to protect *him* if the need occurred.

He was glad he'd been there when Vinnie grabbed that ruler; he had no idea how much torment it would take for gentle Rock to turn on her—no idea how badly the kid might have hurt the innocent animals. Ryan rose at last to rummage in a drawer for salve and Band-Aids. All the while, little Tessa looked on from her own chair at the table beside Clyde. Her brown eyes were huge, filled with a different emotion than Vinnie and their mother, and when she looked at Joe her eyes shone with a shy wonder. Tessa liked it fine, that he had nailed her sister, maybe she even envied him, that he had the nerve to do that.

The child was seated on two phone books tied to the seat of her chair, with a pillow over them. Beside her, Clyde grinned at Joe conspiratorially as Debbie doctored Vinnie's wounds, and Vinnie yelled louder. "Hold still," Debbie snapped, staring at Joe with an expression that made him want to ease away.

Ryan said, "Whatever Joe did, he had good reason. Look at me, Debbie." Debbie looked up, scowling at her. "You are to leave our animals alone, do you understand? You, and Vinnie both. If you so much as touch one of our animals or torment them in any way, you're out on the street pronto." She stared at Debbie until Debbie turned away. At the table, both Clyde and Tessa hid a smile, and Tessa reached up and took his hand.

Joe, feeling righteous and smug, leaped onto the table beside them. Ryan took her seat again, returning to her pancakes and bacon. Debbie sat down at her half-finished plate, glaring at them all as Ryan took up the conversation where they had apparently left it. "As to the battered women's shelter, Debbie, you need to contact them this morning, see if they have room."

"How could *I* get in?" Debbie said, scowling. "You need a judge or a cop to get you in one of those places."

Joe wasn't sure that was true, but it sounded good. Ryan said, "There's one other option. We have an empty cottage that just closed escrow." Was she out of her mind? "It needs a good cleaning, inside and out, and the yard needs weeding and trimming. If you want to work for your rent, you can stay there—for a limited time," she added. Ryan would do almost anything if she thought a person or animal was in need, but she wasn't knuckling under to Debbie Kraft's demands. "The cottage is old and small and neglected. There's no furniture, but the water and electricity are on. If—"

"We don't *have* any furniture," Debbie said. "You can see we have just what's in the car. All our furniture belonged to that landlord. Erik has expensive furniture in the condo, here in the village, but we didn't see much of it. Expensive clothes and car, too, but nothing like that for his family—he says he has to look well, for business."

Clyde said, "There are a number of resale stores, sometimes with good furniture. Salvation Army, Goodwill."

"Oh, I wouldn't buy anything *used*."

"And why is that?" he asked.

Ryan said, "You can pick up what you need at a bargain, the better charity shops have some really nice things. Or, you could check out the furniture-rental places."

"Oh, I wouldn't—"

"The place is empty," Ryan said. "If you want to work for your rent."

"You don't understand. I wouldn't have time to—"

"We can go up as soon as you finish your breakfast," Ryan said, "and you can take a look at it. Bring your suitcases and things, and we'll take some cleaning supplies." She gave Debbie a big smile. "You'll be all set."

"But I can't take the children into some filthy shack. Who knows what kind of germs they'd pick up. You'll have to get someone else to do your cleaning."

Ryan rose, fetched a couple of buckets from the laundry room, and began filling them with supplies: Clorox, disinfectants, rags, brushes. She set a broom and mop beside them, looking evenly at Debbie. "Use these. The children will be fine. It's that, or the shelter."

"You're saying I can't stay here? Why not? You have plenty of room. I could never go into a shelter, it's too degrading. And that's the first place Erik would look.

I've always known that. Whenever I wanted to leave him, I knew I couldn't go to a shelter—and then he left me, stranded." She looked intently at Ryan. "I don't think you understand how cruel he is. There's no telling what he'd do if he found me in one of those places. He wouldn't allow it, that would make him look bad, if anyone found out. And of course I don't have any money to rent a place, Erik took everything. He stripped the checking account that I used for groceries, and that was *all* I had."

Oh, right, the tomcat thought. *And why, if she'd ever wanted to leave Erik, or suspected he might leave her, why didn't she set something aside? This woman is all about grabbing everything she can, to provide for her own comfort. There's not a chance in hell she's broke.*

Dropping down from the table and leaving the kitchen, he wondered if Ryan had told Debbie about her mother's death. Of course she must have, but Debbie sure wasn't grieving. He couldn't see that she'd been crying, and so far he hadn't heard her mention Hesmerra. Nor did the death of her mother seem to have affected her appetite, he thought, as she greedily shoveled in pancakes. Heading for the guest room, he felt Vinnie watching him. Expecting her to follow, he lay down in the hallway beyond the kitchen door.

He heard her sliding out of her chair, and Clyde said, "You follow that cat, Vinnie, I'll take a belt to your backside."

No one spoke. The silence was profound. When Vinnie didn't appear, Joe fled for the guest room. Slipping in between the open suitcases spread across the floor, he saw Debbie's purse lying on the seat of the little chair that was pulled up to the desk. In a flash he was up there, pawing open the bag and nosing out her billfold.

He made quick work of clawing through the money compartment. Twenty bucks? Come on, she wasn't that broke. He could feel a little change in the side pocket, but that was all. Three credit cards, and those could already be maxed out. Dropping the billfold delicately back into the bag, he concentrated on the zippered side pockets.

Nothing but women's stuff, lipstick, emery boards, Band-Aids, old bills and receipts. Abandoning the purse, he dropped to the floor, and considered the open suitcases.

The children's clothes and Debbie's were all mixed together, most of them none too clean. Carefully pushing each item aside, he searched between them, and looked in the side pockets among panty hose, a dingy bra, children's tattered little T-shirts and panties. In

Debbie's makeup case he rummaged among bottles and tubes, wary of meeting a stray safety razor or a pair of sharp scissors, and getting unpleasant smells on his paws. Nothing, no hidden cash, not even loose change.

He went through the second suitcase and into the side pockets, he was losing hope when his reaching paw stroked a thick packet of folded paper with the greasy texture of paper money, and secured with a rubber band. Listening for any movement from the hall, hearing only Vinnie's shrill voice from the kitchen, he pawed out the bundle.

It smelled of uncountable human hands, the oily scent of well-circulated greenbacks. Rifling through with a finesse more suited to Dulcie, he counted fifties and hundreds to a total of two thousand dollars. Well. That should pay rent on a simple room and groceries until she got a job. If, in fact, a job *was* in Debbie's plans.

Straightening the stack, he put the money back in the side pocket, fought the zipper closed, and sauntered out of the room. Heading for the kitchen, he stopped still, hearing Tessa's voice for the first time. She was crying. "I did, too," she sobbed. "I dreamed about Pan and in my dream he talked to me."

Vinnie laughed rudely.

"Don't make up impossible stories," Debbie said. "That's the same as lying."

"I didn't make it up, I dreamed it."

As Joe padded into the kitchen, Debbie was saying, "That's the cat we had, I think it was in the picture I sent. It was only a stray, but the kids made such a fuss to let it stay that I gave in. Tessa decided its name was Pan, she said it told her its name," Debbie said sarcastically.

Joe thought about the many times Misto had talked about his son, Pan. How many cats were named Pan?

"I did dream it!" Tessa said boldly, and Joe watched with interest the way she'd suddenly come alive. "He told me in my sleep, his name is Pan." She looked hard at her mother. "After that, when I called him Pan, he always came to me." Tears were rolling down her cheeks, tears of anger at her mother, tears of grieving for her friend who'd vanished, an innocent friend her mother hadn't ever bothered to look for.

Ryan said, "How long did you have the cat?"

"I guess a year or so," Debbie said. "It showed up at suppertime wet from the rain, slipped in when I heard a noise and opened the door. Got muddy water all over the carpet. I tried to push it out, I didn't want to pick it up and get scratched," she said, glancing meaningfully down at Joe. "Tessa pitched a fit until I fed it, it was easier to give in than listen to her bawl. Next morning she started calling it Pan," Debbie said, amused.

"What happened to it?" Ryan said. "You said something in your letter, but—"

Debbie shrugged. "It left again, that's what cats do."

Clyde said, "Did you look for it?"

Debbie laughed. "How can you look for a cat? There one day, gone the next. Tessa bawled and bawled." She looked at the little girl with disgust.

"You didn't think it might have been hurt?" Ryan asked, trying to control her temper.

"With two kids to take care of? When did I have time to look for some stray cat?"

Tessa had stopped crying, retreating into her silence but staring angrily at her mother, her face red and splotched, the tears still running down. *This little kid,* Joe thought, *is going to be trouble when she gets older—trouble for Debbie but, most of all, trouble for herself, so hurt and miserable and unloved.*

And, he thought, *how does she know Pan's true name?*

The nursing home in Eugene hadn't known, they had called him Buddy. In the dead of night, *did* Pan tell Tessa his name? Was that young cat foolish enough to talk to the child as she slept? Had he crept into the little girl's bed late at night, whispered to her over and over, *The kitty's name is Pan, your kitty is called Pan,* and when she woke up she thought she'd dreamed that whispered message?

Joe was turning this over in his mind with a strange little shiver when there was a knock on the front door and Max Harper's voice came through the intercom. "Anyone home? Any breakfast left?" The chief seldom stopped by early in the day, his sudden unannounced visit startled Joe. Clyde glanced at Debbie and rose to let him in.

Had Ryan or Clyde called Max to tell him Hesmerra's daughter was there, one of the two sisters Max needed to notify of the old woman's death? Or had a patrol unit spotted Debbie's station wagon parked in the drive, called it in because of the *Be On the Lookout* that was out on it? A BOL not only because of the need to notify Debbie, but because of the manner in which Hesmerra died, because of a possible murder, because Debbie Kraft might have information useful to the department.

Max came on back to the kitchen, shook hands with Debbie, sat down at the crowded table, and accepted a cup of coffee. At the far end of the kitchen, Joe stretched out in the flowered easy chair where he could watch

Max and Debbie without calling attention to himself. Debbie didn't seem comfortable in the presence of the law, and that was interesting. But then, some people just naturally became defiant and angry at what they considered the intrusion of uniformed authority. Debbie was, under Max's scrutiny, as silent and withdrawn as her smaller child.

11

When John Firetti left the veterinary clinic at midmorning, crossing the garden to his own small cottage to retrieve some paperwork, he stepped through the doorway into the empty house and paused. He listened, puzzled, to the faint echo of voices coming from his study.

Mary's car was gone; he knew she'd left early to work with the cat rescue group setting up another shelter. No one else lived with them, and this wasn't cleaning day, the housekeeper's car wasn't in the drive. He could hear nothing that sounded like burglars, no stealthy sliding of drawers or wrenching open of locks, just soft voices, one of them female, and John smiled. Was Misto entertaining guests? Pausing beside the fireplace, he listened.

Sunlight shone in through the big living room windows onto the two flowered couches and glinted across the coffee table that was littered with flyers and veterinary magazines and decorated with paw prints etched into a faint coat of dust. Beyond the fireplace, through the door to his study, he could see the pale, cool light of his computer screen. Silently he approached, looking in.

Three furry backs were silhouetted against the screen's glow. Three pairs of upright ears, one pair orange, one pair tortoiseshell, and Dulcie's dark tabby ears. Three tails hanging over, swishing in unison like metronomes for an unheard symphony. The attention of all three cats was fixed on the picture of a red tabby tomcat. But as John approached, they started, looked around at him like children caught at a forbidden prank—and Misto's yellow eyes reflected such a strange mix of excitement and pain that John leaned down for a better look.

The cat on the screen was younger than Misto, but with a broad head and with Misto's same long, bony face. The same wide-set ears, the same wide, curving stripes, but in shades of rusty red. The swirl mark on his left shoulder was startlingly like Misto's own. Sitting down in the desk chair, John peered around the cats to read the accompanying article.

Did Nursing Home Cat Die in Fire?

The remarkable red tabby cat who began, on his own, to visit infirm patients at Green Meadows Nursing Home nearly a year ago has not been seen since a midnight fire burned the complex to the ground. "We're terribly afraid he died in the fire," said nursing supervisor Jamey Small. "We haven't seen him since three hours before the fire broke out, since the alarms went off and we began to evacuate the patients. He came to us as a stray, but he was a most unusual cat. He not only spent nearly every waking moment with the patients, he always favored the most depressed and lonely among them, or the sickest. He would stay with a very ill patient for hours, snuggled close. He would leave for only a few minutes, to eat or drink or visit one of the sandboxes we provided, then he'd hop back on the bed again, purring and rolling over. He gave affection, and enjoyed whatever affection the patient was able to give back. Many of his charges began to sit up in their beds, to smile and talk with the nurses for the first time in months, even to enjoy their meals again."

Even after all the patients were evacuated to safety, to temporary quarters in nearby motels, no one had found Buddy. The night of the fire, which was caused by a faulty furnace in the basement of the building, off-duty personnel searched the rest of the night and into the next morning, searched all over the grounds and in the surrounding neighborhoods, but they found no sign of him.

"If he's been taken in by a nearby family," Small said, "we would very much like to know that he's safe. The nursing staff and the attending doctors have raised a reward of two thousand dollars for information leading to Buddy's return. If he was injured in the fire, we will be happy to repay all his veterinary bills, in order to have him back safe. Buddy is part of our family, he's a remarkable cat, our patients miss him and we miss him, we all pray that he is alive and has not been harmed."

"This is Pan?" John said, stroking Misto. "Your son, Pan?"

The old cat twitched an ear, and touched the picture with a soft paw. "He's too quick to get trapped in a fire—maybe it was Pan who set off the alarm, alerted them at the first smell of smoke, but then he would have beat it out of there." Misto's eyes were filled with a stubborn hope, and John, watching him, prayed that he was right.

When Dulcie scrolled down the screen, two more pictures of Pan appeared, sharing the beds of other patients. In one shot he was curled up against a woman's shoulder, in the other an old man sat up in bed, his arm around the red tomcat, both looking into the camera, the cat's amber eyes bright, his smile laced with humor. Kit, too, lifted a paw to the screen, to touch the young tom's nose. She looked at the picture a long time, her fluffy tail twitching—as it did when she was deep in thought or was deeply enchanted.

But while John Firetti and the three cats browsed online searching for clues to the lost Pan, down at the Damen household Clyde had lit a fire on the hearth, and had left the living room to Max Harper and Debbie. The big room was no longer done in black and brown African patterns, which Hanni's studio had created for Clyde in his bachelor days. That primitive mood had given way to sunny yellow walls, flowered linen covers on the couch and chairs and, over the couch, an arrangement of Charlie Harper's drawings, portraits of Joe, Rock, Dulcie, Kit, and Snowball, all handsomely framed. Three tall schefflera plants softened the corners of the room, and over the mantel was a Charlie Harper etching of Dulcie and Joe and Kit hunting through the tall grass of the Molena Point hills. The white linen draperies were new and fresh, the wood floors gleaming. The only furnishing left over from earlier days was Joe Grey's faded, claw-shredded, fur-matted easy chair, and even its fate was under negotiation. Joe said if his chair went to Goodwill, he went with it. Ryan had proposed a washable linen cover, which, with reservations, he was considering—he wasn't fond of the smell of laundry soap.

Debbie sat at one end of the couch, Max across from her in Clyde's reading chair. Joe, padding into the room, leaped into his own chair and curled up for a nap, as if he was quite alone in the room; he soon let himself snore a little, his head tucked under, his closed eyes slitted open just enough to watch Debbie's reaction as Max questioned her. The chief started out friendly enough, and low-key; he told her how sorry he was about Hesmerra's death, and asked gently when she had last seen her mother.

"I didn't see her much," Debbie said, pretending to wipe at a tear, a gesture Joe thought singularly unconvincing.

"A few months, would you say?"

Debbie shrugged. "Maybe."

"Do you come down during the winter months, when Erik's working down here?"

"I haven't the last few years. Erik was . . . He's always busy with work. I have the children to care for . . . Tessa's so little, she takes up a lot of time. And Vinnie's in school. I don't like to pull her out, move her back and forth between schools, that's very unsettling for a child." *My,* Joe thought, *the ever-caring mother. This, from a woman who patronizes her littlest child until she cries.* "It's bad enough," Debbie said, "that she has to change schools now. But now, of course, I have no choice. We couldn't stay in Eugene, I have no money at all."

"The children are how old?" Max asked.

"Vinnie's twelve, Tessa nearly five." She looked uncomfortably away, causing Joe to wonder about the seven-year gap between the two little girls. Family planning? he wondered. Or long-standing marital troubles?

"If you didn't come down with Erik," Max said, "you must at least have talked with your mother on the phone, or written to her?"

"She didn't have a phone. I wrote to her sometimes," Debbie said evasively. "We weren't . . . We had differences," she said shortly. "I didn't see her much."

"You want to tell me what that was about?"

"She . . . We didn't see eye to eye. I don't under-stand why you're asking me all this. Is this really nec-essary?"

Max said, "What, exactly, was the problem between you?"

Debbie sighed. "For one thing, that boy she's rais-ing. My dead sister's child. My mother isn't . . . wasn't fit to raise a child, with her drinking. When the child was born, I told her she should take it to Child Welfare, where he could be adopted."

"What about his father? Couldn't he have taken Billy?"

"We have no idea who the father was. Some boy from her high school, too young and irresponsible anyway to take care of a family. Greta would never say who he was, only that his family refused to help."

"And your other sister, Esther? She didn't want Billy?"

"Esther didn't want children," she said shortly. Joe, listening to Max bait her, ask her questions to which he already knew the answers, wondered where this was going. Did he think Debbie was involved in Hesmerra's death? Or was he, indeed, simply gathering background information?

"You were sixteen when you married Erik Kraft? Wasn't that pretty young, too?"

"But we got *married,* we didn't just . . . ." Again she sighed, as if losing patience with his lack of insight. "I wanted out of there, I didn't like living with my mother, I didn't like her drinking. All right?"

"She was drinking then?"

"Not as much as now, I've heard. Not every day. She worked in an office then, some kind of clerk. Some weekends she'd go on a tear, then call in sick on Monday. We were living up in the hills above the village, renting a backyard guesthouse. My mother's a loud, mean drunk. She yells and cries. I'm surprised they didn't kick us out. Esther and Greta and I would get out of the house, go our separate ways. When I left to get married, she and Greta moved to that shack. Esther was already married and gone. What does this have to do with the fire and with my mother's death?"

"Just trying to get a picture of her situation," Max said quietly. "Did your mother try to get financial help from the state or county to raise the child?"

"I don't know. Probably not. Who would give her help when she lived in that shack, and the way she drank? They'd just take the kid away from her. No, she would never apply for help, she didn't like government do-gooders."

"Did Hesmerra drink after the baby came?"

"I don't know, I wasn't there. Once in a while, I talked with my sister Esther. She said Mother was about the same."

"You didn't talk with Esther often."

"She and I had a blowup. These questions have nothing to do with my mother."

"They help to give me a picture of your mother's life," Max said, "to understand what might have happened."

"What's to understand? She got drunk and burned the house down. How *did* the fire start?"

"Fire investigators determined she left a skillet on the stove, with the burner on high. The grease in the pan got too hot, flamed up. Flames ignited the wall and then the ceiling. The house went up like tinder."

Debbie's face drained of color. But, strangely, her hands lay relaxed in her lap. Joe watched Tessa creep in and slip behind the couch. Vinnie appeared behind her, as if not to be left out. She found a place on the floor beneath a schefflera plant, sat there silent for once. Was Vinnie, too, intimidated by the law? Joe wondered, amused.

"It was about twelve years ago that you and Erik first separated?" Max asked. "That you left the village and moved up to your uncle's, in Eugene?"

"Yes, but first I took what little money Erik gave me, and some I'd stashed, and enrolled for a summer semester at San Francisco Art Institute. Moved into the cheapest room I could find. I hardly had enough for food and for paper and paint. I don't know, I thought it would lead somewhere, I really didn't know what I wanted to do. I just knew I had to get away.

"Halfway through the semester, I found out I was pregnant," she said bitterly. "When school was out, I moved up to my uncle's—just before Vinnie was born."

"And then some five years later you and Erik got back together?"

"Yes, but what does—"

"That's when you left your uncle's farm, and Erik rented the house in Eugene?"

She shifted her position on the couch, glancing impatiently toward the door. "I still don't see what this has to do with my mother."

"Just trying to get the whole picture," Max repeated. "There's some question about the cause of her death. In the investigation of a murder, we need to have some sense of the victim's family as well as of her own life."

Debbie stared at him. "A murder? Someone killed her? Someone set that fire and . . ." Her hands went to her face. "Someone burned . . . ?"

"She was dead before the fire started," Max said. "But possibly not from natural causes."

Debbie's brown eyes remained fixed on Max. Joe tried to read her, as Max was reading her, but the chief was more skilled at this stuff. At first she had been too calm, too cool. Now, was her shock and distress genuine, or a good act?

Max said, "We don't have many answers yet. I'm sorry to press you, but can we go back in time again, for a moment? Try to bring me up to speed?"

Debbie nodded, mute and still.

"When you and Erik moved into the Eugene house, he worked in that office during the summer months, came down to the Molena Point office for the winter, while you and the children remained in Eugene?"

"Yes. Tessa was only a baby."

"And that is still the arrangement?"

"Until last fall, when he filed for divorce," she said. "September. He sent child support money until just after Christmas, then the checks stopped. A month ago he stopped paying the rent, too. The landlord said we had to get out. I told him we had nowhere to go, and no money. I *told* him Erik took everything, but he didn't care, all he wanted was money. I had to close out my household account, it was down to nothing. We have nothing."

Nothing, Joe thought, *but the two thousand bucks tucked away in your suitcase.*

"Since you arrived in the village," Max said, "have you been in touch with Erik? Or with Esther and Perry Fowler? Have you asked them for help in getting resettled?"

Joe knew Perry Fowler, the older of the two partners. You'd see him around the village dressed in tennis clothes, sometimes Fowler and Erik together. He was tall and slim like Erik but strangely pale despite the fact that he must be outdoors a lot. Pale hair, whitish skin, pale blue eyes, a hesitant way of moving. Joe had never seen Fowler's wife headed for the tennis courts; he guessed Esther wasn't interested in the game. He wondered what kind of tennis player Fowler was, as uncertain as he seemed.

"Erik doesn't know I'm here. I don't want him to know, so of course I haven't contacted Perry, either. He'd be sure to tell Erik." She looked at Harper pleadingly. "Erik would knock me around for coming here where he works. He doesn't want people to know he left me. He won't think I'd come here, this is the last place he'll look. He'll think I headed north, away from California. Maybe just keep going until I found a job."

"How long did it take you to drive down from Eugene?" The chief knew she'd moved out of the rented house ten days ago; he'd called Eugene just after the autopsy, Charlie had told Ryan that. Apparently, while Debbie had left the landlord's furniture intact, she'd taken everything else, down to the curtain rods, the towel racks, and the lightbulbs. Joe wondered if she'd left that little lightbulb in the refrigerator. He watched her fidgeting in her chair, her hands busy now, moving nervously, and then going rigid as she tried to keep them still. Max said, again, "The trip down from Eugene took you how long?"

"I . . . about a week and a half, I guess. We camped along the way. I needed time to think, I didn't know what I was going to do, I needed time to work out a plan. I didn't think he'd look for me in the campgrounds. I wouldn't normally camp, I don't like the dirt and the inconvenience."

"It takes money, even to camp."

"We brought what food we had in the cupboards, canned food, crackers. Ryan and her sister Hanni are the only friends I have, we had enough to get here, to them. I need to think of some way to make a living, some kind of job where I can take care of the kids, I don't want to impose on Ryan any longer than I have to."

Joe rolled over in his chair, hiding a silent cat laugh.

Max said, "If he left you, Debbie, why would he look for you at all? Why would he care where you went?"

Debbie sighed again. "He might think I'd make trouble. He . . . he was into some real estate scams, some deals he made in Eugene. If he found out I knew about them, he'd want to hush me up, he'd come looking for me." She pulled up the sleeve of her sweatshirt. "The purple is faded now, there were always bruises. That scar . . . he cut me with a paring knife, just before he left." The scar on her inner forearm was maybe four inches long. "That wasn't the first time. When he was in Eugene, and even when he wasn't, I was afraid to run away, I knew he'd come after me. I was glad when *he* left. Maybe he doesn't suspect what I know. But," she said tremulously, "I can't be sure of that."

"You want to tell me about the scams?"

"I . . . would really rather talk about it later," she said, glancing at Vinnie. "That can't have anything to do with my mother."

"Did Erik get along well with your mother? Did he ever visit her?"

"I don't know why he would. They'd get along all right, I guess, if he ever saw her. But why would he bother with her?"

"Could Hesmerra have known about his real estate deals?"

"How could she possibly know something like that? Why would she care?"

"How did you know about the deals?" Max said. "Did you see contracts, sales agreements?"

"That would take a while to explain. Ryan's waiting for me," she said, "to take me up to her cottage."

Max rose. "We can talk about this another time," he said easily. "Meanwhile, we'd like you to stop by the station, get your fingerprints on file."

"What for? I'm not being investigated. Why would you need my fingerprints?"

"We need family prints to eliminate from others we might find at the scene."

"It's years since I went there, before Greta's child was born. Whatever prints I might have left wouldn't still be there."

"You're family," Max said. "It's customary. We'll need Billy's prints, of course, and Esther's, as well as yours."

When Debbie rose, Vinnie leaped up and grabbed her around the legs. Max looked at the child a moment, then let himself out the front door. Debbie stared after him, then turned away toward the guest room, dragging Vinnie. The child acted as if Debbie was private property, to push and pull as she chose. Just as, Joe thought, Debbie seemed to view those people around her, who might be useful.

Alone in the living room, except for little Tessa, behind the couch, a number of questions nudged Joe. The more he saw of Debbie Kraft, the less he liked her.

He wondered what *had* happened to the family cat. Had Pan, the night of the fire, tried to return to the Krafts' rented house? If he'd shown up there, maybe injured from the fire, would Debbie have chased him away? Run him off, even if he needed help? She'd already dismissed the young tom as no more than a discarded toy: a cat her little girl loved, a cat who was quite possibly smarter, and surely more decent, than the woman he had come to for shelter.

12

From the back of his well-clawed easy chair, Joe watched through the front window as the chief drove off in the direction of the station. He watched Clyde carry out a load of plastic bags and duffels, kiddie blankets and stuffed toys, and push everything into the back of Debbie's station wagon. Debbie followed him, scowling, bearing a tangle of clothes and stray shoes, none too happy to be shuffled off so quickly. Joe sat enjoying the drama until he heard Ryan's footsteps in the studio above him, then, leaping from his chair, he hightailed it up the stairs, where they could talk in private, hopefully without Vinnie charging in to catch her hostess and the house cat in a private discussion.

Ryan stood beside the tall studio windows looking down to the drive, the sun teasing a shine across her short hair. There was a more relaxed look on her face as she watched Clyde and Debbie pack up the car. Leaping onto the mantel beside her, Joe gave her a wicked smile.

"What?" she said, turning from the window, her green eyes looking into his. When he'd left the kitchen earlier, she knew he was taking advantage of the moment to toss Debbie's room. "What did you find?" she said softly.

"She's not so broke, " Joe said with sly satisfaction.

"How much?"

"Two thousand, in cash. I didn't find a bankbook, so maybe that's all she has, but that's hardly the same as broke. That should hold her until she gets a job—if she plans to get a job. I wonder," Joe said, "how much money she had when she left Eugene. Aren't there some pretty nice resorts in southern Oregon and on down in Mendocino?"

"You do have a suspicious mind, tomcat."

"And you don't?"

"Cop's kid," she said. "Comes with the territory. That's why we survive, suspicion breeds safety. Two thousand bucks! Poor thing. Talk about destitute." Standing on tiptoe, she kissed him on top his head. "You did good, tomcat." If a cat could blush, he'd look like a pink plush kiddy toy. Licking a paw to hide his embarrassment, he watched her make her way back downstairs, heard her in the living room hurrying Debbie along. When he peered down again through the window, the two kids were in the car, enthroned among the blankets and duffels, and Clyde was stuffing the last load in around them. Dropping down from the mantel, he pawed open the sliding glass door and slipped out onto the deck. Looking over, he watched Ryan hand Debbie the want ads, listened to her suggest job venues, including a contact with their friend Chichi Barbi, who had recently bought Charlie Harper's cleaning service. Chichi was expanding the business, taking on a long waiting list of homeowners who wanted their houses cleaned and maintained on a regular basis. She was interested in any possible new employee who could pass the background check and was a good worker. He wondered if Debbie could pass on either count?

But maybe he was being too hard on her, maybe with encouragement she'd knuckle down and get a job—or maybe, he thought, she'd run quickly through the two thousand, and then start whining again.

Debbie was saying, "I need to stop for groceries." She sighed, looking toward the car. "Something to feed the kids." Joe imagined them pulling up before the little village grocery, imagined Debbie asking Clyde to come inside, to show her where things were, so it wouldn't take her so long. And then at the checkout, giving Clyde that helpless, big-eyed look when she discovered she was short of cash. *Right,* Joe thought. *And Clyde's going to sucker up to that?*

As Ryan and Clyde headed for Ryan's pickup to lead Debbie up to the cottage, Joe thought to scorch on down and ride with them, see how this played out. Except, he'd had more than enough of Debbie Kraft and Vinnie for a while. Instead he raced away across the roofs for Molena Point PD, where he could relax among easy cop talk, away from Debbie Kraft's lies and fake smiles; he pitied Rock, who had already scrambled up into the backseat of the truck.

If Max was back at the station, maybe he'd already called Eugene to check on Debbie's movements, see when she *had* left Oregon for California. He wondered if he should call Eugene himself, to try to get a line on the red tomcat. The nursing home must have set up a temporary office, maybe even with the original phone number. Running across the roofs, with an icy wind at his back, he hurried for the station, thinking that winter had turned serious and bold. Dark clouds hung low over the village, the damp air smelled of rain and of a deeper cold yet to come. Well, but February weather on the central coast was never to be relied on. Racing beneath the wind, sailing across the occasional narrow alley, he hit the cold tile roof of the courthouse, ran its length, and dropped down to the roof of MPPD.

He was just backing down the oak, headed for the front door, when a black-and-white pulled to the curb below. Hidden within the prickly oak leaves, he watched two uniformed officers step out, force their handcuffed prisoner out of the backseat and through the glass door, into the little foyer: a young, skinny fellow, long face, long greasy hair. Even from the tree Joe could smell the oily stink of his old leather jacket. As they marched him inside, Joe hit the ground behind them and slid in, too. The arrestee looked startled to see a cat race in past his feet, but the officers paid no attention. They stood at the dispatcher's counter, portly Officer Brennan booking the guy in, printing him, listing his personal effects that Brennan had laid out on the desk; a dirty handkerchief, a little greasy coin purse, a squashed candy bar.

Joe strolled past them and down the hall, thinking that there was a lot to be said for the ambience of a small-town police department. He couldn't imagine being allowed this kind of freedom in the vast, impersonal complex of San Francisco or LAPD. He'd seen the pictures of those daunting establishments with their complicated security, bulletproof glass walls, locked doors. He'd heard the officers discuss the many divisions of the metropolitan hierarchies, and couldn't envision a feline sleuth trying to function in that high-powered maze.

Surprisingly, though, cats *were* serving their own important role in big-city PDs. Even in L.A., feral cats were doing important work. Not sleuthing, but protecting the criminal files and records. Several L.A. precincts, whose buildings were plagued by rats, had brought in colonies of feral cats, housing, feeding, and caring for them, setting them loose among the offices to handle the out-of-control rodent population. Rats in the offices. Rats in the lunchroom. Rats running down the halls into the storage rooms, eating paper supplies and, more alarming, destroying old criminal files: a felon's record quickly expunged, vanished into the belly of a hungry rodent. And it wasn't only L.A. that was employing ferals who might otherwise be killed. Other large city police departments were taking notice, bringing in their own bands of ferals, working with foundations of volunteers like Alley Cat Allies or Animal Friends. Feline exterminators were now working at city offices, college campuses, all kinds of institutions—stable cat populations that did not produce unwanted kittens, but went happily about their business destroying the rats, not only saving valuable paperwork, but saving lives, too. For every rat the cats killed, they destroyed a potential carrier of hantavirus that was fatal to humans, and for which there was no vaccine and no cure. Dogs, Joe thought, weren't the only four-legged professionals serving human needs. Those cats could be as important as Red Cross nurses, giving folks a helping paw.

Slipping into Max's office, into what he considered his personal lair beneath the credenza, he sniffed the sweet scent of horses from Max's Western boots. The chief was on the phone, glancing up now and then at Detective Juana Davis. She sat in one of the leather chairs, leaning over massaging her left knee where a prospective felon, now in Soledad Prison, had graced her with a well-placed kick while she was cuffing his partner. Orange cat hairs clung to Juana's dark uniform, evidence of the kitten she'd recently adopted. Juana seemed more relaxed since the kitten had come to share her condo; the little creature was born nearly in the middle of a murder case that Juana, and Joe himself, had worked in tandem, Juana happily unaware of the identity of the snitch who alerted her to the murder, unaware of the three cats' roles in the timely demise of the killer. Max hung up the phone, looking across at the detective.

"As far as Eugene PD can tell, Debbie did leave ten days ago, about the time she mailed Ryan's letter. Landlord said her lease was up three months ago, but she refused to move. He called her husband here in the village. Erik was out of town, but he got him on his cell. Kraft told him he was divorcing her, said if she wanted to stay she'd have to sign her own lease, pay her own rent. Landlord went over there three times with a lease. Her car was there but she wouldn't answer the door. Brown, 1998 Suzuki station wagon. Eugene has our BOL on her but hadn't spotted her. Strange, if she was camping, they watch those campgrounds pretty close. Well, she's here now, arrived last night, stayed with Ryan and Clyde. I went by this morning, talked with her, asked her to come in and get printed. She doesn't want Erik to know she's here, claims she's afraid of him. Claims he's into some kind of real estate scam."

"If she's avoiding him," Davis said. "Why would she come here?"

Max shook his head. "Says he won't expect her here, that he'll think she's headed north."

"His condo's right in the middle of town," Davis said. "Pretty hard to keep out of his way. The Brighton, that second-floor penthouse." In Molena Point, as in much of California where the buildings were designed to resist impending earthquakes, even a second story often rose above the surrounding rooftops. Joe knew that penthouse well; its walled back patio was a favorite for the village cats, a sunny spot out of the wind on cold days. The little terrace had no access from the roofs around it except to the pigeons and seagulls, and through open aspects at the base of the wall meant for rain runoff, where the local cats could easily slip inside. With Erik gone so much of the time, it was an ideal hunting preserve. One could enjoy a sunny afternoon nap, wake when a pigeon landed, snatch him up before he knew you were there. Warm nap and instant feast, how could any cat resist?

Max said, "Kraft's still out of town, expects to be gone for another month or more. I talked with Fowler. Says he's down in Orange County reorganizing the branch office there, some kind of staff shake-up. Says from there, he's headed for the Bahamas on vacation."

Davis smiled. "Pretty tough life."

Max laughed. "For sure, Debbie's current digs won't match that kind of luxury. Ryan and Clyde are moving her into one of the cottages they bought, that dilapidated one up near the meth house we raided." He frowned, none too happy with that operation.

"They sure saw that coming," she said. "Empty house, nothing left but the smell. Crime-scene cleanup service should be in there this week. Took us a while to locate the landlord, the house sold six months ago to a Jarvis James, in Chicago." They exchanged a look of disgust. Someone out of state buys an old cottage, next thing you know they're making meth.

And, Joe thought, *most likely ruining the house for future sale.* Even if the house was torn down, the land could be useless if it was sufficiently soaked with lethal chemicals.

Davis said, "We have computer copies of the deed and the closing papers. Most of it was done online." Neither Davis nor the chief liked the shift from paper contracts to those completed online, which the real estate and escrow companies had so eagerly embraced, and which made evidence harder to nail down.

"Kathleen's working on the contract," Davis said, "trying to pick up the trail." Kathleen Ray, the newest of the three detectives, had brought with her a fine expertise in the world of computers, and both older detectives were more than happy to see her take on that annoying aspect of their work. Davis said, "She's found other purchases for James, so we'll see where that leads. Looks like Ryan and Clyde, and Hanni, are stuck with those places for a while. Besides the economic slump, no one wants to buy near a meth house."

Max said, "Hanni's nearly done with her renovation. Ryan and Clyde mean to go ahead, too, and then wait it out." He tilted back in his chair. "The meth house isn't the only problem up there. The papers on some of those places are in a hell of a tangle. City attorney's beginning to see illegal foreclosures, false documents, the works. Could keep that area depressed for some long time."

"Anywhere else," Davis said, "I'd worry. But land's too valuable in Molena Point, city council's too concerned, city attorney rides too close when these things begin to happen."

Joe thought about the cats that the rescue group had trapped in that neighborhood. Many members of their local CatFriends group had taken three or four cats apiece into their homes, to shelter on a temporary basis. He thought some of them would turn out to be so charming they'd end up as permanent family members. Juana had already told Charlie she'd take another young cat, that her orange kitten was growing bored, home all day alone, that he was clawing and chewing up the furniture. Davis hoped that two cats, if they were compatible, would chase each other, climb the cat trees, play tag, rather than spend their energy as a two-cat demolition crew.

"Anything more on the burn?" Max asked.

"We lifted three sets of prints from the whiskey bottles and the carton, besides Hesmerra's. Sent the whole thing for contents analysis to the lab, along with the shattered remains of the bottle she had in bed. The few dishes, glasses, pans, knives and forks were melted, but we sent a collection of that to the lab. I'm guessing, even with the new methods, they won't be able to lift much. The rest of the burn, Dallas and I lifted four sets of prints besides hers."

Joe had taken a good look at those transformed blobs of glass, smoky and milky and as weird as artifacts from an alien planet. The pots and pans, too, the knives and forks, all were melted into misshapen monstrosities that might have been turned out by some misguided, first-year art student.

As for the wood alcohol that had killed Hesmerra, that was as common as bargain brand cat food; a person could buy the stuff anywhere, any grocery or drugstore. Slip into Hesmerra's cave, ease off one of the little plastic cap covers, remove the lid. Pour out some of the whiskey, replace it with denatured alcohol. Slip the plastic back on, and wait for her to retrieve that particular bottle and suck it down. The hitch was, the killer couldn't be sure of the timing; it might be months before she picked up the poisoned offering—unless he'd doctored all the bottles.

Or had the killer slipped into the shack, maybe when Hesmerra was sleeping or passed out? Added the wood alcohol to her already open whiskey?

Davis said, "Billy told you that Erik Kraft and Hesmerra were friends?"

Max nodded. "Billy thought that was because Debbie, herself, never went to see her. Neither sister did, Billy said it's been like that since his mother died. Greta was the youngest, maybe her sisters felt protective, felt Hesmerra was remiss in letting her go out in the storm that night. Though that doesn't really explain such rigid, long-standing anger."

"Doesn't explain a lot of things," Davis said. "Doesn't explain Hesmerra's maneuvering for jobs that gave her access to the Kraft offices, and to Alain Bent's house."

Max said, "I asked Emmylou Warren to come in for prints, I want to talk with her, maybe she can fill us in. Up at the burn this morning, she was pretty nervous. Billy said she and Hesmerra had a falling-out when she was evicted."

"You want a BOL on her?"

"Not at this point. If she doesn't show, have the patrols watch for her, give her a little nudge."

Of course she was nervous, Joe thought, *if she lifted that file box from the crime scene.* It had sure smelled, and looked, as if it had been buried in the earth beneath the fire. Question was, would she bring the box to the chief? And, a more worrisome question, how much had Max seen in the backseat of her car when he grabbed one guilty tomcat and tossed him out?

Joe thought he must have seen the box. But before he grabbed Joe, did he see the letterheads that were barely sticking out, had he seen enough so that when he did have the box, he'd focus right in on the gray tomcat pawing through the evidence—if that *was* some kind of evidence?

Or would Emmylou decide to keep those papers to herself, maybe hide them, and not get involved? He was wondering if he should make a call, fill Max in on the letterheads in case she didn't give the papers to him, when a woman's querulous voice cut loudly down the hall. "I'll see him now! He left three very curt calls on my machine, when one polite message would have done, and I don't expect to be kept waiting."

The dispatcher mumbled an answer Joe couldn't make out. The woman said, "I've been out of town. Now that I'm home, I have better things to do than waste my time in this place, with the implication that if I don't show up I'm under some kind of arrest. I'm not in the habit of being summoned by the police, by a public servant, and then kept waiting."

With a look of sorely tried patience, Max rose from his desk and headed up the hall. Davis was slower to rise. Limping, she moved out close behind him. Silently Joe followed them, his claws itching for action. MPPD was his second home, and he didn't take kindly to rude humans throwing their weight around.

13

Three hundred miles north of Molena Point, the red tabby tomcat sat in the cab of a U-Haul truck as it roared down Highway 101. Perched comfortably atop the driver's duffel bag, he watched the pine-wooded hills race by, broken now and then by green pastures. For most of the trip, the sky had been clear, the sea to their right sparkling blue, but then as they neared the Oregon paper mills they'd hit that area's overcast, as thick as curdled milk, the sky hanging low and gray, the sea as unappealing as a smear of mud.

Whatever the weather, though, hitchhiking was a blast—if you chose your mark with care, if you didn't hook up with some nutcase who had no respect for a lone tomcat. Lazily washing his paws and whiskers, he glanced at his hefty driver. She was a big, square woman dressed comfortably in faded jeans, a khaki shirt, a soft brown leather jacket, high brown boots that could stand a good polish if one cared about such matters. Her U-Haul rental agreement, tucked carelessly into the visor above her head, gave her name as Denise Woolsey. She was maybe sixty-some, though he had trouble discerning the exact age of a human. Cats were easier, advancing age providing the clear signs, lengthening chin, graying muzzle, spreading toes and dropped belly; and of course the changing smell of old age.

Denise had told him, conversationally, that she was moving house; she talked to him as she might to any hitchhiker, and he liked that. She was hauling her furniture, all her worldly goods, from Astoria to her new home in Stockton. She said she'd given away half of what she owned, meaning to simplify her life. She seemed hungry for conversation, even if it was one-sided. Maybe she'd taken him aboard simply for someone to talk to, imagining that he couldn't repeat any of her shared secrets. She hadn't a clue he could have contributed to the conversation, could have entertained her, himself, with tales of his own travels. The cab smelled of ancient dust, fresh coffee from her thermos, and the stink of the southern Oregon paper mills, the sour, acid smell of ground-up wood pulp trapped beneath an increasingly heavy fog that hugged the coast.

"You wouldn't catch me living in this stink," Denise told him. "Bad enough to have to drive through it. I guess if you have to make a living, though, if you have a family to feed, some folks don't have a choice.

"Me," she said, looking over at the tomcat, "you won't catch me tied down. Any more than you, right? Single, footloose, a little money in the bank, and I go where I want, when I want." She didn't seem to consider that cats don't have money in the bank. Maybe she thought mice in the fields took the place of hard cash.

She'd picked him up early that morning at the rest stop, a long way from where he'd left his last ride. From the minute he'd approached Denise's U-Haul, she'd been kind to him. When he hopped in the cab waiting expectantly for her to head out, she hadn't even done a second take. She had simply laid a folded blanket atop the duffel, so he could be comfortable and enjoy the view. They had shared her burger and fries in equal portions, and her remarks to him were direct and comfortable—making him wonder what she *would* do, if he answered her.

But he'd never find out, his commitment to secrecy was way too deeply embedded. Caution was bred irrefutably into his every cell, passed down for thousands of generations, and reinforced by parental discipline. The occasional transgression of some individual cat, they all knew, was recklessly dangerous.

While beyond his partially open window the sea lay flat and gray, the sluggish waves smothered by the fog, on their left they passed an occasional small lake that, despite the fog, gleamed blue and clear against a background of dark pines, lakes with no houses around them, the surrounding forest dense and wild. He watched an osprey arrow down into the fresh water; a violent splash and it rose again with a fish gleaming in its talons. The great bird's powerful flight made him dream of soaring high above the hills, effortlessly winging the long, long miles, high above the killer wheels of speeding cars and trucks—made him wish he could dive down out of the clouds with such power as that bird, drop straight down onto his destination. And the photographs from Debbie's album filled his mind, the little seaside village with its sheltering pines and cypress, its white beach and fishing dock, the ocean bright and clear, so very like the home his pa had described for him, when he was young. That was the first place Pa could remember, from his lonely kittenhood.

He couldn't be sure he was headed for the same place. For that one spot, on this vast coast, where

Misto, facing old age, might have gone, in the way so many animals longed to do. He could only pray Misto had returned there, and that he could find him.

He had left Eugene three days earlier in the backseat of a 1992 Toyota Camry, sweltering in the lap of a fat old lady who smelled of mothballs and pee. Even when he lifted an armored paw and growled at her, she couldn't stop petting and hugging him. He had stayed in the car because they were headed south, the woman's daughter and son taking turns driving. And because they seemed a harmless threesome, didn't seem like people who would hurt a cat. A prime path of learning, in a young cat's life, was to listen to his own instinctive fears, to go with what they told him—or not, and learn a hard lesson.

He had picked up the little family just outside Eugene, just two miles west of the burned-down nursing home. Their car had been parked at a lunch stop. The family had sat nearby at an outside picnic table eating hamburgers, studying an unfolded Oregon map, discussing where to stay for the night. It was already late in the day, they had come down Highway 5 from Seattle, were headed over to the coast, to Coos Bay. He'd bummed some hamburger by charming the old woman, and then conned them into a ride. He hadn't counted on the woman's overheated lap and her endless petting. At Coos Bay, where they pulled into a motel with a lighted VACANCY sign, he'd streaked out of the car the minute the old woman opened her door, had vanished among a tangle of shops, small gardens, and garbage cans. Had sat among the overgrown bushes listening as they called and called him, "Here, kitty, kitty, kitty." He'd watched them set a half sandwich torn in small pieces, and a used Styrofoam bowl of water, outside the motel door. He'd slept hidden in the bushes ten feet from their door, listening to their blaring television tuned to an old sitcom, and to the frequently opening door as they looked for him, and to their annoyed and worried calls.

"Maybe this was his destination," the old woman had said querulously, just before they turned out the light, "maybe he didn't want a home at all, maybe he was just hitching a ride."

"Cats don't hitch rides, Mama. Go to sleep," and the room went dark, leaving only the faint sounds of covers rustling as the three got settled.

They called him the next morning, too, before and after partaking of the motel's free breakfast, but at last they gave it up. Leaving a torn-up sweet roll for him from the motel's free continental breakfast, they went on their way. As the car grew smaller and then merged onto the highway, he'd eaten the sweet roll then settled down among the bushes just at the edge of the parking lot, waiting to cop another ride south. His dreams filled with pictures from Debbie Kraft's photo album, shots taken when Vinnie was small, before Tessa was born, apparently before Debbie and Erik began fighting and carping at each other. Pictures of a shore that blended exactly with the tales his daddy had told him, pictures of a rocky cliff above the white beach, the blue and roiling sea, the white-crested waves.

There was no picture of the man his daddy had told him about, who brought food to the feral cats, who talked to them as if they could understand him. Misto had been only a kitten when he was part of that feral band, but he'd known enough not to answer back to the man. How could it be, that Misto had been a kitten in the same village where Debbie Kraft grew up, where her husband still spent part of his working year? How strange was that?

For months after he abandoned the Kraft household, after Erik threw one too many shoes at him, he had searched Eugene for his sisters and his daddy. He'd gone to the house he remembered, from when he was a kitten, but Misto's scent wasn't there. Even after he went to live in the nursing home, he'd go rambling at night searching for Misto, but he never found his scent; he hadn't seen Misto now for well over a year.

Once, after the fire, he'd returned again to the Krafts' house, imagining Erik might indeed have abandoned his wife and children as he'd sometimes threatened, imagining he could be with Tessa again. But, lingering in the overgrown yard and then leaping up a tree to peer in through the dirty windows, he'd seen and smelled the emptiness, the abandoned trash, the discarded clothes, and knew they would not be back. And he'd gone away again, missing Tessa.

After the "mothball woman" and her family departed Coos Bay, he headed south again, traveling on the berm and through the tall grass of pastures that bordered Highway 101, warily crossing the occasional side road. It was late afternoon when he'd come at last to a rest stop set beside the highway among the pine woods. He was paw weary. The clearing was deserted save for two cars parked together near the restrooms, beyond a cluster of picnic tables. A dusty willow tree sheltered the cinder-block building, while a second willow provided shade for a half dozen picnic tables with attached benches, all bolted to concrete slabs buried in the earth. Could you trust humans with nothing? The dusty earth was embossed with numerous tire marks crossing over each other, and these were dissected by lines of long, thin paw prints that stank of coyote. He'd backed away from these, and looked the two cars over, wondering about a ride.

But both were muscle cars, an old fishtailed Chevy painted red and white, and a low-riding orange roadster with the top down; and he could hear the bantering voices of several young men echoing from the restrooms. Moving into the bushes at the edge of the clearing, he'd settled down, listening, wanting to know where they were headed and to assess their character, see whether it would be safe to try to make nice and con a ride—he was feeling desperate to move on—but already their strident voices made his skin twitch.

The voices grew louder and more raucous, then two young men emerged laughing and idly shoving each other, scruffy-looking fellows, a Caucasian and a Latino, long hair hanging down their backs, black jackets and baggy black jeans sagging wrinkled over dusty black boots. Ducking down, Pan remained still as they swung into the Chevy, watched the driver race the engine with a heavy foot and take off in a storm of dirt and gravel. With his eyes squeezed closed, he'd felt gravel pepper his face. Soon three more guys followed. Laughing loudly, they didn't bother to open the doors of the roadster but swung in over the top, took off with a roar, another shower of dirt and rocks and blast of exhaust.

Then, blessed silence.

Pan came out of the bushes. The rest stop was deserted once more, the sun low, the only sound the hushing of the sea. Heading for the willow tree beside the restrooms, he scaled its rough bark through its lacy fronds, leaped to the warm metal roof, and curled up in the willow's late shade. On the roof, safe from dangerous humans and coyotes, he slept. The coyotes yipped and yodeled all night.

He dreamed he was crouched, not beneath the willow tree, but in an oak outside the nursing home. In his dream, the night was red with flames, his elderly friends were being led out, or wheeled and carried out to safety from the licking flames. Then the flames were mixed with other fires: hearth fires, bonfires, blazes from other times, ghostly flames echoing from past centuries. He heard bits of conversation that were not of this time, saw strangers' faces tangled together without order. Only when a late car pulled into the rest stop did he wake.

The wind was up, the night growing cold. He looked the driver over, but didn't like what he saw. Between midnight and dawn only three cars came, stayed a little while as the drivers used the restroom, then left again. Pan remained where he was, on the tin roof. Dawn broke late, beneath dark clouds, the sky heavy, the wind icy. He watched a U-Haul truck rumble in off the highway and park at the edge of the pine grove just beyond the picnic tables—and that was how he met Denise Woolsey.

The driver got out, sat down at one of the tables and opened a brown bag that apparently contained her breakfast. A large woman in jeans, flat-heeled boots, soft leather jacket over a faded khaki shirt. Interested, Pan had slipped to the edge of the roof to look her over, had watched her feed a nervous squirrel a portion of her sandwich, watched her fill a paper cup of water for the little beast, and knew she'd be his next ride.

He rode with Denise as far as the San Francisco Bay Bridge, where she meant to head inland for Stockton. He tried not to think about getting out of the safe and cozy cab when she stopped for gas and to use the rest-room, he didn't relish going it alone on the mean and windy streets of the city. But he'd find his way. He always did. Somehow he was always able to sniff out an accommodating soul to carry him. In the world of concrete and fast cars he didn't have much choice, it was either con some softhearted human, use all his charm and panache, or perish.

14

Slipping into the conference room, Joe watched Juana and the chief escort their loud, pushy female visitor back to Max's office, both officers trying to hold their tempers. She was a big, square woman, solidly constructed, her skin tanned and coarsened from the sun as if she might be an avid golfer, her sun-streaked hair hanging limp to just below her jaw, her scowl lines deeply embedded. Where Debbie cultivated a helpless demeanor, her older sister, Esther, exuded an overriding bad temper, her dark brown eyes flat and cold, a woman Joe would prefer not to tangle with.

Following behind the chief, slipping inside his office and quickly beneath the credenza, he watched Esther settle heavily into the leather couch facing Max's desk. Juana sat tentatively on the arm of the leather chair to

Esther's right, easing her sore knee, her black uniform stark against the tan leather. Max stepped to the credenza, reached for the coffeepot that smelled of the usual overcooked brew, turned to Esther and offered her a cup.

"No," she said defiantly, with no touch of a graceful refusal. "Why did you call me here? Is this about my mother? What's she done now? I just got back in town, I haven't even unpacked. Whatever kind of trouble she's gotten into, I'm not responsible for her, and I don't appreciate your messages. My husband uses that answering machine for business."

"Your husband is with Kraft Realty?" Max asked, knowing perfectly well that Perry Fowler owned half the business. She nodded curtly. He said, "I was at your house twice, Mrs. Fowler. I left messages on the door, and then two e-mails asking you to come in."

"I'm here now. What do you want?"

"I asked you in here with bad news. To tell you that your mother died yesterday morning."

The woman's eyes widened, her mouth pursed tight, but Joe couldn't read her expression. Was it pain? Remorse? Some sort of distaste? "What did she die of?" she said. "Did she drink *that* much, to go into some kind of alcoholic seizure?"

"Why do you say that?"

"That's the first thing you think of, with a drunk. Or did her heart give out, from abuse?"

"There was a fire," Max said. "Her house burned, there was little left, just blackened timbers and ashes." Put off by the woman, was he goading her to see what she might reveal? For sure, he was taking a cop's keen pleasure in seeing her squirm. He didn't trust this woman, and the tomcat felt completely in tune with the chief's sentiments.

Esther sat pressing one hand to her mouth, her other hand fisted so tight her knuckles had whitened. Max said, more gently, "She was dead before the fire broke out."

This seemed to ease her, help her regain her composure. "Who have you notified?"

"Your sister, Debbie. She preferred that we notify you."

"If Mother died before the fire, how *did* she die?"

"She was poisoned."

"Poisoned? What did she get hold of? Or, what was she taking?" she said suspiciously. "Was she on some kind of pills?"

He didn't answer.

She was quiet for some time. "You're not saying she . . . that someone *gave* her poison? Oh, you must be mistaken. You're not saying she was murdered? Why would someone do that? Who would take the trouble? Not for money. She had nothing, whatever money she earned, she drank away."

"She could have drunk the poison by accident," Max said, "though it doesn't seem likely."

"I can't believe someone would do that. Are you saying they burned her house, too?"

"We're not sure yet whether it was arson."

"I can certainly imagine her setting the house on fire by accident, you know how they are when they drink. She was never careful, she'd leave the electric heater too close to the bed, leave something on the stove with the burner on high, dash over when she saw flames, smother them with a wet towel."

She didn't ask how Debbie was taking their mother's death, she didn't ask if Debbie was on her way down from Oregon. She showed little sign of pain or loss, no pity. Nor did she ask about Billy. Didn't she care that her sister's little boy might have died in the fire or been badly burned? Max glanced at Davis, whose stern face was ungiving, then turned back to Esther. "When did you last see your mother?"

Esther hesitated as if thinking back. "This last Christmas. She was in jail overnight for drunk driving. I had to come down here Christmas morning to bail her out, so you can understand why I dislike this place.

Check your records, you'll see. Seven o'clock Christmas morning, I have to bail my mother out of jail."

"She spent Christmas with you, then?"

"No. I dropped her off at her place. We were having people in. She . . . doesn't mix well with our friends. As it was, I had to leave all the preparations to the housekeeper."

No wonder that old woman drank, Joe thought, knowing she'd raised a daughter like that. Except, he thought, which came first? Did Hesmerra drink because of her two sour daughters? Or did Esther turn mean-spirited, and Debbie self-centered and manipulative, because of their mother's drinking? Who was the cause and who was the victim?

But now Hesmerra was the final victim, the prey of someone spiking her drinks, offering an embellishment she hadn't even tasted in her early morning toddy. Max said, "Before you saw her at Christmas, how long since you'd last seen her?"

Esther shrugged. "Maybe a year."

"What was the problem between you?"

"The drink," Esther said shortly. "And other things. Family matters, from the past."

"Such as?"

"Captain Harper, that is private business, that has nothing to do with her death. I still can't believe you think she was murdered."

"It's always possible she took her own life," Max said. She didn't answer to that. He said, "Are you not concerned about your nephew? You might like to know that he wasn't hurt in the fire."

She looked at him coldly. "I'm not taking the boy in, if that's what you're thinking. Is that why you summoned me here? I'll make this plain, Captain Harper. I want nothing to do with that boy, I'm perfectly content to see Child Welfare take him."

Max and Juana simply looked at the woman. He turned away only when the phone buzzed, the dispatcher ringing through though he knew Max was interviewing. Through the intercom, the young rookie's voice sounded tinny and uncertain. "Captain, you might want to take this one." The way he said "this one," Joe felt his heart quicken. Everyone in the department knew that certain, informative calls were to go directly to the chief. As Max picked up the phone, switching off the speaker, Joe bellied closer beneath the credenza. With his ears sharply forward, he could barely make out the higher tones of a female voice, though he couldn't tell what she was saying, couldn't even tell whether it was Dulcie or Kit. He watched Max hesitate, his gaze returning to Esther. "Hold on a minute." Then, to Esther, "Detective Davis will take you up to the front for fingerprinting. Thank you for coming in."

Esther rose, glaring at him. "I don't appreciate that you demand I come in, and then dismiss me just as rudely. I don't appreciate that you order me to submit to fingerprinting, like some common criminal."

Juana Davis put a hand on Esther's elbow, guiding her to the door. "Mrs. Fowler, this is standard procedure, we need the prints of all family members, to eliminate them from other prints we might lift at the scene."

Esther said, "If the house burned to the ground, how could you find any fingerprints at all?"

Max waited until Davis had removed the woman and had pulled the door closed behind them. Leaning back in his swivel chair, he flipped on the speaker—testimony, Joe thought, to the comfortable way the chief now related to these anonymous calls. Years ago, when Joe and Dulcie first began using the phone to pass on information, every call from the unnamed snitch had made the chief edgy, as nervous, himself, as his four-legged informants. But now a rapport had developed, a trust and ease as if between old friends that made the tomcat smile.

"Sorry," Max said into the phone, "someone was in my office."

Now, with the speaker on, Joe smiled at his tabby lady's voice, innocent but businesslike, a savvy young female quite in charge of the situation: "You wanted to talk with Emmylou Warren?" And now, with Esther Fowler gone and the door shut, Joe strolled out from beneath the credenza, yawned and stretched, looked idly at the desk, leaped, and curled up in Max's overflowing in-box, yawning in the chief's face.

"Yes, we'd like to talk with her," Max was saying. Joe closed his eyes and tucked his nose under as if concerned only with a soothing nap.

"She's up near where you raided that meth house," Dulcie said. "I'm watching her as we speak, she's going from door to door, asking about some lost cat. I think she's living in her car, an old green Chevy, full of blankets, household stuff, clothes. It's parked at the corner above Clyde and Ryan's place, she just . . . Gotta go!" she said with alarm. Joe could almost hear her hiss of fear. There was a click, and the phone went dead. Involuntarily, Joe's claws raked into a Department of Justice report. What had happened? Had she been caught using someone's phone? Had she slipped into someone's house, near where Emmylou was working the neighborhood, and the householder caught her? But Ryan and Clyde were there, why hadn't she used one of their phones? Or had she, and Debbie walked in on her? Or Vinnie? The very thought made him shiver. And, what was Emmylou doing, looking for a lost cat, when her own cats were safe with John Firetti?

Beside him, Max sat frowning, looking irritated and impatient, then he buzzed the dispatcher and sent a patrol car to pick up Emmylou. He looked up when Davis returned, and he filled her in. Davis said, "What's she doing in that neighborhood? Well, hell. Is that old woman part of the action up there?"

"Could she be looking for a place to rent?" Max said. "Half those houses are empty, maybe she thinks she can find a cheap room." Then, "Didn't one of the Kraft Realtors live just above that neighborhood? Alain Bent? Three or four blocks above the meth house, that white brick with the big front patio? Wasn't she Erik Kraft's sales partner, until she moved away?"

Davis nodded. "I understand she kept the house, waiting for the market to pick up."

Sprawled across the in-box, Joe lay trying to put it together. Alain Bent had lived just above the active foreclosure area, with its suspicious occupants and a busy meth operation. Alain's partner was the husband of Debbie Kraft, Hesmerra's middle daughter; the wives of both Kraft partners were her daughters. Hesmerra held cleaning jobs that gave her access to Alain Bent's house and to the Kraft offices. What the hell did all this add up to? No good telling himself this was a matter of coincidence; it wasn't. It was simply a tangle of knots neither he nor the department had yet sorted out. He was burning to race out and find Dulcie, find out what else she'd seen, make sure she was all right after that aborted phone call. But he didn't want to miss anything. Max said, "Why exactly did Alain leave town? She had a successful following, I heard she did very well."

"Left about six months ago. The story I got, a client complained to the real estate board that she was trading down. I'm not sure this is illegal, but it's right next door. She takes a buyer and seller into escrow, buyer deposits a check for the down payment, at the agreed price. Then, while the sellers are distracted packing up their moving boxes, she brings in a second appraiser, tells the sellers this is common practice. When the house is appraised for less, she tells them they'll have to lower the price—and they're already in escrow, or supposed to be.

"The way I heard it, she pulled this on old people who might be a little confused, often naïve about real estate transactions, old couples anxious to sell out and get moved into assisted living quarters, people with no adult children to look out for their interests. An old couple, maybe one of them sick, both of them worn out sorting through their household goods and packing up. Sometimes it doesn't take much to get them to agree to the lower price, anything to close the sale—and all the time, they're supposed to be already in escrow.

"Of course the loan officer's in on the scam. If the sellers get edgy and make a fuss, loan officer claims the check for the down payment was never actually deposited into escrow, that it's still waiting in the file for the final price resolution." Davis smiled. "What happened this time, the sellers weren't having any, they went to the real estate board." Her square face, so often too solemn, lit with pleasure. "Everything hit the fan. Loan officer and mortgage officer were fired. Mortgage company made good to the seller. I'm guessing either Kraft Realty sent her packing, or she left before they could fire her."

The two officers were silent, their satisfied looks matching closely the tomcat's own hidden smile as the three enjoyed a rare moment of justice.

Max said, "Alain Bent and Erik Kraft were partners, they worked most of their sales together. Makes you wonder if he was in on the scam."

Davis nodded. "Apparently Fowler wants nothing more to do with Alain. Their latest ads, he's removed her picture. As to Esther Fowler—what *will* happen to Billy? I'm sure he wouldn't choose to live with her, even if she did want him."

Max shook his head. "For all intents and purposes, the kid's an orphan. I don't want to bring in Children's

Services. Right now, he's staying up at our place. He has a permit to work part of the school day; I talked with the principal this morning, and that's all in order. I didn't say much, just that he was doing some work for me, didn't mention where he's living and, interestingly, he didn't ask."

Joe hoped Max could keep it that way. Maybe, one way or another, Erik Kraft had used some pull to stifle questions about Billy. When Davis left, the tomcat slipped up the hall and out through the glass door, on the heels of an unhappy young woman who had just paid a stout traffic ticket. Scrambling up the oak tree, he headed fast for the hills and the neighborhood where Dulcie's phone call had so abruptly ended. It was always touchy to break into a house and use a stranger's phone and not be overheard, to get out again fast, before you were discovered.

Even the matter of using their own phones, at home, was stressful. Clyde's and Ryan's, and Wilma's phones all had caller ID blocking, but you never knew when it would fail. After the Damens' phones had done that twice, Clyde did a daily check on the house phones, to be safe. Wilma had researched the possibility of falsifying their numbers, but such a call had to be made through a computer, and that was more than a cat in a hurry could deal with.

No, there had to be a better way. He hadn't really addressed the problem fully, but one idea had promise— he should have checked it out when he had the chance, before he woke to see flames licking at the sky, before all hell broke loose. Annoyed at himself for his procrastination, he headed fast up the hills. Leaping from oak limb to roof and across the chasms of narrow alleys, he could only pray his lady hadn't, while making that call, stepped with all four paws into a tangle of trouble.

15

The rough wood siding of Ryan and Clyde's remodel badly needed paint, the roof looked frail even for a cat to walk on, the yard resembled an untended vacant lot given over to stray dogs. The neighborhood, even at midday, seemed dark, the clouds low, the giant cypress trees, originally planted far apart as spindly saplings, now spread their reaching arms over the frail cottages as if to bury them. The Damens had bought their gray board-and-batten shack just after Christmas but so far had done no work at all as Ryan finished up Hanni's remodel, and a new house, pushing their own investment aside. The one-bedroom dwelling was as grim inside as out; Debbie Kraft would have to make do with a good cleaning, provided she was willing. Having pushed into their lives uninvited, demanding bed and board, how could she refuse to work for her shelter?

How, indeed? Ryan thought as she pulled the king cab onto the cracked drive, waving Debbie in to park beside her. It was over an hour since they'd left home in their two-vehicle parade, she and Clyde trying not to lose their tempers as they detoured for Debbie to buy groceries, again when she insisted they swing by the school Vinnie would be attending, and the nearest day care for Tessa. "So I'll know where these things are," Debbie said. "Life will be hard enough if I have to get a job, with two children to take care of." She didn't ask if Ryan and Clyde had time for side trips, or if this particular day care was safe and caring; her concern was that it was convenient, as close as possible to the cottage. "If I have to go to work, I can't be running all over dragging kids, I won't have the time for that." Even Rock looked disgusted, he'd had enough of Debbie's brassy voice. Ryan had to grin when she thought what Joe would have said. She didn't know where he'd gone, but he'd disappeared in a flash the minute they started loading the car.

Now, the minute Debbie parked, Vinnie piled out, stood scowling at the frame shack, the front door peeling long strips of gray paint, the rusty window screens deeply dented, two of them torn, and a long crack across the corner of the front window.

"I'm not staying here," Vinnie said. Turning, she stared between the trees, up the hill to where the woods ended, where the houses were larger and well kept, the gardens trimmed and bright with sun, and her gaze fixed on the rambling white brick house with its deep front patio. "I want to stay up *there*, I want to go back *there*, that's—"

"Go unload the car," Debbie snapped, grabbing her arm.

"Why can't we—"

"Unload the car. Now."

Ryan and Clyde, glancing at each other, watched the two with interest. Why would the child fix on a strange house, what did she mean, "go back there"? What was that about?

Earlier, stopping at the little village grocery, they had taken the two little girls into the king cab while Debbie went in to do her shopping. Watching the kids gave them an excuse not to accompany her, not to be present at the checkout to watch her fumble over her purse, making excuses that she was short of cash. In the pickup, Vinnie had sat in the front seat between them, sulking, while Tessa crawled into the backseat and snuggled up with Rock. It wasn't long until Vinnie crawled in back, too, crowding her sister. Taking off her shoe, she began to poke it at Rock, jamming the toe into his silky hide so that Rock was forced to either snap at her or scramble away to the far corner. He scrambled, lunging away as Ryan reached over and snatched the shoe.

"You do that again, Vinnie, you'll get this shoe, hard, across your backside."

Vinnie had stared at her defiantly, while four-year-old Tessa moved closer to Rock, smoothing her hand gently down his sleek shoulder. The Weimaraner nosed at her with infinite patience, though her small hand must surely have tickled. As Tessa stroked his satiny warmth, a little smile bloomed on the child's face. Only when Vinnie began talking about Hesmerra's death did Tessa's face crumple. "Our grandmother burned to death," Vinnie said, standing up on the seat watching with satisfaction as Tessa's tears welled up.

"Your gran did not burn to death," Ryan said. "Your grandmother was already in heaven when the fire started. The fire didn't hurt her at all."

"There's no such thing as heaven. How do you know she was dead?"

"I read the coroner's report. The doctor who did the death investigation."

Vinnie smiled wickedly. "That's where they cut your body open, take out all your insides, and cut them up in little pieces."

Tessa went white. Clyde looked like he could happily take the coroner's knife to Vinnie. *What can you expect?* Ryan thought. *Look how Debbie was about Hesmerra's death, hard as nails. Her own mother.* She reached back and took Tessa's hand. "Your grandmother is in heaven. When she died, she left her body behind. She flew right out of that body, she doesn't need it anymore, she's an angel now, and she can fly free." This might be unorthodox, might seem trite to an adult, but it was what four-year-old Tessa needed to hear—and it was infinitely effective. Tessa clutched Ryan's hand, looking up at her, her brown eyes trusting, wanting very much to believe her.

"Do you know how a caterpillar makes its little nest?" Ryan said.

The child nodded. "A cocoon. They showed us in Sunshine School."

"That's right, it wraps itself all in silk and goes to sleep. And do you know what happens when it wakes up?"

Tessa wiped at her tears.

"When it crawls out of its silk nest, it's no longer a caterpillar. It has turned into a beautiful butterfly, as beautiful as a princess. It spreads its wings and flies away on the soft wind." Ryan stroked Tessa's hair. "For a person to be dead is just the same. When your gran died, she slept for a little while all warm and safe just like the butterfly. She woke up in a most beautiful place, and she had turned into a lovely young woman, even more beautiful than when she was young, in this world." Ryan didn't dare look at Clyde; she could feel him raise an eyebrow. She only knew that she believed what she said, she believed something like that happened—and that right now, Tessa needed to believe it, she needed not to dwell on her sister's ugly interpretation.

"Mama doesn't want a funeral," Vinnie told them. "She said—"

"That's enough, Vinnie."

"If there's a funeral she has to see Aunt Esther. Mama says no one can choose what kind of sister or relatives they get."

Ryan sighed. "I'm sure that's true. If Tessa could choose her sister, she'd surely choose a kinder and more caring child than you."

Vinnie glared, and turned away scowling, fiddling with the button on her sweater. She looked up again only when Debbie passed by the pickup wheeling a grocery cart full of bulging paper bags, heading for her car. Clyde put his hand on the door meaning to get out and help her, but Ryan stopped him with a scowl. She didn't enjoy being cruel, but if you gave Debbie an inch, she was all over you. They watched her cram the bags into her car, into the spaces the children had left when they changed cars. The meal choices Ryan could see sticking up looked to be all boxes of crackers, cookies, and quick-fix meals full of unpronounceable chemicals. No sign of fresh fruits or vegetables, the items that would ordinarily be on top. When the car was loaded, Ryan headed for the day-care center where Debbie meant to park Tessa while Vinnie was in school. Their two vehicles paused before the one-story redwood complex only long enough for Debbie to take a look, then they led her on up the hill eight blocks to the rambling elementary with its dark-shingled roofs. Location, close proximity to where she'd be living, was apparently far more important to Debbie than the safety and quality of either establishment. Ryan had pointed out where the school bus stopped, and then headed on up to the cottage.

Two centuries earlier, this hill had been open grazing land, part of the vast open ranges inhabited by longhorn cattle, and by deer, cougar, and grizzly bear. When civilization overtook the wild, when the land was broken up and cross-fenced into smaller ranches, and then later into farms, this hill had become pasture for dairy cows. In the nineteen thirties, several small adjoining hillside farms were bought up by a retired

civil engineer who thought to construct a community of vacation cottages and rent them out. He built
the little houses solidly enough, but without any discernible imagination. As he grew older he had sold
off many of the cottages as second homes or income
rentals. Some of the buyers added porches, second-
floor bedrooms, walled patios. In subsequent years the
houses were turned over again and again as the market
inflated. Everyone made a profit as real estate prices
soared. Then suddenly, under changed federal laws,
mortgages were easier to obtain: One hardly needed a
down payment or any collateral at all. A buying frenzy
began among families with little or no savings. Soon
the new owners were maxing out their credit cards on
new cars, a motorcycle, an RV or fast boat, trusting the
government to bail them out when they let their mortgage payments slide. There was always tomorrow, they
and the government were in this together, Uncle Sam
would help them out. Thus was the beginning of the
financial landslide, repeated a million times over com-
bined with more complicated economic manipulations,
at government level, until the bottom fell out, the stock
market dropped, businesses began to close, folks lost
their investments and lost their jobs.

When the default on home loans mounted, homes
were repossessed and the occupants left the area. Folks

who had kept cash and real assets at hand began to buy up abandoned, repossessed homes. Ryan and Clyde bought three cottages with cash from the sales of the antique cars Clyde had so lovingly restored. They meant to improve their purchases, wait for the market to pick up again, make a good profit, and leave something nice in the place of neglected and empty dwellings.

Erik Kraft was one of the first and heaviest buyers, making purchases all over the village. Though he had made no discernible improvements in the shabbier places, he had already turned over nearly half of them at a profit. He'd give a place a rough mowing and trimming and, in the worst cases, a coat of cheap paint. Ironic, Ryan thought, that Erik's estranged wife would be living—practically in poverty, as she put it—in the very area where Erik must already have made a couple of million dollars' worth of clear profit.

But the saddest victims of the downturn, Ryan thought, were the abandoned pets left behind like broken toys for trash pickup, innocent animals who had become victims of a vast financial war. So far Cat-Friends, her volunteer group, had taken in nine dogs and trapped twenty-three abandoned cats, settling them all in volunteer foster homes until new and permanent homes could be found. Ryan wasn't sure how many creatures the local Animal Friends group had saved, as well, but the two organizations tried to help each other. Yet even with the work of over two dozen volunteers, the police continued to field complaints about stray cats.

Calls came in not only about abandoned animals around the empty homes, but about the cottages themselves. Often, lights came on late at night in empty, unoccupied houses, then soon went dark again. Rented houses had half a dozen decrepit cars parked in the drive and on the street, and many had trash piled up in the yards. And then, of course, there was the meth house, bulging black trash bags stacked in the side yard, to be hauled away in the small hours. That was why the department had been alerted, the black plastic bags smelling strongly of chemicals. Strangest of all, perhaps, was a FOR SALE sign going up in the weedy yard of a decrepit cottage, soon to come down again as if the house had been sold, but then to be replaced a week later. Another FOR SALE sign. Another apparent sale, then soon another sign, in a seemingly endless two-step.

Ryan's sister, Hanni, had bought one of the cottages early on, before the blight was apparent, and had at once set about restoring it, contracting with Ryan to do the heavy professional work; Hanni was an interior designer, not a builder. When events in the neighborhood began to make her nervous, still she moved ahead. Now, the renovation was almost finished, waiting for the interior hardware and window shutters, while Ryan and Clyde hadn't yet begun on their own remodel. At least now their shabby investment would have an occupant. When Ryan pushed the front door open the cold, damp wind caught it, slamming it against the wall. She stepped aside so Debbie could enter, directly into the living room.

Standing in the open doorway, you could see right on into the bedroom and the tiny bath beyond, and with a full view of the kitchen to the left. There was no furniture, only a very old refrigerator in the corner of the little kitchen and an ancient gas cook stove that Ryan had been assured by her plumber wouldn't blow up or asphyxiate anyone. If the house had any virtue it was the high, raftered ceiling and strong beams, the surprisingly solid construction. This was its one redeeming feature—plus the location and price, she thought, hearing again Joe Grey's caustic remarks about their obsessive bargain hunting.

As Clyde joined her on the tiny porch, putting his arm around her, Vinnie crowded in past them, scuffing her shoes across the dusty gray linoleum that floored all the rooms. She peered with disgust into the small, dim bedroom and ancient kitchen. "I'm not staying here, we can't live *here*." Moving to the grimy window, she stood looking up the hill. "There's real beds up there, we—"

"We have our sleeping bags," Debbie snapped. "Bring in your toys and shoes."

"But I don't—"

"Now!" Debbie said, her glare silencing the child. Clyde had started to speak when, above them, a hard thump hit the roof. They all four stepped back, as if the ceiling might give way. Next minute, a scrambling of claws shook the cypress tree beside the house, and Joe Grey leaped down to the hood of the king cab. While Debbie's attention was diverted, Vinnie raced out across the yard and was gone, running up the street, her long blond hair whipped by the cold wind, her fists clenched. Behind her Tessa appeared from nowhere, racing after her. Debbie ran after them, yelling as if they were runaway dogs escaped from their leashes. Ryan pressed her face against Clyde's shoulder, trying hard not to laugh.

Vinnie made it almost to the white brick house, Tessa trying in vain to keep up. Passing Tessa, Debbie grabbed Vinnie by the arm, jerked her around, shouting. Clyde turned away, disgusted, and went to unload Debbie's car. Ryan looked at Joe, on the hood of the king cab. "What's Vinnie after, up there? Can she have been in that place? In Alain Bent's house? How could she have been?"

"Maybe she looked in the windows," Joe said. "Saw furniture and beds." He turned to look at Ryan. "Or *has* the kid been inside?"

"They only arrived last night." Ryan's green eyes looked into his. "She's been with us all morning."

Joe stretched out on the pickup's warm hood, wondering, his back pummeled by the cold wind, which smelled of rain. Together they watched the family saga as Debbie dragged Vinnie home, scolding all the way. Ryan scratched Joe behind his ears then picked him up, draped him over her shoulder in a manner few people were allowed, listening to his purr as they watched Debbie haul Vinnie into the house, and Tessa slip in behind. Debbie's angry scolding seemed overkill— what was she so mad about?

16

In the dumpy little kitchen, Debbie had torn open the wrapper of a loaf of bread and was hastily putting together sandwiches for the children, maybe hoping to keep Vinnie from whining any more about the white brick house. The kitchen counter was crowded with grocery bags that were still not unpacked except for the bread and peanut butter. Joe watched from Ryan's shoulder as Vinnie grabbed the open jar, stuck her fingers in, retrieving a big glob, and licked them clean, her small face pinched with anger.

Though Joe had come up looking for Dulcie, hoping she'd escaped whatever tight squeak she'd gotten herself into with that aborted phone call, he'd found no sign of her. No scent of her, nothing. Coming up the hill, he'd passed two cops he knew, dressed in blue coveralls with the water department insignia on the pockets and sleeves. They were kneeling together at the curb beneath a spreading cypress tree, pretending to examine a water meter, their position giving them a straight-away view beneath the branches to the meth house. Did Harper expect other members of that ragtag gang to return to their little home business? He had passed Ryan's sister Hanni, too, pulling her blue Chrysler van up to the one-car garage of her own remodel. Ryan was nearly finished with the exterior, had covered the gray board siding with white stucco and added a new tile roof as deep blue as an autumn sky.

Now as Ryan headed outdoors from her own cottage, away from the crowded kitchen and away from Debbie, Joe looked from her shoulder up the hill, scanning the rooftops for Dulcie. He looked past the rambling white house, but then quickly back as two dark streaks flashed across the roof into the shadow of the pines that sheltered the double garage; the sight of Dulcie, safe, made him inadvertently dig his claws into Ryan's shoulder.

"Hey!" she said, pulling his claws free.

"Sorry." He patted her cheek with a soft paw. "Gotta go, explain later," and with a leap into the overhanging cypress tree, he left her, heading up the hill from roof to rising roof, looking for his lady.

There, they appeared again, two dark shapes barely visible atop the garage, two pairs of sharp ears silhouetted against the low clouds. Racing to join them, he greeted Dulcie with nose pushes and purrs. "What happened to you? You were caught with someone's phone? I was in Harper's office when you clicked off."

"Emmylou saw me."

"Oh my God. She heard you using the phone? She—"

"She didn't *hear* me," Dulcie interrupted, "she saw me through the glass. When I saw her looking in, I pretended to be batting at a moth. She was outside, and I was talking softly, she couldn't have *heard* me."

"I hope to hell not," he said crossly.

"We saw her on the street, going door to door asking about two lost cats. She came up into the patio, sat down on that low wall beside the camellias. Took a sandwich out of her pocket, unwrapped it, one of those dry-looking sandwiches in yellow paper. I was inside the house, it was a perfect time to phone, without losing her."

"How did you get in?"

Dulcie smiled. "A basement window, all locked but the last one." She lashed her tail smugly. "Broken, rusty lock, and when we pushed the window it swung right in. Come on, I'll show you."

But Joe paused, watching Kit. All this time, she hadn't said a word, she sat apart from them, staring off into space. Watching her, Joe twitched an ear at Dulcie. "What?" he said softly.

"We were with Misto," Dulcie said. "Her head's full of stories, that's all. He talked about Pan, too. He misses Pan, and he's worried because of the nursing home fire. Kit's worried for them both."

Joe shifted uneasily, wishing Kit had never told Misto about Pan, that she had never upset the old cat. The tortoiseshell was so damned impulsive, as unpredictable as the leaps of a grasshopper. Well, what was done, was done. He said, "What about Emmylou? What did she do when she saw you?"

"She looked puzzled to see a cat in there, and when she finished her lunch she walked all around the house, looking to see how I got in. I watched from above, from the windows." Dulcie smiled. "I'd kicked the window closed when I jumped, she didn't have a clue, she went right on by. The next thing I know she's at the front door and it sounded like she had a key, trying to get inside."

"But she—" Kit began, suddenly paying attention.

"That's when Kit appeared," Dulcie said.

"I watched her from the roof and the key wouldn't turn," she said. "She tried and tried and seemed really sure it was the right key, so maybe Alain Bent changed the locks when she moved and Emmylou didn't know and—"

"Where did she get a key?" Joe said. "From Hesmerra? Did Hesmerra have it copied when she was with the cleaning crew? Maybe on her lunch hour, then turned the keys in as usual at the end of the day?"

"Why not?" Dulcie said. "Maybe Emmylou found the key in the burn, maybe knew where she kept it?"

"So, *why* did she?" Joe wondered. "What did she do when she couldn't get in?"

"She sat down on the patio wall," Dulcie said, "sat there looking at the house as if deciding what to do next."

"But then Ryan's pickup came up the hill," Kit said, "and Debbie's car behind it, and when Emmylou saw them she slipped away through the backyard and that's the last we saw of her, she vanished like when a rabbit smells a coyote, and there's something else, too. Debbie's been inside, you can smell her and the little kids all around the door on the threshold and then inside the house."

Joe said, "I'm guessing they stayed there, maybe one night, maybe more, before they ever showed up at our place." He told them about Vinnie saying there were beds to sleep in, up there in that house, and then racing away up the hill.

"What's Debbie up to?" Dulcie said, looking down the hill to where Debbie was hauling in a last load from her car. "What would she want in Alain Bent's house? How did . . . ?" She looked at Joe. "It has to do with Erik. He and Alain were partners—or were they more than partners?"

Joe smiled. "If they were, maybe Erik had a key. Say Debbie found out they were lovers," he said, "found a key she suspected was Alain's . . . How tempting to copy it and then do a bit of snooping, get the goods on him."

"But why?" Dulcie said. "She wouldn't need to know he was sleeping around, to get a divorce in California."

"Maybe for child custody," Joe said. "Except," he said, "who'd fight to keep Vinnie? Maybe some other reason. Looks like Alain was into some real estate scams or maybe, who knows, Erik and Alain together. Debbie wants to know more, to make some mischief for them. She decides to get into Alain's desk, into her personal papers. Who knows what she'd find, what trouble she could make? She could have come down here from Eugene any time she chose. Catch a commuter flight, round trip just for a day while the kids were in school and nursery school? But as it worked out, she drove down, left Eugene for good."

"With Alain's key in her pocket," Dulcie said. "Alain *is* beautiful, so slim, and her dark sleek hair done up in that fancy chignon, and her elegant suits. You've seen her pictures, of course Debbie would be jealous."

"Beautiful," Joe said, "and as cold as a mannequin in Saks's window." He looked down into the wide front patio with its angles and nooks and lush plantings, its different level walls and neatly tended flower beds. "Alain might have been fired and moved away, Perry Fowler might not be in touch with her any longer, but she isn't neglecting her property. Maybe she does have it listed, with another firm, and they're seeing that someone's watering."

"And pruning," Dulcie said. There wasn't a dead bloom or fallen leaf anywhere, and they could see fresh cuts where the red geraniums had been clipped back. "Or could Emmylou be taking care of the yard? When Alain moved away, could she have hired her? Was that why she was here? Maybe . . . maybe when she was pruning she found a key hidden under a flowerpot, the way people do? Found it just today, and thought she had a way in? She *is* homeless, she *does* need a place to stay. She finds the key and thinks she's found a place to crash. Only, Alain has changed the locks."

"Maybe," Joe said. But something about the scenario was off. As little as he'd observed of Emmylou, he wasn't sure she'd be bold enough to move into someone's house, when workmen might be scheduled to come in, or maybe other Realtors, to have a look, if the house *was* going on the market. The garage roof was in shadow now, around them, the clouds low and heavy above them. Moving closer together with their backs to the chill wind, the three cats tried to sort out what they knew about Alain Bent: She was Erik Kraft's sales partner, and maybe his lover. She'd not only been fired, but moved away, maybe before her other scams caught up with her. How much *did* Debbie know about Alain? What had she been after, when she broke in?

"And what's Emmylou Warren's connection?" Dulcie said. "Will that lead back to Hesmerra and maybe to Hesmerra's murder?"

Joe looked down into the patio of the silent, locked house. He rose, nudged Dulcie, and the three cats skinned down a bougainvillea trellis to the warm paving and headed for the basement window.

Pushing the little window open, they peered down into the dark cellar. Its cold breath chilled their noses; it smelled of damp cement, sour earth, and mouse droppings. "How deep?" Joe said, frowning down into the blackness. "Looks like about seven feet. How did you get out? The boxes?"

"Yes," Dulcie said. "I pushed that stack of boxes over," she said, glancing down at the dark cartons piled against the wall directly beneath them. "I could just see them there in the corner where more daylight comes in; my shoulder's still sore from shoving them. The labels say 'dishes' but who knows what's packed in them. They smell sour, like old clothes." Slipping in through the window, she dropped down onto the stack, and to the floor. Kit followed, and then Joe, each one careful not to tip over their means of escape.

The cellar was L-shaped, following the lines of the house above. The dark corners and the spaces behind the furnace and water heater were thick with cobwebs, and garlands of cobwebs hung down from the floor joists. Three folded aluminum chairs leaned against one wall, their plastic seats frayed, and gray with mildew. There was no scent of Debbie or the little girls down here, and they padded up the dusty wooden stairs. Leaping at the knob, Dulcie curved her paws around it, swinging and kicking until the door flew open.

The house was dim, the rooms lit coldly as the coming storm gathered. They had come up into the front entry, the basement door at right angles to the more impressive front door with its deep carvings, and that did indeed smell of Debbie and the children.

A smear of chocolate candy had been smashed into the grout between the floor tiles.

Across the tile entry, six steps led down to a sunken living room, which was only half furnished. The clay tile floor was bare, but Dulcie could imagine richly colored throw rugs. There was a creamy leather couch but no end tables or coffee table or lamps. White walls, vast windows looking out on the lowering gray sky and the trees and roofs below, white ceiling crossed by burnished oak rafters. The house was silent, no hush of footsteps, no thump or rustle of someone hurrying their way, summoned by the sound of the cellar door. Already, Kit had left them, racing down into the sunken room to look at the fireplace wall.

The entire wall was painted in an intricate mural, a floor-to-ceiling scene in rich colors, though Joe and Dulcie couldn't see the subject clearly from the angle where they stood, up on the dining balcony. Moving out from beneath the carved table and chairs, Dulcie leaned out through the rail, to look.

"Medieval," she said softly. "Oh, my. It's beautiful." Below her, Kit sat in the center of the room looking up at the mural, her fluffy tail wrapped around her, twitching with excitement, her front paws kneading at the tiles in nervous concentration as she absorbed each detail of the ancient scene. From the look on her face,

Dulcie knew the tortoiseshell was already transported back into time, how many centuries ago?

"It's a beautiful home," Dulcie said. "Even if Alain was fired, it's strange she'd leave this, and leave the village, when Molena Point's doing better than much of the country. Couldn't she get a job somewhere else, another real estate firm? You've seen the ads. The high-end houses are still selling, some of the really wealthy people are doing just fine. Where else could a Realtor make better money?"

Joe said, "Word gets around. If she was pulling scams on her buyers, who else would hire her?" Out through the wide living room windows, they could see down the hill to the roof of Ryan and Clyde's cottage, Ryan's truck still parked at the curb. Two blocks over was Hanni's deep blue roof, her own van parked halfway into the garage, and two blocks to the right of Hanni's, forming a rough triangle, the meth house stood forlorn with its curled shingles and overgrown yard. A neighborhood in transition, people forced to move away, uneasy events among the homes they left behind, dramas that could well fit together like the pieces of a jigsaw. Was a pattern taking shape here that would lead directly back to Hesmerra and to the fire, and to the poison that killed her?

Below them, Kit sat with her back to the view, her attention centuries away on a narrow, cobbled street between houses built of wattle and thatched roofs, a medieval street that must speak deeply to the tortoise-shell's romantic dreams. To Joe, dreams of the past were pointless, ancient history was, after all, forever gone and useless, and uncomfortably he turned away. Silently Dulcie followed him, amused and annoyed by her practical and hardheaded tomcat.

The house wasn't large. A hall led back to a bedroom and bath on the right, and to a master bedroom straight ahead that took up the whole back of the house. The bed in the smaller room smelled of the two little girls and of chocolate candy, but it was neatly made. Padding into the master suite, they looked out through the glass doors to a back patio, its tile paving matching the interior floors. An empty swimming pool just outside the glass was covered with heavy, transparent plastic that sagged beneath a pile of pine needles and oak leaves from the woods beyond the white brick wall. Against the wall itself stood oversized pots of tall, drought-resistant grasses in shades of bronze and gold.

In the bedroom, the only furniture remaining was a king-sized bed that smelled of Debbie, and a large office desk along one wall, with a swivel typing chair. The closet was all but empty, a few limp jackets hanging at one end, a lone hanger fallen to the floor. A large suitcase lay on the floor, too, and was heavy when they pushed at it; and when Dulcie leaped up to the closet shelf, its dusty surface showed the marks where two smaller bags had been removed. She glanced down at Alain's expensive leather suitcase. "Why did she leave that?" The shelf smelled of Debbie, too, and she could see where Debbie had smeared the dust, probably reaching above her head, searching, for what? She dropped down again to sniff at the leather bag. It was secured with a little padlock; maybe they'd find the key, maybe not. The whole room smelled of Debbie, as did every drawer in the master bath, as if she'd gone through the entire house.

While Dulcie went to inspect the kitchen, Joe had a go at the desk. This was not a desk someone would pay to have moved, just an ordinary office-supply model made of fake oak laminate. The dusty cubbyhole that yawned in the left-hand pedestal was pocked with small black marks where a computer had stood. A thick, old-style monitor had been left behind. The blotter was still in place, dog-eared and incised with various notations, phone numbers, little floor plan sketches, used perhaps to clarify Alain's memory of some particular house as she talked with a client. Beside it, a rectangle with less dust showed where something the size of a briefcase, or laptop, had lain. There was no dust on the drawer handles, and Debbie's scent was strong. The desk's file drawer was marred and dented with fresh scratches, as if someone had jimmied the lock. When Joe fought the drawer out, pulling with stubborn claws, he could see that the lock's little metal arm was broken off.

Rearing up, he pawed through the hanging folders. Most were empty, folders labeled for house insurance, car insurance, medical records. Alain had left behind files of notes about old sales, but nothing more recent than four years. If there'd been anything of interest to others, had Debbie made off with it? Climbing into the dark drawer, he pawed under the files. He felt the broken metal bar, cold against his paw. Lying beside it was a small cardboard folder. He clawed it out, was backing out with it in his teeth when Dulcie returned from prowling the kitchen and leaped up beside him. Dropping the folder on the desk, he flipped it open.

It was one of those studio photographer's folders with a picture inserted inside, into the cardboard frame. The photo was of a couple, maybe in their sixties, a small, thin man, and a big square woman, both with sour looks on their faces. A younger version of the hefty woman stood in front of them. A daughter, perhaps? Didn't any of them know how to smile? Both women were frumpy, looked as if their clothes had come from a markdown rack, perhaps from the middle of the last century. The women had mousy brown hair, square faces, and pasty white skin, and were surely mother and daughter. The man, by contrast, was a neat little fellow dressed in a three-piece suit, white shirt and subdued tie, his thin cheeks clean shaven, narrowing down to a precisely trimmed goatee. There was not any notation to indicate their identity.

"Flip it out of the frame," Dulcie said. "Maybe there's something on the back. Here." Hissing with impatience, she pawed the picture out.

But there was nothing, only Debbie's smell, though she hadn't been interested enough to take the picture with her. Dulcie slid it back into the cardboard frame, and pushed that into the drawer. "They stayed here more than one night. Leftover pizza in the refrigerator, half a hamburger, a carton with some vile-looking spaghetti. A little carton of milk that's just going sour. Wrappers and takeout cartons in the trash, too." She frowned, her ears at half-mast. "What was Debbie looking for? If this is about custody of the children, about proving Erik's having an affair, why bother? If he wanted the kids, why would he leave them in the first place, why not take them with him?"

"Why would either of them want Vinnie?"

"Debbie would, they're exactly alike, Vinnie's one of her own. Maybe she's afraid when Erik gets back from his vacation, finds out she's here in the village, he'll claim custody, jinx Debbie's claim for support payments. No kids, no child support. Maybe that's all this comes down to, Debbie's grab for support money."

But Joe didn't think so. "Say Erik *is* into some kind of scam, Erik and Alain together. Debbie would look for proof and, who knows, maybe Hesmerra was after the same thing, when she cleaned for Alain."

Dulcie licked her paw. "If Alain is doing more than trading down, she gets out when that's discovered, wants to cover her tracks before she's charged with real estate fraud? She skips, leaves Erik holding the bag?"

"Maybe." Joe smoothed his whiskers with a quick paw. "Maybe Hesmerra was spying for Debbie, maybe they weren't as estranged as Debbie let on. That would explain the Kraft business papers in the metal box Emmylou lifted. Erik finds out the old woman is snooping, and he silences her. Say he killed her, looked for whatever papers she'd taken, but didn't find anything? So he sets the house on fire, to destroy the evidence."

In the dining loft, when they looked down through the wrought-iron railing, Kit was still engrossed, rearing up on her hind paws before the mural studying every smallest detail, her dark nose twitching as if she could actually smell the cobbled streets, the wandering sheep and chickens, the homely scents of suppers cooking in the stone and wattle cottages; they watched her dreaming away until suddenly she looked up and saw them, looked embarrassed, dropped down and turned her back as if she had no interest at all in that lost world.

They left Alain Bent's house through the cellar window. Leaping up one at a time from the cardboard cartons to the sill, swinging and kicking, they fled up and over, and down into the garden beneath a holly bush bright with red berries. Crouching beneath their stickery shelter, they looked down at the neighborhood laid out below them. At the Damen cottage, the front door was open and they could see Ryan and Clyde kneeling just inside on the living room floor.

"They're praying?" Dulcie said, twitching a whisker.

"Praying it'll hold together," Joe said, "that it won't collapse when they drive the first nail." Rock stood on the little porch outside the open door, his long leash looped around one of the stanchions. He was looking up the hill, his ears erect, watching them or maybe listening, where they hid among the holly shadows. Weimaraners were sight as well as scent hounds, they could spot a bird in the sky when it was less than a speck, when even Joe and Dulcie could see nothing.

Ryan and Clyde seemed to be examining the linoleum, they had one corner up and were peering at the floor beneath. Joe said, "Maybe they plan to rip it out. Who wants linoleum in a living room?" The minute he spoke, as far away as they were, Rock's tail began to wag madly, he jumped off the porch, tightening his leash and whining. Amused, they went still; they didn't speak again, they let him settle down so he wouldn't break his leash and come charging up the hill.

Two blocks over, at Hanni's remodel, someone was at work clearing out a flower bed, turning the earth as if preparing it for the bright cold weather cyclamens that stood in flats along the drive. "Billy Young," Joe said. "Maybe Hanni hired him for the day." They didn't see his bike, Hanni must have picked him up at the ranch. Billy looked up as Detective Juana Davis's Toyota came down the street and parked in front of the cottage. A black-and-white was right behind her, and the department's SUV pulled up behind it. "What's this?" Joe said softly. "What's happened?"

Leaving their prickly shelter, they headed down through the tangled yards. Below them, young Officer Jimmie McFarland stepped out of the van, his brown hair falling in a boyish cowlick over his forehead. He and Davis stood talking with Hanni, then moved into the garage. The two officers in the black-and-white stayed where they were. Not until the cats were halfway across the yard could they see inside the garage clear to the back, where Juana Davis had set her black satchel on the workbench and was removing a camera. Slipping closer, they settled down among the yard's overgrown geraniums to see what they had missed.

17

The U-Haul was headed slowly through the jammed-up traffic of downtown San Francisco when Pan reared up against the passenger window and began to yowl and paw against the glass.

"What?" Denise said, scowling over at him. "You can't get out here, in the middle of the city. You out of your mind? You have to go? I knew I should have fixed up a sandbox. You'll have to hold it, tomcat. There, there's a Chevron station up ahead, bound to be some dirt, a patch of garden or lawn."

Pan hissed at her, turned back and continued to paw the window, peering out at the busy city.

Denise saw nothing out there that a cat should get excited about. A white passenger bus traveling alongside them in the slow lane, the driver signaling that he wanted to get over, maybe wanted to make a left. Slowing, she let him in. The bus was full of older women, frizzed hair, long faces and round faces, all as wrinkled as old apples. All of them seemed to be talking at once, gabbing away having a good old time. Some kind of senior outing, she guessed, maybe a group from some retirement home. The script on the bus's white side said *MOLENA POINT FOUNDATION,* whatever that was. The driver gave her a wave as he cut over and made a left, into the Chevron station. She pulled in behind him. The minute she did, the tomcat settled right down, for all the world as if he knew she'd pulled in so he could take a leak.

Smartest cat she'd ever seen; she was already thinking of him as her cat. She'd picked up an unusually handsome and intelligent stray, and she surely meant to keep him. At the first Target or Walmart she passed, she'd pick up some decent cat food, a cat bed and sandbox, all the supplies to make a cat comfortable. She was wondering what to call him, what name would fit the big red tom. He'd do well on her acreage outside Stockton, he was bold and strong and looked like he'd be a good mouser. Her last two cats had died of old age and she was more than ready for a new companion.

Beyond the three rows of gas pumps and the office and restrooms was a patch of scruffy lawn and a bed of ragged pink geraniums barely surviving in the dry sand. She pulled over there, parked, and because he had come right back into the truck on previous stops, she let the tomcat out. He bolted out in a hell of a hurry, straight into the geraniums. Smiling, she swung out herself, and went to use the women's more private facilities.

When she came out, the cat was gone. He wasn't in the cab, where she'd left the door open. He wasn't in among the geranium bushes. She searched the paved gas station area, the open bay with its two lifts, and the surround. She called him, sounding foolish shouting, "Kitty, kitty."

Afraid he might have been hit by a car, she walked the edge of the highway and then the access road, looking carefully. Returning to her U-Haul, she talked with other drivers who had stopped, but no one had seen him. Finding no clue to where he'd gone, she borrowed some paper and a stapler from the cashier and put up half a dozen signs, on the posts and trees, giving the cat's description and both her cell number and her Stockton phone number. She went on after several hours, praying for the tomcat and sick with the loss of him.

Maybe he'd turn up, maybe someone would find him and call her, but she didn't hold much hope. Moving on through the city, she pulled onto the Bay Bridge with a heavy heart. Why had he vanished like that? There'd hardly been time for someone else to pick him up. Could that cat have had his own agenda and left her on purpose? Was he traveling maybe to rejoin his family, as in some of the strange stories in the paper or on the Web? Cat gets accidentally locked in a truck and carried off, a year later has found his way back home again?

Whatever this was about, she had lost a friend. Even as short a while as she'd known him, it would take her a long time to get over his loss. She didn't think, after traveling with this handsome tomcat, there would be another cat in the world who could mean anything to her, who could touch her heart as he had, in that short drive down from Oregon. Heading inland, she made sure her cell was on, in case anyone did call.

That was the last Denise Woolsey ever saw of the big red tomcat. The last she ever heard of him, though his objective, single-minded destination wasn't sixty miles, as the crow flies, from her own new home.

The women on the bus talked nonstop, they were worse than a yard full of chickens announcing their egg-laying scores. Pan, crouched out of sight on the dusty, rough-riding floor, wedged between a bulging cloth shopping bag and a shoe box that smelled of sausages, tried to shut out the shrill voices that had already begun to pound like hammers in his head. Twenty-three women, all of them marathon talkers. Peering out from beneath the last seat, riding practically over the rear wheels and bumpy as hell, he counted two dozen conversations rambling on all at once. A woman sitting right up in front was quizzing the driver querulously. "When will Tom be back? He's our regular driver. Did you say he's your cousin? Then you're Wallace, nice to meet you, Wallace. I hope Tom's not sick, we all enjoy him, he's such a riot."

The driver didn't answer, just kept his eyes on the road, as if this shepherding of loquacious women wasn't his preferred portion of the job description. All Pan could see of him was his gray uniform, wide shoulders, and protruding ears beneath a gray cap. The woman behind him, talking with her face inches from his ear, wore a black slouch hat pulled down as if to hide a bad haircut. Three rows back, two women exchanged a look between them and began to whisper, glancing up at Wallace, then drifted into a discussion of the funniest television shows, a subject that would have put Pan right to sleep except for all the other women talking and giggling among themselves. Too bad he hadn't spotted a busload of men headed for the same village, at least men's voices were lower. By the time Wallace had put the city traffic behind them and they were out on the highway rolling along, Pan was wild for solitude, for the restorative peace of the woods and fields that he had left behind him. But then four of the women began to talk about Molena Point, and he came wide awake and alert.

"We've worked on that auction for months," said a frail little brown-haired woman as bony as a wren. "We're hoping to bring in at least fifty thousand, maybe more." At mention of that amount of money, Wallace came to attention, too, his hand tightening on the wheel, his shoulder and head shifting as he positioned himself to hear better. "Fourteen local artists have given work," the little wren was saying, "four of the nicest hotels have donated luxury weekends for two, and—"

"*That* much money?" interrupted a big woman across the aisle. She was dressed in a jacket embroidered with pink flowers, her white-blond hair arranged in an elaborate knot, the white roots showing around her face. "I can't believe that much money for a bunch of stray cats." She shook her head, her long gold earrings jangling. "That kind of money should go to fight disease or help starving children. Cats can take care of themselves."

"The cats were abandoned," the wren told her. "They're house cats, they *don't* know how to fend for themselves. Little frightened animals dumped by cold, uncaring people without any feeling," she said pointedly, "thrown away like garbage."

A woman with long dark hair turned around in her seat to stare at the round, complaining woman. "*I'm* fostering five of the rescue cats. They're so dear, I don't know if I'll want to part with them at all. As for the auction, I'm helping out, and I'm certainly going. I have my eye on one of Charlie Harper's etchings. There'll be a mob, I mean to get there early."

"What's troubling," said a tall, skinny woman in a white sweater and cream-colored slacks, "the auction's on Sunday, and the banks won't be open. All that money they take in, a lot of it will surely be in cash. What will they do with it until Monday morning?"

"Surely no one would steal from a charity," said a woman whose black hair was so thin you could see her scalp, like spaces in a poorly made bird's nest. "Surely not from a charity for homeless animals." Pan thought about the abandoned cats who'd started showing up around Eugene as the economy faltered, hungry, pitiful cats who'd never been on their own. He thought about the Animal Friends' rescue truck setting out traps, which he had watched with a fierce ambivalence.

On the one hand, those cats didn't know flip about hunting. Pan himself had hunted for a few of them, but they were frightened and shy, even of him. Sometimes he'd thought, *They're better off in a shelter,* but then he'd think, *They're better off trying to learn, better off taking the challenge to survive or die,* and he'd argued with himself, back and forth, until he didn't know what he thought. Sometimes he'd dreamed of starving cats, too, thin and scruffy cats that lived in ancient, rough villages, centuries past, cats from the stories his pa had told when he was just a kitten. His pa's tales of other times had frightened him, the cruel life among the wattle and stone cottages that crowded close along dirty, cobbled streets. Pa told of rats bigger than a kitten, as big as a dog, lurking in the thatched rooftops, of stinking sewers slimy with offal, of thin, shaggy donkeys straining so hard to pull their over-loaded carts that they collapsed, lay untended until they died.

As he grew older, those stories made him think a lot about staying alive, himself. This world was better now, but in a way, it was more dangerous, the machines and fast highways, a world not built for a cat's survival. Especially when you hitched rides with humans, folk who might truly care about a lone cat—or might only take him in to torment him.

Well, he *was* traveling south, and these women were harmless enough. He could only pray this bus *was* going to the right destination, to Pa's rugged cliff along the sand, with its little caves and fishing dock, tall pines and crowded cottages, to the shore his daddy had painted for him with such longing.

At last the women ceased arguing and settled down to nap or read, looking up now and then as the tall bus was buffeted and rocked by a rising wind blowing from the west, carrying the smell of the sea and of coming rain. He woke twice, thirsty and hungry. He eyed the shoe box that smelled so enticingly of sausages, but it was taped shut all around the edges, and tied with heavy, knotted string. What did the owner think, that someone would try to tear into it and rob her of her sausages? He considered the matter, but he would make too much noise ripping the tape off. He tried to force himself back to sleep, to avoid thinking about food and water.

He woke fully when the bus slowed and turned off the highway, descending a residential hill. Below, small cottages crowded close together, a tangle of shops among pines and cypress trees, that already looked familiar. A misty rain veiled the village, and the wind smelled briny, too, deeply of the sea. As tree branches swept across the bus windows, the passengers stirred and began to gather up their belongings. Bags and bundles and jackets, scarves and water bottles. When the round, gray-haired woman waddled to the back and pulled her shoe box of sausages from his lair, Pan pressed under the seat against the wall, hiding himself from her view.

He waited until the bus had parked, the engine died, the doors opened, and the ladies had all filed out, then he slipped out on their heels. The minute he hit the ground, the rainy wind swept at him and the smell of the sea came stronger. Overhead, a gull screamed, making him smile. He could hear the breakers crashing, but as he reared up, drinking in the smells, a passenger spotted him.

"A cat! Oh, look, a little cat! It can't have been on the bus with us!" When she dove to pick him up, he headed away fast down the sidewalk, dodging shoes and pant legs and leashed dogs that lunged at him, their barks echoing between the crowded shops.

He evaded them all and soon left them behind, leaving the main street for a side street, trotting down a less crowded sidewalk past small and charming shops built of stone, adobe, stucco. Tubs of flowers by their doors, the smell and the hushing of the sea ever stronger as he wove past shop doorways and their bright gardens; the crashing surf ever louder, and the smell of brine stronger, and the sure sense this *was* the right village.

There—the first gleam of choppy water, and a wide white beach. He reared up, looking, then headed fast for the sand, dodging humans and dogs, slashing a lunging nose, and racing on.

Only a few people on the shore, a few hardy children running, chasing their unleashed dogs. To his left the land rose up, big houses sprawled up there behind a grassy meadow. The meadow stopped suddenly in a steep cliff that dropped straight down to the sand. The view was familiar from Pa's words, and from Debbie's photographs, too. This was his father's place, this was Pa's first home, he was sure of it.

As he hurried up the steep cliff, the sea was soon below him. To his left beyond the meadow, the handsome houses stood, built of stone, of brick set in fancy patterns, of pale stucco with roofs displaying richly curving shingles. Between the houses and the meadow ran a narrow street, lined on his side with spreading cypress trees.

Not many cars were parked along the street, and those were spaced far apart where the cypress branches didn't hang so low. An old battered sedan was nosed in between the trees, its back door open and a thin woman leaning in rummaging in the backseat among a tangle of paper bags and boxes, her jeans worn pale and threadbare. Thin, knotty legs. Worn jogging shoes.

A short-sleeved T-shirt clinging so he could see her spine. A whiff from the car smelled of cat, but he saw no cats. He wasn't sure what made him stop to watch her, but he eased deeper into the tangle of grass, held by an amused curiosity. Maybe the old woman and her cats would lead him to the cats his pa said lived on this shore. Maybe he'd even find cats who knew his pa, maybe elderly cats as lanky and lean as this old woman herself. Maybe, he thought, hardly daring to think it, maybe somewhere here, on this strip of shore, he would find his pa.

18

Earlier, while the three cats were busy tossing Alain Bent's house, down the hill among the smaller cottages Ryan's sister Hanni had pulled her van into the drive of her own remodel. Billy Young sat in the cab beside her, feeling shy of the beautiful woman. Even in frayed jeans and a faded T-shirt she was elegant, her short white hair curling carelessly around the perfect oval of her smooth, tanned face, her dark lashes and brows making her hazel eyes look huge, her hands long and elegant, busy with a clanging of jade and silver bracelets.

Hanni glanced over because he was looking at her, and gave him a wink. Now, with her construction work nearly finished, she'd brought over a load of plants, and had picked Billy up at the ranch knowing he'd be glad of the work. She'd chosen pink and red tea trees, two mock orange bushes, and a dozen breath of heaven plants; their common names pleased her more than the Latin ones, which she never bothered to remember. All of these were showy, but so hardy they lent themselves well to a rental. She had wanted oleander with its bright red or pink blooms but the bush was poisonous, and that would rule out renting to a family with little, leaf-eating children.

The sky was low and threatening, and the wind chill. Getting out of the van, she pulled a warm cap over her short white hair, pulled on a ragged jacket to keep out the wind. Preoccupied with planning the garden, she was unaware she'd had a visitor during the night. While Billy unloaded the plants, trying to shelter them from the wind, she opened the garage—and stopped.

The back door was ajar, swinging back and forth in the wind, wasn't locked as she'd left it. She remembered distinctly pushing in the simple thumb lock before she turned out the light. When she crossed the garage and stepped outside, she could see where the faceplate was bent and pried half off, fresh tool marks on the newly painted door and on the frame. She touched nothing. Stepping back inside, she stood quietly assessing the rest of the single-car garage to see what building supplies and tools might be missing.

The boxes of hardware she'd left stacked on the worktable were still there, and the cartons of new lighting fixtures that stood on the floor against the wall. Nothing seemed to be missing, but, in fact, there appeared to be more boxes than she'd left there, the pile was half again as large.

Examining the cartons, still not touching, she found seven that were unlabeled, no brand insignia or bar codes or shipping instructions. Reaching for a screwdriver, she chose the largest blank carton, pulled on her gloves, and pried the lid open—maybe that was dumb, she knew she should have handled it differently but she was too curious.

There were cleaning materials jumbled inside, a collection of solvents, ammonia, drain cleaner and, strangely, several drugstore bags containing cold medications: a combination that made chills creep up her back. She stood looking for only a minute, then closed the box and used her cell phone to call the department.

Coming up the hill she had seen the police stakeout still in place, two officers she knew, wearing water company uniforms, kneeling at the curb tinkering with a water meter, watching the meth cottage that had been raided. Now, as she talked with dispatcher Mabel Farthy, she returned to the driveway; she didn't want to move around in the garage and maybe scuff through someone's faint footprints, didn't want to destroy anything more than she already had.

When she'd hung up she stood by her van looking in the side mirror, pretending to adjust her cap, watching the uphill reflection. She saw Officer Blake answer his phone, glance briefly down at her and then away again. The two officers didn't leave their post, she assumed they'd been told to stay put.

But it wasn't five minutes until a car appeared answering her call, not a black-and-white, but Detective Juana Davis's pearl-colored Toyota slipping up the hill to pull into the drive behind her van. A black-and-white appeared behind Juana, pulling to the curb. As the detective stepped out, Hanni had to hide a little smile. Juana always looked so serious, her square face so forthright and no-nonsense, the severity of her dark uniform and black stockings and hard black shoes, black cap pulled down over her smooth hair, dark Latino eyes that could look as flat as a wall. Or could, with her friends or with an unfortunate victim, turn deeply kind and caring. Now, most likely, Juana would make Hanni's cottage part of the crime scene, locking it into their investigation of the meth operation.

That was fine with her, if they rooted out this scum. At least four men had been seen by neighbors coming and going from the meth house, two Caucasians, one

Asian, and the Latino man who was now taking his meals courtesy of Molena Point Jail. She joined Juana, pulled on the cotton booties Juana gave her, and followed the detective into the garage, where Juana first used an electronic device to scan for footprints. Behind them, a white police van slid to the curb, a vehicle big enough to haul away the cartons. Officers McFarland and Crowley got out, young McFarland with his clean good looks, Crowley towering over him, his big-boned body maybe six foot five, broad shoulders, the broad hands of a farmer.

Juana pulled off her booties and stepped out to talk with them, then the two men began to walk the perimeter of the house, moving with care, scanning for anything dropped, and for footprints. Hanni watched them, thinking about the drug dealers hiding their supplies in her garage. Had they thought that because she was Detective Garza's niece, the cops wouldn't search here? Maybe they thought she wouldn't notice the extra boxes right away? Maybe they'd meant to haul them out again in a day or two, maybe they were setting up a new operation somewhere else. She didn't like that some of these guys were still around, she'd made an investment in this neighborhood, and so had Ryan and Clyde, they wanted to see this area turned back again into the charming neighborhood it had once been.

She'd bought the house eight months ago, before the surrounding houses began to stand empty, and before that enterprising parolee, who was now in jail, had started his mom-and-pop meth business, before the neighbors began to wonder about the many different cars suddenly parked on that street, and so many strangers going in and out, and called in a report. Early on, though, she'd begun to see stray cats slipping around the empty houses, wary and hungry, and she'd put out food in unset traps, luring them in, getting them used to the open wire cages. So far, she'd trapped five, who were now in a temporary shelter, but she was still seeing strays.

This morning when she'd told Billy about the trapping operation, driving down from the ranch, he'd asked a lot of questions about how the trapping was done, about the people who were sheltering the cats. He was an animal-oriented kid, good with horses and dogs as well as the cats he'd taken in. Before they'd left the ranch, he'd shown her their new home—he was touchingly proud of his little brood and really happy with their cozy new accommodations.

But then when he'd gotten in the truck and they were headed down the hills, he was quiet again, and looked so sad. She knew he was grieving for his gran, but thought there was something more. "What is it?" she'd said softly.

He'd looked at her helplessly. He didn't say anything for a long time, then, "I just hung up from talking with my aunt Esther. Why would *she* call me? How did she know I was there at the Harpers'?" He went silent, looking down at his hands, then looked up at her, his dark brown eyes questioning. "I don't want to live with her," he said angrily.

"She asked you to live with her?"

"No, she didn't ask me. But what else could it be? She said she wanted to come up and see me. Why would she want to see me, she never has before. She never came to see Gran, even right after Mama died. She never came when Mama was alive, either, not that I know of."

"You must see her around the village?"

He nodded. "She acts like she doesn't know me, never speaks to me or looks at me."

"This morning, did she say anything else?"

"No, but she had something on her mind. She asked about the fire, asked if *everything* was gone, if we'd saved anything." He was quiet, then, "She sounded real caring and friendly. She said twice that she'd be coming up to see me."

"What did you say?"

"I said I couldn't talk any more, I had to go to work, that my ride was waiting, and I hung up," Billy said, his cheeks coloring.

Hanni laughed.

Billy looked at her, frowning. "*Can* she make me live with her? She *is* my aunt. Does she have some kind of . . . claim? Some legal way to make me live there? Why would she want me? Except to work, maybe, like in the old days when kids were adopted out to do farm work. But people don't do that anymore."

Hanni reached over, took his hand. "You see that on TV?"

"We don't have TV. I read it."

She smiled. "Esther won't do that, this isn't the eighteen hundreds. Max Harper wouldn't let her do that."

"If I don't go there, will I have to go to a foster home?"

"What do you want to do?"

"I can take care of myself." But then he looked at her shyly. "What I really want?"

She nodded.

"I want to stay with the Harpers."

"And they want you there," she said. "They both do. Max knows a few people," she said lightly, "he has a little pull." She smiled wickedly, gave him a wink that made him blush. "I know enough dirt myself about some of the folks working in Children's Services, enough to pull a few strings."

Billy looked at her, surprised, and then laughed. "Can you do that?"

"Try me."

He looked as if he wanted to hug her, and then as if he wanted ask something more. Instead he looked away, out at the dropping hills and the village roofs below. And that was where they left it, with Billy's worries eased, but Hanni wondering just what Esther Fowler *had* wanted.

The three cats were crowded together on the roof of the house across the street from Hanni's, shivering in the cold; the wet wind was dying now, giving way to colder, misty rain. They were watching Officers McFarland and Crowley load seven large cartons from Hanni's garage into the back of the police van, when Dulcie let out a low hunting cry and took off across the roofs where a thin figure was slipping away behind a sagging fence. Joe and Kit saw little more than a shadow, an impression of jeans and faded T-shirt. Emmylou? Dulcie meant not to lose her again; she'd followed her, lost her twice, seen her trying to get into Alain Bent's house, and then lost her yet again. Now there she was appearing suddenly out of nowhere, but then gone again. She glanced back to see Joe following, pushed along by a last gust of wind, but behind him, Kit had paused.

Lifting her paw uncertainly, Kit watched Joe and Dulcie race away in pursuit of the hurrying shadow, then turned to watch the interesting activity around Hanni's cottage, and she shivered with indecision. But she was caught even more powerfully in her own agenda. Leaving all the human excitement to play out below her, she spun around and streaked down the dropping rooftops for the center of the village, her head full of the medieval painting that so fit Misto's stories, full of lost centuries and ancient dreams, and she raced away to tell the old tomcat about the wonderful mural.

It was too early for the ferals' feeding time, but maybe he'd be there, the day was growing cold and dark and maybe John Firetti would feed early. She was only vaguely aware that something else, besides those ancient times, might be drawing her so powerfully; she raced down across the roofs like a wild thing, her own urgency startling and puzzling her.

Joe caught up with Dulcie two blocks above the Damens' cottage, as she paused to look over the roof's edge down into a scrappy yard: brown earth, bare beneath overhanging branches, the narrow house made of rough brown boards, an old house, dour and neglected. "Emmylou vanished in there," Dulcie said. "Maybe she broke in, I heard glass break."

He moved close to her, in the cold drizzle. "Could she mean to camp in there? Break into a stranger's house to get out of the cold? Is that what she was doing, all along, poking around up here, looking for the best empty house to crash in?" The dark brown house *was* sheltered from its neighbors, jammed in between two huge cypress trees, their heavy branches sweeping the roof like the tails of giant beasts. A tentlike acacia stood at the back, hiding the house behind. The yard itself was thick with broken cypress branches fallen across the cracked cement walk. Backing down a rough trunk, they paused among the browning cypress fronds that were wet now in the mist. On the little cement porch, a stack of wet newspapers lay moldering. Lace curtains, limp and gray, hung crookedly over the windows. The cats could just detect Emmylou's trail, overridden by the fresh scent of a man, a nervous smell and fearful.

"Was that a *man* I saw?" Dulcie whispered. "So thin and tall, so like Emmylou?" They followed his scent in silence, watching the shadows—and nearly plowed into him standing among the multiple trunks of a spreading cypress, his clothes as dark as the rough branches, his face in shadow; they leaped away, startled, then, gathering their wits, they crouched dumb and innocent, looking up at him.

He was dressed as a gardener, but he didn't have a gardener's tan, his face was pasty white. Slim, dark jeans, heavy shoes, faded brown T-shirt, and, slung low on his thin hips, a leather carpenter's belt holding clippers and gardening tools, and who knew what else? When he turned to look at them, his eyes were so cold that the two cats slipped away again, frightened.

When they glanced back, he hadn't moved. But he was paying no attention to *them*, he stood watching, down the hill, the activity around Hanni's remodel, watching the cops and Detective Davis. "Could he be from the meth house?" Dulcie whispered. "One of the men they missed, who disappeared before they raided it?"

"One way to find out," Joe said softly. "Why don't you slip on up to the roofs and keep an eye on him?"

Dulcie smiled and vanished, scrambling up to the shingles, as Joe streaked down through the tangled yards for the Damens' cottage, to find a phone. He was headed for the open front door when he saw Clyde in the backyard and veered in that direction, leaping to Clyde's shoulder.

It took only a minute, Joe clinging to Clyde's jacket, his whiskers tickling Clyde's ear as Clyde made the call. They listened to Mabel pass his message on as, out in front, McFarland answered her call. At once, the two officers stopped loading the van and moved away to vanish among the wooded yards. Listening to their soft, fast footfalls as they ran, then a dry scraping and sliding as if their quarry was climbing a fence, Joe leaped from Clyde's shoulder to the roof, to see better. Yes, there went Dulcie racing across the roofs, looking down, watching them. He sped to join her, but soon she lost the runner between the houses.

Together they watched Crowley circle through the trees to the left while McFarland disappeared to the right. Ahead, a branch snapped. McFarland shouted, dove in among the trees behind the brown cottage; they heard a scuffle, then McFarland's sharp command.

The young officer came out marching the erstwhile gardener ahead of him, hands cuffed behind him. Crowley joined him, moving close to the man, carrying the tool belt. Behind them in the cottage the curtain twitched aside and a figure appeared, watching them, watching the prisoner. McFarland had his back to the window, he didn't see Emmylou—until some inexplicable cop instinct made him turn, and look back.

They halted their prisoner, and moved him away from the window. Crowley took a frowning look at her, and moved up the three cement steps. Standing to the side of the door, he knocked.

There was a long pause. When he knocked again, Emmylou eased the door open, stood looking at the officers, looking at the handcuffed prisoner, at his pale, angry face; and she took a step back. Crowley towered over her, made tall Emmylou Warren look as petite as a doll by comparison.

"Do you live here?"

She nodded, then shook her head.

"Could you tell us your name?" By the look on his face, he knew who she was. When she didn't reply, he said, "You're Emmylou Warren?"

She stood with her veined hands loose at her sides, her wrinkled face impassive but her jaw set tight, a little muscle twitching. "It isn't my house, it belongs to a friend. She's . . . I don't know where she is. You can see the mail's piled up." She nodded toward the mailbox at the curb, its door open, the mail so jammed inside that half of it stuck out. She glanced toward the soggy newspapers littering the porch. "I've been up here several times. When I saw she was gone, I started coming to feed her cats, but now they've disappeared, too. I'm worried about her, and I'm worried for them. She always leaves the key, tells me if she's going away. But it isn't there, and at last, today, I broke in." She looked at Crowley pleadingly. "I'm afraid something's happened to her. Someone's been in here, they've made a terrible mess."

"Does she have any family near? Have you tried calling them?"

Emmylou shook her head. "No one. No one I can call, no one who'd come. Only her brother, and he never comes up here, he's . . . He calls himself a vagabond."

"Homeless?" Crowley said.

She nodded.

"Where does he hang out?"

"Up and down the coast."

"With bad weather on the way," Crowley said, "might he have come here, wanted a place to crash? Found her gone, and broke in?"

She shook her head. "It doesn't look like that, Birely wouldn't make that mess, he wouldn't trash the place. He shows up in the village a couple times a year. When she worked bagging groceries, he'd meet her out in front of the market, she'd give him money, buy him some food. When he's in town, he camps down by the river with the other homeless, or, in cold weather like this, under the Valley Road bridge. Bridge is just behind the market where we both worked, they'd meet there, she'd see him a few times then he'd be gone again."

"Do you think she'd have gone off with him?"

"She'd never do that, she hated the way he lived. Sammie's a homebody, she loves her home. I don't understand where she's gone."

"Would he have harmed her?"

She looked intently at Crowley. "No, not Birely. He's stable enough, he's not a nutcase, he just likes that life, no responsibility. I've met him a couple of times, and the way she talks about him . . . He calls himself a vagabond, a hobo, a wanderer. He's a happy man, and gentle. No," she said, "he would never hurt her, he loves his sister." She frowned. "It isn't like her to leave the village without telling me, so I could feed the cats. She didn't know I'd been evicted but she knows my old car; if she'd wanted me, she'd have found me."

"You want to file a missing persons report? You can do that when you come in for fingerprinting." At her uncertain look, he said, "You'll have to come in, Ms. Warren. We need your prints in the investigation of the fire and of Hesmerra Young's death. When you delay, you're holding up a murder investigation."

She looked at him blankly.

"Hesmerra was your friend?"

"Yes, she was."

"There's a possibility she didn't die naturally." Emmylou was silent, looking at him, gripping the door frame. He said, "You could help her by giving us your prints. You want to ride down to the station with us? I can bring you back to your car."

From the roof, the cats watched the exchange, Dulcie's ears sharply forward, the tip of her tail twitching as Emmylou backed away from the two officers. The cats looked at each other, puzzled. Surely Emmylou hadn't poisoned Hesmerra, they didn't like to think that, though they had no real cause to believe otherwise. "I'll come to the station on my own," she said stiffly. She seemed not to know the prisoner, he might have been a tree standing there in handcuffs for all the attention she paid him. The officers didn't question her about him, nor question him about Emmylou. Maybe they were leaving that up to one of the detectives, who would want to do the questioning in their own way.

Emmylou said, "I'm parked down the block, around the corner." She stepped on out, carefully pulled the door closed, latched it as best she could despite the way she'd pried the lock loose. It looked, Joe thought, much like the jimmied lock on Hanni's garage door. Coming down the three steps, she walked past the officers and their prisoner with her head high, and moved on down the street. She was just approaching Hanni's cottage when Billy looked up from the garden, saw her, and the two officers just behind her with their cuffed prisoner. The boy went still, looking, then he raced to Emmylou and threw his arms around her.

19

"They can't put you in jail," Billy said indignantly, clinging to Emmylou, watching the officers and their prisoner. "What did *you* do? *You* didn't do anything."

"They only want my fingerprints," she said, "they say it's routine. Didn't they take yours?" Billy nodded. She said, "Sammie's house is trashed inside, I don't know what happened. While I'm at the station I'll report her missing, maybe they can find out where she's gone. First the fire, and Hesmerra, and now . . . seems like everything's gone wrong." She saw the hurt in his eyes at mention of his gran, and hugged him hard. "I'm sorry, I don't mean to upset you. I'm just a foolish old woman."

"Have you been staying at Sammie's?" he said so softly the cats could barely hear.

Emmylou shook her head. "She didn't leave the key, I can't find the key. But I did break in, just now, to look inside for the cats. She always comes to tell me if she's going away, she always leaves the key." She looked at Billy, frowning. "She said more than once that someone was watching her, maybe following her. She's been gone since before the fire, and not a word. She could have found me, found my car. And now, where are the poor cats? Muddy raccoon prints all over the back porch, too, and in the house, so maybe it wasn't a person at all, but those beasts . . . Oh, the poor cats."

The raccoons of Molena Point seemed singularly wicked, they killed unwary cats, attacked small dogs in their own fenced yards, attacked the owners when they intervened. Several villagers had been so badly bitten they were taken to emergency for shots and stitches. Twice an angry mother raccoon, apparently rearing her kittens in the bushes of a downtown cottage, attacked small dogs as their owners took them for an evening stroll. It did no good to trap and move the beasts, they either came back or, wherever they were released, became someone else's problem. And the village's no-kill policy regarding predatory wild animals meant the raccoons increased in numbers at their own pleasure. One's only choice was to stay out of their way.

As Emmylou headed away for her car, on the roof above, Dulcie said, "Didn't Chichi Barbi trap a black-

and-white cat last week? Was that one of Sammie's cats?"

"Don't know," Joe said, distracted. Below them, the prisoner either couldn't speak English, or pretended he couldn't. Juana had joined them and was having a go in Spanish. When the guy wouldn't talk to her, either, pretending not to understand her, Crowley helped him into the backseat of the squad car, holding the guy's head down so he wouldn't crack his skull, and took him away. McFarland followed in the SUV, hauling the meth supplies from Hanni's garage, and the cats headed for the Damen cottage, where they could hear Debbie inside, complaining.

"That old linoleum's filthy, I can't live in this mess." Ignoring the cleaning rags and scrub brushes, she said, "I'd better get down to the police, for fingerprints, Captain Harper *did* seem in a hurry," and she fled the house, calling the kids, moving away toward her car. The cats, with both Debbie and Emmylou headed for MPPD, raced away across the roofs, eager to see how this came down, amused that Debbie hated scrubbing the floor even more than facing Harper again.

Running through the cold rain across the wet shingles and the slippery limbs of oak and cypress, Joe and Dulcie hit the courthouse roof soaked nearly to the skin, galloped its length, and dropped down through the branches to MPPD's glass door. Any sensible cat would be curled up on a deep couch before a warming fire. But what the hell, Joe thought, pawing at the door.

Mabel Farthy, behind the counter, rose at once to let them in. There was nothing quite as satisfying to a persistent cat as an obedient human, as to see his training pay off. "Oh, you poor things, you're soaking." The grandmotherly woman fit snugly in her uniform, its dark color setting off her creamy complexion and blond-dyed white hair. She, and the office, smelled of cinnamon buns, testimony to the competence with which Mabel mothered the officers. From beneath the counter she produced a baker's box, which she set beside the in-box. Enticing Joe and Dulcie up, she broke a bun into small pieces, laid them out on a clean paper plate. By the time their rough tongues had snatched up the last sticky crumb, she'd dried them both off with paper towels, all the while scolding them for getting wet. They were washing the damp places she'd missed when they heard Vinnie Kraft's whining from beyond the glass door, looked up to see Debbie hurrying across the parking lot dragging Vinnie and Tessa.

Shoving in through the glass door, Debbie sailed past the bars of the holding cell, past the folding chairs that stood against the wall, bearing down on Mabel.

"I'm here to see Captain Harper. At *his* request, so I don't expect to be kept waiting." The eyes of both children were fixed on the cats, particularly on Joe, who sat center stage on Mabel's counter.

"That's Ryan and Clyde's cat," Vinnie said sharply.

"Don't be silly." Debbie stared at the cats as if something disgusting had been left in a public place. "What would their cat be doing in a police station? Sit down, Vinnie." Moving away from the cats to the other end of the counter, she returned her scowl to Mabel. "*Is* Captain Harper here? He as much as demanded that I come in. I don't have time to *wait*."

Mabel looked her over, her round face expressionless. "Captain Harper is busy. Would you like to take a seat?" Deftly she moved the tray of outgoing mail back from the edge as Vinnie reached a hand up. Dulcie and Joe backed away, too, watching the kid warily.

Debbie huffed and took a seat, pulling the children away with her. Mabel resumed sorting the mail, looking up only when the glass door opened again and two women and a thin little man stepped in. The women were dumpy and soft, faintly unkempt, their hair marceled into rigid waves, their dresses reminiscent of the flowered rayon frocks one saw in old '40s movies. The man was a precise little fellow decked out in a dark three-piece suit, his thin face clean shaven except for a carefully trimmed beard of the same salt-and-pepper gray as his neatly styled, short hair; the trio might have just stepped out of the photo the cats had found in Alain Bent's file cabinet. Their expressions were every bit as sour, though they approached Mabel's counter uncertainly. Behind them Debbie had turned away, leaning down over Tessa to adjust the little girl's hair bow.

Both women were squarely built, as sturdy as pit bulls, they had to be mother and daughter. The older woman's face was pale as milk, her skin thick with small scars as if she'd suffered endless little surgeries. "I'm not sure we've come to the right place," she said, "to report a missing person? Or someone we think is missing? My cousin . . . I'm Norine Sutherland. This is my daughter, Betty, my husband, Delbert," she said abruptly. "My cousin is Alain Bent. The Realtor?" She launched into a long and complicated explanation of why they thought Alain was missing—but the cats' attention was on Debbie. She watched the three warily, and when the older woman glanced idly at her, she leaned down again as if dusting lint from her shoe. She knew these people—but perhaps they didn't know her? Could she know them only from the same picture, which was tucked into Alain's file cabinet?

Yet if they didn't know her, why was she so wary? One more glance from the older woman and Debbie rose and left, hurrying the kids out, her expression hard to read. Behind her on Mabel's counter Joe and Dulcie sat washing their paws, highly entertained by the little drama. But across the village, another, subtler drama was unfolding.

On the cliff above the sea where the rainy wind swept cold, the big red tom stood still, looking. Something watched him, something hidden among the blowing grass; while beyond him, at the street, the lone woman still rummaged in her car, the rain blowing in on her backside as she looked for something or maybe tended to her vagabond housekeeping. Then suddenly among the shifting grasses the darker shadow moved again, staying downwind so he could get no scent at all.

He'd come a good way along the cliff, looking down at the shore below, searching for the little fishing dock. Maybe it had been torn down or perhaps swept away by a high sea, was no longer there, where Misto had remembered it from his youth? But now again Pan searched the grass, and again his skin rippled from the shadowy presence. Who would follow him, and why? No cat knew him here. This wasn't a dangerous predator, he didn't sense that at all, but still he crouched, ready to fight or run, whichever was expedient. Above him the dark clouds heaved lower, heralding an early dusk, and the drenched grass forest began to fill up with shadows—but there, where a tangle of blackberries wove dense and dark, something solid crouched, poised. A darkly mottled shadow, a pair of eyes bright as marigolds, holding steady on him. He eased forward, and caught the scent of her, mixed with the smell of sea and rain. He could see the tip of her fluffy tail twitching, her only movement as she watched him.

Slowly she emerged from among a tangle of blackberry vines into the grass, and shyly she slipped closer. Her long, wind-rumpled fur was a mix of black and brown, her face mottled black and brown, her yellow eyes keen with curiosity. Very close to him she stopped. She looked deep into his eyes, studied his face, and then again she moved closer. She looked him all over. She tasted his scent on the wind. She looked closely at the circular mark on his shoulder.

"Pan?" she said, startling him. "You *can't* be *Pan*?"

"I'm Pan," he said warily. "How could you know me?"

"Where did you come from? How did you come here?"

"How do you know my name?"

"Who is your father?"

"My father is Misto," he said. "Do you know him?"

"He's here," she said, twitching her wind-tangled tail. "Misto's here, he talks about you. How did you know to come here, how did you know where to find him?" Beyond them at the street the old woman had backed out of the car with a paper bag in her hand. Closing the door, she turned and headed straight toward them, wading through the blowing grass soaking her jeans, carrying a bundled-up brown blanket. Immediately the two cats hunkered down, made themselves small, peered up side by side through the blowing stalks. Both felt a rippling urge to run, an inborn alarm that she might throw the blanket over them—yet they remained still. Had she even seen them?

Unaware, she moved past them to the cliff's edge. At the very brink, she began to trample the grass, pressing it down in a circle. Spreading out the old blanket, she sat down in the center, ignoring the fitful rain.

The tortoiseshell relaxed, laughing softly as the old woman took a strip of paper towel from the bag, smoothed it down on the blanket, and laid out her thermos, an apple, and a cellophane-wrapped sandwich.

"Suppertime," she whispered. She looked Pan over again, her yellow eyes so clear and bold they quite unsettled him. "My name is Kit. You've come to find Misto. But how . . . ?"

"Is he here?" he said with excitement, lashing his red-striped tail.

"Yes, but how did you find him? Oh," she said, "from his tales? You found this place from his stories?"

"Yes, but how do you know that? Then I saw pictures of the village, exactly the way he described. There are lots of villages all along the coast, but none quite like this one, not the same cluster of cottages so cozy beneath the spreading trees." He looked at her intently. "Is there a fishing dock farther along the shore? Do ferals live there?"

"They live there. And Misto comes every morning and evening, he'll be there soon, now," she said, laughing at the light that blazed in his russet eyes. "You came all this way, because of a picture?"

"Lots of pictures, color pictures in magazines in the house where I lived, and then photographs, and I knew this was the right village." Pan wiped at his ear with a front paw, where the grass seeds tickled. "I saw this place and thought about Pa, I knew he was growing old and would miss his kittenhood home, and I guessed he might come here.

"Once I lived in a nursing home," he said. "I listened to those old folks, how they longed for the places of their childhood, and I thought Pa would be longing, too, wanting to return to where he was a kitten. After the nursing home burned down I set out to follow him. Do you know what it's like not to have any notion where your pa is, or even if he's still alive?"

"I never knew *who* my father was," Kit said. "I never knew him at all. My mother . . ." She went silent as a police car came up the narrow street cruising slowly, nosing to the curb in front of Emmylou's car as if to block its departure. Officer Brennan sat a moment talking on the radio, glancing at the empty car and then scanning the cliff. His bulk completely filled the driver's seat; and the cats could hear the faint, tinny reply of the dispatcher—but so could Emmylou. She ducked down below the tall grass, cowed there as still as a cat, herself.

But not still enough. Brennan, seeing movement, stepped out of the black-and-white, moving lightly considering his weight, and approached through the rustling grass asking her to come out. The weight of his equipment belt made him look all the heftier, his holstered gun, the radio and phone and nightstick, the holstered pepper spray and Taser. The third time he spoke, Emmylou rose up out of the grass like a wind-blown scarecrow, scowling at him, clutching her thermos and lunch bag to her as if for protection.

Brennan said, "The chief's looking for you to come in, Emmylou, for fingerprinting, right?"

Emmylou said nothing, she just looked at him, clutching her lunch bag closer.

"Why don't you come on in with me? It won't take long, and I'll bring you back." He nodded toward her old Chevy. "You can leave your car, I'll see it isn't ticketed."

Emmylou's expression was such a comical mix of defiance and helpless resignation that both cats, peering up through the tangle of green blades, had to stifle a laugh—but Kit watched Pan shyly, too. He was the handsomest tomcat she'd ever seen, he was big, well muscled, his rust-red coat beautifully striped, wide dark tiger stripes, and as sleek as silk. And he was Misto's son, she could see Misto's own kindness and honesty in his face, in his copper-colored eyes. She daren't look at him too long, his returning gaze left her as giddy as a kitten on its first tumble of catnip.

As Officer Brennan helped Emmylou into his squad car, Kit led Pan along the edge of the cliff above the pale sand and dark and rolling sea, led him toward the dock and the feral band where John Firetti would be setting out the evening meal, led Pan to where he'd find his pa again after so long a searching, and she could hardly wait.

20

The three visitors to Max Harper's office sat lined up on the leather couch as rigid as three schoolkids facing an unsmiling principal. Square and pudgy Norine Sutherland and her matching daughter. And the small, tight-looking man of the house. Their uncertainty out at the front desk seemed to have vanished. Norine had told Mabel, "We weren't sure where to come, where to report a possible missing person. To the police? To the county sheriff? Or to some welfare agency? Well, if there *is* anything to report, if Alain really *is* missing. Officially, you know. *Do* you take missing person reports? Someone we *think* is missing?"

But now that they had an audience with the chief, as they'd been angling for, the two women were bolder.

Now they sat sizing Max up, seeming to assume that he would take immediate action.

Delbert, on the other hand, still looked apologetic, uncertain whether they should be there at all, bothering the police with their family dilemma. Perhaps only Joe and Dulcie, crouched out of sight beneath the credenza, caught the sharpening of Max's attention at the mention of Alain Bent, a tightening of his jaw that the cats knew well.

"Alain doesn't answer her phone nor our messages," Norine said, "we haven't spoken with her for months, she never answers her calls. She used to have an answering machine. Maybe it's full. We've been up to her house three times since we arrived in town, but no one is ever there. We thought we had a key for emergencies, but it doesn't work. We drove down from Redding because we didn't know what else to do, we're worried about her. The house looks cared for, the walks have been swept, we've found no mail in the box, no newspapers on the drive, but still the place seems deserted. We looked in the windows. No magazines or mail left about, the beds are neatly made, no clothes thrown across a chair the way Alain leaves them. You can't see into the kitchen from the ground but you can glimpse her desk through the bedroom slider, and it looks so neat. Usually there are stacks of papers, flyers, files. The computer's there, at least the monitor is, but not her laptop. Well, wherever she is, I guess she has that with her." The woman was rambling, but the picture she painted was familiar enough to the cats. The house, when they'd prowled there, had indeed looked neat and deserted. Now, in their shadowed lair beneath the credenza, both Joe and Dulcie wondered if they had missed something, some clue to Alain's supposed disappearance. Maybe, Dulcie thought, if Alain was Erik's lover, she was off in the Bahamas waiting for him, planning on a romantic vacation they didn't care to advertise.

"You've had no contact with Alain at all?" Max said. "Since what date?"

"That's the strange part, that's what makes us so uncertain," Norine said. "She *has* been in touch, we've e-mailed back and forth, and that's what we don't understand. We told her we need to talk with her by phone. There's some family business we need to discuss, and I'm never sure how private these electronic messages are. We asked her to please call or give us a number where we can reach her, but she keeps making excuses. At first she said she was on the East Coast, that she'll be back soon and will call us then. Then she said she'd been delayed, that some business had come up, but she'll call soon. She could call from the East

Coast, what's the problem with that? This has gone on and on. We can't understand why she's so evasive. We're beginning to wonder if those messages *are* from Alain at all.

"Anyone," Norine said, "could be sending them, if they had her password. I know it sounds paranoid, but this has gone on too long. A month ago when we called her office, they said she'd moved away. But she didn't tell us that, she didn't say anything like that to us. If she's moved, why on earth wouldn't she say so?

"When we identified ourselves as family, and asked for her new address, they gave us my parents' address. Well, she's not *there*. They say they haven't heard from her at all, and one of the owners of Kraft Realty, Mr. Perry Fowler, said since she moved months ago they're directing what personal mail they get to a post office box in our own town. He said it hadn't been returned, so she must be getting it, but that doesn't make sense. He was very short with us, as if he really didn't have time for our silly questions."

Betty Rails said, "The post office won't tell us anything. They won't say whether there's any mail in her box, won't even say whether she has a box, won't tell us whether she's picked up any mail. We went to our local police but they wouldn't help us. They said we'd have to come here, because she lived here." The two women looked helplessly at Max, all their early confrontation gone, only uncertainty remaining. They looked up when Detective Davis appeared in the doorway.

Max nodded to Davis. She stepped in and laid a piece of paper on his desk, glancing briefly at the trio, a quick assessment, like the flash of a fast camera. The cats noticed she was limping again, her bad knee giving her trouble. She'd talked about surgery, but kept putting it off, said she didn't have time. Max read what appeared to be a short note, and a little smile touched his face. "Go ahead and interview her, Juana. She find a place to live?"

Juana shook her head. "Still on the streets. She said she was arranging to stay with a friend." She shrugged, gestured dismissively, and moved away up the hall toward the front desk to fetch Emmylou, to take her on back to her office. Beneath the credenza, Dulcie gave Joe a questioning look. When he twitched an ear, she bellied out under the side rail and melted into the hall behind Juana, vanishing beneath Max's line of vision. It was little indiscretions such as Max seeing them suddenly veer off to follow a witness that could prompt the chief to study them with undue attention. Joe heard the faintest sliding of paws on the hard floor as his lady streaked into Juana's office.

Max was saying, "If you want to sign a missing persons report, we'll talk with Kraft Realty. It's possible, if she's moved, that the house is on the market, and that they have a current key. If so, we might get a court order and have a look."

"We couldn't find an ad in the paper that it's for sale," Norine said, "and there's no sign in the yard."

"Sometimes a sale isn't advertised," Max said, "a silent sale, handled strictly within the office, for any number of reasons."

But Joe was thinking, *Maybe she doesn't* like *these relatives, maybe she doesn't* want *to be in touch.* Except he thought there was more to Alain's disappearance than that, there were too many disappearances all at once. *Was* Erik Kraft down in southern California, soon to head off on vacation? Where was Alain, and, for that matter, where was Emmylou's friend Sammie, who lived not a block down the hill from Alain? Three absences, was that a coincidence? More like the first odd pieces of a puzzle just short of making sense, just short of forming a coherent picture.

High on the cliff above the shore Kit sat alone, a small tortoiseshell silhouette against the gathering evening, her fur damp and cold, her ears down in the icy gusts. Below her on the shore, despite the cold drizzle, the two tomcats strolled side by side looking deeply content at their sudden reunion. Their voices were drowned by the breakers and the wind, their pawprints quickly filled with water behind them as the tide crept in. Kit, watching them, felt as happy and proprietary as if she'd arranged their meeting all by herself, as if it was all her doing that had brought father and son together.

Well, she *had* guided Pan the last quarter mile of his vast journey, had escorted him along the cliff top until he'd seen, below, the feral band gathered around the little dock at their supper dishes. She had watched Pan race down the cliff in three long leaps, a red blur plowing in among the startled strays, scattering the shy ones, alarming the bold ones into hisses and raised claws. He had plunged at Misto, nearly knocking him down—and hadn't the old yellow tomcat exploded into kittenish cavorting at the sight of his grown son. The two had erupted into a wild race that sent them streaking up the cliff again and down beneath the dock, scattering the ferals, and both of them talking up a storm, *Where did you come from, how did you get here, how long was your journey, how did you know where to find me . . . ?* On and on until Kit had rolled over, laughing.

Kit knew Mary Firetti watched them from the cliff above, silent and entranced. She had come tonight instead of John, loaded down with a bag of kibble and water bottles. She had fed the ferals, was leaving when she caught sight of Pan. She froze to see a new cat trotting beside Kit, had sat down at the edge of the cliff nearly hidden in the tall grass. She'd remained as still as a stone, watching the meeting of father and son. Now, as the two toms raced to the end of the dock, their voices drowned by the waves and by the fitful gusts, Kit and Mary watched them, filled with a giddy joy at their atartling reunion.

When Kit had first met Misto some two months earlier, the old yellow cat had told her he'd longed for three things. Three wishes, like a fairy tale, Kit thought. Misto had arrived in Molena Point just before Christmas, traveling all alone, paw weary from a journey that had taken many months, traveling down the Oregon coast and then the California coast hoping to find his kittenhood home. That was the first wish, to return where he was born, to find a safe haven there. That wish had been granted when John and Mary Firetti begged Misto to live with them.

The next wish had gone unfulfilled until this very moment, was answered when Pan appeared, as if by magic, right out of the old cat's dreams.

Now only the third wish remained. But this last desire *would* remain a dream, a longing as ephemeral as the wind itself. No cat could return to his past lives, no cat could go back to times and places he might indeed remember, to lives long since gone to dust. Misto could not step back again into some fabulous past, he could only bring those times alive by painting the stories for others.

Now as dusk pushed in more willfully, Mary rose from the grass, brushing off her jeans. When Misto led Pan up the cliff to greet her, Kit hung back, feeling suddenly out of place. Watching father and son so happy, watching Mary's quiet joy in them, she felt shy and uncertain, and she turned away. She was headed away for home and her own family, was trotting away through the blowing grass when Pan came racing after her, "Come with us, Kit." And Misto behind him, "Come with us."

Kit fidgeted. "Lucinda and Pedric are waiting. Lucinda said—"

Mary caught up with them. She didn't argue, she picked Kit up, cuddling her over her shoulder. "I'll call her, maybe they'll come to supper." And, carrying Kit, she headed for the van. *Oh, my,* Kit thought, glancing at Pan shyly now as they all crowded onto the front seat together. Mary said, "John will be home soon, he'll be so excited. I have steaks to cook. Shall I open the smoked salmon appetizer, and maybe some artichoke hearts?"

Kit and Misto licked their whiskers, but Pan laughed aloud with pleasure. "I didn't eat like that in Eugene. Debbie favored the cheapest cat food. And nursing home leftovers—they run to strained squash and instant potatoes."

"Tonight," Mary said, "you will dine royally. And you will sleep on feather pillows, not on the bare, hard roadside."

And that's the way it was, dinner for seven, four humans, three cats. Seven chairs at the table, three fitted out with sturdy file boxes from John's office, to raise the cats up so they could easily reach their plates. Kit's tall, thin housemates came down from their hillside home, bringing a large tray of Kit's favorite flan for dessert. Neither Lucinda nor Pedric Greenlaw, both in their eighties, a tanned, active couple, had lost their appetite for a good steak. The fillets *were* good, rare and tender, the artichoke hearts swam in butter, the caramel custard was so good it made a cat's whiskers curl. And all evening, neither Lucinda nor Pedric could take their eyes from Pan. Their wonder at another speaking cat suddenly among them was overridden, perhaps, only by the suspicion that this red tomcat might have brought with him a heartbreaking change in their lives.

To see Kit and Pan together, see their looks at each other even this early on in their acquaintance, to see the sharp chemistry already sparking between the two, was to imagine a future in which Kit might draw away from them, or perhaps leave them altogether. The concept saddened the Greenlaws for selfish reasons, but it thrilled them for Kit's sake. After all, they wouldn't be around forever. Now at last, maybe Kit had found someone good enough, strong enough, wild but loving enough, to share the next stage of her life. Pedric gave Lucinda a smile and a wink that said all was well, all would be well. He looked down at Kit, sitting next to him, and he prayed that that was so.

When the table was cleared and they'd gathered before the fire, Pan's russet eyes closed sometimes as he told of his travels, as he brought back the little, quirky moments, the rough fishermen in an Oregon harbor drinking a mix of wine and beer for breakfast, the story of Denise Woolsey in her U-Haul truck. But then his gaze would turn to watching Kit as she tried to imagine such feats: cadging rides from strangers, dodging fast trucks and then riding in them, nimbly sidestepping dangers that made her shiver clear down to her paws.

"One thing I wouldn't have liked," Kit said, "is living with the Kraft family all those months."

Pan said, "I stayed because of Tessa. Vinnie could be mean, but she was afraid of me, I could make her back off from Tessa. Debbie never bothered. But," he said, "it was Erik I was afraid of. I stayed out of his way. I was glad he was gone so much of the year, it was more peaceful then." He gave her a sly smile. "Debbie liked it that way, too. When Erik was gone, or at work, she'd go through his desk, pull out files and make notes. I could never get a good look, she'd push me off the desk. I never saw her copy anything on his Xerox, I think she was afraid he'd find out. Maybe he kept track of the copy count on the machine. Sometimes she'd copy things in the files by hand, too. She sent them all to her mother, she wrote to her mother a lot. I'd jump up on the desk to look, and she'd shove me away. Letters about Erik, though, I saw that much. About his real estate transactions. When she finished a letter she'd seal it right away, drop it in her purse and be off to the post office. As if she was afraid to leave it even for a few minutes where he might come home and find it."

Kit said, "Debbie's nephew, Billy, told Max Harper that Debbie never wrote to Hesmerra, that Debbie would have nothing to do with her mother." And Kit burned to tell Joe and Dulcie that there *were* letters, that either Billy had lied or he didn't know about them. Between this new bit of intelligence, and the presence of Pan himself, Kit was so wired she could barely settle in Pedric's arms, as Pan asked Misto for a tale. This was the story Misto told, of a deep cold winter such as Kit could hardly imagine.

"In a village five centuries before Dickens's London, in the frozen cold of winter in a cottage as rude as a cow byre, a child huddled alone, chilled on the icy hearth, her father gone to fight the invaders. The cries beyond the sod walls and banks of frozen snow were the cries of pain and death. The child hugged herself with fear and cold; the only movement in the dim hut was that of a half-wild village cat, as he crept to the child and lay up against her, to share his meager warmth. She put her arms around him, and only when the shouts of the hordes drew close did the cat rouse the child, hissing and pawing; he led her out into the dark and snowbound streets, and quickly on beneath a hill of frozen snow that covered a village haymow. He led her deep into the heart of the hay, where the fermenting heap had made its own warmth. There they remained huddled as the night passed, until the screams of the dying, and the trample of hooves, at last grew faint.

"At dawn the Huns had vanished, and child and cat came out. Beside the hill of snow and hay lay a warrior, dead. The child's own father lay there, the reins of his steed tethered among his armor. The child wept as the cat took the reins, freed the mount, and leaped into the saddle. When he pulled the child up before him, he was a cat no more, but a fine young knight dressed in catskins, with a lashing tail. And the child . . . . Her cheeks grew rosy, her frail body bloomed stronger, until her beauty shone with the light of love, out over all the bodies of the dead.

"Together they left that place, knight and damsel. They rode away in the dawn to where the land grew warm and sweet and the crops lay untouched by fire. There they gathered around them strong warriors and kind, they gathered a fine army, and there among plenty they waited, armed and strong, to turn away the Goths or to slaughter them," Misto ended, his golden eyes smiling at Kit.

The evening ended, too, with Kit still in Pedric's arms, looking back over her shoulder where Pan and Misto stood together in the open doorway. The wind had died, but, strangely, the night air felt as cold as that medieval winter. As she looked back at the two tom-cats, she could see the hearth fire blazing behind them, in a scene that seemed as magical to the tortoiseshell as Misto's ancient tales. And then Pedric was slipping into the car, holding her, and home they went through the cold night to their own warm house, Kit carrying the tales with her, carrying dreams with her of times long past—and, perhaps, of amazing times yet to be known.

21

It was earlier that evening, the icy wind rattling the trees and fingering down among the darkening cottages and shops, when Debbie Kraft and the little girls returned to MPPD. They came in shivering in their thin coats. Maybe because of her long wait and having to return, Debbie seemed chastened. She was silent as a deputy fingerprinted her and then ushered her and the children back to Max's office.

The two cats were sprawled on Max's couch when, over the intercom, the dispatcher announced her. Now, at her approach, Dulcie slipped beneath the credenza, but Joe wasn't in a mood to move. He stayed where he was, but the next minute he was sorry, when Vinnie bolted in ahead of Debbie, spied the tomcat and grabbed him up, nearly strangling him.

"Why is Ryan's cat in here? Why is this cat always in the police station? Is it lost? *I* know where it lives," she said, staring up boldly at the chief, squeezing Joe so hard it was all he could do not to bite the kid's grubby fingers. What was this preoccupation with cats? She didn't even like cats. He remained very still, trying to keep his claws sheathed. Not easy. Passive acceptance wasn't in his nature, he wanted to bloody the little brat.

Debbie pushed in, with Tessa behind her. The little girl slipped into the nearest leather chair where she curled up like a sleepy kitten. Debbie tossed her jacket and purse on the couch and sat down huffily, scowling at Max as she wiped the last smear of fingerprinting ink on the leather cushion, then reached into her purse for a tissue. Vinnie, still clutching Joe, squirmed up next to her. Joe pushed his hard paws into her bony chest, finally growling as she wriggled to get settled. Vinnie didn't see Dulcie peering up from beneath the credenza, whiskers twitching, green eyes bright as the tabby tried her best not to laugh aloud.

"I came in to be fingerprinted," Debbie said. "They did that. I thought that's all you wanted. What is it now? I have to get back, I have work to do."

"You arrived in the village when?" Max asked her.

"I told you that, we got to Ryan's last night," Debbie said.

"I understand you have a key to Alain Bent's house."

"Alain gave my husband a key. She works with him."

"She gave Erik the key for what purpose?"

"I suppose in case he needed to pick up papers, sales contracts, like that."

"And he gave the key to you?"

"No, he went off without it. I didn't want to leave it in the vacant house, and I didn't want to throw it away. I put it in my purse. As long as I had it, I stopped there at Alain's last night to pick up some clothes she borrowed, stopped on the way to the Damens'. What is this, some kind of interrogation?"

"Only a few questions," Max said easily. "Alain Bent borrowed clothes from you? You were friends, then?"

"No, not close. Once when she flew up to Eugene, they lost her bag. Erik insisted I loan her some things, and she never returned them."

"She borrowed clothes. Isn't she somewhat taller?"

The irony seemed lost on Debbie. "She's taller, but she's thin. What in the world does that have to do with anything?"

"What kind of clothes did she borrow?"

"A couple of long vests, and some smocky blouses. Things she could manage to get into."

Max had to hide a smile. This woman didn't even lie well. "When you arrived in town, then, you went into the Bent house to get the clothes. You and the children slept there that night, the night before you went to the Damens'?"

"No. I told you, we went there just before we went to the Damens." Beside her, Vinnie looked up at her mother and began to fidget. Debbie scowled down at her until Vinnie settled back, Debbie so tense that even her scent had altered. Joe was surprised Max had let the children stay in there, when he'd meant all along to interrogate her. He could have had one of the officers watch them and give Debbie some privacy. But maybe that was his intention, to pressure her, to see if Vinnie, the talkative child, would make some comment and give her mother away.

Though what really pleased Joe was that, while Max had only *his* word that Debbie and the kids had stayed at Alain's and slept there, the chief was taking his word against hers; Max was running with what Joe had told him, and that made him feel pretty good.

Max looked at Debbie a long time, letting the silence build, then abruptly switched the subject. "You said you came here because Erik wouldn't expect you to, that he'd think you'd go somewhere else?" Debbie nodded. "Were you afraid of him?"

Another faint nod.

"Can you tell me why?"

"Sometimes he hit me," she said sullenly. "When he got really mad, he'd knock me around. I told you that before."

"What was it about Erik's work that caused friction between you?"

Debbie scowled at him, and looked down at her lap. Max said, "What was it he didn't want made public, that he was afraid you'd talk about?"

She didn't answer.

"It will be easier to tell me now, than to explain later why you withheld information from the police."

Still, she didn't answer. Beside her, Vinnie was quiet. When she relaxed her grip on Joe, he thought of bolting. He tensed, then decided to stay put, even if she was hot and sweaty. Debbie's brown eyes had gone flat. "Alain and Erik worked most of their real estate listings together."

"Why would that upset you?"

"I didn't say it upset me."

Max seemed to change tack again, as if to keep her off balance. "You knew your mother was cleaning the Kraft offices, that she was working with the night crew of Barton's Commercial Cleaning?"

"I knew she worked with some cleaning service. I didn't know she cleaned Erik's offices. How long had she been doing that?"

"Do you have any idea why she wanted to work nights, when she had to leave Billy alone? That must have been hard for them both."

"Maybe it was the only work she could get. The way she drank. I guess the boy was independent enough, he'd have to be, with no one but my mother to look out for him."

"You think, then, that it was coincidence she was cleaning the Kraft offices?"

"What else would it be? What choice would she have? I imagine she worked where they told her. After all, she *was* working, despite the drink. Earning enough to buy booze," she said bitterly.

"Debbie, did your separation from Erik have to do with Alain Bent?"

She didn't reply.

"Were they lovers?" Max asked.

"They . . ." She glanced down at Vinnie, then nodded.

Max sat relaxed in his swivel chair, looking interested but kindly. "And what else about their relationship troubled you?"

Debbie fiddled with her purse, opened it, found a tissue, crushed it in her hand. It took her a while to speak. "They . . . were into some kind of . . . something outside the regular real estate sales. Something they kept secret." She looked up at him, perhaps not aware she was busily shredding the tissue. "Some kind of transactions that weren't . . . That I don't think were legal." She glanced down again at Vinnie. "Could we talk about this another time? The children . . . I need to get them home, fix their supper."

"We can talk again," Max said. "Do you think Perry Fowler would have been a part of their scams, if that's what this turns out to be?"

"I have no idea."

"Was Fowler close to Alain?"

"I really don't know. Fowler is . . ." She shook her head, didn't finish. When Joe thought of Fowler, he thought of a slick, slippery man, pale and soft and evasive.

Max rose, buzzed Mabel, and sent the two children on up the hall to her. "I can't force you to tell me what these scams are about, Debbie. But if this involves criminal activity, you're better off coming to us with what you know, than to face a charge of withholding information, and perhaps as an accessory. You're better off telling us what you know, than facing criminal charges yourself."

Debbie looked at him uncertainly, coloring with a sudden hesitancy that made Joe wonder. Was she telling the truth? Or was she setting Erik up for her own purposes, for something he hadn't done? As Max wrapped up the interview he asked Debbie about Hesmerra's funeral.

"It's just a graveside service," she said. "Sunday morning at ten, at the Pacific Sea Cemetery. Esther arranged it. Just the family, I guess. But you can come, if you want." Joe watched from the couch, and Dulcie from her shadowed lair, as Max escorted her out. The cats followed, could see from the hall out the glass door as Debbie hurried the children away to her car; her walk was quick and angry, as if she'd escaped a dominance she found hard to handle.

Why, Joe wondered, hadn't Max questioned her more intensely about just when she *had* arrived in the village and what she *was* doing in Alain Bent's house? Why had he let her sidestep so many questions? Still, though, Max had asked enough to see she was lying, that was clear enough.

Maybe he didn't want to distress her so badly she'd slip back into Alain's to set the house to rights, to clean off fingerprints and any other telltale evidence of her presence before the department had a chance to search the place? She'd have to clear the food out of the refrigerator, Joe thought, carry away the trash, get rid of the wet towels.

Out in front, Davis's car pulled into the parking lot and up to the red curb before the station. The detective got out, gave Max a little crooked grin as she pushed in through the glass door. The scent of cinnamon drifted around her, from the small white bakery bag she carried.

"Just drove Emmylou back to her car," she said. But clearly she had something more to tell him, and the two headed back to his office, Davis limping badly again. The cats followed, sniffing the aroma of cinnamon buns with an interest that would seem, to the two officers, as natural as if Juana had brought in a bag of live mice; neither officer would imagine the cats' interest lay, rather, in police business, in whatever secrets Emmylou Warren had passed on to Juana Davis.

22

W hat do you cats want?" Davis said, opening the bag of cinnamon buns she'd dropped on Max's credenza, and pouring two mugs of coffee. Joe and Dulcie looked at her hopefully, drinking in the cinnamon smell. She broke apart one of the buns onto a napkin, laid it on the floor, put the bag, Max's coffee, on the desk before him. "Emmylou didn't much like being picked up, but nothing seemed off. She grumbled about being printed, but she settled in, and let me question her." Carrying her coffee, she sat down in the leather chair that was still warm from little Tessa Kraft.

"Said she was up the valley at the time of the fire, had pulled off onto a side road, was sleeping in her car, said she heard the sirens. She described her friendship with Hesmerra pretty much as she told you. What made her nervous was when I asked her about breaking into Sammie Miller's place. She claimed to be worried about Sammie but didn't want to file a missing report, said she thought the woman would turn up soon. She sounded more worried about Sammie's cats. I'd like to have a look at the place, but without a missing report we have no cause. I dropped her at her car, told her not to leave the village."

"She's living in her car," Max said.

Juana nodded. "I didn't press it. Said she had two cats herself and that John Firetti had taken them in." Ever since Davis had adopted a kitten, courtesy of Joe and Dulcie, she'd been more aware of the cats that might suffer when she made an arrest or during a domestic dispute. Among all the officers, Davis was quickest to bring in the SPCA or CatFriends to care for the family pets. She had always been willing to help abused women, too, advise them on how to escape to safety. "I called three women's shelters to find Emmylou a place but they're all full. Called Chichi Barbi, they're full, too, extra beds in all four rooms. Chichi has a PI running background checks on the women she's taken in, he's cleared five and they're all working for her."

Just before Christmas, Chichi and her housemate, Maria Rivas, had bought Charlie Harper's cleaning service. Charlie had started the business with very little money, working out of an old, used VW van badly in need of repair. When she sold the business it included four new vans, a staff of sixteen cleaning women and two handymen. Now Charlie had the workday to herself, no more bookkeeping, no more scheduling and unforeseen disasters. She had time to finish the drawings for her second book, attend to the final editing of the manuscript, and complete five commissions for animal portraits, two of local Thoroughbred stallions, three of champion shorthair pointers. Max said, "What about the boxes in Hanni's garage?"

"We lifted three sets of prints." She grinned. "Matches for those from the meth house, including the Romero brother we picked up this morning, Raul. No ID yet on the others. Kathleen's canvassing the local retailers, running the bar codes on the chemicals. A long shot, to find a clerk who remembers a Latino customer with a big purchase, but worth trying."

Joe wondered how long it would take to get an ID on the other prints. Depended on what was in the system, on how backed up the lab was, and how complicated those particular prints were to identify. Licking the last cinnamon crumbs from his paws, he wondered if the hoods from the meth house had had some warning about the raid, giving them time to move their chemicals to Hanni's garage. Hanni had left the house unattended for nearly two weeks while she finished up an extensive interior design installation, plenty of time for them to make the shift. He kept wondering, too, about a connection between the meth house, Alain Bent's place, and Sammie Miller's cottage—and, wondering why Emmylou *had* broken in.

Licking their cinnamon-flavored whiskers, the cats curled up on Max's Persian rug and pretended to doze, as if lulled asleep by the monotonous drone of the officers' voices. But when Davis left and Max headed for Dallas's office, they hurried up the hall, their minds on those three neighborhood houses and on Sammie Miller's jimmied front door.

Outside, the night was still. An icy cold radiated through the door, nearly frosting their noses. A green van stood in the red zone just outside, its back doors open and a courier in a green and white uniform emerging, carrying a brown manila envelope. As he ducked his head beneath the dripping oak, and pushed the glass door open, the cats slipped quickly out past his hard shoes. The parking lot was wet, reflecting the overhead vapor lamps in yellow pools. Scrambling up the wet trunk of the oak to the roof, they headed across the slick tiles, their paws already freezing. "Feels like snow," Dulcie said.

"Oh, right," he said, cutting her a look. How many years since the central coast had seen snow flurries?

This was California. What felt like snow, and smelled like snow coming, was no more than a fanciful illusion.

"Do you think," she said, "we should swing by Jolly's alley? I'm more than starved, that cinnamon bun only made me hungrier. If we go by my house, Wilma will start asking questions—she'll worry for sure if we head out again in this weather."

"She'll worry more if you don't come home."

"Well, she has to know what's going on," Dulcie said to ease her conscience. "Maybe she'll think we're still in Max's office, cozy and warm and picking up information." Wilma Getz was as close with the department as were Ryan and Clyde, she knew about the meth house, and she would already know about the cartons of chemicals. Dulcie, lashing her tail with irritation because her housemate too often looked over her shoulder, swerved away in a sharp detour, heading for Jolly's alley. Joe galloped close behind her, thinking of smoked salmon, crab salad, scraps of rare prime rib—then they'd search Sammie Miller's cottage. He wondered, as they dropped down into the picturesque alley, if Emmylou had hidden Hesmerra's metal box there in the house, when she broke in. Would she do that, with cops all over the neighborhood?

He still wasn't sure whether Max had seen the box half hidden in the backseat of Emmylou's car and whether he'd glimpsed the Kraft letterhead sticking out. Wasn't sure what Max had thought at seeing *him* there. He told himself the chief was used to seeing him in strange places—he was, after all, an annoyingly nosy tomcat. Given the chief's matter-of-fact take on life, what else could Harper think?

"Oh, my," Dulcie said, licking her whiskers at the smell of roast chicken drifting up to them from Jolly's alley. Scrambling down a potted bottlebrush tree into the brick-paved alley, they were about to make a dash for the food bowl when, from the shadows, a dark little shape leaped away and vanished, a little black-and-white cat, diving behind a potted geranium where, in fact, they could easily corner the little thing. They remained still, hoping it would come out again; they didn't want to scare it all the more. The scent was of tomcat, a little young tomcat.

"Sammie Miller's other cat?" Dulcie said. "Did he have a mustache mark?"

"I don't know," Joe said. "I'm starved."

"We'll share," she said, "we'll leave him some, he'll come out when we're gone. I'll tell Wilma, maybe he'll come out for one of the volunteers." No one wanted to trap a cat unnecessarily, if he was friendly. And Jolly's alley didn't make good trapping, with so many neighborhood cats stopping in for handouts. Odds were, they'd have to release two dozen cats before they caught this one. Dulcie headed for the bowl, and Joe shouldered in next to her. It took great restraint to leave any chicken for the stray, they slurped up the deli's offering as eagerly as if they, too, were homeless and starving.

When they'd finished, leaving a generous portion, they scaled the bottlebrush tree back to the roof, and waited nearly half an hour for the little cat to come out. When at last he did creep to the bowl, he inhaled their leavings in six big bites. "If they can catch him," Joe said, "he'll be happy to see his sister, and they'll be fine at Chichi's." Chichi Barbi's cages, set up in her airy daylight basement between the guest rooms, were large and clean with multiple levels for each cat; the cats, according to Ryan, got plenty of petting and attention from the women Chichi was sheltering. Leaving the young cat licking the bowl, they headed for Sammie Miller's. This was a lot of fuss for a box of business papers that could turn out to be nothing; but something prodded Joe to find it, his instinct about those papers was as urgent as the curiosity of a stubborn cop.

No exterior lights burned around Sammie's cottage; Molena Point neighborhoods didn't have streetlights, the only illumination was what homeowners chose to install on their own. Sammie's yard was not only dark but smothered by overgrown bushes clutching the walls, reaching toward the grimy windows. The frame building was no wider than a double garage, maybe six hundred square feet at best. Even from outside, the house had the sour smell of accumulated dirt and rotting wood, a house overripe for a teardown. In better economic times someone would already have bought it, razed it, and be building a new little retreat in its place. Or would have bought several adjoining houses, torn them all down, and built yet another overlarge, too impressive residence; even in this unpretentious neighborhood, every square foot of land was valuable.

The little front porch was no more than a slab of flaking concrete with three cement steps leading up. The front door was painted a dark, sticky color undetectable in the night, sealed with a new hasp and padlock, courtesy of MPPD, where Emmylou had pried the old lock open. There was a small window at either side, but no cat door. Trotting around the side of the house, they pushed downhill through patches of thorny pyracantha bushes, moving to the back where the dropping lot allowed for a taller basement, enough space for another pair of small, dirty windows. Twelve wooden stairs led up to a wooden landing supported by four-by-four pillars. The steps smelled rank and wild. "Raccoons," they said together, hissing with disgust.

The back door was narrow, decorated with the same dark sticky paint. To the left, a cat door had been cut into the wall, a homemade affair closed by a flap of warped plywood hanging on rusty hinges. Raccoon fur was caught around the edge, where the beasts had pushed inside. "This," Joe said, "might not be such a breeze, if we corner one of those mothers in there."

"You want to leave? Wait until the department has a go? If they can get a search warrant. We could tell them we think maybe there might be a box hidden in there and maybe it contains information . . ."

"All right. Enough." Laying back his ears, he shoved beneath the plywood flap into the kitchen. The place stank of raccoons and, even more viral, it smelled of soured milk and spoiled food from the refrigerator. They paused, listening.

There was no sound, no scuffling or snarling as if they had surprised some rough-furred bandit. The linoleum was gritty beneath their paws, the floor scattered with kibble where the animals had torn open a large bag of dry cat food. A five-foot length of counter held the sink, its dark cabinets featuring the same sticky paint as the front and back doors. The ancient gas stove was small, round cornered, pale enamel with chrome trim, short curved legs and curved feet. It stank of old grease and of the gassy pilot light, those smells blending with the aroma of cat kibble and the stink of raccoon.

A cracked white bowl stood on a rubber mat just inside the cat door. It was empty, licked clean save for two muddy, long-toed pawprints marking the white interior. Together, the cats pawed the cupboards open.

Old dented pots and pans in the bottom, five cans of soup in the top cabinets, a bag of flour with bugs crawling out, and half a dozen ants wandering aimlessly as if discouraged in their hopeless scouting trip. The inside of one cupboard door held a row of cup hooks where Sammie had hung a beer opener, a flat grater, a key on a ring, a set of measuring spoons, and a little rusty strainer. The refrigerator, when Joe swung on the handle and kicked the door open, offered half a loaf of moldy bread, a bottle of curdled milk, a bowl of spaghetti green with mold, three rotten tomatoes. The freezer, the size of the glove compartment in a compact car, held two packs of rotten meat. Had Sammie neglected to pay her bills, even before she vanished? The power company, with so many folks moving away with rent and bills unpaid, had grown rather surly in such matters.

Moving into the front of the house, they found one long room, with a notch cut out for a bathroom that left a narrow sleeping alcove with a brown curtain drawn halfway across. The same dark walls as the kitchen.

A fusty gray carpet, gritty beneath their paws. Toppled stacks of newspapers cascaded against the furniture, some of the papers shredded among torn-apart paperback books. Had the raccoons done this? Or had someone else? Rumpled clothes were tossed across a fat, overstuffed couch and matching chair of undetermined color.

The room had four small windows, those each side of the front door, and two artlessly placed in the center of the side wall, half covered by graying lace curtains hanging crookedly. Sammie might have a roof over her head, in contrast to her wandering brother, but this environment seemed far more grim than his open roads. Beneath the smell of raccoons and the smell of dust came, faintly, the hint of young cats, an old and fading scent. No cats were visible. They started at floor level, scenting out like bloodhounds looking for the tin box, trying to pick up a whiff of water-soaked ashes, nosing into every pile of papers, old sweaters and rumpled T-shirts, feeling with careful paws for the smooth cold feel of metal. But only Joe thought the hunt might be worth the effort; Dulcie really didn't think Emmylou would have hidden Hesmerra's box in here, it didn't seem to her a safe place at all—if the papers *were* of any value.

The heavy sideboard and two end tables were coated with the same dark paint as the doors and kitchen cupboards. Had Sammie bought a barrel of the stuff and kept painting until it was all used up?

The receiver of the phone had miraculously remained in place but when Joe pushed it off and listened, the line was dead. With all the letters jammed in the mailbox, it was likely Sammie hadn't paid her bills; the phone company wasn't charitable about such oversights. The cats, prowling and poking, lost track of time as they dragged stacks of debris aside to search among the next layer. Together they fought out heavy drawers, looked under the couch and chairs, burrowed beneath the cushions, wondering what Emmylou *had* been doing in here. Outside the grimy windows, the pines pressed against the house heavy and dark, the night sky beyond forming small, pale islands between the shaggy limbs.

"This is dumb," Dulcie said. "Emmylou wouldn't hide anything in here. Why would she, when whoever was here might come back?"

Joe was silent, rummaging in the little closet. "Come smell this," he said, his voice muffled from beneath a bag spilling out old towels and linens. She bellied under, and then into the bag. Over the smell of very old cloth, she breathed in the scent of smoke and wet ashes.

But there was no box, nothing like hard metal beneath their seeking paws.

"If she did hide it there," Joe said, "then moved it again, why would she? Unless it *was* of value?"

"Well, it's gone now," Dulcie said crossly. "I just know, if we have to toss a house, I'd rather search anywhere else than this depressing mess. How could she live like this?" Lashing her tail, she looked down with disgust at the old metal vent set into the carpet. "Even the heat vents are rusty and dirty and . . ." She paused, and approached closer. She sniffed at the metal grid then backed off, making a flehmen face.

"What?" He was beside her in one leap, sniffing at the grid and then backing off, too, with the same grin of disgust.

She said, "Maybe it's a dead raccoon. Or . . . Oh, not one of the cats. One of Sammie's cats? Oh, the poor thing can't have gotten trapped down there, trapped under the house?"

"I don't know, Dulcie," he said impatiently. While the smell was certainly of something dead, of a body left to perish, the faint stink wafting up from the basement could be anything. Gopher? Ground squirrel? Dead dog?

But whatever it was that lay moldering down there, there was only one way to find out. "Come on," he said, and headed back through the kitchen, through the homemade cat door and out, to find a way underneath.

23

The wind had stilled as Joe and Dulcie prowled outside the house looking for a way into the dank cellar, to the source of the dead smell. The thin rain was sullen, and colder, hiding any hint of moon or stars. It was strange, fitful weather, its penetrating cold made them shiver and move closer together beneath the dense bushes; and even under the wet bushes the smell of death clung in their nostrils. Easing around to the far side of the house where they hadn't yet explored, where the land dropped down, they at last found a small door into the basement, a crude affair built of matching wooden siding and crowded by early-budding mock orange bushes whose sweet scent blended strangely with the stink of decay. The door was locked.

Leaping up, Joe pawed at the rusty hasp and padlock hoping the screws might be loose. He knew that, in his desire to get inside, he was destroying fingerprints with his grasping paws, but it couldn't be helped. He was fighting the lock when Dulcie said, "Wait, Joe. Come this way."

He could see only her backside, she was halfway under the house where the siding had rotted, leaving a ragged slit barely high enough for her to wriggle through. Joe dropped down, and joined her, pushing under, the wood so soft that pieces of desiccated siding clung to their fur as they bellied through into the dark, earthen cellar.

Drooping cobwebs hung down from the floor joists, so thick and long they brushed their ears. The dead smell led them into the blackness toward the front of the house, where the ground rose.

"If it is a human body," Joe said, "there's not much room for a cop to crawl back in there." In most of the cellar, there was hardly belly space for a cat. Only where a swale ran along between the rough wooden wall and the earth, was there room for a human to move, bent over. The thought of a human body stuffed up into that claustrophobic crawl space made Joe's fur rise along his back. Hard clods of dirt bit into their paws. Splintered scraps of wood and bent nails cut their pads, and the longest cobwebs clung to their whiskers like sticky tape. "This is what we do for entertainment?" Joe said.

"No. This is what we do because we can't help ourselves. Because we're cats. Because we're cursed with too damn much curiosity." She moved ahead of him into the blackness like a stalking tiger, every fiber honed to the quarry. He could see the ancient furnace deep in, a hulking black box sprouting fat pipes that led up through the floor, a squat, low affair beyond which Dulcie vanished.

Soon he could hear her digging. He picked out her dark shape, half hidden, clawing at the earth. How could she stand the stink? When she gave a sudden squeak and flew backward, he jumped nearly out of his skin.

When he pushed up against her, she was shivering. When he nosed at her, her paws smelled so bad he backed away. Hastily she pawed at fresher earth, trying to wipe the smell off, unwilling to lick her paws and force the taste into her mouth. "Fingers," she said, looking at him.

"Fingers?"

"Human fingers, Joe. A hand, an arm. I left them half buried. Let's get the hell out of here. We need to call the station."

They fled for the crack where icy air wafted in together with the clean cold smell of rain. This wasn't the first body they'd dealt with, they'd reported plenty of deaths over the years, but this one smelled the worst, sent them scrambling out beneath the rotted siding sucking fresh air and then racing straight up a juniper, inhaling its sharp, clean scent.

Only high in the branches did they stop, looking down, and consider the implications if they called the department. To report what appeared to be a murder, to report those frail skeletal fingers and arm—to try to explain how the department's two best snitches, supposedly human snitches, had "just happened on" a body buried in a space hardly high enough for a child, half hidden behind a furnace in a pitch-black cellar that could be entered only through a padlocked door.

Whatever they said, or didn't say, was going to generate any number of unanswerable questions. Queries to which they couldn't even imagine a believable reply. Uncomfortably they looked at each other, trying to figure out how to handle this new level of deceit, this even more complicated web of lies, to the very officers they wanted only to assist.

The rain had all but stopped, the drops seeming to have slowed until they were almost floating. The midnight village was wrapped in a strange silence, even the rhythm of the sea hushed. High in the hills, Kit could hear not even a passing car; no sound at all until suddenly a great horned owl boomed, too close to her. From her tree house she watched him descend above her and on down over the village gardens; he would be sensing the warmth of some small creature. *Not me,* Kit thought, *you won't take me, you daren't come in my tree house, you'd snatch nothing in here but a beakful of pillows—and my claws in your face.*

She and Lucinda and Pedric had been home from the Firettis' for nearly an hour but she couldn't sleep. She'd started out in the house on the bed between the old couple but she was too restless, too warm, her blood pounding too hard. Slipping down off the quilt to the floor, she'd trotted through the house to the dining room, leaped to the table, across to the sill, and pushed out through her cat door along the twisted oak in the icy night and into her tree house, where she'd burrowed deep beneath the pillows.

She listened in the silence until another owl answered from farther up the hill; she thought about Pan, and that was why she couldn't sleep and her claws kneaded sharply into the pillows. She thought how the firelight glanced off his red coat, thought about his travels, thought how she and Pan had listened together to Misto's tales. Pondering the stories and adventures of both tomcats, she grew so restless that at last she left her warm cushions, too, scrambled down out of her oak tree, and raced across the neighbors' yards until, where the houses rose closer together, she hit the roofs again. Putting the call of the owls behind her, farther and farther behind her, she prowled the roofs above the village shops, scrambled over peaks and dormers feeling bold and wild, looking into second-floor penthouses, trotting, racing, stopping again to peer into the rooms of strangers. She looked into Erik Kraft's elegant penthouse, slipping under the terrace wall. It still looked neat and unlived in, the bedroom elegantly furnished and totally unused. Quilted black bedspread made up just so, thick black towels folded perfectly on the shelf in the master bath, one black towel perfectly aligned on the rod, as neat as if a decorator had placed it there. Even the white ceramic drinking glass and tray by the basin were placed just so.

It hadn't been so neat when he was in town; then, looking in, you'd see his clothes dropped here and there, and often a woman's things, sleek nightgown, satin slippers tossed under the bed, a mess of jars and tubes on the bathroom counter—Alain, she supposed, or maybe some other woman; human men were so fickle.

She prowled until her paws felt like ice cubes and then she spun around and headed for home. She was freezing when at last she clambered up her own oak tree and back under her own soft pillows, just her nose and face sticking out where she could see the street and yards below. From her high vantage she sighed once, purred twice, and was nearly asleep when she saw, down on the street, Emmylou's old car moving slowly along. What was she doing out at this hour? Looking for a place to park for the night? Somewhere the cops wouldn't hassle her?

Strange old woman, Kit thought, very independent even with the law. She guessed Emmylou didn't like the cops or anyone else telling her what to do—didn't like to be bossed around, any more than a cat did. Maybe in ancient times, Kit thought, letting her imagination run, maybe Emmylou would have been a homeless loner then, too, always at odds with the world, an outcast faring no better, then, out in the cold looking for a place to rest and get warm.

Rambling along in her old Chevy, with the heater turned on full blast, easing along beside the village shops looking in their softly lit windows at wares she couldn't buy, Emmylou at last turned up into the narrow residential streets, to find a place to park. But she stopped now and then where a living room light burned, sat watching the flicker of firelight against drawn curtains, imagining the cozy room within. Then, moving on, she tried to think what she should do; she had to find a job but she so hated the regimentation. She'd tried, at three groceries, to get on as a bagger, had filled out applications, left her name, but no one needed her. Maybe, like others down on their luck, she should steal just a little, just enough to get by, if she could do it without getting caught.

The cops were right, she *had* meant to stay at Sammie's. Until she saw the mess, until she thought someone had been in there—or some*thing*. Something she didn't want to share a bed with. She'd hidden the metal box there earlier, but then had gone back to retrieve it. The trashed house had frightened her so that, even if the cops stopped watching the place, she wouldn't go back inside.

Earlier in the evening, driving around looking for Sammie's cats as well as for a place to get warm, she'd stopped outside Dr. John Firetti's clinic, thinking about her own cats. Wondering if they were still there, if she could get them back when she did find a place, or if he had already found homes for them.

Maybe better homes than she could give them. He'd known when he questioned her that she was lying about their shots, but he'd been willing to help them anyway. She liked him for that. The clinic complex was a hodgepodge affair, the two small cottages joined by the big solarium and then, across a little patch of lawn, the doctor's own small cottage. Two outdoor lamps burned in the yard, their glow smeared by rain, lighting the way between the house and clinic. Neat flower beds flanked the front door, and through the shuttered windows the undulating light of a hearth fire gave her a sharp jolt of loneliness. Listening through the car's open window, she caught soft laughter, a happy sound that twisted at her and made her move on, feeling left out, knowing she wouldn't be wanted there.

Chilled by loneliness as much as by the icy night, she headed up among the winding hillside streets where the cottages were crowded close and the streets didn't have parking limits, where if she could find an empty spot among the residents' own cars, she could safely stay the night. She was searching for a parking place, thinking the cops didn't usually bother a person up here, when a black-and-white approached her from the rear, startling her, coming fast, its tires throwing up sheets of water. Slowing, she pulled over. What did *they* want? They had no reason to follow her, no reason to hassle her.

But the squad car didn't slow, it sped on past, and another behind it, and then two civilian cars, all of them heading straight up the hill—in the direction of Sammie's neighborhood. She looked after them with unease.

But hundreds of people lived up there, in those little pocket neighborhoods separated by ravines or outcroppings of boulders too rugged to build on. Why would she think they were headed for Sammie's? They had no reason to go to Sammie's, she was worrying for nothing.

She was just tired, exhaustion always left her edgy and nervous. Turning onto a short dead end, she found a parking place no one else had wanted, really only a swale, a runoff that directed rushing rainwater down into a little ravine, sheltered by a dripping willow so her car would be nearly hidden.

She backed parallel into that portion of curb, her front and back wheels straddling the low dip. She locked her doors, rolled up her windows to just a crack. Crawled over into the backseat, stacked the bags and boxes on the floor as she did every night, to make a flat surface. Shook out her blankets and quilt and pulled them around her. The backseat still smelled of ashes from Hesmerra's metal box. Hesmerra had called it her safe, and she'd been partially right. It wasn't insulated like a fire safe, but the metal had been enough to protect the papers from the dampness of the earth where it was buried; and the earth in turn had protected it from the fire.

The problem now was, should she take it to the police, or keep the papers to herself as Hesmerra had done? Maybe at some future time, she thought uneasily, the papers would serve as a payback? A payback for Hesmerra's death?

"And what," Joe said, stretching out along the juniper branch where the rain didn't reach, "what do I tell the department? I just happened to crawl under Sammie Davis's deserted house? I, a grown human, just happened to squeeze through a space not big enough for a miniature Chihuahua?"

"Tell them . . . that the cellar door was standing open and you smelled something. *I* can't call, they might think it's Emmylou. She's been in that house, nosing around. That would sure make her a person of interest."

"Maybe she *is* a person of interest. I have to tell them the cellar door was open, how else would the killer, or the snitch, get in? So how come it's locked now? What, I tell them I locked it when I left, after discovering the body? Oh, right."

"We'll have to unlock it," she said sensibly.

"You're going to pick the lock. Like some trick movie cat? Jimmy the lock with your clever little claws."

She narrowed her green eyes at him, the tip of her tabby tail twitching. "Maybe that's what the key in the kitchen was for. You think? It looked like a padlock key." Scrambling backward down the tree, she disappeared around the corner, was up the back steps in an instant and in through the cat door, leaving the little square of plywood banging in Joe's face.

This was a long shot, but who knew? Joe watched her leap to the counter and open the cupboard, watched her ease the key off its hook with a delicate paw, trying not to smear any existing fingerprints. Maybe the killer had used this key. Or not, Joe thought. Maybe he had a key of his own. Either way, they didn't need paw prints. Cat prints might be just as unique as human fingerprints, if any of the three detectives decided to follow a hunch and check out the markings they found.

So far, they had been lucky no one had thought to compare paw prints found at a scene, with prints an officer could lift within the department itself. Joe imagined Juana or Dallas offering them little treats, and then restraining them long enough to ink their paws, to produce a set of fingerprint cards that would go into the office files. The idea gave him chills. Could he get used to wearing gloves? Pulling on little cat mittens?

Dulcie, taking the key carefully in her teeth, dropped to the floor looking smug, and they beat it out again, down the steps and around to the cellar door. Carefully Joe took it from her, and climbed up through the brittle branches of the nearest bush, trying not to drool, not get the key wet and slippery. Clinging within the bush, he found a steady position and pulled the lock to him with a careful paw.

Holding it steady, turning his head at an angle, he tried to ease the key in. Just a little finesse, and he'd . . .

He dropped it.

Silently Dulcie retrieved it, and climbed up through the bush; he took it, and tried again, but it wouldn't go. He turned his head, adjusted his balance. Another try, but it didn't fit. This wasn't the right key. Ears back, he tried forcing it, but still it wouldn't go. He turned around in the branches, poised to leap down.

"Try again, Joe. Is the lock rusty?"

Of course it was rusty. This baby'd been out in the weather since locks were invented.

"Take your time," she said. "Try just once more." In the female mind, any impossible problem can be solved with sufficient patience. Ducking lower, he tried again, bowing his back so the key wasn't angled, giving it a straighter approach.

Nothing. Nada.

"Turn it over."

He'd already tried that. It wouldn't fit. He couldn't talk with his mouth full, couldn't even hiss at her. He was fighting it, the metal hard against his teeth, when he dropped it again. Dulcie gave him a look, dove into the bushes, rustled around, and came out with the key safe between her teeth.

Motioning with her head for him to get down, she climbed, silent and quick. Around them, the rain had quickened again, they were both soaking wet, the raindrops on Dulcie's back pale and icy. His paws felt like blocks of ice. Above him Dulcie was fiddling and fussing as she eased the key up to the lock. Females were so nitpicky, not direct like a tomcat.

Within minutes she had it open. With a quick paw she pulled the padlock off, let it fall, the key still protruding, a rustle and dull thud as it dropped to the ground among the bushes.

She didn't brag or tease him. "What shall we do with it?"

"Lose the key, keep the lock. If anyone else knows the key was inside the locked house, that leads right back to Emmylou. Maybe she's innocent," he said doubtfully. "Maybe she's not." He watched Dulcie remove the key and, with it safe between her teeth, they scrambled up the nearest pine and headed across the roofs.

They carried it six blocks away where two steep peaks angled together, and tucked it down beneath the overlapped shingles. Then shoulder to shoulder they headed for Dulcie's cottage, and a phone.

"I just hope Wilma's asleep, we don't need to drag her into this, in the middle of the night."

"You don't want to listen to her scold," Joe said, grinning. Though, in fact, Dulcie's housemate was as tolerant of the cats' involvement with the law as a human could be. Wilma had been, for twenty-five years, a federal parole officer, she knew very well the intense fascination of sorting out a crime, she knew how it felt to be deeply involved with a case.

But that didn't stop her from worrying, she knew the disasters, too. She worried because they were small and vulnerable, and because they were, in her opinion, far too brash and bold. Worry made her overprotective, and so she fussed at them. Joe followed Dulcie in through her cat door, stopping midway to ease the plastic flap down along his back, to keep it from swinging, thump, thump, and waking Wilma. She slept attuned to that sound, to any small noise that would herald Dulcie's return home.

Crossing the laundry, they left wet paw prints on the blue kitchen floor, left a wet trail across the oriental rug in the dining room, and when Joe leaped to Wilma's desk, again a damp row of prints incised across the blotter. As he pawed at the phone's speaker, pressing the arrow down until the sound was as soft as it would go, Dulcie slipped down the hall to the bedroom, peering in, to make sure Wilma was asleep.

Yes, she slept, breathing deeply, her back to the phone on the night table. Dulcie, watching her, decided she really was asleep and not faking, that she wouldn't see the phone's flashing light. Trotting back through the dim house and leaping to the desk, she watched Joe key in 911 and prayed, as she always did, that Wilma's ID blocking was working as it should. She'd heard a number of stories where the service had failed, incidents too alarming to bear thinking of, at that moment.

The night dispatcher came on, a young man they didn't know well. Joe asked for the chief or whichever detective was on duty.

"If this is not an emergency, you—" the dispatcher began.

"It *is* an emergency. Do it *now*. Max will be mad as hell if you fool around. And no, I won't give my name. Just *do* it!" There was a short silence, then Kathleen Ray came on. She knew his voice, she didn't interrupt as he described the location and probable condition of the body.

"In the crawl space of a dark cellar? How did you find that?"

"I was walking my dog, he smelled something. The body must be pretty rank."

"You crawled back in there, to look?"

Joe went silent, and clicked off. "Does she have to be so damned nosy?"

"She's a police detective. That's her job."

He hissed at her companionably and they waited, listening, looking out at the cold night. The raindrops had turned suspiciously white and slushy. Dulcie said, "It's going to snow."

Joe turned, gave her a look. "Snow. Right. Since when did it snow on the central coast?"

But even through the glass, the night felt cold enough to freeze the rain solid. They were peering out when a lone siren cut through the silence from the direction of the station: one whoop, like a squad car clearing traffic as it sped away. They imagined the black-and-white moving fast through the village followed by another and maybe by Kathleen's white Ford two-door. Dropping from the desk, they slipped quickly out of the house, scrambled to the roofs again through the rain, which was heavier now, almost sleeting, and they followed where they knew the cop car was headed. The immediacy of the police response took precedence over the cold, over their sharp hunger, and over their need for sleep—even over their caution to remain unnoticed at the soon-to-be-busy crime scene.

24

Wilma was awake when the cats quietly left the house. She'd heard them come in just moments earlier, the faint brush as they slipped through the cat door, and she'd thought Dulcie was in for the night. But then when Dulcie didn't trot in to leap on the bed, and she heard Joe's soft voice from the living room, she'd rolled over to look at the phone.

With the red light for the main line flashing, she knew the phantom snitches were at work, calling the department, she knew the scenario too well. She hadn't dared turn on her speaker to listen in, the little click would have alerted them at once. Swinging out of bed, shivering even in her flannel gown, she'd slipped barefoot to the bedroom door and listened, only mildly ashamed of herself. She could hear the faintest mumble, not Dulcie's voice, but Joe's, serious and urgent, too faint to make out a word he was saying.

She daren't slip closer, they'd hear even the faintest brush of her gown against the wall or door, or would scent her approach. The next moment, the whoop of a siren rose from the center of the village, a squad car leaving the station. How cold the night had grown, her bare feet were freezing. She'd stayed by the bedroom door debating whether to go on out, but then she heard them leave as stealthily as they'd entered. Searching for her slippers, she pulled them on and went up the hall to the living room, turned on the desk lamp, and hit the redial button.

The number 911 came on the screen, and quickly she clicked off.

She couldn't ask the dispatcher what was happening. How would *she* know they'd just received a tip from the snitches? That lone siren could have been a patrol unit pulling over a speeding driver, but from the cats' stealth and haste, she didn't think so. Something was happening out in the night, and she knew she wouldn't sleep again. Wide awake, she turned out the lamp and pulled the curtain aside.

The rain had turned to slush, the cold was as sharp as knives. Closing the curtain again, she moved into the kitchen, flipped on the light over the sink, got the milk from the refrigerator, and a saucepan, and made a cup of cocoa. Carrying it back to bed, she opened the curtain, then tucked up under the covers, getting warm as she sipped her cocoa and looked out at the night. The slushy rain was falling more slowly, in a strange, drifting pattern.

She sat up straighter when she realized it was snowing, small flakes floating beyond the glass. Snow, here on the coast. And the weatherman apparently hadn't had a clue.

This hadn't happened in a decade, smatterings of snow in the village, deeper drifts up in the surrounding hills, an amazement that had brought the whole village out to look. There were newspaper articles in the library's local history collection, pictures of heavy snow some fifty years ago when, one article said, Molena Point High School students abandoned their cars to throw snowballs in the drifts, getting to class hours late. That was the year that the steepest grades were too icy to drive on, and the Bing Crosby Pro-Am Golf Tournament was postponed because the golf course was covered with snow. The newspaper pictures made the higher elevations look like ski country, hills and roads solid white, roofs and the tops of the fence posts heaped with snow. The papers said that all day a steady stream of drivers headed up the valley to have a look and take photos.

And now here it was again. The real thing. She imagined the village waking in the morning to a white world, everyone running outdoors, excited by the novelty.

But right now, tonight, the two cats were out in it freezing their busy little paws. If they had alerted a patrol car, you could bet they were headed back to the scene, to whatever violence had occurred, that they'd be in the middle of the action, peering down from some freezing rooftop into the glare of strobe lights, hardly able to hear the officers' voices for the harsh radio's grainy insistence. Two little cats out in the icy night with no thought to frozen ears, their entire attention on the investigation unfolding below them.

It seemed so long ago that Dulcie was just a giddy kitten, with no thought to human crime, human evil, and with no notion of her true talents.

Though even then, that tiny little thing was strange and different. So covetous, for one thing, stealing the neighbors' sheer stockings and bright scarves right through their bedroom windows, even then a clever little break-and-enter artist. And look at her now, a bold, grown-up, crime-solving lady, too often wired for trouble.

The day Dulcie first spoke, that was a shock to them both, had left them both shaken, staring at each other,

Dulcie's green eyes huge with amazement, Wilma trembling as if with vertigo. Dulcie's disbelief had made her laugh, and hearing her own human laugh, she was startled all over again.

And now, besides her aggressive fascination with village crime, look what else the feisty little tabby was up to. She was suddenly filled with poetry, caught up in a whole new obsession, *"What a lovely cat she is, Posed behind the curtain's gauze..."* And tonight, when Wilma stopped by the library after leaving the Damens', and had turned on the computer, she found a new poem waiting. She hoped this was only the first verse, only the beginning, because it did make her smile.

> *All along the cliff top blowing*
> *She stalks her prey in grasses growing*
> *Forest tall and thick above her*
> *Quick and silent feline hunter*
> *Queen of the high sea meadow*

She thought there would surely be more verses, that Dulcie might even be toying with the lines as she crouched beside Joe out in the freezing night, watching the police at work. She longed to follow them, but sensibly she ignored the urge, finished her cocoa and set the mug aside. She drew the curtain again and switched on the lamp, dispelling the comfortable dark, and reached for her book. Sliding deeper under the covers, she read for the rest of the night, or tried to. Even through the book's gripping mystery she kept seeing the cats out in the cold, seeing the squad cars, the busy officers, wondering which detective had come out, which officers were on duty, all of them illuminated in theatrical unreality by the harsh strobe lights; she kept wondering what had happened to bring them out, what *was* happening, called out by the phantom snitches.

The cottage roof next door to Sammie's was quickly growing white with snow, and the cats' backs and noses were dusted with snow. This wasn't a five-minute flurry, destined soon to melt away again, this snow was building, it was clinging, it seemed to be serious. The harsh lights below them picked out each drifting flake, and reflected from the cops' slickers, and from the snow-covered patrol cars. One black-and-white was parked just below them in the side yard, one out at the curb beside Kathleen's white Ford. In the drifting snow, two officers were stringing crime-scene tape; they had already cordoned off the open cellar door, which spilled light out into the yard brightening each drifting snowflake. Only a few minutes ago,

Detective Kathleen Ray had gone down into the cellar alone, carrying more lights and her black crime-scene bag. "Where's Davis?" Dulcie said.

"Her knee's worse," Joe said. "I heard Brennan talking, said it was swollen twice its size, said she was meeting the doctor at his office. Brennan says she'll probably have to have a knee replacement." Dulcie shuddered, she didn't like to think about surgery. When Wilma had had gall bladder surgery, that was bad enough, she'd worried herself into a frazzle until her housemate was healed and well again. Below, more lights came on in the cellar as Kathleen got to work. The tall, slim brunette had arrived dressed in jeans and a yellow slicker, her long dark hair stuffed up under a yellow cap. Entering the cellar, she had pulled on cloth booties over her running shoes. She reached out the door twice as Officer Crowley handed her additional lights and her camera bag. Kathleen was, in Joe Grey's opinion, too beautiful to be crawling around in the dirt, crawling back under there into that putrid stink.

"*I* crawled in," Dulcie said. "You didn't worry about *me* spoiling *my* looks, or gassing myself or getting splinters in my paws."

"You're tougher than a human woman," Joe said, cutting her a look. "And far too beautiful to ever spoil your looks, even with dirt in your fur."

They could see into the cellar for only a little ways, could see, in the painfully bright lights, deep marks in the earth where the body had been dragged in. Kathleen hunkered along at the side, away from these. Twice she paused to look at Dulcie's paw prints, and both times, she'd photographed them. The first time, she had called out to the waiting officers to ask if Sammie had cats.

"Did she have to notice that?" Dulcie said.

"Of course she'd notice, that's her job," he said smartly.

Officer Brennan, looking like a tent with legs in his wide black slicker, had said Sammie had two cats, that when they found Emmylou Warren in the house she said she had come up to feed them, said she couldn't find them. Kathleen had nodded, and disappeared. There'd been a long silence in which they imagined her inching her way back toward the furnace, placing her lights as she went.

They imagined her finding the partially buried fingers, envisioned her carefully uncovering them until she had, like Dulcie, revealed the buried hand and arm; she would photograph them, and photograph the surround. She would be kneeling on a small sheet of plastic, and as she resumed digging, she would brush away a few grains of earth at a time with a soft paintbrush.

To find what? Only the hand and arm? Or the murder victim? Was this Sammie Miller? And, beneath this bloated but intact body, what would she find to account for the far more sick-making smell that seemed to come from underneath?

Sounds were becoming muffled as the snow accumulated. On the snowy roof, the two cats huddled together shivering as the temperature dropped degree by falling degree. Dulcie hoped Wilma's garden wouldn't freeze, she hoped Wilma wasn't out there in her slippers and robe, covering her prize plants with newspapers and old sheets.

In the cellar, the position of the lights changed again and again, coming from different angles as Kathleen photographed the grave. They heard her talking on her cell phone, there was a little silence when the call ended, then the lift of her voice as she made a second call. At the third call, Dulcie eased forward. "Maybe I can just slip in and listen."

"No way," Joe said, hauling her back with a nip to the butt that got him a swat on the nose. "You want to get caught in there? She's already wondering about the paw prints."

Sighing, she settled back, pawing snow off her ears. Silence again, only the soft mutter of the police radios. Kathleen would have a black-and-white camera in there, one for color, and a video. She would already have photographed the drag marks and, who knew, maybe she'd found a trace of the killer's footprints. By the time Dallas Garza's tan Blazer pulled up next to Kathleen's car, Sammie's yard and drive were more white than brown, and the pines and cypress trees looked like a Yosemite postcard.

Dallas stepped out of the Blazer looking as if he had just rolled out of bed, his heavy boots pulled over the gray sweats he might have slept in, his black slicker hanging crookedly, his short dark hair mussed from sleep. Walking the narrow path between two barriers of yellow tape, to the lighted cellar door, he knelt down, looking in, touching nothing as he talked with Kathleen.

"We have a body," she said. "Smells like more than one. I called the state forensics lab, two techs are on the way. We'll have another in the morning, and possibly their entomologist. And I called Ryan. I'm thinking we could cut away the outside wall nearest the grave, give them space to work, room to move back and forth, and get the body out without trampling the surround."

Dallas considered this, and nodded.

Atop the roof, Dulcie said, "Working in there, with that stink, has to be like working right inside the grave. Why does anyone do that, why do people choose this kind of work?"

"The need to know," Joe said. "Why are we here freezing our butts and starving? You ever think what life would be like, if no one went after the bad guys?"

Dulcie sneezed. "So, all this work, and the courts let half of them loose again."

Joe didn't have an answer to that. They were licking snow from their fur when Ryan's red king cab came up the street. Parking just beyond the squad cars, she moved down along the house following the officers' footsteps on the narrow, muddied path between the yellow tape. Crouching beside her uncle Dallas, she peered in. The conversation came in snatches as they considered ways to keep the scene from being trampled and contaminated by sawdust as she removed a portion of the wall.

"I can prefabricate a frame," she said, "then bolt it together inside the cellar, a barrier between the basement wall and the grave. Staple a sheet of plastic to it, seal off the site before we start the tearout."

Dallas nodded. "That should contain the debris, keep it off the surround and body." They discussed the details of the construction, then he headed around the house to the front, to work the scene inside. Joe wanted to follow him, but there was a limit to how much they could push. Cats in the office. Paw prints at the scene. Cats following him around that little crowded space inside wouldn't be a good idea. Dulcie said, "I'm freezing and I'm starving, and there won't be much more action for a couple of hours, until the techs get here."

He looked at her like she was abandoning the mission.

"Even then," she said, "it could take them the rest of the night to free the body, bag the evidence underneath, take samples, get the corpse onto a gurney. And maybe have to dig out a second body. While we freeze our tails and starve, and then they're off to the lab, and we don't know any more than we do now."

"I guess," he said reluctantly. If he'd been alone he'd have stayed all night, hungry and cold or not. But he saw how cold she was, her ears down, her tail tight around her, trying not to shiver, and he knew she needed breakfast and a warm bed. "I guess they won't bring the first body out until daylight," he said. Another patrol car had arrived with two officers to help secure the scene if onlookers or the press began to gather. Maybe, with the amazement of snow, the villagers' attention would be elsewhere. As the officers worked, one or another would look up at the falling snow, look around at the white yard, the accumulating snow weighting down the trees, and they'd start to grin. Snow, and it was nearly Valentine's Day.

Nearly Valentine's Day, Joe thought, nearly Ryan and Clyde's first anniversary. And here Ryan was, pulled out of bed on a freezing morning to work in the middle of a foul-smelling murder scene—plus, the happy couple was saddled with Debbie Kraft, whining to be taken care of. He looked at Dulcie again, at the way she was shivering. "Let's cut out of here, my ears are freezing off." He looked toward Ryan's truck. "If we hurry, we can hitch a ride." They were poised to drop down the nearest tree and race to the truck bed when Ryan turned away from the cellar, headed for her king cab to go gather the materials she'd need, and swung in. The cats were halfway down the tree when she started the engine, and backed out and pulled away.

Hadn't she seen them? It had looked as if, when she glanced in her side mirror, she was looking right at them. "Well, hell," Joe said. Sopping wet and cold, they looked after her longingly, then took off across rooftops, bounding like rabbits in the cover of snow. Hadn't she guessed they'd be there? Who did she think called in the report? When she was summoned out of her warm bed, didn't she wonder why Joe didn't come bolting down from his tower? Where did she think he was, but already at the scene? When she saw it was snowing, didn't she worry about her poor little cat, out in the freezing night? And where was Clyde? Still home in bed sound asleep and not a worry in his thick skull? Humping across the white roofs beside Dulcie, freezing his paws, he had worked himself almost into a temper when, two blocks from the crime scene, they saw the red king cab parked at the curb, the engine running, its exhaust flume rising white on the cold air.

Ryan was standing out on the curb, looking up.

Within seconds they were inside, snuggled warm against her, drenching her jeans and her red leather seats as they licked their sopping fur. Heading down the hill, she looked over at them with a little smile. "How did you explain to the dispatcher that you just happened on a buried body in the back of a deep crawl space, in the middle of the night?"

"I didn't," Joe said. "I hung up."

"Three squad cars," she said, "six uniforms and two detectives, the San Jose techs on their way down that icy freeway, a contractor called out in the middle of the night. All of this, Joe, hanging on one short, unidentified phone call." She looked at him and smiled and shook her head. "So how *did* you find the body?"

"A little break-and-enter," Dulcie said innocently. "From there, one thing just led to another."

Ryan sighed, reached in the backseat, found a towel ripe with the smell of dog, and dropped it over them. "I guess the department has decided not to ask questions, just to be thankful for what they get." Letting the truck ease over an icy patch without touching her brakes, she coasted to the curb in front of Dulcie's house.

The front windows were dark. But they could smell smoke from the woodstove, and could see a light at the back, glancing up the hill, so Wilma would be awake in bed, reading. "Awake and worrying," Dulcie said guiltily.

Ryan reached over the cats, opened the passenger door, watched Dulcie streak for the house and vanish through the plastic flap. When she looked down at Joe, he was laughing. "What?"

"She'll climb in bed ice-cold and sopping wet, push right in against Wilma."

That, in fact, wasn't a bad idea. Snuggle up next to Clyde, thaw his frozen paws on Clyde's warm, bare back.

Ryan scowled at him. "You can do what you're thinking, Joe. Shock him out of a nice sleep—and go to your own bed hungry. Or you can endure the hair dryer to get warm, and finish up the fillet I saved for you, from supper."

Well, hell. What choice did a little cat have? "Rare?" he asked.

"Of course, rare," she said. "With a side of kippers on a warm plate."

And that, of course, was no contest.

25

The Harpers kept the barn closed up at night, the big doors at both ends drawn shut against the wind and cold, and against predators, two-legged or four. Now in the early dawn, the alleyway was dim, but the light was strange, unnaturally pale. Billy woke in his box stall to a glow more white than shadowed, white light seeping in above the stall door, and the air was freezing. His face and hands were icy while the rest of him was too hot. Six cats were piled on top of him, and one curled up between his shoulder and chin, all seven snuggled close trying to keep warm. Sliding his hands under them, he luxuriated in their body heat and warm fur. For a moment, he didn't know where he was. He wasn't in his own bed on the thin pad through which you could feel the rough slats, this bed was soft, and saggy in the middle, and he was tucked between real sheets, smooth and smelling of laundry soap, and the blanket was soft and thick, too. And the air—the cold air didn't stink of whiskey and throw-up, it smelled of horses and of fresh, sweet hay. All this in an instant, and then he sat up spilling cats every which way, realizing he was in the Harpers' barn.

He swung out of bed, and stood looking out through the hinged mesh barrier that formed the top half of the stall door. Down at the end of the alley, the light seeping in around the big doors was bright white, the faint movement of air freezing cold. The horses were stirring in their stalls, restless and wanting breakfast. When he turned to look at the cats, they were hungry, too, all seven lined up in a row, now, waiting to be fed—but they, too, were puzzled by the light, they sat glancing up at the door and up at the ceiling, watching a shaft of white light that fingered through, where the timbers joined the wall. Striped Sam, and black Lulu, they were Gran's favorites. He thought of Gran and felt his stomach go hollow. The image would never be gone, Gran lying dead on that stretcher, her charred body, his not wanting this to be real, wanting it not to have happened, wanting to believe that such a thing couldn't happen.

He had seen the fire as he came up the highway, pumping hard up the steep hill, saw the EMT van turn in and had raced to catch up, raced behind in its cloud of dust down the dirt lane, saw the fire truck and cop cars and felt his stomach turn hollow. Like he felt now, hollow and sick. Gran on the stretcher, her clothes and skin burned black. They had pulled him away, wouldn't let him near, he couldn't touch her. She was gone, she wasn't his gran anymore, she was a foreign thing. He had stood by the wet, black timbers, the live red coals, the smoke and steam and the stink of burning rags, trying to understand that Gran was dead, stood there until the hollow sickness in his belly made him retch and turn away.

But then later a jolt of something else hit him and he was immediately ashamed. Part of him felt *free*. Free of Gran's drinking, of dragging himself awake in the middle of the night to hold a bucket so she could throw up, free of cleaning up after her and cleaning her up, having to change her nightie and get her back into her bed. He hated trying to clean up the rough wood floor, you could never scrub that stuff out, never get the smell out, the place always stank of throw-up. And then every night when she went off to work, seeming to be sober, worrying she'd have a wreck, get hurt, or hurt or kill someone else.

Now he was free. So free he felt like running, like he could fly, he was free of an old woman who refused to take care of herself, refused to take any responsibility for what she did to them both.

He loved Gran, but even right after she died, right after the fire, the burst of lightness and freedom inside him had felt pretty damn good.

Did you burn in hell for such thoughts?

The bag of kibble stood on a cardboard box that Charlie had brought in for him to use as a table. He poured the dry food into the cats' dishes, set them on the hard dirt floor, and the cats dove in growling softly at each other. No one tried stealing, they were pretty good about that. Out in the stable, Charlie's sorrel mare nickered for her hay and banged the door, and the two big dogs, who were shut loose in the alleyway at night, stood up on their hind legs, their front paws on the stall door, looking in. Both were fawn colored, they were litter brothers, Charlie had said, most likely of a Great Dane mother and maybe fathered by a German shepherd. Both were huge and ungainly and still acted like puppies, until Charlie or Max took a hand with them. After the fire, Charlie had shown him the smoke alarm that was wired from the barn to the house, and the speaker that, if there was trouble, if there was fire or a break-in, would let her and Captain Harper hear the dogs barking.

Opening the stall door, he pushed the dogs back, stroking and pummeling them, and stepped out into the alleyway. Moving out between the two rows of stalls past the restless horses, he approached the barn door with curiosity, where the white streaks of light shot in.

When he slid it open, the yard was white around him, the pastures white, the far hills, the roof of the house, the tops of the cars, all white, snow piled up in a white dazzle, snow on the sills of the bay window framing the lighted kitchen where he could see Charlie inside, getting breakfast.

The dogs had already bolted past him bouncing and barking and biting at the snow. Still wearing the old sweatsuit he slept in, he ran to join them and pummeled and pelted them with snow, rolled in the snow with them, laughing as they barked. Not in his whole life had he ever seen snow, only in pictures in books. He played in the snow with the dogs until he was freezing and soaking wet and then turned back inside the barn to get dry. He put on his day clothes, and fed the horses, measuring the grain carefully, following Charlie's instructions, flaking off just the right amount of hay for each, filling their buckets with clean water. By the time he'd turned the horses out into the pasture and cleaned their stalls, the smell of bacon and pancakes was nearly more than he could stand. The two big dogs had long since gone in the house, and as he headed across the yard he could see Max Harper at the table hurriedly eating his breakfast, as if something pressing was pulling him away.

The minute Billy pushed into the warm kitchen, Charlie dished up his plate. Even as he pulled off his boots, Max gulped the last of his coffee and was up and headed for the door.

"A murder victim found last night," Charlie said when he'd hurried away to his truck. "An old murder." She said no more and he didn't like to ask. The thought of murder made him queasy. She moved to the bay window, stood looking out at the white world, the snow-deep pasture. "Who would have imagined?" She watched her mare shying at the snow and acting silly, and Max's buckskin gelding pawing at the white stuff with his usual single-minded determination, as if to clear the world of this unwanted intrusion. The kitchen table was piled with papers and flyers where she'd been working on the Cat Rescue Auction. A stack of posters lay on the sideboard showing pictures of three rescued cats, with a list of the donations to be auctioned: a weekend for two at the fancy Molena Inn, six months' housecleaning service, a year's car maintenance donated by Clyde Damen, three of Charlie's original etchings of dogs and horses and two paintings. The impressive list went on and on down the page, making

Billy wonder what he'd bid on if he had any money for such luxuries. Sitting down at the table, he reached for the syrup and butter, spread his pancakes liberally and began to shovel in breakfast.

Emmylou woke stiff and uncomfortable, bent nearly double in the too-short backseat. No matter how long she slept in the car, she couldn't get used to not stretching out. She had pulled all the blankets over her, but still she was cold. What time was it? Her watch said seven, barely dawn, but a curious white light shone in, pale and icy. Rising up holding the blankets close around her, she peered out.

The world was white. The ground and roofs white, the tree branches patched with white, snow stuck to the car windows. *Snow.* In Molena Point, that wasn't possible. But during the night it had snowed. The very fact of it made her joints ache.

Snow was fine if you had a warm little house and a fire on the hearth, a hot shower, something warm to eat and drink. She had none of these comforts, and she was damned cold. And soon she'd have to leave even this poor nest, before people came out and saw her, she'd have to get back in the cold driver's seat and move the car before some do-gooder reported a homeless woman camping on the street and the damned cops hauled her in.

She longed for a hot shower. Longed to be inside a warm house with the furnace turned up all the way and maybe a blaze on the hearth, too, and a nice hot cup of tea. And the only place was Sammie's.

Yesterday, she hadn't thought to see if Sammie's power was on, hadn't had time before the law showed up. Even if the heat wasn't on, the house would be warmer than outdoors, and there was the fireplace.

Slipping to one end of the backseat, she folded her covers neatly. Laying them over the bags and boxes, she thought about Hesmerra—wouldn't she have been amazed at the snow. Waking with her usual hangover, she'd look outdoors, startled, and then turn the old stove up high and call across the yard to her, tell her it was snowing, tell her to come on over for coffee and they'd fry up some breakfast.

Hesmerra would do that, would have done that. She thought about Hesmerra dead, maybe poisoned, and a sick reality filled her, she couldn't really believe Hesmerra had been poisoned. By whose hand?

But Hesmerra was dead, and Sammie had disappeared. And the fact that the two events were related was her secret.

Even the fact that that Realtor's house stood empty, up there so close above Sammie's, that could be a part of it, too. All a part of what Sammie knew.

Shivering, she crawled over into the front seat and, on the third try, started the engine. She let it idle a while, the poor thing was as cold and stiff as she was herself. She backed out clumsily from the swale, the water in it running fast enough to keep from freezing solid, and she headed up the hill toward Sammie's. Despite whoever or whatever had made the mess in there, despite what she knew that no one else knew, it was the only place she could think of to get warm. If the cops weren't nosing around again, if the cops would leave her alone.

She drove slowly, didn't use her brakes, or barely touched them in little feathery motions, staying in the tracks of other cars, which had crushed the snow and ice to slush. She drove the last two blocks within the wide prints of some heavy vehicle, but when she came in sight of Sammie's she stopped suddenly, braking in spite of herself, skidding sideways into the snowy berm.

There were cops all over. A black-and-white sitting in the side yard, two more in front parked beside a couple of civilian cars with bubble gum lights attached to the top. A white van with the logo of the state of California. Whatever this was, it wasn't good, she guessed those patrol cars last night *had* been headed up here.

She could see where they'd cut a great hole into the cellar and dragged bright lights in under there, and that made her hands begin to shake. Two men stood leaning down, looking in, talking to someone. She sat looking for only a minute, then backed up beneath a low-hanging willow, halfway into a driveway where she might be able to turn around, unnoticed. They had found Sammie. She knew they had. She sat for a moment hugging herself, thinking about what she was seeing. She cracked her window open, wondering if she could hear the cops talking, and then wished she hadn't, she went sicker, at the smell.

From this moment, she was going to need all her strength. She couldn't let herself fall apart. First she had to get warm, and eat something, or she would be sick. She had to take care of herself, and then think about this, think about the cops in there under Sammie's house.

Backing deeper into the drive, she looked up across the hill between the other houses, where she could see part of Alain Bent's place. The windows were dark, the paler shades and curtains looked just as they had for weeks. Reaching under the seat, she fished out the crowbar she kept there, completed her turn, and headed over to the next block and up toward Alain's.

Joe woke at dawn, the king-sized blankets bundled around him. By the silence, he knew the rest of the bed was empty, Ryan gone, finishing up the hole in Sammie's basement, Clyde already up and gone. No sound of the shower pounding, no buzz of the electric shaver like a swarm of hornets loose in the bathroom. Why wasn't he up on the roof, in his own tower? The bedside clock said 7:15. A lingering smell of coffee drifted up the stairs, but no smell of breakfast cooking or having been cooked. A pale white light filled the room. Through the open curtains a clear white glow streamed in across the walls, as weird as if he'd awakened in some alternate world—and then he remembered. *Snow! It snowed last night!* The bedroom even smelled different, and the air was so cold it burned his nose. Leaping off the bed he flew to Clyde's desk, glancing down at Snowball asleep on the love seat bundled in a quilt. Snoring softly, she didn't stir. Leaping up to the rafter, he bolted along it and out his cat door—into the blinding white light. The world was so bright he felt his pupils slitting closed, white roofs all around him, snow piled up six inches around his tower, hills of snow against the neighborhood chimneys, snow weighting down the pine and cypress branches. When he looked over the edge of the roof, the white yards and street were patterned with shoe prints where the neighbors had walked. One set of dark tire tracks snaked through between the white curbs. Children's voices screamed as kids raced by pelting each other with snowballs. In his own yard was a trampling of big paw prints, the snow matted down where Rock had apparently performed a doggy snow dance. Clyde's prints came out of the house to join Rock, and the two sets led away as if on an impromptu walk through the village, a walk in the incredible snow.

And left me asleep, he thought irritably. But in his own fascination at the snowy world, he raced away over the white roofs, swerving around chimney drifts and leaping weighted branches, running until his paws were so numb with cold that he had to stop and lick them.

In the center of the village he watched half a dozen early-rising locals cavorting in the snow, as excited as kids themselves. He watched several pairs of tourists, emerging from the motels, head for one or another of the village bakeries, stomping off snow in the door-ways, pushing inside to warm up on coffee and strudel or cheese Danish. Dulcie would say, the village looked like a scene from Dickens. Where was she? Why wasn't she out in this, racing through the frozen morning? Leaping away, he headed for her place, but on the pris-tine rooftops he saw not one paw print, not Dulcie's, not Kit's or Misto's, not even a squirrel. Maybe Dulcie was already at the crime scene, maybe watching the early-arriving forensics team.

He thought of the techs driving two hours down from San Jose on the icy freeway, eating doughnuts and coffee in the cab of their warm van. Once they got to work, they'd bundle up, heavy sweaters under their lab coats, faces masked against the smell. Maybe they'd be warmed a little by heat from the high-powered spotlights shining beneath the beams and cobwebs as they brushed away earth from the first body. A pair of techs crouching low in the tight space, dropping bits of trace into evidence bags: fibers, hairs that might be other than the victim's, maybe a button or a fragment of shoelace. He hoped not cat hairs. Maybe a broken fingernail, but not a broken claw. Maybe the forensics entomologist was there, as well, waiting for the second body to be exhumed, to diligently consult the colonies of insects that had created their own tiny worlds within and, in fact, might turn out to be the only living witnesses to the time of death.

Inside Sammie Miller's house, Dallas finally had the lights on, after an earlier call to the power company. It was cold as hell in there. He'd left the furnace off, keeping the atmosphere in the house as he found it, and so as not to disturb the scene below where the old furnace, which had to be far from airtight, would suck and expel air and disturb all manner of evidence. The house and yard were cordoned off, and most of the overgrown lot, and they'd established a control center where Officer Brennan was handling the documenting. He'd told Davis to stay home, her knee was pretty bad. She'd said it was damn near as big as a basketball, and she was trying to wrap her mind around the upcoming surgery.

He had photographed the interior of the house, which, in this mess, had taken the better part of two hours, had done three rolls just of close-ups of the tangle of clothes and scattered household debris. What was a part of Sammie's lifestyle, and what disarray the vandals had caused—raccoons or humans or both—was pretty much up for grabs. He had gathered trace evidence, including the intrusive raccoon fur, and begun lifting prints and scanning electronically for footprints, working one section at a time as he tried to figure out what might be out of place and how much of the mess Sammie had left herself. So far he had prints for what looked like four separate individuals, besides those of the damned raccoons. Talk about contaminating the scene. One set would be Sammie's, one possibly Emmylou Warren's. The stink of the raccoons, mixed with the smell of death and the smell of spoiled food from a refrigerator without power, made him sorry he'd eaten breakfast. No wonder Emmylou Warren, when she came in here, hadn't smelled the body. Below him in the cellar, the forensics team should be pretty close to lifting the victim, sliding a stretcher under it and easing it out onto a gurney. The question was, what would they find underneath?

And the real question was, how the hell had the snitch *found* the damned grave? What was he doing snooping around underneath Sammie Miller's house, in the middle of the night?

Or had this call not been from their regular snitch at all? Kathleen wasn't as familiar with the snitch's voice as he and Davis were. What if it was someone else?

Had that meth bunch broken in, thinking to hide more chemicals under there? Or to stash the meth itself, get it out of their possession where they thought no cop would look?

Or had someone broken in under there to get out of the cold, maybe meant to sleep safely hidden beneath the house? Maybe Emmylou Warren had returned but afraid to go back inside after they ran her off? She slips in underneath, maybe thinks the furnace is running and it will keep her warm. But then she smells the stink and makes a hasty retreat?

But *she* didn't call the department, it was a man who called—unless she was pretty good at disguising her voice.

He thought about the snitch, this guy, and the gal, who were so unlike the usual informant with whom you maintained a quiet relationship; someone you knew and could talk to, a barkeep, a mechanic, city clerk, someone who had contact with a lot of people, and who liked the high of helping the law, liked to feel they were on the inside. And, he thought, smiling, liked seeing their marks go to jail.

They knew most of their snitches and nurtured the relationships, yet for some six years now they'd been getting anonymous calls from this man or the woman and they didn't have a clue to either one. Yet not once had they been led astray, every tip was a good one, though too often perplexing in the things they turned up. Evidence no cop might have come up with, items lifted that no one could have gotten their hands on without a pretty elaborate break-in. Information that didn't involve locked houses or cars but seemed to have been overheard under the most unlikely of circumstances. It was almost as if they had a ghost on the payroll, someone skilled beyond any normal ability to get their hands on all manner of evidence, someone almost uncanny at eavesdropping, and at slipping in and out of locked houses and offices unseen. An invisible snitch who left no smallest mark of jimmied lock or fingerprints, no trace of any kind.

Sometimes a few cat hairs at a scene, as if maybe the snitch kept cats. But what were you going to do with that? Half the people in the world owned cats. What, run DNA on the cat hairs and then run DNA on every cat in the village until you found the right owner?

As Dallas mulled over the puzzle of the snitches, he had no idea his two informants crouched just above his head on the neighbors' rooftop. When Joe first arrived he'd found Dulcie already hunkered down there against the brick chimney where the snow hadn't gathered. Freezing their restless paws, they'd listened to the faint voices of the two crime-scene investigators working in the cellar, and they could see down across the narrow scrap of yard through the hole Ryan had cut in the wall, could see the men's shadowed movements. They had watched Kathleen find and bag the open padlock, and had prayed that if the lab found fingerprints, they wouldn't find cat prints badly smearing them. Dulcie said, "If the lab picks up a few good fingerprints, why would they bother with the smears? With even one good print, plus whatever information they get from the body itself, maybe they won't be so nosy."

"And maybe they will," he said. "Nosy is what makes good police work." He wished the sun would come out, he'd had enough of the cold. Snow was fine as a novelty, but this freezing morning, snow was best seen from a snug house as you lay curled before a crackling fire.

They had watched Dallas enter the house, glimpsed him through the windows as he worked the scene lifting prints, taking blood samples, taking roll after roll of photographs of the detritus from every angle, a hard job, sorting out anything that might be linked to the murder, among that chaos. Seemed like Dallas had been in there forever before the front door opened, he stepped out, and secured it with the department's own lock. He stood on the little porch looking around at the snowy neighborhood as if he'd expected, when he came out, the snow would have started to melt.

It hadn't.

Where the snow was exposed to the full morning sun, it *had* begun to soften, but then the heavy drifts slicked over again as the temperature dropped, the morning sun gone again behind a pale mist. Black ice glittered in the gutters, icicles hung from the trees. Dallas paused on the porch as Ryan came around the corner of the house, her frown stern and uncomfortable.

"What?" he said, looking down at her.

"There *are* two bodies, just as Kathleen thought. Two bodies, Dallas, crammed into that terrible, dark place."

He came down the steps, put his arm around her. "You okay?"

"Yes. Just—maybe the smell gets to me. Two graves, the earth packed down with the back of the shovel, shovel marks where the footprints were smoothed away."

Joe hoped Dulcie's prints were all smoothed away.

"They are," Dulcie whispered, cutting him a look. "I brushed them away, I *hope* I got them all."

26

Warmed from his breakfast of pancakes and bacon, Billy was coasting his bike down the steep two-lane, down the hill from the Harpers', headed over to the Harmann ranch to feed their horses when, passing the narrow lane to his burned house, he saw Gran's landlord standing at the edge of the burn, his silver-colored pickup nosed nearly out of sight against the hill. Billy stopped, softly dragging his foot, silently braking his bike. The stink of burned wood still hung in the air, souring the clean cold smell of the snow. The old man stood just at the edge of the fire-chewed timbers, his back to him, and as Billy watched, he stepped in over the crime-scene tape, carrying a sharp-nosed shovel.

He stood a moment, looking, then began to poke the shovel in among the wet, burned walls and debris; the shovel made an ugly, grating sound as it sliced through ashes and charcoal. The crusty old man had every right to be on his own property, but the burn was still off limits, Max Harper had told Billy that. Maybe not even Zandler should be disturbing the scene until the cops released it. Zandler always looked like an ancient crow in his dusty black suit with its old-fashioned vest. Stained white shirt open at the collar, grizzled gray hair combed sideways over his balding head, hanging down around his collar. Short gray beard as stiff as a scrub brush. He was a tall old man, long angled face under the bristle, and small angry eyes that could fix on you like the eyes of a mean-spirited old crow wanting to peck and strike. Didn't he know he shouldn't be in there? But there was no cop around, so what did he care?

Zandler's footprints led from his truck across the snowy yard to Emmylou's shack and then to the collapsed one. Had he gone to see if Emmylou had moved back in, on the sly? Or if Billy himself meant to stay on there hoping he wouldn't be caught? The old man was always sure someone was taking advantage of him. He was nosy, too, asking Gran, when he came to get the rent, if she had enough money set aside for the *next* month's payment, saying he hoped she had it in a safe place. Gran always said the same, *What I have is none of your damn business. If I can't pay you, we'll get out.* But she always had the money, and Zandler always remarked slyly on her frugal ways. Every time, the minute he'd gone, Gran would say, *Nosy old goat.*

The burn was still warm enough so no snow clung to the black rubble, and Zandler was just poking and prodding with his shovel, bending down to look sometimes, or to pick something up. What was he looking for? And why was his pickup parked right beside the old lumber and doors that hid Gran's cave?

He had to know about the cave, but Billy didn't think he'd ever shown any interest or snooped around there. The land and buildings belonged to Zandler, but Billy wasn't sure the cave did. It might even be on the Harper property, cut back into the hill the way it was, only a few feet from their pasture fence. Gran had always been secretive about it, didn't want anyone snooping in there, sure not Zandler. She might have been drunk a lot of the time, but she knew if even one board in that pile had been moved. If Billy went out there to count the bottles, to see how much she was drinking, he'd better be sure she was asleep, and be sure to replace the boards exactly right. Now, easing his bike down into the gulley that ran alongside, he laid it down in the weeds that grew at the bottom. Climbing back up the bank, he stayed close to the hill where Zandler might not notice him, walked silently and tried to melt into the hill.

The old man still hadn't seen him. He was scraping around the remains of their burned table, and then scraping at Gran's burned bed, pushing aside what was left of it. Billy thought to try to stop him, but common sense held him still. Zandler might be old but he was strong and he had a mean temper, he handled the big shovel as if it weighed nothing, shoving aside melted pots and pans, melted dishes and burned rags, then gouging at the floor beneath Gran's bed, squinting and poking at whatever might lie beneath. If someone *had* started the fire on purpose, Zandler's rummaging could destroy important evidence, and . . .

Was that what the old man had in mind?

But why would Zandler hurt Gran and burn his own house? Surely not just for her whiskey money. Billy watched him scrape aside the remains of their cupboard and the two chairs with their legs burned off. He wished Max Harper was there to see what he was doing and to stop him. He watched Zandler kneel, examine the burned wooden floor under where the cupboard had stood, and then begin to dig. When the old man rose, Billy melted into the hill among the grayed lumber and bushes.

But the old man found nothing, his hands were empty except for the shovel. Idly swinging it, he headed for his truck, started it, and spun a turn kicking up snow and gravel, sped up the lane, and a right turn onto the highway heading for the village. When he'd gone Billy hauled his bike out of the ditch and took off fast for work, thinking he'd call Captain Harper from the Harmann place, tell him Zandler sure was looking for something.

Misto was lame with the cold, but despite his paining shoulder, father and son raced across the snowy roof-tops wild and laughing, amused by this sudden surprising touch of displaced Oregon winter. Eugene hadn't had snow every year, but when it did they'd found it highly entertaining, the whole family, even when the kittens were small, plunging through the drifts like demented hound dogs. There was never much snow on the valley floor, in the business section of Eugene. But up in the residential hills snow formed drifts high enough to bring cars to a halt, people clueless how to drive in it, cars skidding, drivers honking or stalling or both—while Pan and his sisters, watching from the snowy rooftops, could barely contain their laughter.

Now, below the two cats, the same drama was at work, cars sliding sideways, drivers going super slowly hanging their heads out of ice-blind windows; and Misto and Pan, as they headed for Kit's house, delighted by this familiar circus of winter confusion.

The morning was so cold that twice, when a car pulled to the curb to park, they waited for the occupants to hurry away then bellied down a tree, leaped to the car's hood, and sat warming their paws and backsides before they raced on again. When they reached Kit's house, the smell of waffles and syrup drew them like bees to honey, despite their own ample breakfast. Licking his whiskers in anticipation, Misto led Pan up the fat trunk of Kit's oak tree and into her tree house— where Pan halted, staring around with amazement.

"This is Kit's? All hers?" He looked up at the timbered roof and out at the surround of twisted oak branches that formed an extended bower. "All *hers*?" he repeated.

"All of it," said Misto, laughing, "the fancy pillows, the velour lap robe, the works." The cushions smelled deliciously of Kit, and there was a fine mat of her tortoiseshell fur embedded in the velvet and brocade. Drifts of snow had piled up outside one edge of the planked floor, but the tree house itself was fine and dry. Pan lingered, looking, followed Misto only reluctantly as he headed for the smell of breakfast, padding along a snow-covered branch to Kit's cat door. The old cat pushed in under the plastic flap onto the window-sill, a leap to the dining table, and he paused, listening.

The house was silent. The smell of breakfast was immediate and rich, but the table had already been cleared. Peering into the kitchen, they could see dirty plates hastily stacked, sticky with syrup, as if Lucinda and Pedric and maybe Kit, too, had gone off in a fine hurry.

But at the far end of the table, two small saucers had been left on a single white place mat. Each plate presented a waffle, cut small and glistening with butter and syrup, and a slice of bacon broken into small bites. On the place mat itself shone one perfect, syrupy paw print carefully incised: a pretty invitation to breakfast, which they could hardly ignore. Pan said, "How did she know we'd come here?"

Misto smiled. "How could she not? She knew I'd be showing you the village, and where else would we start?" He turned his attention to breakfast, handily licking up every bite of his own share, and the good food warmed them right down to their icy paws. When no one appeared, they circled through the empty house, then returned to the tree house. Backing to the ground, their claws deep in the rough bark, they circled the house on the outside, as well, and finding Lucinda's and Pedric's boot prints leading away, and Kit's paw prints trotting along beside them, they followed.

"They're heading for the murder scene," Misto said. The grave had not remained a secret for long, word never did in this small village; news traveled from friend to friend, neighbor to neighbor, and back again. The Firettis had heard it over breakfast from a busy-minded neighbor, and where else would Kit go?

The two tomcats galloped along in the wake of the Greenlaws' footprints, amused when Kit's paw prints vanished suddenly, to appear again after a block or so— little forays to the rooftops, or sometimes where Pedric had picked her up and carried her, most likely tucked inside his coat until her paws grew warm again. The two toms followed them up into the neighborhood of the Damens' remodel and on up to where the yard and street were full of cop cars. Ryan Flannery's red truck, too, and a white van marked with the seal of the state of California. There were cops everywhere, and over all came the sick smell of something dead for a very long time. Warily they scrambled up into the low, weeping branches of an acacia tree, crouched there behind its leafy curtain, looking out, their fur dusted with yellow pollen from the tree's early blooms. The snow outside the tree was stained yellow, too, as was the bare ground within, sheltered by the tent of branches.

Lucinda's and Pedric's footprints made patterns among the tangle of other prints as if they had stood talking with the officers, then their trail headed away again, while Kit's prints vanished at the base of a pine tree. And there she was above them, on a neighbor's roof, Kit and Joe and Dulcie, three dark small shapes silhouetted against the milky overcast, watching the action below. Pan and Misto didn't race to join them, there were too many people to see them, too many cops. Enough to see *three* cats together there on the rooftop so intently watching. What would they make of five? Such a gathering would stir far too puzzled an interest.

From among the drooping branches they could see directly into the big hole that was cut in the side of the small brown cottage, the raw earth within picked out with bright spotlights, blinding in their intensity. A slim, dark-haired woman in faded jeans stood looking in, her dark glasses shielding her from the searing light. "Detective Ray," Misto said. A curtain of clear plastic had been hung over the opening, pulled to the side and tied back like a hastily devised shower curtain. They couldn't see what was happening inside but could hear the soft brush of careful digging, as delicate as the brush of a cat's paws.

But then soon, another decaying smell reached them, a bit different from the cellar's taint of death. Pan, following his twitching nose, looked down beneath the tree where the ground was bare of snow, where rotted leaves were matted between the tree's exposed roots: smooth gray roots as thick as human arms, twisted together, and over the aroma of death from the cellar, and the honey scent of the acacia blooms, this other faint, metallic smell. Dropping down from the low branches, Pan sniffed at the roots and at the dark stains on their smooth gray surface, and curled his lip in a flehmen face. "Blood." He looked intently up at Misto. "Human blood."

Misto jumped down and sniffed, too, flehming, trapping the smell on his tongue. "Old blood, not fresh," he said. There was no scent of anyone having recently entered under the tree's low branches, and he looked away to where the officers were at work. "How could they miss this? Stay here," he said, and slipped out through the leafy curtain.

Easing across the snowy yard among the white-crested bushes, he scrambled up through the dark pine that crowded the neighbors' house, and across a swaying branch onto the neighbors' roof to join the other three, and excitement filled the old cat.

When first he'd arrived in the village just before Christmas, the three village cats had been nosing into another murder investigation; he'd fallen eagerly in with them, and found this work even more interesting than his many travels. Now, he whispered to Joe and led him down the pine and through the bushes into the leafy tent. Joe looked at the bloodstained roots and smelled them. He gave Misto a whiskery smile and a nod, then he melted away again, along the edge of the yard heading for Ryan, making straight for his housemate.

Within minutes Joe and Ryan were in her truck, her cell phone lying on the seat where Joe could punch in 911. Before he made the call, Ryan got out again, left the far door cracked open, and stepped over to join Kathleen. Joe was crouched on the seat, his face close to the phone, when dispatcher Mabel Farthy picked up. Knowing his voice, she was quick to put the snitch through to Kathleen, Mabel never wasted time on useless questions.

"Why did you wait until now?" Kathleen said. "When did you find this blood? No one's been *in* the backyard, last night or this morning, there are guards all over. When did you—"

Joe broke the connection, then peered carefully up over the edge of the window, watching Kathleen as she dropped the phone back in its holster.

Slipping out of the truck, Joe was crouched in its shadow as Kathleen turned to Ryan. "The snitch," she said. "What the hell is this? How does he do this?

Couldn't he give us a little more information? Why so damned secretive? What's the point in calling, when he . . . ? Oh, to hell with it," she said, looking away toward the acacia tree.

Kathleen was the newest detective on the force, she was still tempted to cross-examine the unknown informant. Not that it ever did her any good. She stood frowning, then headed for her car, pulled out her evidence bag from the trunk, hung two cameras around her neck, and headed for the acacia. As she approached its drooping branches, she didn't see a pair of shadows slip out from the other side and vanish among the neighbors' yards. When Kathleen knelt down to peer under, the space was empty.

Before crawling in for a closer look, she circled the tree and poked her camera in through the leaves, taking shots of the trunk, the roots, the faintly disturbed mat of dry leaves. When at last she entered, looking unconvinced she'd find anything of value, Misto and Pan were on the roof with Dulcie and Kit, only Joe was absent.

From their high vantage, they couldn't see in under the falling branches, the tree was like a little tent; but they could see Kathleen's shadow, kneeling as if she was shooting close-ups of the dark stains on the pale roots.

The detective took her time beneath the tree, lifting blood samples and then digging carefully through the leaves looking for any smallest item of evidence, a human hair, a torn fingernail, a shell casing. She was thus occupied when Kit caught a glimpse of something shiny, just by Kathleen's left boot—a leaf had been turned over as she shifted position, and something bright shone out. They all saw it, they all stifled a mew, and Kit drew back her paw where she'd reached as if to alert Kathleen.

But the next instant something, some unknown sense, made Kathleen turn and look, too.

Carefully she lifted the leaves away.

A cell phone lay buried among the mat of leaves, its bright surface plastered with damp acacia leaves. Carefully Kathleen photographed it in the position she'd found it and then, with her gloved hand, she slipped an evidence bag over it, and dropped it in her pocket. Whatever was there, phone numbers, notes, or perhaps photographs, she would examine back at the department, once she'd finished working the scene. The cats looked at each other, and grinned, and they felt high on the discovery. What *would* she find? Had the killer dropped it? Or had one of the victims buried it there, unseen, hoping to pass on what evidence?

Or had the phone nothing at all to do with the killer, maybe had lain there long before the victims died? The detective continued to search among the moldering leaves, and then she rose to examine the tree itself. She started when her exploring fingers found a tiny dimple within the damaged bark.

Photographing this, and then exploring it with a small dental tool, carefully she bent away a small sliver of bark, to reveal a spent shell.

She cut out a piece of the tree itself, leaving the slug embedded, and carefully she bagged it. She had the bullet. It would be too much coincidence to think this slug hadn't killed one of the victims—though stranger anomalies had happened. The cats were considering this when two of the CSIs came out of the cellar, and fetched a stretcher from their van and a body bag; as the four watched from the roof, Joe Grey slipped out across the yard and quickly up to the roof to join them, pushing beneath the shadowed branches.

The CSI team, having photographed the first body and its surround, had covered the victim's hands for more careful examination at the lab, then had spent several hours lifting trace evidence. Now they wanted Dallas and Kathleen in the cellar before they eased the corpse into the body bag, wanted to see if either of them knew the woman. With the bloating and discoloration that takes place even in a week or two, a victim is not always easy to identify. The cats watched the two detectives slip in through the hole in the wall.

The detectives were in there for some time; when they came out again, the expressions on their faces told the cats clearly that they didn't recognize the victim. Now, in the cellar, the team would be bagging the body. Below the cats, Dallas was on the phone to Mabel Farthy. "I want a BOL on Emmylou Warren, you have the description. We need her to look at a body. If she's picked up within the hour, let me know, before the CSI unit takes off."

Otherwise, Joe thought, they'd have to haul Emmylou up to San Jose, to the crime lab, to ID the body. If that *was* Sammie Miller buried under her own house. As reclusive as Sammie seemed to be, and with most of her neighbors moved away, Emmylou might be the only one who did know her—besides the killer, and Sammie's vanished brother. As Dallas ended the call, the five cats slipped away, disappearing like ghosts among the snowy rooftops.

27

Before Billy fed the Harmanns' horses, he had called MPPD from their stable. By the time he'd pumped his bike back up the hill to the burn, Detective Garza was there, his tan Blazer parked in the yard, and old man Zandler was long gone. Garza wore jeans and a faded down jacket, his dark Latino eyes smiling when he looked at Billy. Billy had done some thinking since he called the station, and he was debating just how much he should keep to himself. If Gran did have money hidden in the cave—and what else could have made her so protective?—what would the cops do with it? Would it belong to Debbie and Esther? They were her daughters, but he was only the grandson. That money would be all he had to take care of himself, except for what he could earn, and at twelve, that still wasn't much. He hadn't helped take care of Gran all these years without learning the value of money, seeing how much she spent on whiskey that could have bought something to eat besides beans and potatoes and cheap sausage, could have bought new tires for his bike, might have paid rent on a house where the wind didn't blow through the walls. If he told the law about the money, would he have to give it to his aunts? He hoped Zandler hadn't found it, but maybe not, the boards and old doors didn't look disturbed. Detective Garza was photographing the burned house all over again, where Zandler had dug into the rubble. When he finished taking pictures, he began to dig around in the rubble, himself, photographing wherever he could see that Zandler had disturbed anything. "You got moved in okay," Garza said, talking as he worked. "You and the cats?"

"Yes," Billy said, "just fine."

"You have any idea what Zandler was looking for? He wouldn't have been looking for the cause of the fire, he knows it was a grease fire." Max Harper had told Billy that, that it looked like Gran had started making her breakfast, put potatoes on to fry and then went back to bed, forgetting the burner was on. She'd done that more than once, their skillet was blackened and crusty where she'd burned it. That was mostly at supper, though. She'd put something on to cook, then forget it, but Billy had been there to smother the flame before it got going.

That morning, he wasn't there.

Garza poked around for a while longer, then rose, looking across at Billy. "The week or two before the fire, was Zandler up here?"

Billy shook his head. "I doubt it, Gran didn't say anything, and it wasn't rent time. That's the only time he ever came. Maybe he came up to be sure Emmylou was gone, though, after he evicted her, make sure she hadn't come back."

"Hesmerra was working regularly?"

Billy nodded.

"Did she have a bank account?"

"She didn't like banks, she kept the money somewhere around the place. She never even told me, she'd never get into her stash when I was home. She said once, if I knew where her money was, I'd take it so she couldn't buy what she wanted. She meant, so she couldn't buy whiskey."

Billy knew what the next question would be: Could the money be in the cave? He was surprised when Dallas didn't ask it. The detective said, "We'll compare these shots with the photographs we have, maybe they'll show us if he took anything."

Billy waited until Garza left, made sure he'd turned onto the highway, then he pulled some boards away from the cave's entrance, and moved the old door just enough to slip inside, into the smell of sour earth and rotting timbers. Maybe the money *was* here, maybe she'd saved back more than he'd thought, between what she'd earned and what Mr. Kraft gave her.

He never knew how much Kraft gave her, Gran was so closemouthed, he only knew that *that* money made him feel strange, he never understood why Kraft gave her money. Kraft said it was because Debbie, Gran's own daughter, wouldn't help her out, he said it was Debbie's duty to help her mother and if she wouldn't, he would. To Billy, that didn't make sense; his other aunt didn't help Gran, or hardly speak to her. The idea of family helping each other wasn't something he was used to.

If Gran's money *was* in the cave, he wanted it before someone else got it. He might be only twelve, but he knew that money laid by meant freedom. You could eat, you didn't have to work *all* the time, you could keep your bike running so you could get around. Gran had hidden her whiskey here, so why not the money?

Or, he wondered, had there been more to hide than money?

He'd wondered sometimes when Gran's car pulled in at midnight but she was so long coming in the house, wondered what she was doing. Sometimes he'd rise and look out to see a faint light shining out between the old door and the boards. He thought she'd gone to get a bottle, thought she'd forgotten there was a nearly full bottle under her bed. But maybe she was hiding something else there.

In the cave, he found the flashlight she'd kept by her whiskey case, and flicked it on, shining the beam along the rough dirt walls. Besides the sour smell of damp earth, the cave stank of mice or rats, and of rotted potatoes from a bag Gran had stored months before. Even the smallest rotted potato smelled like something dead. Billy explored the earthen floor where the whiskey case had stood, which Detective Garza had taken away, then he pushed on back into the darkness.

The dirt between the supporting timbers was packed hard, the dirt walls and ceiling seemed as solid as concrete behind the grid of rough planks. He hadn't been back in here for a long time. After his mother died, he'd spent weeks in here alone, way at the back, hoping Gran wouldn't come in and try to cheer him up, which only made him cry. Moving slowly toward the back, he looked along the walls and above him where beams held the earth up, shining the light into earthen crevices behind the timbers.

At the very back there was rubble, loose rocks, three old empty baskets made of half-rotted wooden slats. He searched among these and searched overhead. He was halfway back to the opening when he heard a sound outside, the scrunching of a foot on the rough ground. He switched off the flashlight, stood quiet and still.

The opening darkened as a figure knelt, looking in. "Billy?"

He breathed again, switched on the flashlight. Heard a horse snort, then one of the dogs pushed in past Charlie, nearly knocking him over. "I'm here," he said, "I'll be right out." He was trying to settle the dog, who was rearing up as tall as Billy, licking his face. He was trying to wrestle him away, the flashlight still in his hand when its beam shone low against a four-by-four support.

Where the floor met the rough earthen wall, light reflected off a sliver of something white, shining white.

It was only a speck, which he'd missed from the other side of the rough timber. Kneeling, he dug the earth away, and pulled it free.

It was a plastic sandwich bag stretched thick over a packet of folded white paper. He could see a stamp, could see awkward hand printing, clumsier than his own handwriting that Gran had been stubborn about teaching him: Debbie's printing. Pushing the dog away more forcefully, he shoved the packet deep in his jeans pocket, hiding it from Charlie. He felt his face heat. He didn't know why he did that; and he moved on out to join her.

"You okay?"

Billy nodded.

"Dallas stopped by, when he left here. I'd just saddled Redwing, I said I'd ride down this way." Her green eyes searched his. "That Mr. Zandler was here earlier? I don't like him much."

Again Billy nodded. "I won't tangle with him, if that's what you're thinking."

Charlie grinned, and glanced at her watch. "I thought I'd take a little ride and then, if you want to, we could go shopping." He thought she meant he could help her carry groceries. "Clothes for Gran's funeral," she said. "Maybe chinos and a new polo shirt?"

Billy looked down at his worn jeans with the frayed bottoms, at his run-over boots. He didn't want her to buy him things, he had his own wages, but he didn't want to spend them on clothes.

She said, "We could go to J.C. Penney's."

Well, he guessed he could do that.

"It isn't a gift," she said, "you'll earn it back soon enough, taking care of our spoiled animals."

He hadn't thought of working for clothes. Well, that was all right, he did want to look nice for Gran. He watched her ride away easing the mare into a canter, the two dogs racing ahead. When she'd gone, he opened the plastic bag, took out the letters.

He read them twice, but didn't understand much. He didn't want to think about what the earliest ones might mean, the ones dated twelve years ago just after he was born. The surprise was that Debbie had written to Gran at all, when Gran always complained she never heard from her. Why would Gran lie about that? There were twelve letters, the envelopes roughly printed. In the two bulkier envelopes, the letters had been torn into tiny pieces, wadded up, stuffed back inside, and the flap loosely stuck closed again. Besides these, the letter with the earliest postmark was only a few lines:

"No, I don't want to come there. How can you even ask that. Why would I want to see her and why would I want anything to do with that child? I certainly don't want to see you again, after you let this happen, what you did was way worse than simple lying. Well, you've always lied to us. I thought, in my stupidity, that it was only about your drinking, not about something like this."

Then came the two torn-up letters, the envelopes postmarked just a few months later. Then nothing for eight years. The next letter was very short.

"How do you know that's what happened? Go to the cops, if that's what you think, he deserves whatever he gets. But remember, I won't help you. And you don't have an ounce of proof. You go to the cops, they'll just laugh. As to the other, I'll have to think about that."

Whatever this was about, Debbie was sure vague. Was she afraid someone else would read it? What *was* this about, what was she afraid of?

There was another long space, nearly two years. The letters after that were different and there were more of them, as if she and Gran had talked on the phone maybe, and maybe made up a little. There was no phone in the cabin, but maybe Gran had called her from work. Now, it seemed like they were into something secret, something they didn't want to write much about. In one, Debbie said, *"I have nine sets of papers,"* and she had enclosed a list of names and dates, with one single address at the end. That street was up near the Damens' and Hanni Coon's remodels. In the next letter she asked, *"Did you copy the statements? Call me on my cell but do it soon, it might not be working after next week, not sure I can pay the bill."* Later there was mention of some kind of contracts, and terms Billy didn't understand. Further on, she complained about a woman. *"I hope she double-crosses him, that's what he deserves."*

The last letter was dated a month ago: *"Copy all the discs you can find. Just follow the instructions I gave you. Don't be afraid of the damn machine. Maybe I should come down there. I wish you knew more about computers."* Whatever they were into sounded illegal. What he wondered was, did this have anything to do with why Gran died?

Emmylou couldn't lock the bedroom slider once she'd pried it open and stepped inside Alain Bent's house. She pushed it shut and closed the draperies over it, making sure there was no crack for light to shine out. There was no one back there in the woods, surely no one to hear her prying metal against metal as she'd jimmied the door, but still she was nervous. She had parked on a little side street down the hill where her car might not be noticed. The house was stuffy inside, and cold. Moving up the hall, she found the thermostat, she felt a thrill of satisfaction as she turned it up to nearly eighty and heard the furnace click on. She wondered if the water heater had been turned down, too. She made a quick tour of the house to be sure she was alone, then returned to the master bath, with its peach-tinted tiles and peach-colored marble, and ran the hot tap in the basin.

When the water ran hot she smiled, shed her clothes, dropping them on the floor, turned the shower on full blast and got in, luxuriating in the hot water and steam. She stayed in a long time, scrubbed real good and washed her hair. When at last she came out she found a thick towel in one of the drawers, and dried off beneath the heat blowing from the furnace vent. Moving into the bedroom, she pulled a blanket off the bed, draped it around herself and tucked it in. Carrying her clothes into the alcove by the kitchen, she found the laundry soap and threw them in the washer, jeans, shirt, socks, panties, everything. While the wash ran she ransacked the kitchen cupboards. Finding canned soups and fruit, she pulled a saucepan from a lower cupboard, warmed a can of black bean soup, and opened a can of apricots. She had found the bowls and was gulping her breakfast when she heard the bedroom slider open—she was so startled she burned her mouth on a big spoonful of soup. She half rose, pulling her blanket tighter, looking to the front door for escape.

She was too late. One second's hesitation, and here came a woman down the hall, silent and quick, a tall woman dressed in jeans and sweatshirt, long dark hair down around her shoulders, and she was wearing a holstered gun. Emmylou had seen her around town, but only in uniform. Cop. Woman cop. She stepped to the table.

"Having breakfast?"

Emmylou stared at her.

"Smells good. I guess you're doing a load of laundry, too?"

Emmylou said, "You were down at Sammie Miller's house. What's happened down there? How did you know I was in here?"

"Someone saw smoke, they thought it was from the chimney. I came up to see if Alain had returned." She glanced down over the rail at the cold fireplace. "I guess what they saw was hot air from the furnace vent."

Kathleen didn't mention that Ryan Flannery had already come up here to have a look, had circled the house and then slipped inside while Emmylou was in the shower. Kathleen didn't mention—because she didn't know—that it was not, in fact, Ryan who had first spied the white trail rising up from the chimney, it was Joe Grey. He saw the condensation, alerted Ryan, and, because Kathleen was busy with the CSI technicians, she'd walked up the snowy street, walked along the front of the house and through the patio, had knocked then rang the bell. When no one answered, and she could hear water running, she'd gone around to the back, found the glass slider to the master bedroom jimmied, the frame bent, the door not quite closed, and a crowbar lying inside tucked against the wall. After slipping in to look, which she knew was foolish, after seeing that it was only Emmylou in there, she'd called Kathleen on her cell.

Ryan had remained in the bedroom while Kathleen cleared the house. She could hear them talking, Kathleen and Emmylou, she heard the washer stop and in a moment the clothes dryer kicked on. When Kathleen came back down the hall, her expression was both annoyed and amused; the detective had trouble, sometimes, maintaining the unreadable façade of a seasoned cop. "Emmylou's having breakfast. Wrapped in a blanket, cozy as a cat in a basket."

"It *was* pretty cold last night," Ryan said, straight-faced. She followed Kathleen into the kitchen, where Emmylou had found some tea and had put a saucepan of water on to heat. They watched her drop teabags into three cups. She poured hot water over them, looking up inquiringly. Kathleen nodded, and they sat down at the table, Kathleen facing both the front door and the hall. It might be out of order for an arresting officer to socialize with someone breaking and entering, but Ryan didn't think, from Emmylou's behavior, that Kathleen had made an arrest. The detective was watchful and silent—there was something in the moment as tentative and frail as a whisper.

Did Emmylou *know* that was Sammie Miller down there? Ryan wondered. Was that what this was about? Was she on the verge of identifying the body without ever seeing it? Or even, perhaps, on the verge of confessing to killing her? Ryan remained still, sipping her tea, trying not to telegraph her interest, trying to keep her thoughts, her whole demeanor, blank and withdrawn.

Whatever their individual thoughts, none of the three women, not even the detective, was aware of movement in the master bedroom, of someone else slipping in through the glass door and down the hall to listen: an intruder padding stealthily, his shadow low to the floor; no one heard the hush of his soft paws.

Joe slipped closer through the shadows of the hall, crouching where he could see all three women. Now, he realized, Alain Bent's house was an adjunct to the case, a part of the crime scene: It had been broken into at least twice by players in this tangle, once when Debbie searched it, and again this morning by

Emmylou—to say nothing of the phantom snitches. With this much interest, one had to wonder what the connection was, what *was* here of such value, or what had been here? What did Debbie, and Emmylou, think was hidden here? How did their interest tie in with the murders, and with Alain's absence? How, in fact, might this house play out in the scenario of Hesmerra's death? Kathleen was saying, "We'd like you to have a look at the body, Emmylou, see if you can identify the woman."

"You think it's Sammie," Emmylou said, her face going pink as if with suppressed tears. "Who else would be buried there, under Sammie's own house? When did this happen? I saw her two weeks ago, and I've been up here nearly every day since, looking for her cats. Was she lying there all that time?"

Kathleen said, "You told Officer Brennan you had a key. I'm surprised you didn't stay there in the house, as cold as it's been. You've been living in your car?"

"She kept the key under the porch. I *told* the officers it wasn't there, that it's gone. Yes, I broke in but when I saw the mess I was afraid to stay there, someone's been in there. Maybe only raccoons, maybe not. Someone has the key, and that scares me."

Kathleen said, "If the body is Sammie Miller, did she have family, someone to be notified?"

"No one," Emmylou said. "Just her brother, and Birely would be hard to find. He does have a cell phone, the number's in Sammie's Rolodex, you could try that. He doesn't have a home, he calls himself a hobo, he comes to the village now and then and phones her, that's why she bought him the prepaid phone. She meets him down near the river, the homeless camp there. Or up at the bridge where they all camp in bad weather." She looked evenly at Kathleen. "There's no one else who cares about Sammie. No friends I know of, only me."

"Which bridge is that?" Kathleen said.

"The one on Valley Road, just off Highway One, just above the market where Sammie worked, where I used to work." Her answer brought Joe Grey's ears up. He rose, slipped down the hall where he could better watch Emmylou from the shadows.

Ryan said, "The bridge where Hesmerra's daughter Greta died?"

Emmylou nodded. "That was a long time ago," she said vaguely.

"Four years," Ryan said. "Billy was eight when his mother's car went off the bridge. I heard it was a really bad storm, driving rain, heavy winds, the kind of storm where you can't see the road at all."

Emmylou's face colored, she busied herself with her bowl of apricots and the last of her soup; Joe studied her with interest. She wanted to tell them something, she was on the verge of it, was filled with an urgency that she found hard to conceal. The ghost of something hung in the room, as dark as a storm cloud, some new information, vital and unstated. Watching Emmylou, both Ryan and Kathleen tried to hide their intensity, but their curiosity was as keen as that of the gray tomcat.

"What happened that night?" Kathleen said softly. "What happened when Greta's car went off the bridge?"

Emmylou rose, never taking her eyes from the detective. "I'll come down with you now, to look at the body. Afterward, if you like, I'll come into the station. I'll tell you about the bridge. As soon as we . . . as soon as I've gotten through this, seeing . . . seeing Sammie. If that is Sammie, down there."

But Joe Grey's skin rippled with suspicion. *You know that's Sammie, don't you? You're already certain! What do you know, Emmylou, that you haven't told?*

28

Kathleen Ray's office was half the size of the chief's, just enough room for her desk crowded between file cabinets, a console that held her little coffeemaker, and a small leather armchair. The desk faced the door, neatly stacked with papers and reports, and carefully arranged bookshelves stood behind. On the adjoining walls Kathleen had hung well-framed photographs of the rugged Molena coast, close-ups of stone escarpments and tide pools and stormy skies, fine work done half a century earlier by the region's famous photographers. The only place to hide was beneath the minicredenza, and quickly Joe and Dulcie slipped under, into the shadows against the wall.

By the time they'd left the crime scene, after watching Emmylou identify the body, which was indeed

Sammie, after watching her turn away shaken and sick, the day was growing warmer, the snow starting to melt. The sun did its work quickly; even as they headed for the station, the rooftops and streets below were turning dark and glistening wet, and snowmelt dripped from every crevice and weighted branch.

With a new officer behind the desk, they had padded quickly past, slipping into the empty conference room as Kathleen came in the front door ushering in Emmylou. They'd watched from beneath the conference table as Kathleen snagged half a dozen fresh doughnuts from a tray by the coffeemaker, and herded Emmylou on to her office. Silently they'd followed.

Now, from the shadows beneath the console, they watched Kathleen make Emmylou comfortable in the small leather chair, easing her back into the rapport Kathleen had established at Alain's table, before Emmylou went down to identify the body. Much of the identification was based on Sammie's hair color, on her watch and little silver bracelets, on her silver locket that opened to pictures of her two black-and-white cats. Emmylou knew who Sammie's dentist was, and Sammie's dental records had been sent up to the lab. The CSI techs estimated the date of Sammie Miller's death at two weeks; they would have more information once the lab had finished the autopsy. Kathleen poured two cups of coffee; Emmylou refused sugar or milk, took the cup from Kathleen along with two doughnuts on a little paper plate. The two were silent, sipping coffee.

Both women were tall and slim, Emmylou sinewy and bony with sun-leathered skin, Kathleen pale and smooth, her shining dark hair back carelessly at the nape of her neck, the grace that had made her a good model very much apparent, even in her severe uniform. Her dark eyes studied Emmylou kindly, without a cop's closed shield of authority, and her voice was soft.

"What did happen, that night on the bridge, Emmylou? You told me, in the car, that Sammie's murder could be connected to the death of Hesmerra's daughter?"

"Her youngest daughter," Emmylou said. She broke her doughnut in two, concentrating on that, and said no more.

"I have the accident report," Kathleen said, picking up some papers from her desk. "There was heavy rain that night, a strong wind, hardly any traffic on the roads. The report shows one witness to the accident. He wouldn't give his name, he claimed to have no address, no relatives." She glanced at the report as she talked. "Says a car came up fast behind Greta's car, pulled up beside her and swerved into her, forcing her off the road. The witness saw her car crash through the rail, land on its side on the concrete abutment below." She looked up. "What do you know, Emmylou, that isn't in the report? Was this man Sammie's brother?"

Emmylou nodded. "She was with him that night, they saw it all. The car came up fast on Greta's left, started to pass, then swerved over straight into her car. He had some kind of bright spotlight in his hand, he shone it in her face, the light must have blinded her. Sammie said Greta looked startled, like a deer in your headlights. She swerved hard, lost control, and rammed into the abutment. Crashed right through, right through that corrugated rail, Sammie said, as if it was made of paper. She said the two sections, where they were joined, broke away from the post.

"Sammie said the car rocked a moment, balanced there, then dropped straight down on the concrete and rolled. I guess Greta didn't have her seat belt on, she was thrown around and then thrown out, and the car rolled on top of her. That's how Sammie told me. She saw it, and Birely saw it, they were together at the foot of the bridge. Sammie called 911 while Birely ran to help her—but Greta was already dead, she was beyond help.

"When they heard the siren coming, Birely told Sammie to run, to get away, not let anyone know she was a witness. Even then, he was afraid for her, he thought the killer must have seen her face in the spot-light, and would come after her. Birely waited for the cops, gave them a statement. They told him to stay in town, but he disappeared. Left town, vanished."

Joe, crouched beneath the little console, saw not only the scene Emmylou described, he saw the earlier scene as well, saw his nightmare, the driving rain sluic-ing against the little shack in the windy night, saw and heard the two women yelling at each other, Hesmerra and Greta. Saw the young woman race out to her car and take off into the stormy night, saw the second car, dark and sleek, skid against the hill as it raced to follow her.

Emmylou said, "The killer saw Sammie that night. He knew there were two witnesses, not just a homeless man."

"But if he knew that, why . . . If *he* killed Sammie, why did it take him four years? It couldn't have taken four years to find her, in his small village."

Emmylou shook her head. "He found her before that. Maybe a year ago. He must have been looking for her. Yes, it's a wonder it took him that long. She was real careful, stayed away from people, shopped when the stores were busy so she could get lost in a crowd. Other times, she kept to herself, that was the way she lived anyway.

"He found her when she was walking up in the hills, just at dawn, barely light. A car passed her, a dark two-door. It slowed, the driver did a double take, swerved into a driveway, turned around and pulled to the curb. The minute it slowed she slipped away through an overgrown yard. She watched him from there, and then ran. Through the backyards to another street, through the backstreets and then through yards where a car couldn't follow.

"But days later," Emmylou said, "he tracked her down, he discovered where she lived, and he began to watch her—just to watch, and follow.

"She thought he meant to scare her, keep her afraid so she wouldn't talk. She thought maybe he was afraid to kill again. Or," Emmylou said, "that he hoped she'd lead him to the other witness. Sammie pretended to be unaware of him, she thought that was her best protection. She thought sooner or later he'd decide she wasn't going to the law and he'd back off, would give up watching her."

"Why didn't she file a report, that she was being followed? Why didn't she tell us what this was about?"

Emmylou shook her head. "What was she going to say? She said the cops, even with Birely's report on file, did nothing to find the man the first time, so what were they going to do now?" Emmylou gave Detective

Ray a wan smile. "Sammie wasn't fond of cops—of the police. Maybe because of her brother. The law hassles him a lot."

"He has a record?"

"Not that I know of, but he's been picked up for loitering, and . . . the homeless get hassled, that's the way things are. He calls himself a hobo. Travels up and down the coast, stops in the village now and then and calls her. He won't stay at her place, though. When he shows up . . . when he showed up," she said, "he wouldn't stay with her. She'd bring him a meal, wherever he was, and they'd visit a while. If the weather was bad he'd stay there under that bridge with the other homeless, that's where he was headed that night. Or he'd stay down by the river where you always see smoke rising, and in a few days he'd move on again.

"That night, Sammie had come up to the bridge to meet him, she was working as a checker at the same market where I worked. She worked a different shift than me. She got off at nine, pulled on her slicker, left her car in the parking lot and walked up there in the rain, brought him some deli chicken, hot coffee, and a piece of apple pie in a plastic bag. They were headed under the bridge to get out of the rain when the Jaguar hit Greta's car, she said it happened so fast, and they were just a few feet from where the car came over."

"*Did* they ever get a look at the driver? The report says Birely didn't."

Emmylou shook her head. "Only that bright light in their eyes, blazing on Greta's face, and past her onto them. But Sammie remembered the car, those sleek Jaguar lines. Birely told the police that, that should be in the report.

Kathleen nodded. "If they couldn't see the driver, how could she be sure, later, who was following her?"

"She didn't know who else would follow her, who would watch her, and watch her house. She was certain, even though he had a different car, a black Audi. Maybe he sold the Jaguar, or maybe he hid it away. There must have been damage to the right fender, though I guess he'd have had that fixed, maybe up the coast somewhere."

"Once he started following her, and she saw him, did she know, then, who he was?"

Emmylou reached to the desk, took another doughnut, began to break it into little pieces on her paper plate. Beneath the console, the cats waited, glancing at each other.

Kathleen said, "Emmylou?"

She looked up at Kathleen. "She knew him. I know him."

"Do you want to tell me? Do you want to see Sammie's killer caught?"

Emmylou just looked at her.

"If you know him, Emmylou, do you have any idea why he would kill Greta?"

Emmylou said, "He was her lover. He was the father of her child."

Quietly, Kathleen waited.

"Greta was sixteen when Billy was born. No one knew who the father was, except Greta herself, and Hesmerra. The father gave her money to support the child, if they'd keep quiet. But after eight years, apparently Greta wanted more. Maybe decided she wanted to live better, that he wasn't giving her enough. She threatened him, threatened to tell his wife the truth."

"And his wife was?" Kathleen said softly. Only the silent tap of her toe on the little rug beneath her desk signaled her impatience.

"Debbie Kraft," Emmylou said. "Erik Kraft is Billy's father. Debbie's own husband got her little sister pregnant, not some high school boy."

In the shadows, the two cats were very still. Amazing where human lust could lead, the resultant twists of human deception. Kathleen said, "Hesmerra knew he killed Greta? But still she was friends with him? She accepted money from him, when she knew he'd murdered her daughter? She let him buy her whiskey, like some kind of cheap bribe?"

"Money to support Billy," Emmylou said, "such as it was. And, yes, to buy whiskey. Payments from the man who murdered her child, to keep her from going to the police, from telling what she knew and starting an investigation."

Joe could feel his claws kneading at the hard floor as the little bomb of truth pulled the various fragments together: a married couple, the husband dallying with his wife's little sister. Impregnating the girl, paying to keep her silent. And then when Greta rebelled, he killed her. Afterward he paid the boy's keep or paid Hesmerra blackmail money, whichever way you wanted to put it.

And then when matters changed between him and Hesmerra, he killed her, too? When for instance he found out Hesmerra was snooping into his business affairs, into his illegal transactions, he poisoned her whiskey and set fire to her house? A grease fire, on the stove. How simple to replicate, once Hesmerra lay dying.

Kathleen said, "Does Billy know that Erik Kraft is his father?"

Emmylou shook her head. "I'm sure he doesn't. If that's the case."

"What does that mean?"

"Hesmerra had some suspicion it could have been Perry Fowler. Fowler was nosing around Greta for a while, about the same time Erik was seeing her. He came around the house a number of times. He said, to see if Hesmerra needed anything. She was his mother-in-law, too, and she thought he felt guilty Esther didn't have much to do with her. Hesmerra always thanked him, but then sent him on his way. He always came just at suppertime, when he knew Greta would be home, never earlier in the day. She said sometimes there would be a look between them, that made her wonder. Later, after Billy was born, Fowler didn't come anymore."

"But Fowler never gave her money, presumably to support the boy? It was always Erik? And Billy had no clue to the truth?"

"As far as I could tell, Hesmerra managed to keep it all from him. I didn't repeat to her anything Sammie told me, but Hesmerra figured out for herself about the bridge 'accident,' she was certain Erik had killed Greta, she was certain Erik was Billy's father.

"Billy's aunts never came there to see her," Emmylou said, "so Billy wouldn't have overheard any comments from them. He thinks Erik came to see Hesmerra out of guilt because Debbie wouldn't visit her. And because Erik seemed to be truly fond of Hesmerra."

"Was he?"

"Erik's very smooth, always so charming. I never liked him. When he came, Hesmerra would ask me over for tea, but I was never comfortable. I always felt his friendliness, and the money and whiskey were like a sales pitch, like window dressing."

"Did Hesmerra see that? Why did she go along with it? She could have come to us," Kathleen said again. "We could have reopened an investigation into Greta's death."

"Hesmerra had something else in mind," Emmylou said. "Something more."

Kathleen waited. When Emmylou didn't continue, she said, "You had a box of papers with real estate letterheads, and with the Kraft letterhead. Do they tie into this?"

"Yes. They were in a metal box, under her bed. I dug it out of the burn." She reached into her canvas tote, withdrew a thick packet of business papers and letters and laid them on the desk; she had the grace not to deny she'd lifted them. "That's everything that was in the box. Captain Harper saw it in my car."

Kathleen nodded, and picked up the stack of papers. Below in the shadows, Joe was so edgy to have a look that Dulcie had to nudge him to be still. Kathleen shuffled through, pausing to read passages, her expression growing more intent as she compared a number of pages. She looked up at Emmylou. "Where did Hesmerra get these? Some of the dates are recent, business that seems still in progress. Hesmerra stole these from Erik?"

Emmylou looked down at her hands, then shyly up at Kathleen. "This was Hesmerra's retribution. It took her a long time to collect these, working in his office at night, and cleaning Alain's house, too. It took too long," she said bitterly.

"Those papers," she said, "together with what Debbie has, should be enough to put Erik Kraft in prison. Erik may never serve time for Greta's death, there may be no sure way to prove he killed her. But Hesmerra meant to see him pay."

"But Sammie saw him kill her, she could have come forward."

"Sammie was afraid. She felt she had no real proof. She was afraid she wouldn't have enough to convict him, that he'd go to trial but then go free, and would come after her."

"He'd be a fool to do that, to harm someone who'd testified against him."

"No one said he wasn't foolhardy, that he didn't make stupid choices." Emmylou frowned. "Only recently did Sammie seem bolder. I think she was getting tired of being watched and followed, tired of his sly bullying."

Kathleen sat looking at her. "All along, while Hesmerra was taking his money, she was working to destroy him."

"Yes. She made copies at night, from Erik's personal files, then put the originals back. Evidence of fraud, real estate scams, and theft. That's what she and Debbie were working toward, together."

"But Debbie—"

"Debbie hated her mother, yes. In her opinion it was Hesmerra's fault, that Erik was able to lure Greta into bed. Allowing Greta too much freedom, not keeping track of where she was. As if Hesmerra could have done much. Greta was never an angel, Hesmerra said she was headstrong, defied her at every turn. And Erik. I see him as sly and smooth, I think he may be totally without conscience.

"A year or so after Greta was killed," she said, "though Debbie still hated Hesmerra, they came together in this. Mother and daughter, teaming together to ruin him, each to have her own revenge. Working together, they thought they could put him in prison. If not for murder, then for fraud, for as many felony counts as they could provide."

In the shadows, Joe and Dulcie were both thinking the same. Right now, Erik was still in control, he had ended each life that crossed him: Greta. Hesmerra. Sammie Miller. So far, all but Debbie herself.

29

Yesterday's snow seemed long forgotten, the morning was nearly too warm, the birds and squirrels were out everywhere, soaking up the sun. At the edge of the cemetery, Joe slipped down from the branches of a thick and twisted oak onto the manicured lawn. February weather on the central coast was always fitful, cold one day, hot the next, but on this day the events to occur were even more at odds: Hesmerra's burial this morning that marked the end of an unhappy life. The auction this evening that should bring happiness to any number of lives, human and cat. And then, tonight, a late supper to mark what Joe hoped would be an incredibly long and happy married life, as Ryan and Clyde celebrated their first anniversary—and to top it off, it was Valentine's Day, a strange day, indeed, for Esther Fowler to choose to bury her mother.

This was Esther's bit of twisted irony? Sending Hesmerra off on a day of love, when there had been little love between them?

The early dew had nearly burned off, its last glitter broken by trails of cloven hoofprints leading away to the woods that surrounded three sides of the small cemetery. Joe could see deer among the shadowed trees, quietly grazing, relinquishing their nighttime pasture to the unpredictable whims of the human world.

The grave markers were all set flat into the velvet grass, its expanse broken only by three miniature hills: outcroppings of boulders that thrust up out of the earth as if shoved up by an unseen hand, and from which, oak trees had managed to grow. Joe headed for the rocky hill nearest the open grave.

Leaping up the boulders, he lay down among them, between the gray oak trunks so he was nearly invisible except for his white nose and white paws. Below him the freshly dug grave was discreetly covered by a sheet of blue plastic edged by a scattering of black earth to hold it in place. The pile of removed earth, too, was dressed in plastic, like a low blue tent. The plain oak casket stood to one side, facing five neat rows of metal chairs, a box that looked to Joe like the cheapest one available. It was a wonder Esther hadn't nailed together the slats from old orange crates.

The little access lane that ran near the grave was already filling up, a line of cars parked along the edge, two wheels on the macadam, two on the grass. Clyde's yellow roadster, in which Joe himself had ridden to the funeral in style with the top down and sitting on Ryan's lap. Charlie's red SUV was parked behind it, then a couple of police cars. Then Max's truck, Emmylou's battered green sedan, a sleek tan Mercedes belonging to Esther Fowler, and a number of cars he didn't know. He was surprised to see so many folks turn out for Hesmerra. Esther and Debbie stood far apart, at opposite sides of the gathering, pointedly ignoring each other. Tessa clung to Debbie, who had Vinnie firmly by the hand. A half-dozen more cars drew in and parked, the drivers' windows open to the warming morning, and behind them, Wilma's car came up the street.

She paused at the turn-in, her driver's door opened, Dulcie and Kit leaped from her lap and vanished into the woods. Joe could see Lucinda in the front seat beside Wilma, Pedric in the back. Wilma drove on in, parked, and they got out, all three respectfully dressed, no casual jeans today. Lucinda wore a long, slim black skirt, black boots, a soft shawl in muted tones. Pedric was nattily dressed in a tan suit, white shirt, and plain brown tie, his tall, slim figure fashion perfect. Wilma had resurrected what looked like a dark business suit from her working days, narrow skirt, soft white blouse, flat dark shoes. Among the women present, only Debbie wore high heels, apparently unaware that she could not walk across the grass without sinking in. Joe watched her tiptoe over the turf, hunching in her short, tight skirt. An usher escorted her to the front row beside Esther, who was dressed more appropriately in a plain brown suit and flats. Neither looked at the other, neither spoke.

Joe heard a rustle of leaves and then Dulcie was beside him; and when he looked up, Kit crouched on a jutting ledge of granite, her yellow eyes shuttered against the sun. At the grave, four men in black suits stood to one side of the chairs, cemetery employees as rigid and expressionless as plastic department store figures. There would be no indoor service for Hesmerra, just this simple burial. Among the rows of folding chairs, people were sitting down, talking in whispers and occasionally glancing at Billy where he stood to the side between Charlie and Emmylou. Charlie held his hand, and Emmylou's arm was around his shoulders. When Charlie bent to ask him something, he shook his head. Maybe he didn't want to go up to the front, beside his two aunts. During the short service, Max Harper stood watching Debbie. Did that make her nervous?

She seemed more aware of him than of saying farewell to her mother.

The minister wore the requisite black habit, his spiel short, dry, and generic. Until this morning, he had probably never heard of Hesmerra Young. He prayed dryly for her soul, then prayed for Billy, which made the boy look down in embarrassment. Joe had never imagined he'd find something as grim as a funeral too short, but this service seemed cruelly abrupt. The four attendants stepped forward, removed the plastic cover from the grave. Lifting the casket by the two heavy black ropes that had been laid under it, they lowered it down into the hole, and deftly pulled the ropes out. Either the cemetery hadn't seen fit to provide, or Esther hadn't wanted to pay for, one of those machines that lift the casket securely into its last resting place without the possibility of it falling on its side and dislodging its contents. Esther picked up a handful of earth and tossed it in. Debbie rose and did the same, as Tessa hid in her chair. Vinnie stepped forward, snatched up a big clod of dirt, threw it hard down onto the casket.

Billy was the last to take up a handful of earth and scatter it. He stood a moment, his back to Joe, his head bent, then turned away, perhaps as much from the gaze of his aunts as from this last and final contact with his grandmother. What Billy was feeling had to be as mixed and confused as had been his young life. A child doing a grown-up's work, taking care of an old woman who preferred to remain as helpless as a child herself, a child held captive by his grandmother's weaknesses and by her twisted life. Watching the boy filled Joe with a heavy sadness, and when he looked at Dulcie, his dismay was reflected in her green eyes. Kit's ears were down, too, her yellow eyes sad, hurt that a young boy's life could be so without joy. For all three cats, the mysterious balance between joy and pain was the deepest mystery they knew, the real meaning of that conflict was too confusing to sort out, in this life.

Billy and Charlie didn't linger over the grave, the cats could see he wanted to get away. Within minutes, he and Charlie got into her SUV and pulled on around the curve behind one of the black-and-whites, making the circle through the cemetery to the main road, heading away toward the ranch. Nearly everyone seemed glad to escape, moving toward their cars, including Wilma and the Greenlaws. Kit looked back toward Dulcie and Joe, but then she went on, wanting to be with her old couple, caught perhaps in the sadness of the funeral and the fragility of life.

Quickly Debbie turned to leave, too, she was dragging the children away when Max caught up with her. "Debbie?" She turned to look at him, frowning.

"Would you want to come on down to the station? We have some papers we'd like you to look over, they were among your mother's things. Do you have someone to watch the children for a while?" Joe glanced across at Ryan and Clyde, they were just about the only people remaining. If Max was going to press them into babysitting, he was out of there.

"No," she said, "I don't have anyone to watch the children. We just buried my mother, this is not a good time. What is it, that can't wait?"

"The papers were just brought to our attention, and could be important. You can bring the children, it won't take long. One of the officers will watch them."

"This really isn't an appropriate time."

"It's a good time for me," Max said. "I don't see the need to arrest you, just for questioning, if you're willing to cooperate. I'll follow you down to the station."

Debbie gave a dramatic sigh, and headed for her car. Opening the back door, she pushed the girls in the backseat.

"Well," Dulcie said, smiling.

"Come on," Joe said, racing for Clyde's roadster just ahead of his housemates. As the cats leaped in, the little cemetery tractor came lumbering along the lane. It stopped at the open grave, uncovered the mound of earth, and began to scoop it over the casket, patting it down with the tractor's toothy bucket. Soon the two gardeners would lay squares of sod over the raw earth; in a few weeks the grass would fill in, and the velvet lawn would look as if no hole had ever been dug there. Deer would graze on Hesmerra's grave, leaving cloven hoof prints in the damp grass. Joe wondered if Debbie or Esther, or Billy, would bring flowers to put in a little vase. Off in the woods, two deer had stopped grazing and stood watching the tractor at work, and for some reason, their interest made the fur along Joe's back prickle. Then Ryan and Clyde were there at the car and, at Joe's direction, Clyde headed obligingly for MPPD.

The two cats beat Max to the station by minutes, as the chief dawdled along behind Debbie, who in his presence seemed compelled to obey every village speed limit. By the time the two little girls had been settled in the conference room with Officer Brennan, Vinnie complaining all the while, Dulcie and Joe were under Max's credenza. They watched Debbie flounce in, into one of the leather chairs as if she owned the place. Behind her, Max was saying, "I can't give you any guarantees. We'll do what we can. If he's put away for a while, you won't have to hide from him." He sat down at his desk, leaning back. "Were the transactions all on Molena Point property?"

"Some were here," Debbie said. "Most of them, they couldn't have pulled off here, in their own territory. They had deals going in five states, sales I'm sure can't be legal." She looked at him pleadingly. "If he finds out I was here, that I told—"

Max said, "You have no choice. You were ordered to come in." That seemed to ease her, she looked uncertain, but relaxed a little. He said, "How did you get your hands on the papers without him knowing?"

"Late at night, when I was sure Erik was asleep. I photographed whatever papers were in his briefcase that day. I didn't dare use his copier, I was afraid he'd check that little counter thing that keeps track. I took digital photos, put them on my computer, printed them out, put them on a disc, then erased the hard drive." She looked intently at Harper, a more intelligent look than the cats had seen, a look not just of anger now, at being hauled into the station, but of a canny malice. "They'd sell one house several times. Sell it over and over again."

"You mean buy it back, and sell it again?"

"No, they didn't buy it back. They just kept selling it. Out-of-state buyers, people who never even flew out to see what they'd bought. They looked at the pictures and maps he sent, took his word for everything. People who wanted investment property. Erik invented fake titles, drew up fake escrow papers, fake deeds. He and Alain made the sales just after the yearly property taxes were paid, so no one would inquire about a tax bill, find it was in the wrong name." She went quiet, looking down at her hands. Max waited, relying on that void in a conversation that will prompt an interviewee, uncomfortable in the silence, to frantically fill up the empty space, revealing perhaps more than he intended.

Debbie fidgeted, and sighed. "They'd buy old, run-down foreclosures, too. Take pictures, doctor the pictures on the computer to make them look like a nice renovation, nice landscaping. Advertise them on the Web, for sale by owner. They'd double the price, again sell to some out-of-state buyer who didn't have time to come out and look at the place, who wanted coastal real estate for investment. I know of one buyer, bought five houses. Erik's agreement was, he'd rent the houses out for them until the market went up and they could make a profit, he'd keep ten percent of the rent, send the buyer the balance. That part was legitimate, and why not? He'd already made a hundred percent profit on the deal. It was easy to find tenants, people scrambling for low rent. They did all this under fictitious Realtor's names, so if the buyer wanted to sell, or came out here and got a look at the house, he couldn't track them down."

"Did you plan to bring this to the attention of the police or the real estate board, either here or in Eugene?"

She looked down again. "I . . . Eventually, I meant to. I made the copies so I'd have some power over him. So he'd give me a decent support settlement and child support." She looked up at him pleadingly. "If I went to the cops right away, I'd lose what power I had. I thought . . . I meant to wait until I could bargain for a cash settlement. Then give him the papers I had, and that Mama had, and promise to leave it alone. Maybe, then, I'd bring you copies. It . . . It was for the children," she added lamely.

Max didn't look like he was buying all this. Nor were Joe and Dulcie. What made her think Erik would believe her when she promised to back off? What made her think he wouldn't get really angry and turn more violent? Joe guessed that now, with Hesmerra dead, and Sammie dead, Debbie was feeling a little less cocky in her expectations.

Or, he thought, was she only making up Erik's scams? Maybe for some agenda of her own? Maybe setting him up for something he really hadn't done? Joe had little doubt Erik Kraft had knocked her around, he could see the fading shadows of bruises on her face and neck—unless she was an artist with the makeup, he thought with interest. A little purple eye shadow, carefully applied? Yet it made perfect sense that Kraft, known for his ironfisted business ways, would be raking off all he could, and that he wouldn't be soft with Debbie. If Kraft and Alain *were* into illegal deals, and he found out Debbie had proof, Joe didn't doubt that he'd turn more violent, just as Debbie feared.

Max said, "Your mother was in on this? You knew about the papers she had?"

Debbie just looked at him.

"You knew your mother was cleaning the Kraft offices," he said patiently. "That she took that job with the night crew of Barton's Commercial Cleaning, in order to gather evidence."

Reluctantly, Debbie nodded. "I knew."

"Did you put her onto that company?"

Again, a nod.

From the shadows, Dulcie glanced up at Joe. Everything seemed to fit, just as Emmylou had said. Debbie and her mother working together to bring Eric down, Debbie in contact with Hesmerra all along, unknown to Billy. Was it possible that Hesmerra had, at some point, balked at any more spying? Decided to pull out? Maybe she wasn't sure that Eric *had* killed Greta, after all? Maybe she'd wondered if Perry Fowler had? Maybe she'd grown to like Eric, didn't want to think him guilty of murder or of the scams?

Or maybe Hesmerra grew afraid of him, became nervous that he might find out what she was up to? Maybe she decided to go to the cops with what proof she had, before Erik turned on her.

But going to the law would destroy Debbie's power over Erik before she had a chance to extort money from him. Would that make her angry enough to stop Hesmerra? To kill her own mother? From the looks of the sales contracts and letters, the rake-off for this operation could have run into the nine figures, and people had killed for a lot less. In a way, that seemed a far stretch: No matter the bad blood between them, they *were* mother and daughter. Except, Joe thought, murder within a family wasn't all that unusual, it was often the first place the police would look, in an investigation.

But what of Alain? Where was she now, having left town when her deals went awry? Where had she gone when she pulled out to save herself?

As for that, was Erik down in southern California straightening out the branch office as Fowler claimed? Or had he already flown off to the Bahamas on vacation? Or had Erik and Alain both skipped? The two lovers gone off together taking with them the money gleaned from their various scams?

If they had, did Perry Fowler know that? Had Fowler, all along, been in on their operations and lied to protect Erik? Or was he, as he appeared, aware only of Alain's wrongdoing and ignorant of Erik's own involvement?

It didn't matter where Erik was the morning of the fire when Hesmerra died; what mattered was, where was he when someone poisoned her whiskey? As to that, where was he when Sammie was killed?

And wherever he was, Joe thought, smiling, did he know how vulnerable he had become? Did he know that, from the evidence laid out on Max's desk right now, plus whatever else the detectives and the CSI team might find, there could soon be a warrant out for him, an order that could perceptibly change his opulent lifestyle?

Joe was sorry to have missed Max's interview of Fowler; he hadn't known about it until he glimpsed a notation among the papers on Max's desk. He pictured the pale, wimpy Realtor slouched in the leather chair farthest from Max's desk nervously answering the chief's questions—nervous simply at having to deal with the police, or from more than that?

From what Joe could see of Max's notes Fowler had known nothing about Erik's scams. Possibly, Joe thought, Fowler had suspected what Erik was up to but hadn't wanted to think badly of his partner? Hadn't wanted to rock the boat, hadn't wanted to confront

Erik? Hadn't really wanted to find out what was going on? Some people were like that, didn't want to know all the facts, to see what was too awkward, too painful.

And how convenient that many of Erik's scams had been made through bogus real estate firms and nonexisting escrow companies, venues that Erik had fabricated, and were not connected to Kraft Realty. Given that Fowler didn't appear to have much backbone, he might latch onto that fact as exonerating the firm itself from any connection to Erik's crimes, ignoring those that did involve their partnership. *Foolish,* Joe thought, *and self-destructive. But hey, we're dealing with humans, here. What's a cat to expect?*

30

Kit didn't join the other cats high on the balcony of the Aronson Gallery as they looked down on the auction party nor, in the soft evening, did she slip in with Lucinda and Pedric when they entered among the jostling crowd; nor did Pan appear. Misto arrived in style riding from the Firettis' van on John's shoulder. But as John and Mary approached the front door, the old cat left them, leaping up into a tangle of jasmine vine that climbed the stucco wall. Clawing his way up to the high little window that opened above him, he could see Dulcie looking out. He disappeared inside, onto the gallery's balcony, and there he sat with Dulcie looking down through the railing, watching the party crowd below. "Where's Joe Grey?"

"Out in Ryan's truck," she said. "He'll be along shortly. He'd never miss supper." She glanced down at the fine buffet laid out below, licking her whiskers at the aromas that rose up to them.

The Aronson Gallery, along with the café and bookstore that joined it, was a favorite meeting place for the villagers. Wide archways linked the three airy shops, and a walled patio opened through glass doors at the back of the café. The gallery's high white walls featured tonight not a carefully selected art exhibit, but the items to be auctioned: five vibrant oriental rugs that hung on the exhibit panels, flanked by small pieces of handmade furniture, some intricately carved, some painted in vivid patterns by one of the cats' human friends. There was sporting equipment, even a canoe. Charlie Harper's animal paintings and etchings occupied one long wall and included portraits of several of the rescue cats— while out on the patio the rescue cats themselves were housed in oversized cages among the potted flowers and little tables, each of the ten cages featuring two to three friendly felines looking for new homes.

As the auction party gathered, out on the street Ryan and Charlie sat in Ryan's truck, Joe Grey on the seat between them as Charlie passed on what Max had told her as they'd headed for the auction. "Autopsy's finished on the second body. They don't have a positive

ID yet, but they're pretty sure it's Alain Bent. They found a .32 slug that had entered near the temple. Same riflings as the .32 slug Kathleen dug out of the acacia tree, which appears to have passed through Sammie's throat."

She looked down at Joe. "Those white marks on Sammie's back? CSI's photographs of them, and Kathleen's shots of the acacia tree roots, are a perfect match. Looks like the killer shot her there as if maybe she was hiding from him. Left her lying there for several hours. As the body cooled, her blood pooled around where the roots pressed in, that's what made the white marks, pressure from the roots, pressing all the blood out."

"Maybe he left her there until dark," Joe said, "then dragged her into the cellar."

"That's what they think. Pathologist says the blood on the acacia roots is O positive, same as Sammie's, though that type's common enough. You know how long it takes to get DNA, with the lab backed up."

Joe knew some two- and three-year-old cases were still waiting. Outside the truck he could hear folks talking and laughing as they hurried inside. "What about the cell phone Kathleen dug from under the tree?"

"It's Sammie's, all right," Charlie said. "Complete with photos to add to the evidence. Kathleen printed out five shots of a tall, lean man dragging a woman's body across the yard—that could be the first victim. From the angle of the shot, looks like Sammie might have taken them from the cottage window. Kathleen made some enlargements where you can see a portion of the woman's face, and an old scar on her upper left arm, and it sure looks like Alain. CSI has contacted Alain's dentist for a positive ID. The man's face wasn't visible, only his back. Dark hair, tall. From his haircut, and the angles of his body, looks very much like Erik Kraft. Forensics is working to lift prints from the victim's clothes."

"No gun?" Joe said.

"Not yet," Charlie said.

"You want it all, right now," Ryan said, laughing, unceremoniously picking Joe up. "Come on, we're missing the party." She and Charlie swung out of the truck, Ryan carrying Joe over her shoulder. Going in through the gallery door, she stopped just beneath the balcony—gave Joe a little toss, and he leaped up to the second floor, scrambling through the rail, where Dulcie and Misto sat looking down on the crowd, still eyeing the buffet, and Dulcie assessing the women's attire with as keen an eye as any fashion model.

Joe settled down between them and, in whispers, repeated what Charlie had told him; and didn't that make Misto smile. The old cat liked their clandestine role, he liked helping the cops. He liked the mix of human skill and electronic techniques, with the skills that only a cat could have offered.

"Where's Kit?" Joe said. "Where's Pan?"

"Not a clue," Dulcie said innocently.

Misto looked at them and smiled. Beyond the windows, the evening was balmy, the sky so clear that every star shimmered. "A perfect night for a hunt in the hills," the old cat said. "Or, for a bit of romance on the rooftops?" he said thoughtfully.

Dulcie gave the two toms a sly little smile.

"She's a charming lady," Misto said.

"She's very young," Joe said in a fatherly manner that made Dulcie laugh.

But in truth Kit and Pan weren't preening and flirting, not at the moment. Nor were they hunting the starlit hills—though they *were* stalking some human game, following Erik Kraft.

Did anyone know he was back in the village? Had they spotted him before even the cops had? They had been on the roofs, wandering in the direction of the auction, when they saw lights on in Kraft's second-floor condo; they had galloped across the roofs to the rear of his penthouse, where the little walled terrace shut away any ugly view of roof vents and heating units and of the narrow back stairs that led down to the street.

When they peered in under the low, wide arches that had been left along the bottom of the stucco wall for drainage, a soft light shone out through the wide glass doors, and the closed curtain shifted in the breeze where the slider stood open. They could see the flickering light of a television, too, and could hear its tedious recap of yesterday's snowfall, details already far outdated, on this balmy evening.

They could see a round teak table against the terrace wall with two folding canvas chairs, and three flowerpots containing dead geraniums as dry as old hay. They saw no movement beyond the glass, no shifting shadows. "Come on," Kit said, and bellied under, emerging to paw roofing gravel from her fur, shake gravel from her paws. The air drifting out smelled of steam and shaving soap. Kit reached her nose to push the curtain aside, sniffing at the aroma of lime soap and at the scent of male human. Carefully they peered in.

The apartment was stark, very modern and not to either cat's taste, all done in black and chrome against cold blue walls: chrome headboard, chrome chairs with black leather slings, a glimpse of chrome kitchen cabinets beyond the bedroom. They could hear him in the bathroom, where a brighter light shone through the cracked-open door with a glimpse of black marble floor, mirrored walls, they could see his shadow moving about. Warily they pushed on into the bedroom, their paws sinking into the deep black carpet. They paused with the curtain still across their backs, listening.

The bedcovers were tumbled in a heap, white silk sheets, soft black comforter, a sleek black phone on the nightstand beneath a chrome lamp. A closed suitcase, made of expensive black leather, sat on a chrome stand near the closet doors, just below the recessed TV that was still belaboring bygone snow scenes. A pair of jeans lay dropped on the carpet beside a pair of black Italian boots, worn and dirty. Brown shirt thrown over the back of a chrome chair, black leather jacket folded across the chair's arm. When Kit approached the clothes, they smelled of smoke and ashes, smelled exactly like the burn. As she pressed forward to look closer, Pan's hiss stopped her; the sound of a sliding door made her dive beneath the bed.

But then they heard the shower come on, water pounding. As a cloud of steam ghosted out to them, Kit approached the clothes again, sniffing. His boots smelled of ashes, and were streaked with gray. The pounding of the shower was broken by the sluicing sounds of someone vigorously washing. She said, "He's been at the burn, he's been up at Hesmerra's, so what was he looking for? The papers she stole?" Then, "Oh!" she said, as she turned. Rearing up, she peered at the top of the dresser. "Oh my, what's this?" she said, smiling.

On the dresser stood a thin black laptop, its case open, its cord plugged into the wall, its lighted screen not as bright as the TV, writhing in an abstract pattern of purple and red squares that changed and retreated and appeared again as the screensaver did its work. Leaping up, Kit reached out a paw, then warily drew it back, looking down at Pan. "You any good with these things?" She wished she had Dulcie's expertise.

"I never had the chance, Erik was as secretive with his computer as he was with his files and papers. I can adjust a patient's oxygen, I can work some of the levers on a folding bed and ring the alarm for a nurse. But computers, no way—I could erase everything."

Kit was afraid she'd do exactly that. The laptop was not at all like Pedric and Lucinda's big computer at home, everything seemed different, there wasn't even a proper mouse. One wrong stroke, and whatever evidence it might contain could vanish forever. She studied the keyboard. Uncertainly she reached out again, and drew back again, looking down helplessly at Pan.

But she had to do something. It wasn't in Kit's nature to back away. She had to make *something* happen.

Carefully she pressed the flat space that she thought might be the built-in mouse. The screensaver vanished, and a page of e-mails flashed at her: two short messages, the first signed by a *Betty*. Could that be Alain Bent's cousin? But why . . . ? The second was signed by Alain herself, dated three days ago, long after she was murdered. Kit caught only a few words when the pounding of water stopped, " . . . Toronto, promise to be home next week and we can . . ." They heard the shower door slide open. As the bathroom door opened, she dropped to the floor and under the bed expecting Pan to follow. He didn't, she heard him hit the bed above her and burrow under the covers. As she peered out, Erik came out of the bathroom naked and headed for the closet as if to retrieve clean clothes. He moved quickly, tense and in a hurry.

When he slid the closet door back, the rod and shelves were nearly empty. He removed one of three shirts and the only pair of jeans. From behind the fallen covers she watched him jerk the suitcase open, grab a pair of black Jockey shorts and black socks, and begin to hurriedly pull on his clothes. Why the rush? Was he afraid a police patrol would see the light, find out he'd returned? Why had he come back at all?

As nervous as he was, and with a suitcase packed and waiting, this time might he be gone for good, taking with him the evidence to fraud and murder? What, in fact, could be more damning than that he'd been faking Alain's e-mail—while she lay rotting in her grave?

She wondered if he had just now heard about the fire? If he had poisoned Hesmerra's whiskey months earlier, had he just now learned that she was dead? Had he come back to find the papers he knew she'd stolen, papers he'd searched for before she died, and had never found?

The laptop lay on the dresser just a few feet above her. Once Kraft vanished again, even as efficient as MPPD was, there was the chance he'd somehow evade them. If she knocked the little computer off the dresser onto the soft carpet, she and Pan could drag it, between them. She was trying to think how to get it out the door unseen when Erik finished dressing and turned to the bed; silently she slid deeper out of sight.

She heard him throw the covers back, perhaps meaning to lay the suitcase on the bed and open it. With a swish of sheets, the quilt fell to the floor—she thought Pan would leap clear of it and run, maybe distracting Erik so she could snag the laptop.

Pan didn't run, she heard him hiss and growl, and knew he must be standing boldly where Erik had jerked the covers away. She slid out behind Erik, to look. Oh my. Pan stood facing Erik, snarling like a cougar, his claws bared, his daggered paw lifted to strike.

Kraft backed away. Clearly he recognized the tomcat, this cat he had tormented—clearly he thought that if the cat was there in the village, Debbie must be there, that she must have brought the cat with her. His puzzlement made Kit want to laugh, but his rage scared her so bad her paws began to sweat.

Was he wondering if Debbie had come back because of her mother's death, if she suspected *he'd* killed Hesmerra? Seeing Pan seemed to ignite all his anger at Debbie. When he lunged for Pan, the tomcat struck, his bared claws tearing long slashes down Erik's arm and hand, then he leaped away and fled for the open glass door, Kit beside him looking back, reluctant to leave the laptop.

But Erik was fast, he blocked the opening, kicking at them, jerked the door closed, and lunged to grab them. They vanished under the bed, waiting with claws lifted for his hand to reach under. He kicked the bed and swore, but he didn't kneel down and reach in. When he couldn't drive them out by kicking and pounding on the bed he turned away, as if to waste no more time on stray cats.

Peering out, they watched him snatch a handkerchief from the suitcase, wrap it around his hand, and toss the last of his clothes in, watched him fetch a batch of papers from the top dresser drawer and drop those in on top. Before closing the suitcase, he returned to the bathroom. Kneeling before the vanity, he removed a drawer, and then slid a portion of the cabinet's inner wall aside.

A small metal safe was set into the wall. Deftly he worked the dial, swung the little door open, and began to remove thick packets of money, bills bound together with paper strips. From behind these he pulled out a dozen plastic tubes, each half as big around as a tiny cat food can, but longer and made of pale, thick plastic.

"Gold coins," Pan whispered, his words barely a breath. "He had cylinders like that in Eugene, I watched him count out the coins, each one as bright as the sun."

As Erik tucked this fortune into the suitcase and locked it, Kit crept out from beneath the bed and hid among the black folds of quilt. She watched him turn off the laptop and unplug it, watched him wind the cord and slip it into a side pocket of the computer case, watched him zip the case and set it atop the suitcase. As he returned to the bathroom to lock and conceal the safe, the cats were a blur. They leaped on the suitcase, dragged the laptop off and to the door, and they were out of there, their hearts hammering as they fought the door open and hauled the laptop through, their teeth deep in the leather case. They dragged it across the patio, noisily across the scatter of gravel, and out of sight beneath the patio wall. Kit was ready to race away with it, when Pan set down his end and vanished under the wall again into the terrace. She peered under.

Kraft was still in the bathroom, she could see his moving shadow. She watched Pan take a roofing pebble in his mouth, leap to the glass door, and push the pebble down into the bottom track, wedging it in just where the door would shut, a tiny black pebble that might never be noticed within the creases of the dark metal track.

Pan returned from beneath the wall, saying nothing. He picked up his end of the laptop, and they carried it between them, their teeth firmly in its padded case. They dragged it across the roofs and up a sharp peak, and down again within a sheltered niche where three roofs joined—down into a dark and shingled crevice not easily accessible to a human, only to someone smaller and more agile. Sliding the laptop into deep darkness, they scrambled out again and ran. Erik Kraft wasn't likely to climb up those peaks and look down.

They raced down the stairs and up the street into the shadows of a narrow alley, and there they waited for Kraft to appear. "He'll think it fell on the floor," Pan said. "Black laptop, black carpet, black folds of comforter. Take him a minute to realize it isn't there. When he sees the slider open . . ." He went still, listening. They heard the glass door open, heard Kraft race across the terrace, heard the patio table rattle as he scrambled over the wall. They didn't run. Backing deeper among the shadows, they wanted to see what he would do, listened to his footsteps pounding across the roof and down, watched from their dark recess as he raced up the sidewalk stopping strangers, asking questions, looking for an escaping thief. Watched him peer into parked cars, race from one little alley to the next, stop to stare in through the doors of closed shops.

"When he gives up," Kit said, smiling, "when he knows he won't find it, what's he going to do? Call the cops? File a report for one stolen laptop, that's ripe with evidence?"

Pan gave her a satisfied look as they followed Kraft around the corner, watched him double-time up the front stairs.

"He'll grab his bag and be out of there," Kit said. "We need to see his car, get his license, *then* we call the station." She turned to look at Pan, her green eyes widening. "The pebble!" she said. "*That's* what the pebble was for? So we can get back inside."

31

Looking down from the balcony to the crowded room, Joe cut a look at Dulcie. How easy to drop down onto the buffet table, right between the sliced turkey and the salmon mousse, grab a few bites before anyone even noticed.

"Don't even think about it," Dulcie said. Misto smiled, the older cat, too, envisioning a grand leap into the heart of the feast—what a stir they'd make in the crowded room.

People were still arriving, eager for the auction, and Joe thought about all the money CatFriends would raise tonight, to pay for cat food and medicine. Out through the tall windows on the patio, the rescue cats themselves, safe in their cages, were drawing as much attention as the treasures to be bid upon. They were of every color, every disposition. Some rubbed against the bars or reached out a friendly paw to whoever spoke to them. Only a few backed off, keeping their distance, still distrustful since their own humans had abandoned them. Sammie Miller's two black-and-white cats snuggled together on a blue blanket looking up hopefully when anyone approached. Twenty-five unadopted strays, from the sixty-two cats that CatFriends had trapped and placed in foster homes. Those who didn't find homes tonight were destined to become permanent members of their adopters' families—but they didn't know that. They looked out through the bars at a conflicted and perplexing world: They were imprisoned, but they were safe. Surrounded by kind hands and gentle voices, but yet crowded by too many strangers pressing against their cages. Frightened or friendly, they didn't know what was happening to them. "Maybe," Dulcie said, "they'll all find new homes tonight."

The auction would not be a silent affair with a prim sorting out of written offers, this would be a lively free-for-all of bidding, led by a volunteer auctioneer who had driven down for the occasion from Sacramento: a friend of Max Harper's who presided over all manner of auctions including the horse sales, which was where Max and Charlie had met him. Among the prizes to be auctioned, besides various valuable maintenance services and luxurious vacation weekends, and Charlie's drawings, and the decorative rugs and furniture, the bright blue ocean kayak stood upended in one corner of the gallery, crowded by handsome brass lanterns and other select items for the boat lover, a set of state-of-the-art golf clubs, a Stübben English saddle, a carved Western saddle, both saddles on racks, both valued at several thousand, and a locked glass case displaying ten pieces of diamond and emerald jewelry, all donations from various local shops for the abandoned cats. Joe had already spotted a number of MPPD officers among the crowd, all out of uniform, all enjoying the party but watchful, in the event unknown visitors were tempted by the high value of the jewelry and sports equipment.

As the three cats watched the auctioneer take his place on the podium, and the mayor join him to say a few words, they didn't imagine that, away among the dark rooftops Kit and Pan had narrowly escaped an angry and desperate Erik Kraft—with evidence enough to put Kraft in the hands of the county DA and of federal authorities as well.

As Kraft raced up the front stairs to retrieve his suitcase, Kit and Pan crouched near the entrance to the underground parking garage waiting in the shadows to see the make of his car and his license number. Kraft was gone maybe ten minutes, then came hurrying down, two steps at a time, carrying the black suitcase, his black leather jacket slung over one shoulder barely hiding a shoulder holster and the butt of a handgun. Moving swiftly down the ramp, he disappeared into the parking garage. They heard a car door open and slam, an engine start, and in a minute a black, two-door Audi sped up the incline, Kraft's profile sharp against the garage lights. Kit took one look at the California license plate and would remember it for life. The minute his car roared off, they raced around to the back steps and up to his condo, worried that he'd found the pebble and dislodged it, and locked the slider. Or, in his hurry, had he abandoned the faulty door and locked only the front door? Why bother with an apparently broken latch, when he must have taken everything of importance with him anyway? The money, the little cylinders of gold, the real estate papers or contracts? Up the back stairs they streaked, under the wall, and with frantic paws they scrabbled at the glass door.

Together they slid it open and bolted inside, Kit laughing at the resourcefulness of the red tomcat, and leaped to the bed beside the phone. Pan had never had so much fun. Nothing he'd ever done, from comforting the nursing home patients, to the edgy thrill of hitching rides with strangers, could equal the excitement of facing human evil head-on, of attacking this man who seemed so eager to turn humans' lives to ruin.

It took Kit only a few minutes to make the call. By the time they fled the condo again, racing down the back stairs and around to the front, Kathleen was already pulling to the curb, Max in her car beside her. Two black-and-whites pulled up behind them, and on the side street two more police units moved swiftly past, heading in the direction of Highway One. They imagined more patrol cars setting out to comb the area, skimming the night as silent as sharks. Kit had told Max about the laptop and its counterfeit messages from Alain, she told him about the safe, the money, the holstered gun. The call had been a long one, never before had a snitch told an officer so much, or had stayed on the line to answer his questions. She couldn't explain why she did that, why she didn't back off.

"You *took* the laptop, from his apartment?" Max had said. "You broke in and—"

"I didn't break in, I walked in. The back slider was wide open." Her paws were cold with unease, she wanted to race away but she wanted, more, to keep talking.

"You went over the wall into his private patio?"

"Well, yes. I looked over, and saw the door was open."

"What were you doing on the roof?"

"I went up the stairs, I knew the back of his condo was there and I was curious. I looked over, saw the door open, saw the lighted computer screen. Saw there were messages on it, and when I saw they were signed Alain, dated long after she left the village, I thought you might want it." Now, her paws were sweating. "He was all packed and ready to leave. I thought, if I didn't take it, he might erase those messages before you ever saw them."

There was a little silence, as if he'd expected her to hang up. She said, "When he found the laptop missing he burst through the door looking for me, he came after me. I didn't want him to catch me with it, he's bigger, he'd have taken it. I hid it on the roofs, got rid of it where I didn't think he'd find it. Then I ran, tried to lead him away from it, down the back stairs. It's there now," she said, and described the hidden well between the precipitous roofs. "It's waiting for you to get it." And she'd hung up then, worrying that, because the laptop was stolen, maybe that would taint the evidence it contained. What did the law say about that? Had she and Pan, in their hurry to retrieve the evidence, only destroyed it themselves?

But what other choice did they have? Once he was on the freeway, the minute he saw the first cop after him, he'd erase everything, Alain's messages, whatever financial dealings were there. There'd be nothing left, all the proof vanished like smoke sucked away on the wind.

Kit thought later maybe she'd talked so long to Max because, without any explanation at all, their stealing of the laptop and hiding it on the roof, slipping it into that little niche that most humans would never notice, was too far out, too strange. Would create one more uneasy scenario to puzzle Max Harper, make him wonder just what kind of snitch would choose a hiding place that only a pigeon or roof rat might be aware of.

After they'd called Max, and had watched the police deploy after Kraft's car, they watched Max Harper and Kathleen head for the back stairs, watched Kathleen climb in over the steep roofs and retrieve the laptop. Watched her and Max head for her car, saw them grin at each other as they locked the laptop safely in the trunk. As their car turned up toward the freeway, the cats heard gunfire. One shot, two more, and they seemed very close. They had no way to know what was happening, they could only pray Kraft had been taken without any cops getting hurt. Kit debated whether to race for the station where they could hear the calls coming in, could follow the action via police radio. But there would be cops at the auction with their radios. When Charlie heard sirens and gunshots, wouldn't she get the news right away? And when Kit thought of the delicious buffet waiting, hunger won, she leaped away across the roofs for the gallery, Pan beside her, Kit worrying about her human friends, and both cats famished for supper.

32

Galloping over the rooftops for the gallery, Kit and Pan could hear the auctioneer's quick staccato and then in a minute other voices and laughter rising up, as if the auctioning had finished. Kit imagined folks heading for the buffet, and the good smells drew her on, making her lick her whiskers. But running full tilt, Pan stopped suddenly and doubled back, looking down and across the street.

Debbie's car was parked below, in front of the village Laundromat. The windows were open and little Tessa was looking out, both children were there, but not Debbie. They scanned the street and looked in through the Laundromat windows but didn't see her, and Kit flattened her ears, lashing her fluffy tail. "What kind of mother leaves her kids alone at night, on the street, in an unlocked car?"

"Debbie does," Pan said. "She has them sit up in front so if anyone bothers them, they can blow the horn."

"Fat lot of good that would do."

Pan crouched over the roof gutter looking down at Tessa, his expression so filled with longing that Kit reached out a paw, touched his paw gently. "You want to go down there?" she said softly. "We could—"

"I can't let Tessa see me. She'd never stop talking, telling her mother I'd followed them, begging her to look for me. And Vinnie? She catches one glimpse, who knows what trouble she'd make, asking how I got here. That kid won't leave anything alone, we don't need that kind of attention."

"Maybe, though . . ." Kit said, "maybe at night you could slip into the cottage to see Tessa? Wait until she's asleep, until they're all asleep, then talk to her the way you did before?"

"How do you know that?"

"Debbie told the Damens. She laughed at Tessa, made fun of her, said a talking cat was impossible, but Tessa wouldn't back down. She said that in the night, in the dark, you told her your true name. Joe heard it all, he told me and Dulcie. He said it was all he could do not to claw Debbie. No wonder Tessa never talks, when her mother is so sarcastic."

"I wish she hadn't told," Pan said quietly. "I did whisper to her, how else could she have named me? She's so small, and . . . dear," he said, looking embarrassed. "Debbie doesn't deserve her." He looked at Kit, flicking his ears. "Maybe . . . *Is* there some way I could visit her, get her to keep the secret?"

"If you *could* talk to her at night again, maybe you could help her. Show her how to survive that woman. I could be the lookout," Kit said. "I could watch Debbie and Vinnie, make sure they don't wake and hear you, make sure that Debbie, if she's still up, doesn't come sneaking in."

Pan smiled. "Maybe," he said. "Maybe we could do that." His amber eyes were so deep, his look so close and real it made her tremble. "Late in the night," he said softly, "when the house is dark, maybe we can help her, maybe together we can."

Charlie found all five cats in the bookstore, out of the way of the workers who were cleaning up the last of the buffet, folding up the big table and the metal chairs, putting the little café tables back in their usual places. On a bookstore table, Kit and Pan crouched before their empty plates waiting for news, licking the last smears of salmon mousse from their whiskers. Dulcie and Misto sat above them on a bookshelf, as Joe Grey paced back and forth along the shelves, the five cats waiting impatiently to know if Kraft had been caught. They'd heard no more shots, no more sirens, the night was silent, but somewhere out in the dark, officers might still be in danger.

Charlie sat down at the table beside Kit and Pan and flipped open her cell phone, pretending to make a call, to key in a number that never rang at the other end. She said softly, *"They got him."* The cats came to full attention, Joe Grey paused on the bookshelf and lay down just above her, and on the table Kit rolled over, handily drawing closer. All ears were up, all tails very still.

"They spotted the Audi headed north just before the off-ramp to the hospital. When he saw two patrol cars coming up fast behind him, and a CHP cutting across the median from the southbound lanes, he swerved up the ramp, doubled back southbound, weaving in and out. Cut a right at Carpenter, grazed two oncoming cars, headed up into the residential. A Realtor must know those little winding streets like the back of his hand, he must have been convinced he could lose them up there. It didn't work," she said, grinning. "They forced him over, he fired once at Brennan. McFarland took him down with two shots. He struggled out of the car bleeding, his hands up, and didn't fight anymore."

Kit was so pleased she almost laughed out loud.

No wonder we heard the shots, Joe thought. *Those hilly streets, they're only a few blocks from here, just up past the gallery.*

"He's all tucked away in the hospital," Charlie said. "Private room with a guard, regular VIP treatment. Max has talked with the DA, there's enough evidence for an arraignment, he was really pleased to have the laptop." She reached to pet Kit, and shyly to stroke the top of Pan's head. "Kathleen made copies of everything on it, the fake messages from Alain, all kinds of real estate transactions on a dozen different letterheads. From what they've found so far, those are all fake. They searched the condo, got a lock man up there to open the wall safe but of course it was empty. Max has the cash, maybe a hundred thousand and I don't know how much in gold. They're still lifting prints in the condo."

Well, Kit thought, the whole department had been busy. In the time it took the party to break up, and her and Pan to demolish their big plate of seafood, turkey, salmon mousse, and three desserts, everyone at the department had been hard at work, she imagined the computers and phones and fax machine just humming away. Never overly modest, tonight Kit felt pretty smug.

"The murders are in our jurisdiction," Charlie said, "but the real estate swindles reach way beyond California. Oregon, three Midwestern states, North Carolina and Virginia. Max is turning copies of that evidence over to the FBI, everything on the laptop, and the papers from Hesmerra's tin box. I expect our county DA will charge Kraft with multiple counts of real estate fraud, as well as two counts of murder—the investigation of Hesmerra's death is still under way." She glanced up as Billy came across the room. "See you next week," she said, pretending to end the call.

Billy had been helping with the cleanup, with moving tables and folding up cages; he'd worked willingly all evening at various tasks, but now as he approached, his expression wasn't happy, and he looked at Charlie forlornly. Away behind him, Perry and Esther Fowler stood watching.

He stepped close to the table, speaking softly. "They said . . . My aunt Esther said a person from Children's Services will be at school tomorrow morning. To talk to me. To make arrangements for my placement . . ." He looked down, his voice faltering.

"Placement?" Charlie said, trying not to shout. "What placement?"

"To tell me what institution or foster home they're going to put me in."

"The hell they are," Charlie said, scowling past him at the Fowlers. "They're not taking you anywhere. Who are they sending, did you get a name? Did they say what time?" She looked up as Ryan came to join them, passing the Fowlers without speaking.

Billy said, "They didn't say a name. Said first period, around nine." The boy's face was white, he was trying hard not to cry.

"Max and I will be there," Charlie said, her voice low and measured with anger. "You're not going anywhere, you're staying with us. For as long as you like." She looked up at Ryan. "If the Fowlers won't cooperate, if they won't sign the legal papers to let you live with us, I'm sure Debbie will."

"Debbie will," Ryan said. "Or she'll be out on the street looking for a roof over *her* head."

Billy tried to grin at them, but still he was pale and uncertain. Ryan hugged him, and Charlie said, "It will be all right, we'll take care of it. Go on out and help Clyde with the rest of the tables."

The boy walked silently past the Fowlers hardly looking at them. He didn't stop, though they tried to question him. Watching him, Joe hoped a signature from Debbie would be sufficient. He wondered what other leverage Max would have, maybe with Perry Fowler, as well as his hold over Erik Kraft.

There'd been no mention of Fowler's involvement in Kraft's embezzlements, but Joe thought maybe Fowler wasn't clean, maybe he and Esther had known all along, and looked the other way. If that was the case, Max might have plenty of information to use to help Billy.

He guessed the truth would come out when Max and Kathleen had all the loose ends wrapped up. Detectives Garza and Davis were, at this point, pretty much out of the loop. Dallas had started working another case, a domestic violence that had flared up noisily, night before last. And Juana was at home tonight, fasting, preparing for an early morning surgery. She had decided to go ahead with the knee replacement; Ryan had said Officer Brennan would be taking her to the hospital.

Joe thought about his strong and reliable friend having to deal with the pain of surgery and then with a mechanical knee, and he prayed that all went well. Charlie'd said Juana had taken her young cat over to the Firettis, to board, where he'd likely be spoiled just the way Juana spoiled him. Joe thought maybe Misto would play nursemaid, and spoil the little cat, too.

Out in the patio, as Billy helped Clyde arrange the tables, he watched a young couple leaving with their carrier, their new kitty peering out. Every cat had been spoken for, and those folks that the volunteers knew well had taken their cats with them. Others, not so well known, would wait while CatFriends checked them out, talked with their veterinarians, even visited their homes. Charlie said they weren't going to rescue and doctor and nurture a cat, then not make sure it would be well cared for. Billy looked in at George Jolly's two black-and-white adoptees, who waited in their carrier on a table near the kitchen. One reached out a paw to him, while the other rolled over for a tummy rub.

Charlie had told him the last one of George Jolly's three elderly cats had, shortly before Christmas, been put down by Dr. Firetti because of painful liver failure. Charlie said Jolly was now, at last, ready for new housemates. When she described Jolly's house, Billy knew the cats would like it. There were high shelves and all kinds of climbing places, and out in back, a lush garden, Charlie said, with an escape-proof fence. He guessed Sammie Miller's two cats were, for sure, going to a happy home.

But his own cats had lucked out, too, Billy thought, with a whole hay barn full of mice to hunt. He didn't know what made him think about Zandler just then. Except that the landlord had groused about his cats, said they were dirty. Well they were cleaner than that old man. He thought about Zandler prowling the burned house, and wondered again if Gran's money *was* still hidden there—or if Zandler, or someone else, had found it. Maybe he'd never know, but he sure meant to keep looking.

As the remaining volunteers gathered for a good-night celebration, the scent of fresh coffee filled the patio and George Jolly brought out the anniversary cake he'd baked, setting it before the Damens: a three-layered confection iced in white, decorated with a red Valentine heart and a border of running cats. Everyone toasted the newlyweds, and toasted each other at the success of the auction. They had raised over forty thousand dollars, and every last stray had a new home, a more productive night than any of CatFriends had dreamed.

Charlie and Billy left soon after the boisterous toasts ended, Billy yawning, full of good food, sated with too many people talking all at once—and worried about tomorrow. Wondering if his friends could, indeed, stand up to the power of the county authority that meant to take him away. Now, tired and discouraged, he wanted only to climb into his bed, in his cozy stall, among his own furry family.

As Kit and Pedric and Lucinda left the party, Kit looked back over her shoulder hoping Pan would decide to come with them, but he didn't, he only gave her a conspiratorial smile, and hopped into the Firetti van beside Misto. Wilma and Dulcie were leaving, too. Wilma, having done a background check on Emmylou Warren, had thought of asking her home with them, but Emmylou had already vanished; she hadn't stayed long, a silent observer at the edge of the party, then had slipped out again into the night as was her way.

"Where will she go?" Wilma said, turning the car heater up as she and Dulcie headed home. "Keep on sleeping in her old car, among all the bags and boxes?"

"Or maybe off to look for Birely?" Dulcie said. "To tell him his sister has died?"

"How would she ever find him? Oh, but she has his cell phone number." She glanced down at Dulcie. "What about Sammie's house, now the police have released it? You suppose she left it to Birely?"

"What would he do with it?" Kit said. "A wanderer like Birely, settle down in one place? I don't think so. Trapped by a roof and four walls? He'd be about as happy as a feral cat shut in a box."

"I guess," Wilma said. "Maybe she left the house to Emmylou, if she *was* Sammie's only friend. That would be nice" She looked down at Dulcie and scratched the tabby's ears. "You cats did all right," she said. "Cats and cops together."

Joe arrived home yawning, endured Rock's wet licks across his face, gave Snowball a few licks of his own, and then was up into his tower stretched out among his cushions, staring up at the stars.

"Sleep tight," Ryan called up to him.

"You did good," Clyde said, "you all did."

"Didn't do bad yourselves," Joe told them, thinking of their welcome help. And he slept, as did each of the cats, each warmed by their own private mystery: Joe Grey with dreams he hadn't wanted, but wasn't able to forget. Misto filled with visions of his lost past and, maybe, visions of what was yet to be. Dulcie awash in poetry whose source she could never have explained. And Kit, her wild dreams now given over, so suddenly, to an amazement of romance.

And Pan? What did Pan dream? Of past lives, as his daddy did? Of medieval times long vanished? Or did he dream of one tortoiseshell lady? Or, perhaps, dream equally of both, and with equal fascination?

But as the cats dreamed, each reaching out into realms they could not fully define, Wilma Getz dreamed, too. As Dulcie snuggled beside her beneath the quilt, Wilma slept wrapped in her own sense of miracle. Before leaving for the auction this evening, she had switched on her computer and found Dulcie's last, finished poem, and didn't that make her smile. The tabby's sudden creative flare was, to Wilma, the greatest joy of all. The transformation of the thieving kitten she had adopted so long ago, to this most surprising and talented of cats, still left her marveling. Now, more than ever, left her nearly purring, herself, with excitement. And they slept, side by side, Dulcie and her human, dreaming, to the echo of Dulcie's poems.

> *All along the cliff top blowing*
> *She stalks her prey in grasses growing*
> *Forest tall and thick above her*
> *Quick and silent feline hunter*
> *Queen of the high sea meadow*
>
> *Mouse creeps very close to edge*
> *She snatches it from narrow ledge*
> *Sparrow tardy in his flight*
> *Will never see another night*
> *He's gone to feed the queen*
>
> *Through dark to early morn she'll roam*
> *Waves crash below*
> *Gulls scream above her*
> *Scolding as the wild queen passes*
> *Through the swaying summer grasses*
> *Queen of the high sea meadow*

THE NEW LUXURY IN READING

We hope you enjoyed reading
our new, comfortable print size and found it
an experience you would like to repeat.

Well – you're in luck!

HarperLuxe offers the finest in fiction and
nonfiction books in this same larger print size and
paperback format. Light and easy to read, HarperLuxe
paperbacks are for book lovers who want to see
what they are reading without the strain.

For a full listing of titles and
new releases to come, please visit our website:

www.HarperLuxe.com

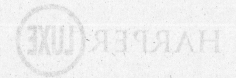